Bronwyn and Stephen
Theirs Was a Love Born in Fury,
to Burn with an Eternal Flame!

"You cannot escape me again . . . you're mine now," Stephen murmured as his lips touched hers.

It was not the first time Bronwyn had kissed a man. But it was the first time she'd experienced anything like this kiss. It was soft and sweet, but at the same time it was taking from her things she'd never given before. His mouth played with hers, touching it, caressing it yet plundering it. She stood on tiptoe to reach him better, turned her head to more of a slant. He seemed to want her to part her lips and she did so. The cold-hot touch of the tip of his tongue on hers sent little shivers down her spine . . . holding her captive more than any chains could.

Stephen chuckled. "You are mine more than you know." He released her and pushed her toward Morag. "Go and ready yourself for our wedding . . . if you can wait that long."

JUDE DEVERAUX
is America's most highly acclaimed author
of historical romances, and

HIGHLAND VELVET
is her most stunning saga—a tale to live forever
in your memory!

Books by Jude Deveraux

The Velvet Promise
Highland Velvet
Velvet Song
Velvet Angel
Sweetbriar
Counterfeit Lady
Lost Lady
Twin of Ice
Twin of Fire
River Lady

Published by POCKET BOOKS

JUDE DEVERAUX

HIGHLAND VELVET

PUBLISHED BY POCKET BOOKS NEW YORK

Another *Original* publication of POCKET BOOKS

POCKET BOOKS, a division of Simon & Schuster, Inc.
1230 Avenue of the Americas, New York, N.Y. 10020

ISBN: 0-671-60073-7

First Pocket Books printing August, 1982

17   16   15   14   13   12   11   10   9   8

POCKET and colophon are registered trademarks of Simon & Schuster, Inc.

Printed in the U.S.A.

To Mia
(the gorgeous one in Louisville)
with love

Author's Note

WHENEVER ANYONE HAS READ THIS BOOK BEFORE PUBLICA-
tion, she has asked me the same questions: Why isn't a
kilt mentioned, and what were the tartan colors of Clan
MacArran?

The early Highlanders wore a simple garment *(plaide*
is Gaelic for *blanket)* that they spread on the ground,
then lay upon and pulled the edges to their sides and
belted. This formed a skirt at the bottom, and the
upper part of the plaid, or blanket, was pinned at one
shoulder.

There are several stories of how the kilt came into
being. One story is about an Englishman who abridged
the costume for the convenience of his Highland iron-
workers. Of course, the Scots deny that this story is
true. Whichever story is true, the modern kilt was not
in existence before 1700.

As for the tartan colors, the clan members wore
whatever color appealed to them or could be made
from dyes from plants in their area. The clans were
identified by colored cockades in their hats.

Again, there are several stories about the origin of
the clan tartans. One is that the export merchants gave
clan names to the yards of plaid they manufactured so
they could be more easily identified. Another is that the
British Army, with its love of uniformity, insisted that
each Scots company wear a tartan of the same color
and design. Either way, there were no clan tartans
before 1700.

Jude Deveraux, 1981
Santa Fe, New Mexico

Prologue

STEPHEN MONTGOMERY STILL SAT VERY STRAIGHT ON HIS horse even after the long night's ride. He didn't like to think of the bride who waited for him at the end of his journey—who had been waiting for him for three days. His sister-in-law, Judith, had had a few choice things to say about a man not bothering to show up for his own wedding, nor making the effort to send a message of regret at his lateness.

But despite Judith's words and the realization of the insult he'd paid his future wife, he'd been reluctant to depart King Henry's estate. Stephen had been hesitant to leave his sister-in-law's side. Judith, his brother Gavin's beautiful golden-eyed wife, had fallen down a flight of stairs and lost the badly wanted child she carried. For days Judith hovered between life and death. When she woke and learned her baby was gone, one of her first thoughts was typically about someone other than herself. Stephen had not remembered his own wedding date nor given a thought to his bride.

1

Judith, even in her grief and pain, had reminded Stephen of his duties and the Scotswoman he was to marry.

Now, three days later, Stephen ran his hand through his thick, dark blond hair. He wanted to stay with his brother, Gavin. Judith was more than angry with him. Her fall had not been an accident but had been caused by Gavin's mistress, Alice Chatworth.

"My lord."

Stephen slowed his pace and turned to his squire.

"The wagons are far behind us. They cannot keep pace."

He nodded without speaking and reined his horse toward the narrow stream that ran by the rough road. He dismounted, knelt on one knee, and splashed his face with cold water.

There was another reason Stephen didn't want to travel to meet this bride he'd never seen. King Henry meant to reward the Montgomerys for their faithful service over the years, so he gave the second brother a rich Scots bride. Stephen knew he should be grateful, but not after the things he'd heard of her.

She was, in her own right, the laird of a powerful Scots clan.

He looked across the green meadow on the far side of the stream. Damn the Scots anyway for their absurd belief that a mere woman was intelligent and strong enough to lead men. Her father should have chosen a young man for his heir instead of a woman.

He grimaced as he imagined what kind of woman could inspire her father to name her chief. She had to be at least forty years old, hair the color of steel, a body thicker than his own. On their wedding night no doubt they'd arm wrestle to see who would get on top . . . and he'd lose.

"My lord," the boy said. "You do not look well. Perhaps the long ride has made you ill."

"It's not the ride that's turned my stomach." Stephen

stood up slowly, easily, his powerful muscles moving under his clothes. He was tall, towering over his squire, and his body was lean and hard from many years of strenuous training. His hair was thick with sweaty curls along his neck, his jaw strong, his lips finely chiseled. Yet now there were sunken shadows under the eyes of brilliant blue. "Let's return to our horses. The wagons can follow us later. I don't want to put off my execution any longer."

"Execution, my lord?"

Stephen did not answer. There were still many hours before he'd reach the horror that awaited him in the solid, bulky shape of Bronwyn MacArran.

Chapter One

1501

BRONWYN MACARRAN STOOD AT THE WINDOW OF THE English manor house, looking down at the courtyard below. The mullioned window was open against the warm summer sun. She leaned forward slightly to catch a whiff of fresh air. As she did so, one of the soldiers below grinned up at her suggestively.

She stepped back quickly, grabbed the window, and slammed it shut. She turned away angrily.

"The English pigs!" Bronwyn cursed under her breath. Her voice was soft, full of the heather and mist of the Highlands.

Heavy footsteps sounded outside her door, and she caught her breath, then released it when they went past. She was a prisoner, held captive on England's northernmost border by men she'd always hated, men who now smiled and winked at her as if they were intimate with her most private thoughts.

She walked to a small table in the center of the oak-paneled room. She clutched the edge of it, letting the wood cut into her palms. She'd do anything to keep those men from seeing how she felt inside. The English were her enemies. She'd seen them kill her father, his three chieftains. She'd seen her brother driven nearly insane with his futile attempts to repay the English in their own kind. And all her life she'd helped feed and clothe the members of her clan after the English had destroyed their crops and burned their houses.

A month ago the English had taken her prisoner. Bronwyn smiled in memory of the wounds she and her men had inflicted upon the English soldiers. Later four of them had died.

But in the end she was taken, by the order of the English Henry VII. The man said he wanted peace and therefore would name an Englishman as chief of Clan MacArran. He thought he could do this by marrying one of his knights to Bronwyn.

She smiled at the ignorance of the English king. She was chief of Clan MacArran, and no man would take her power away. The stupid king thought her men would follow a foreigner, an Englishman, rather than their own chief because she was a woman. How little Henry knew of the Scots!

She turned suddenly as Rab growled. He was an Irish wolfhound, the largest dog in the world, rangy, strong, hair like soft steel. Her father had given her the dog four years ago when Jamie'd returned from a trip to Ireland. Jamie had meant to have the dog trained as his daughter's guardian, but there was no need. Rab and Bronwyn took to each other immediately, and Rab had often shown that he'd give his life for his beloved mistress.

Bronwyn's muscles relaxed when Rab's growl stopped—only a friend produced such a reaction. She looked up expectantly.

It was Morag who entered. Morag was a short, gnarled old woman, looking more like a dark burl of wood than a human being. Her eyes were like black glass, sparkling, penetrating, seeing more of a person than what was on the surface. She used her lithe little body to advantage, often slipping unnoticed amid people, her eyes and ears open.

Morag moved silently across the room and opened the window.

"Well?" Bronwyn demanded impatiently.

"I saw ye slam the window. They laughed and said they'd take over the weddin' night ye'd be missin'."

Bronwyn turned away from the old woman.

"Ye give them too much to speak of. Ye should hold yer head high and ignore them. They're only Englishmen, while ye're a MacArran."

Bronwyn whirled. "I don't need anyone to tell me how to act," she snapped. Rab, aware of his mistress's distress, came to stand beside her. She buried her fingers in his fur.

Morag smiled at her, then watched as the girl moved toward the window seat. She had been placed in Morag's arms when Bronwyn was still wet from her birth. Morag had held the tiny bairn as she watched the mother die. It'd been Morag who'd found a wet nurse for the girl, who'd given her the name of her Welsh grandmother, and who'd cared for her until she was six and her father'd taken over.

It was with pride that Morag looked at her charge now nearly twenty years old. Bronwyn was tall, taller than most men and as straight and supple as a reed. She didn't cover her hair like the Englishwoman, but let it flow down her back in a rich cascade. It was raven-black and so thick and heavy it was a wonder her slender neck could support the weight. She wore a satin dress in the English style. It was the color of the cream from the Highland cattle. The square neck was low and tight, showing Bronwyn's firm young breasts to advantage. It fit like skin to her small waist, then belled out in rich folds. Embroidery entwined with thin gold strands edged both the neck and the waist and fell in an intricate waterfall down the skirt.

"Do I meet your approval?" Bronwyn asked sharply, still irritated over their quarrel about the English attire. She had preferred Highland clothes, but Morag persuaded her to wear English garb, telling her to give the enemy no reason to laugh at her in what they referred to as "barbaric dress."

Morag chuckled dryly. "I was thinkin' it was a shame no man would be takin' that gown from ye tonight."

"An Englishman!" Bronwyn hissed. "Do you forget that so soon? Has the red of my father's blood faded before your eyes?"

"Ye know it hasn't," Morag said quietly.

Bronwyn sat down heavily on the window seat, the satin of the dress flowing about her. She ran her finger along the heavy embroidery. The dress had cost her a great deal, money that could have been spent on her clan. But she knew they would not have wanted to be shamed before the Englishmen, so she bought dresses that would have been the pride of any queen.

Only this gown was to have been her wedding dress.

She plucked violently at a piece of gold thread.

"Here!" Morag commanded. "Don't destroy the dress because ye're mad at one Englishman. Perhaps the man had a reason to be late and miss his own weddin'."

Bronwyn stood up quickly, causing Rab to move protectively to her side. "What do I care if the man never appears? I hope he had his throat cut and lies rotting in some ditch."

Morag shrugged. "They'll only find ye a new husband, so what does it matter if this one dies or not? The sooner ye have yer English husband, the sooner we can go back to the Highlands."

"It's easy for you to say!" Bronwyn snapped. "It's not you who must wed him and . . . and . . ."

Morag's little black eyes danced. "And bed him? Is that what's worryin' ye? I'd gladly trade with ye if I could. Think this Stephen Montgomery would notice 'twere I to slip into his bed?"

"What do I know of Stephen Montgomery except that he has no more respect for me than to leave me waiting in my wedding dress? You say the men laugh at me. The man who is to be my husband holds me up for their ridicule." She squinted at the door. "Were he to come through there now, I'd gladly take a knife to him."

Morag smiled. Jamie MacArran would have been proud of his daughter. Even when she was still held prisoner she kept her pride and her spirit. Now she held her chin high, her eyes flashing with daggers of crystal-blue ice.

Bronwyn was startlingly beautiful. Her hair was as black as a moonless midnight in the Scots mountains, her eyes as deep blue as the water of a sunlit loch. The contrast was arresting. It wasn't unusual for people, especially men, to be struck speechless the first time they saw her. Her lashes were thick and dark, her skin fine and creamy. Her lips of dark red were set above her father's chin, strong, square on the tip, and slightly cleft.

"They'll think ye're a coward if ye hide in this room. What Scot is afraid of the smirks of an Englishman?"

Bronwyn stiffened her back and looked down at the cream-colored gown. When she'd dressed that morning, she thought to be wed in the dress. Now it was hours past time for the marriage ceremony, and her bridegroom had not shown himself, nor had he sent any message of excuse or apology.

"Help me unfasten this thing," Bronwyn said. The gown would have to be kept fresh until she did marry. If not today, then at another time. And perhaps to another man. The thought made her smile.

"What are ye plannin'?" Morag asked, her hands at

the back of Bronwyn's dress. "Ye've a look of the cat that got the cream."

"You ask too many questions. Fetch me that green brocade gown. The Englishmen may think I'm a bride in tears at being snubbed, but they'll soon find the Scots are made of sterner stuff."

Even though she was a prisoner and had been for over a month, Bronwyn was allowed the freedom of Sir Thomas Crichton's manor. She could walk about the house and, with an escort, on the grounds. The estate was heavily guarded, watched constantly. King Henry had told Bronwyn's clan that if a rescue attempt were made, she would be executed. No harm would come to her, but he meant to put an Englishman in the chief-ship. The clan had recently seen the death of Jamie MacArran as well as of his three chieftains. The Scots retreated to watch their new laird held captive and planned what they'd do when the king's men dared to try to command them.

Bronwyn slowly descended the stairs to the hall below. She knew her clansmen waited patiently just outside the grounds, hiding in the forest on the constantly turbulent border between England and Scotland.

For herself she did not care if she died rather than accept the English dog she was to marry, but her death would cause strife within the clan. Jamie MacArran had designated his daughter as his successor, and she was to have married one of the chieftains who had died with her father. If Bronwyn were to die without issue, there would no doubt be a bloody battle over who would be the next laird.

"I always knew the Montgomerys were smart men," laughed a man standing a few feet from Bronwyn. A thick tapestry hid her from his view. "Look at the way the eldest married that Revedoune heiress. He'd hardly got out of his marriage bed when her father was killed and he inherited the earldom."

"And now Stephen is following in his brother's footsteps. Not only is this Bronwyn beautiful, but she owns hundreds of acres of land."

"You can say what you like," said a third man. His sleeve was empty, his left arm missing. "But I don't envy Stephen. The woman is magnificent, but how long will he be able to enjoy her? I lost this fighting those devils in Scotland. They're only half human, I tell you. They grow up learning nothing but plunder and robbery. And they fight more like animals than men. They're a crude, savage lot."

"And I heard their women stink to high heaven," the first man said.

"For that black-haired Bronwyn I'd learn to hold my nose."

Bronwyn took a step forward, a feral snarl on her lips. When a hand caught her arm, she looked up into a young man's face. He was handsome, with dark eyes, a firm mouth. Her eyes were on a level with his.

"Allow me, my lady," he said quietly.

He stepped forward to the group of men. His strong legs were encased in tight hose, his velvet jacket emphasizing the width of his shoulders. "Have you nothing better to do than gossip like old women? You talk of things you know nothing about." His voice was commanding.

The three men looked startled. "Why, Roger, what's wrong with you?" one asked, then stared over Roger's shoulder and saw Bronwyn, her eyes glittering in stormy anger.

"I think Stephen had better come soon and guard his property," one of the other men laughed.

"Get out of here!" Roger ordered. "Or shall I draw my sword to get your attention?"

"Deliver me from the hot blood of youth," one man said wearily. "Go to her. Come, the outside is cooler. The passions have more room to expand in the out-of-doors."

When the men were gone, Roger turned back to Bronwyn. "May I apologize for my countrymen? Their rudeness is based on ignorance. They meant no harm."

Bronwyn glared at him. "I fear it is you who are ignorant. They meant great harm, or do you consider murdering Scots no sin?"

"I protest! You're unfair to me. I have killed few men in my life and no Scots." He paused. "May I introduce myself? I am Roger Chatworth." He swept his velvet cap from his head and bowed low before her.

"And I, sir, am Bronwyn MacArran, prisoner to the English and, of late, discarded bride."

"Lady Bronwyn, will you walk with me in the garden? Perhaps the sunshine will take away some of the misery Stephen has foisted upon you."

She turned and walked beside him. At least he might keep the guards from tossing rude jests at her. Once they were outside, she spoke again. "You speak Montgomery's name as if you know him."

"Have you not met him yourself?"

Bronwyn whirled on him. "Since when have I been afforded any courtesy by your English king? My father thought enough of me to name me laird of Clan MacArran, but your king thinks I have too little sense to even choose my own husband. No, I have not seen this Stephen Montgomery, nor do I know anything about him. I was told one morning I was to marry him. Since then he has not so much as acknowledged my presence."

Roger lifted a handsome eyebrow at her. Her hostility made her eyes sparkle like blue diamonds. "I'm sure there must be an excuse for his tardiness."

"Perhaps his excuse is that he means to assert his authority over all the Scots. He will show us who is master."

Roger was silent for a moment as if he were considering her words. "There are those who consider the Montgomerys arrogant."

"You say you know this Stephen Montgomery. What is he like? I don't know if he's short or tall, old or young."

Roger shrugged as if his mind were elsewhere. "He is an ordinary man." He seemed reluctant to continue. "Lady Bronwyn, tomorrow would you do me the honor of riding into the park with me? There's a stream running across Sir Thomas's land, and perhaps we could carry a meal there."

"Aren't you afraid that I'll make an attempt on your life? I have not been allowed off these grounds for over a month."

He smiled at her. "I would like you to know there are Englishmen with more manners than to, as you say, discard a woman on her wedding day."

Bronwyn stiffened as she was reminded of the humiliation Stephen Montgomery had caused her. "I would very much like to ride out with you."

Roger Chatworth smiled and nodded to a man passing them on the narrow garden path. His mind was working quickly.

Three hours later Roger returned to his apartments in the east wing of Sir Thomas Crichton's house. He'd come there two weeks ago to talk to Sir Thomas about recruiting young men from the area. Sir Thomas had been too busy with the problems of the Scots heiress to talk of anything else. Now Roger was beginning to think fate had brought him here.

He kicked the stool out from under his sleeping squire's feet. "I have something for you to do," he commanded as he removed his velvet jacket and slung it across the bed. "There's an old Scotsman named Angus lying about somewhere. Look for him and bring him to me. You'll probably find him wherever the drink is flowing freely. And then bring me half a hogshead of ale. Do you understand me?"

"Yes, my lord," the boy said, backing out of the doorway, rubbing his drowsy eyes.

When Angus appeared in the doorway, he was already half drunk. He worked for Sir Thomas in some sort of capacity, but generally he did little except drink. His hair was dirty and tangled, hanging well past his shoulders in the Scots manner. He wore a long linen shirt, belted at the waist, his knees and legs bare.

Roger glanced at the man and his heathen attire with a brief look of disgust.

"You wanted me, my lord?" Angus said, his voice a soft burr. His eyes followed the small cask of ale that Roger's squire was carrying into the room.

Chatworth dismissed the boy, poured himself an ale, sat down, and motioned Angus to do likewise. When the filthy man was seated, Roger began. "I'd like to know about Scotland."

Angus raised his shaggy brows. "You mean where the gold is hidden? We're a poor country, my lord, and—"

"I want none of your sermons! Save your lies for someone else. I want to know what a man who is to marry the chief of a clan should know."

Angus stared hard for a moment, then he closed his mouth with his mug of ale. "An *eponymus*, eh?" he mumbled in Gaelic. "'Tisn't easy to be accepted by the clan members."

Roger took one long step across the room and grabbed the mug of ale from the man. "I didn't ask for your judgments. Will you answer my questions, or do I kick you down the stairs?"

Angus looked at the cold mug with desperate eyes. "Ye must become a MacArran." He looked up at Roger. "Takin' that you mean that particular clan."

Roger gave a brief, curt nod.

"Ye must take the name of the laird of the clan, or the men can't accept ye. Ye must dress as the Scots or they'll laugh at ye. Ye must love the land and the Scots."

Roger lowered the ale. "What about the woman? What must I do to own her?"

"Bronwyn cares about little else except her people. She would have killed herself before she married an Englishman, but she knew her death would cause war within her clan. If ye make the woman know ye mean well for her people, ye'll have her."

Roger gave the man the ale. "I want to know more. What is a clan? Why was a woman made chief? Who are the enemies of Clan MacArran?"

"Talking is thirsty work."

"You'll have all you can hold, just as long as you tell me what I want to know."

Bronwyn met Roger Chatworth early the next morning. In spite of her good intentions, she'd been so excited about the prospect of a ride in the woods that she'd hardly been able to sleep. Morag had helped her dress in a soft brown velvet gown, all the while issuing dire warnings about Englishmen bearing gifts.

"I merely want the ride," Bronwyn said stubbornly.

"Aye, and what mere trifle does this Chatworth want? He knows ye're to marry another."

"Am I?" Bronwyn snapped. "Then where is my bridegroom? Should I sit in my wedding gown for another full day and wait for him?"

"It might be better than chasing after some hot-blooded young earl."

"An earl? Roger Chatworth is an English earl?"

Morag refused to answer, but gave the gown a final straightening before pushing her from the room.

Now, as Bronwyn sat atop the horse, Rab running beside her, she felt alive for the first time in many weeks.

"The roses have returned to your cheeks," Roger said, laughing.

She smiled in return, and the smile softened her chin

and lit her eyes. She spurred the horse to a faster pace.
Rab with his long, loping strides kept pace with the
horse.

Roger turned for a moment to glance at the men
following them. There were three of his personal
guards, two squires, and a packhorse loaded with food
and plate. He turned and looked ahead at Bronwyn.
He frowned when she glanced over her shoulder and
spurred her mount even faster. She was an excellent
horsewoman, and no doubt the woods were full of men
from her clan, all eager and willing to help her escape.

He threw up his hand and motioned his men forward
as he set spurs to his own mount.

Bronwyn made her horse come close to flying. The
wind in her hair, the sense of freedom, were exhilarat-
ing. When she came to the stream, she was going full
speed. She had no idea if the horse had ever taken a
jump before, but she urged it on regardless of the risk.
It sailed over the water as if it had wings. On the far
side she pulled the animal to a halt and turned to look
back.

Roger and his men were just approaching the stream.

"Lady Bronwyn!" Roger shouted. "Are you all
right?"

"Of course," she laughed, then led her horse through
the water to where Roger waited for her. She bent
forward and patted the horse's neck. "He's a good
animal. He took the jump well."

Roger dismounted and walked to her side. "You gave
me a terrible fright. You could have been injured."

She laughed happily. "A Scotswoman is not likely to
be injured while atop a horse."

Roger put his arms up to help her dismount.

Suddenly Rab jumped between them, his lips drawn
back showing long, sharp teeth. He growled deeply,
menacingly. Roger instinctively retreated.

"Rab!" The dog obeyed Bronwyn immediately. He

moved away but his eyes, with a warning gleam, never left Roger. "He means to protect me," she said. "He doesn't like anyone touching me."

"I'll remember that in future," Roger said warily as he aided Bronwyn off her horse. "Perhaps you'd like to rest after your ride," he suggested. He snapped his fingers, and his squires brought two chairs upholstered in red velvet. "My lady," Roger offered.

She smiled in wonder at the chairs set in the woods. The grass under their feet was like a velvet carpet. The stream played its music, and even as she thought that, one of Roger's men began to strum a lute. She closed her eyes for a moment.

"Are you homesick, my lady?" Roger asked.

She sighed. "You could not know. No one not of the Highlands could know what it means to a Scot."

"My grandmother was a Scot, so perhaps that qualifies me to have some understanding of your ways."

Her head came up abruptly. "Your grandmother! What was her name?"

"A MacPherson of MacAlpin."

Bronwyn smiled. It was good to even hear the familiar names once again. "MacAlpin. 'Tis a good clan."

"Yes. I spent many evenings listening to stories at my grandmother's knee."

"And what sort of stories did she tell you?" Bronwyn asked cautiously.

"She was married to an Englishman, and she often compared the cultures of the two countries. She said the Scots were more hospitable, that the men didn't shove the women into a room and pretend they had no sense as the English do. She said the Scots treated women as equals."

"Yes," Bronwyn agreed quietly. "My father named me laird." She paused. "How did your English grandfather treat his Scots wife?"

Roger chuckled as if at some private joke. "My

grandfather lived in Scotland for a while, and he knew my grandmother to be a woman of intelligence. He valued her all his life. There was never a decision made that was not made by both of them."

"And you spent some time with your grandparents?"

"Most of my life. My parents died when I was very young."

"And what did you think of this non-English way of treating women? Surely, now that you are older, you've learned that women are only of use in the bed, in creating and delivering children."

Roger laughed out loud. "If I even had such a thought, my grandmother's ghost would box my ears. No," he said more seriously, "she meant for me to marry the daughter of a cousin of hers, but the child died before our marriage. I grew up calling myself MacAlpin."

"What?" She was startled.

Roger looked surprised. "It was in the marriage contract that I'd become a MacAlpin to please her clan."

"And you'd do that? I mentioned to Sir Thomas that my husband must become a MacArran, but he said that was impossible, that no Englishman would give up his fine old name for a heathen Scots name."

Roger's eyes flashed angrily. "They don't understand! Damn the English! They think only their ways are right. Why, even the French—"

"The French are our friends," Bronwyn interrupted. "They visit our country as we do theirs. They don't destroy our crops or steal our cattle as the English do."

"Cattle." Roger smiled. "Now there's an interesting subject. Tell me, do the MacGregors still raise such fat beasts?"

Bronwyn drew her breath in sharply. "Clan MacGregor is our enemy."

"True," he smiled, "but don't you find that a roast of MacGregor beef is more succulent than any other?"

She could only stare at him. The MacGregors had been the enemies of the MacArrans for centuries.

"Of course, things may have changed since my grandmother was a Highland lass," Roger continued. "Then the favorite sport of the young men was a swift moonlight cattle raid."

Bronwyn smiled at him. "Nothing's changed."

Roger turned and snapped his fingers. "Would you like something to eat, my lady? Sir Thomas has a French chef, and he has prepared us a feast. Tell me, have you ever eaten a pomegranate?"

She could only shake her head and look at him in wonder as the baskets were unloaded and Roger's squire served the meal on silver plates. For the first time in her life she had the thought that an Englishman could be human, that he could learn, and desired to learn, the Scots' ways. She picked up a piece of pâté, molded into the shape of a rose and placed on a cracker. The events of the day were a revelation to her.

"Tell me, Lord Roger, what do you think of our clan system?"

Roger brushed crumbs from his doublet of gold brocade and smiled to himself. He was well prepared for all her questions.

Bronwyn stood in the room where she'd spent too much time in the last month. Her cheeks were still flushed and her eyes still bright from the morning's fast ride.

"He's not like other men," she said to Morag. "I tell you, we spent hours together and we never once stopped talking. He even knows some Gaelic words."

"'Tisn't hard to pick up a few hereabouts. Even some of the Lowlanders know Gaelic." It was Morag's worst insult. To her the Lowlanders were traitorous Scots, more English than Scot.

"Then how do you explain the other things he said? His grandmother was a Scot. You should have heard his ideas! He said he'd petition King Henry to stop the English from raiding us, that that would bring more peace than this practice of capturing Scotswomen and forcing them to marry against their will."

Morag screwed her dark, wrinkled face into walnut-shell ugliness. "Ye leave here this mornin' hatin' all English and come back bowin' at one's feet. All ye've heard from him are words. Ye've seen no action. What has the man done to make ye trust him?"

Bronwyn sat down heavily on the window seat. "Can't you see that I want only what is best for my people? I am forced to marry an Englishman, so why not one who is part Scot, in mind as well as in blood?"

"Ye have no choice of husbands!" Morag said fiercely. "Can't ye see that ye are a great prize? Young men will say anything to get under a pretty woman's skirts. And if those skirts are covered with pearls, they'll kill themselves to have them."

"Are you saying he's lying?"

"How would I know? I've only just seen the man. But I have *not* seen Stephen Montgomery. For all ye know, his mother could have been a Scot. Perhaps he'll appear with a tartan across his shoulder and a dirk in his belt."

"I could not hope for so much," Bronwyn sighed. "If I met a thousand Englishmen, not one of them would understand my clan as Roger Chatworth does." She stood. "But you are right. I will be patient. Perhaps this man Montgomery is unique, an understanding man who believes in the Scots."

"I hope ye do not expect too much," Morag said. "I hope Chatworth has not made ye expect too much."

Chapter Two

STEPHEN HAD RIDDEN FAST AND HARD ALL DAY AND WELL into the night before he reached Sir Thomas's house on the border. Stephen had long since left the wagons and his retainers behind. Only his personal guard managed to stay with him. A few hours ago they'd encountered a storm and a river about to burst its banks. Stephen slogged through the muck. Now, as he reined into the courtyard, he and his men were covered with lumps of mud. A tree branch had struck Stephen over the eye, and the blood had dried, giving him a swollen, grotesque appearance.

He dismounted quickly and threw the reins to his exhausted squire. The big manor house was lit by a myriad of candles, and music floated on the air.

Stephen stood inside the door for a moment to allow his eyes to adjust to the light.

"Stephen!" Sir Thomas called as he hobbled forward. "We've been worried about you! I was going to send men out to search for you in the morning."

A man came to stand behind the aged and gout-crippled knight. "So this is the lost bridegroom," he smiled, looking Stephen up and down, noting his filthy, torn clothing. "Not everyone has been worried, Sir Thomas."

"Aye," someone else laughed. "Young Chatworth seems to have done quite well without the belated bridegroom."

Sir Thomas put his hand on Stephen's shoulder and guided him toward a room off the hall. "Come in here, my boy. We need time to talk."

It was a large room, paneled in oak carved in the linen-fold pattern. Against one wall was a row of books above a long trestle table. Completing the sparse furnishings were four chairs set before a large fireplace, where low flames burned cheerfully.

"What is this about Chatworth?" Stephen asked immediately.

"Sit down first. You look exhausted. Would you like some food? Wine?"

Stephen tossed a cushion out of a walnut chair and sat down gratefully. He took the wine Sir Thomas offered. "I'm sorry I'm late. My sister-in-law fell and lost the baby she carried. She nearly died. I'm afraid I didn't notice the date and only realized it after I was already three days late. I rode as hard as I could to get here." He picked a piece of caked dirt from his neck and threw it into the fireplace.

Sir Thomas nodded. "That's obvious from the look of you. If someone hadn't told me you approached bearing a banner of the Montgomery leopards, I'd never have recognized you. Is that cut above your eye as bad as it looks?"

Absently, Stephen felt the place. "It's mostly dried blood. I was traveling too fast for it to run down my face," he joked.

Sir Thomas laughed and sat down. "It's good to see you. How are your brothers?"

"Gavin married Robert Revedoune's daughter."

"Revedoune? There's money in that match."

Stephen smiled and thought that the last thing Gavin cared about was his wife's money. "Raine is still talking about his absurd ideas about the treatment of serfs."

"And Miles?"

Stephen finished the wine in his cup. "Miles presented us with another of his bastard children last week. That makes three, or four, I lost count. If he were a stallion, we'd be rich."

Sir Thomas laughed and refilled both metal goblets.

Stephen looked up at the older man as he lifted his drink again. Sir Thomas had been a friend of his father's, an honorary uncle who brought the boys gifts from his many trips abroad, had been at Stephen's christening twenty-six years ago. "Now that we're through with that," Stephen said slowly, "perhaps you'll tell me what you're hiding."

Sir Thomas chuckled, a soft sound deep within his throat. "You know me too well. It's nothing really, an unpleasantness, nothing serious. Roger Chatworth has spent a great deal of time with your bride, 'tis all."

Standing up slowly, Stephen walked toward the fireplace. Bits of mud fell from his clothes as he moved. Sir Thomas could not know what the name Chatworth meant to Stephen. Alice Valence had been his brother's mistress for years. Repeatedly, Gavin had asked her to marry him. She refused, preferring to marry the rich Edmund Chatworth. Soon after her marriage, Edmund was murdered and Alice reappeared in Gavin's life. She was a treacherous woman, and she had climbed into bed with a drunken, sleepy Gavin, then arranged for Judith to see them together. In her agony Judith fell down the stairs and lost her child and nearly lost her own life.

Roger Chatworth was Alice's brother-in-law, and even the mention of the name made Stephen grit his teeth.

"There must be more to this," Stephen said finally.

"Bronwyn hinted last evening that perhaps she'd be more pleased with Roger for a husband than one who is so . . . discourteous."

Stephen smiled and went back to the chair. "And how does Roger take all this?"

"He seems amenable. He rides with her each morning, escorts her to supper in the evening, spends time in the garden with her."

Stephen drank the last of the wine and began to relax. "It's well known that the Chatworths are a greedy bunch, but I didn't know to what degree. He must be very hungry to endure the woman's company."

"Endure?" Sir Thomas asked, surprised.

"There's no need to be dishonest with me. I heard how she fought like a man when she was surrounded, and worse how even her own father considered her enough of a man to name her his successor. I almost feel sorry for Roger. It would serve him right if I let him have the hideous woman."

Sir Thomas stood with his mouth agape, then slowly his eyes began to twinkle. "Hideous, is she?" he chuckled.

"What else could she be? Don't forget I've spent some time in Scotland. A wilder, more savage group of people I've never run across. But what could I say to King Henry? He thought he was rewarding me. If I stepped aside and let Roger have her he'd forever be in my debt. Then I could marry some sweet, pretty little woman who wouldn't try to borrow my armor. Yes," he smiled, "that's just what I think I'll do."

"I agree with you," Sir Thomas said firmly. "Bronwyn is truly a hideous woman. I'm sure Roger is only interested in her land. But just so you can tell King Henry you were fair, why don't you meet her? I'm sure she'll take one look at you, filthy as you are, and refuse to marry you."

"Yes." Stephen grinned, his white teeth only making

him seem dirtier by contrast. "Then tomorrow both the woman and I can tell Roger of our decision. Then I can go home. Yes, Sir Thomas, it's a splendid idea."

Sir Thomas's eyes shone like a boy's; they fairly danced. "You show an uncommon wisdom for a man so young. Just wait here, and I'll have her brought down the back stairs to this room."

Stephen gave a low whistle. "Back stairs, is it? She must be worse than I imagine."

"You'll see, my boy. You'll see," Sir Thomas said as he left the room.

Bronwyn sat buried to her chin in a tub of hot, steamy water. Her eyes were closed, and she was thinking about going home. Roger would be with her, and together they'd lead her clan. It was a picture she was beginning to conjure more and more often in the last few days. Roger was one Englishman she could understand. Every day he seemed to know more about the Scots.

As Morag burst into the room she opened her eyes. "He's here," the old woman announced.

"Who is here?" Bronwyn asked stubbornly, knowing exactly whom Morag meant.

Morag ignored her question. "He's talking to Sir Thomas but I'm sure ye'll be called for in a few minutes, so get out of that water and get dressed. Ye kin wear the blue dress."

Bronwyn leaned her head back. "I'm not finished with my bath, and I have no intention of meeting him merely because he's bothered to appear. He kept me waiting for four days, so maybe I'll make him wait for five."

"Ye're bein' childish, as ye well know. The stable boy said the man's horses had been run near to death. Ye can see he tried to get here in a hurry."

"Or perhaps he always mistreats his horses."

"Ye're not too big to take a switch to! Now get out of

that tub or I'll throw a bucket of cold water over yer head."

Before Morag could act, the door was suddenly thrust open again, revealing a pair of guards.

"How dare you!" Bronwyn yelled as she sank lower into the water.

Instantly Rab rose from his place at the foot of the tub, ready to attack.

The men had barely a glimpse of Bronwyn before they were knocked off balance by a hundred and twenty pounds of snarling, sharp-toothed dog.

Morag grabbed Bronwyn's thin linen chemise and tossed it to her. She stood in the tub and hastily pulled it over her wet body, the hem of it falling into the water. She grabbed a woolen tartan from Morag as she stepped out of the tub.

"Quiet, Rab!" Bronwyn ordered. The hound obeyed immediately, coming to her side.

The guards stood up slowly, rubbing their wrists and shoulders where Rab had toyed with them. They did not know that the dog killed only on direct command from Bronwyn; otherwise he protected her without doing permanent damage. The men had seen the tub taken to Bronwyn's room, had heard her splashing. They used Sir Thomas's orders as an invitation to see her in her bath. Now she was wrapped from head to toe in a Scots plaid. There was no outline of her body showing, only her face, her eyes shining with humor.

"What do you want?" Bronwyn asked, laughter in her voice.

"You are to come to Sir Thomas's study," one of the guards said sullenly. "And if that dog ever again—"

She cut him off. "If you ever again enter my room without my permission, I will allow Rab to have your throat. Now lead the way."

They looked from Bronwyn to the big wolfhound, then turned away. Bronwyn held her head high as she followed them down the stairs. She would let no one

see her anger at the way she was being treated by this
Stephen Montgomery. Four days late for his wedding,
then, the moment he arrives, she is dragged before him
like an errant serving wench.

When Bronwyn was inside the study, she looked
from Sir Thomas to the man standing by the fireplace.
He was tall, but he was filthy beyond belief. Of his face
she could tell nothing. It seemed to be swollen on one
side, and she wondered if it was a permanent affliction.

Suddenly one of the guards saw a way to repay her
for her sport of him. Grabbing the trailing end of the
long tartan, he gave Bronwyn a sharp shove. She fell
forward, and the guard yanked back on the plaid.

"You!" Sir Thomas bellowed. "Out of my sight! How
dare you treat a lady like that! If you're within fifty
miles of here in the morning, I'll have you hanged!"

Both guards turned and quickly left the room as Sir
Thomas bent to retrieve the garment.

Only momentarily stunned, Bronwyn quickly got off
her knees and stood. The thin chemise clung to her
still-wet body as if she were nude. She started to cover
herself with her hands until she glanced up at Stephen.
He was no longer nonchalantly leaning against the
fireplace but had come to attention, staring at her in
open-mouthed disbelief. His eyes were wide, showing
white all around them, his mouth so agape that his
tongue fairly fell out.

She curled her lip at him, but he didn't even notice.
All he could see was what was below her neck. She put
her arms straight to her sides and glared at him.

It seemed an extraordinarily long time before Sir
Thomas placed Bronwyn's plaid gently about her
shoulders. She wrapped it tightly about her body.

"Well, Stephen, shouldn't you greet your bride?"

Stephen blinked several times before he could recover himself. Slowly he walked to her.

Bronwyn was a tall woman, but she had to look up to

meet his eyes. He looked worse in the dim light. The candlelight seemed to make eerie shadows of the mud and dried blood on his face.

Lifting a curl from her breast, he felt it between his fingers. "You've made no mistake, Sir Thomas?" he asked quietly, his eyes never leaving hers. "This is the laird of Clan MacArran?"

Bronwyn stepped back. "I have a tongue and a brain of my own. You need not speak as if I weren't here. I am the MacArran of MacArran, and I am sworn to hate all Englishmen, especially ones who insult my clan and me by appearing late and unwashed before me." She turned to Sir Thomas. "I find I am greatly fatigued. I would like to be excused, if you can grant this poor prisoner so great a request."

Sir Thomas frowned. "Stephen is your master now."

She whirled to face him, gave him one scathing look, then left the room without his permission.

Sir Thomas turned to Stephen. "I'm afraid she lacks some in manners. These Scotsmen should take a firm hand to their womenfolk more often. But in spite of her sharp tongue, do you still think she is hideous?"

Stephen could only stare at the doorway where Bronwyn had just left. Visions of her danced before him—a body he thought existed only in dreams, black hair and sapphire eyes. Her chin had jutted out at him so that he ached to kiss it. Her breasts were full, hard against the wet, clinging fabric; her waist small and firm; her hips and thighs round, impudent, tantalizing.

"Stephen?"

Stephen nearly fell into the chair. "Had I known," he whispered, "had I any idea, I would have come weeks ago when King Henry promised her to me."

"Then she meets with your approval?"

He ran his hand across his eyes. "I think I'm dreaming. Surely no woman could look like that and be alive. You must be playing a trick on me. You don't plan to substitute the real Bronwyn MacArran on my wedding day, do you?"

"I assure you she is real. Why do you think I keep her guarded so heavily? My men are like dogs ready to fight over her at any moment. They stand around and repeat stories of the treacherous Scots to each other, but the truth is, individually each of them has generously offered to take your place in the girl's bed."

Stephen curled his lip at this. "But you have kept them from her."

"It hasn't been easy."

"And what of Chatworth? Has he taken my place with my wife?"

Sir Thomas chuckled. "You sound as if you're jealous, and a moment ago you were willing to give her to Roger. No, Roger has never spent an unchaperoned moment with her. She is an excellent horsewoman, and he would not ride out alone with her for fear she'd run to her Scots."

Stephen snorted in derision. "It's more like the Chatworth name has too many enemies to ride out alone." He stood up. "You should have locked her in her room and not let her ride with any man."

"I'm not so old that I can resist a face like Lady Bronwyn's. She has merely to ask me for something, and I'll give it to her."

"She is my responsibility now. Do I have the southeast room again? Could you send a bath and some food? Tomorrow she won't be insulted by my appearance."

Sir Thomas smiled at Stephen's calm self-assurance. Tomorrow should prove to be an exciting day.

As the early-morning sunlight fell across the room, Bronwyn stood by the table, a note in her hand, a frown creasing her brow. She wore a velvet gown of peacock blue. The puffed sleeves were slashed, and tiffany silk of pale green was drawn through the openings. The front of the skirt was cut to show more of the green tiffany.

She turned to Morag. "He asks me to meet with him in the garden."

"Ye look presentable enough."

Bronwyn crumbled the note in her hand. She was still angry over the way he'd commanded her presence last night. This morning he offered no apology nor explanation for his behavior or his lateness. He merely requested that she do exactly what he wanted when he wanted.

She looked at the serving girl who waited for the answer. "Tell Lord Stephen I will not meet with him."

"Will not, my lady? You are unwell?"

"I am quite well. Give my message as I said, then go to Roger Chatworth and tell him I will meet him in the garden in ten minutes."

The girl's eyes widened, then she left the room.

"Ye'd do well to make peace with yer husband," Morag said. "Ye'll gain nothing by making him angry."

"My husband! My husband! That's all I hear. He is not my husband yet. Am I to jump at his call after he has ignored me these past days? I'm laughed at by everyone in the manor because of him, yet I am to fall at his feet like an obedient wife the moment he bothers to appear. I don't want him to get the idea I'm a pliable, cowardly woman. I want him to know I hate him and all his kind."

"And what of young Chatworth? He's an Englishman."

Bronwyn smiled. "At least he is part Scot. Perhaps I can take him to the Highlands and we can make a whole Scot of him. Come, Rab, we have an appointment."

"Good morning, Stephen," Sir Thomas called. It was a lovely morning, the sunlight bright, the air fresh from a quick shower the previous night. The scent of roses was in the air. "You certainly look better than you did yesterday."

Stephen wore a short jacket of deep brown worsted. It emphasized the breadth of his shoulders, the thickness of his chest. His legs were encased in hose that hugged every muscular curve of his powerful thighs. His dark blond hair curled along his collar, his eyes sparkled above his strong jaw. He was extraordinarily handsome.

"She refused to see me," he said without small talk.

"I told you her ways were sharp."

Stephen suddenly jerked his head up. Bronwyn was coming toward them. At first he did not see Roger beside her. His eyes were for her alone. Her heavy, thick hair flowed down her back, unhampered, uncovered. The sunlight flashed off it, making it glitter like specks of gold dust. The blue of her dress repeated the blue of her eyes. Her chin was as stubborn in the daylight as it had been at night.

"Good morning," Roger said quietly as they paused for a moment.

Bronwyn nodded to Sir Thomas, then her eyes lingered on Stephen. She did not recognize him. She only thought that she'd never seen a man with such eyes. They seemed to see through her. It was with difficulty that she looked away and continued down the path.

When Stephen recovered enough to finally realize that Roger Chatworth walked beside the woman he was to marry, he growled low in his throat and took a step forward.

Sir Thomas caught his arm. "Don't go after him like that. I'm sure Roger would like nothing better than a fight. And for that matter, so would Bronwyn."

"I may give it to them both!"

"Stephen! Listen to me. You've hurt the girl. You were late, you sent no message. She is a proud woman, more proud than a woman has a right to be. Her father did that when he made her his heir. Give her time. Take her riding tomorrow and talk to her. She's an intelligent woman."

Stephen relaxed and took his hand off his sword hilt. "Talk to her? How could I speak to a woman who looks like that? Last night I could hardly sleep because she haunted me so. Yes, I'll take her riding, though perhaps it's not the kind of riding you mean."

"Your wedding is set for the day after tomorrow. Leave the girl virgin until then."

Stephen shrugged. "She's mine. I'll do as I will with her."

Sir Thomas shook his head at the arrogance of the young man. "Come, look at my new hawks."

"My sister-in-law, Judith, showed Gavin a new lure. Perhaps you'd like to see it."

They left the garden and walked toward the mews.

As she walked with Roger, Bronwyn kept looking about the garden for the man she'd met the night before. The only stranger she saw was the man with Sir Thomas. The rest of the men were the same, staring at her, laughing in the same derogatory way when she passed.

But none of them resembled the ugly, filthy man she'd been dragged before. Once she glanced over her shoulder to where Sir Thomas had been. Both he and the stranger were gone. The man's eyes haunted her. They made her want to run away from him yet at the same time kept her from moving. She blinked to clear her vision and turned to someone safer—Roger. His eyes were smiling and kind and not disturbing in any way.

"Tell me, Lord Roger, what else is there to know about Stephen Montgomery besides that he is an ugly man?"

Roger was startled by her question. He wouldn't have thought a woman introduced to Stephen would think him ugly. Chatworth smiled. "Once the Montgomerys were rich, but their arrogance displeased a king and he took their wealth."

She frowned. "So now they must marry wealth."

"The wealthiest women they can find," he emphasized.

Bronwyn thought of the men who'd died with her father. She would have chosen one of them for her husband, and she would have wed a man who loved her, one who wanted something besides her lands.

As Morag pulled a bucket of water from the well, her eyes never left the quiet young man who leaned against the garden wall. For the last several days Morag had never been too far from Bronwyn's side, though the girl was often unaware of Morag's presence. She didn't like the way Bronwyn was flaunting herself with this Roger Chatworth. Nor did Morag like Chatworth, a man who'd court a woman a few days before she was to marry another.

Morag had heard Bronwyn's ravings the night she'd returned from meeting Stephen Montgomery. She'd heard what a leering, drooling idiot Montgomery was. Bronwyn screamed that she'd never marry him, that he was vile, repulsive.

Morag set the water bucket on the ground. For nearly an hour she'd been watching the blue-eyed man stare at Bronwyn as she sang to a tune Roger was playing on a lute. The stranger had hardly even blinked. Just stood and watched her.

"So ye're the one she's to marry," Morag said loudly.

Stephen had difficulty looking away. He peered down at the gnarled woman and smiled. "How did you know?"

"It's the way ye're lookin' at her, like ye already own her."

Stephen laughed.

"She said ye were the ugliest man created."

Stephen's eyes sparkled. "And what do you think?"

Morag grunted. "Ye'll do. And don't try to get compliments out of me."

"Now that I've been put in my place, perhaps you'll tell me who you are. I take it by your accent that you're a Scot like my Bronwyn."

"I'm Morag of MacArran."

"Bronwyn's maid?"

Morag's back stiffened. "Ye'll do well to learn that we're freemen in Scotland. I do what I can to earn my bread. Why were ye late for yer own weddin'?"

Stephen looked back at Bronwyn. "My sister-in-law was very ill. I couldn't leave until I knew she was going to live."

"And ye couldna' send a message?"

Stephen gave her a sheepish look. "I forgot. I was worried about Judith and I forgot."

Morag gave her little cackle of a laugh. She could feel herself being charmed by this tall knight. "Ye're a good man that ye could care enough about someone else to forget yer own interests."

Stephen's eyes sparkled. "Of course, I had no idea then what your mistress looked like."

The woman laughed again. "Ye're a good, honest boy . . . for an Englishman. Come inside and have some whiskey with me. Ye're not afraid of a little whiskey so early in the day?"

He held out his arm to her. "Maybe I can get you drunk and ply you with questions about Bronwyn."

Morag's cackle rang out across the garden. "There was a time, young man, when men wanted me drunk for other reasons." They walked together into the house.

Bronwyn frowned at the laugh. She'd been all too aware of the man staring at her, and she'd found it oddly unsettling. She glanced at him occasionally, and she had an impression of easy grace, power, and a strength held lightly under control. Morag's too-intimate conversation with the man disturbed her. The old woman didn't usually take to men, especially Englishmen, and Bronwyn wondered how this man could charm her so easily.

"Who is that man with Morag?"

Roger frowned. "I thought you'd met him. That's Stephen."

She stared at Stephen's retreating form, watched how he offered his arm to the wrinkled woman. Morag's head barely reached above Stephen's elbow.

Suddenly Bronwyn felt even further insulted. What kind of man was he that would stand by while another courted the woman he was to wed? He'd been only a few feet away, yet he hadn't even bothered to speak to her.

"Lady Bronwyn, has something upset you?" Roger asked, watching her closely.

"No," she smiled. "Absolutely nothing. Please continue to play."

It was nearly evening when Bronwyn saw Morag again. The setting sun made the room dim. Rab stood close by his mistress's side while she combed her long hair. "I see you had a visitor this afternoon," she said as if it were of no importance.

Morag shrugged.

"Did you speak of anything interesting?"

Again Morag merely shrugged.

Bronwyn put down her comb and went to the window seat where Morag sat. "Will you answer me!"

"Ye're a nosy one. Since when do I have to make an answer about my private conversations?"

"You've been drinking in the afternoon again. I can smell it."

Morag grinned. "That boy can certainly hold his whiskey. I bet he could drink a Scot under the table."

"Who?" Bronwyn demanded.

Morag gave her a sly look. "Why, yer husband of course. Who else would ye be houndin' me for answers about?"

"I am not . . . !" Bronwyn calmed herself. "He is not my husband. He doesn't even bother to speak to me much less appear for his wedding."

"So that's what's still botherin' ye. I figured ye'd see us together. Were ye plannin' to snub him while you had the arm of young Chatworth?"

Bronwyn didn't answer.

"I thought so! Let me tell ye that Stephen Montgomery isn't used to being snubbed by any woman, and if he does decide to marry ye after the way ye've carried on with Chatworth, ye should consider yerself fortunate."

"Fortunate!" Bronwyn managed to gasp. It was all she could say. Another word from Morag and she just might wring that scrawny little neck. "Come, Rab," she commanded and left the room.

She hurried down the stairs to the garden below. It had already grown dark, and the moon shone brightly over the trees and hedges. She walked along the paths for quite some time before she finally sat down on a stone bench in front of a low wall. How she wanted to go home! She wanted to get away from these foreigners, out of these foreign clothes, away from foreign men who looked at her only as a prize of war.

Suddenly Rab stood and gave a low growl of warning.

"Who's there?" she asked.

The man stepped forward. "Stephen Montgomery," he said quietly. He looked larger in the moonlight, towering over her. "May I sit with you?"

"Why not? What say do I have in any matter concerning the English?"

Stephen sat beside her and watched as she controlled Rab with a single hand gesture. He leaned back against the wall, his long legs stretched before him. Bronwyn moved closer to the edge of the bench, away from him. "You'll fall if you move any farther."

She stiffened. "Say what you want and have done with it."

"I have nothing to say," he said easily.

"You certainly seemed to have 'nothing' to say to Morag."

He smiled, the moonlight showing his even, white teeth. "The woman tried to get me drunk."

"And did she succeed?"

"You don't grow up with three brothers and not learn how to drink."

"You merely drank and had no conversation?"

Stephen was silent for a moment. "Why are you so hostile to me?"

She stood quickly. "Did you expect me to welcome you with open arms? I stood in my wedding gown for six hours waiting for you to come. I have seen my entire family slaughtered by the English yet I am told I must marry one. Then I am disregarded as if I did not exist. And now you make no apology to me but ask why I am hostile."

She turned away and started back toward the house.

He grabbed her arm and pulled her around to look at him. She wasn't used to a man so much taller than her. "If I offered you an apology, would you accept it?" His voice was quiet, deep, as liquid silver as the moonlight. It was the first time he'd ever touched her or even been so close. He took her wrists, ran his hands up her arms, gripping her flesh beneath the silk and velvet.

"King Henry only wants peace," he said. "He thinks that if he puts an Englishman in the midst of the Scots, they'll see we aren't so bad."

Bronwyn looked up at him. Her heart was pounding quite hard. She wanted to get away from him, but her body wouldn't obey her. "Your vanity is alarming.

Judging from your lack of manners, my Scots would see the English as worse than they feared."

Stephen laughed softly, but it was obvious his mind was not on her words. He moved his left hand to touch her throat.

Bronwyn tried to jerk from his grip. "Unhand me! You have no right to paw me . . . or to laugh at me."

Stephen made no effort to release her. "You're a delicious thing. I can only think that had I not missed our wedding, I could take you upstairs to my chamber this very moment. Perhaps you'd like to forget the day of waiting for our wedding and go with me now?"

She gasped in horror, causing Rab to growl menacingly at Stephen. She twisted sharply away from the hands that held her. Rab stepped between his mistress and the man who touched her. "How dare you?" she said between clenched teeth. "Be grateful I do not turn Rab onto you for that insult."

Stephen laughed in astonishment. "The dog values its life." He took a step closer and Rab growled louder.

"Don't come any closer," Bronwyn warned.

Stephen looked at her in puzzlement. He put his hands up in a pleading gesture. "Bronwyn, I didn't mean to insult you. I—"

"Lady Bronwyn, may I help you?" Roger Chatworth asked, stepping from the shadows of the hedges.

"Have you lately taken to skulking in shadows, Chatworth?" Stephen snapped.

Roger was calm, smiling. "I prefer to think of myself as rescuing ladies in distress." He turned to Bronwyn, his arm extended. "Would you like an escort to your chambers?"

"Chatworth, I'm warning you!"

"Stop it! Both of you!" Bronwyn said, disgusted at their childish quarrel. "Roger, thank you for your kindness, but Rab will be all the escort I need." She turned to Stephen and gave him an icy glare. "As for you, sir, I am grateful for an excuse to leave your vile company." She turned away from the men, and Rab followed her closely as she went back to the house.

Roger and Stephen stared after her for a long while, then, without looking at each other, they turned away.

Bronwyn had difficulty sleeping. Stephen Montgomery disturbed her a great deal. His nearness was unsettling, and tonight she hadn't been able to think properly while he was touching her. Was this the man she was to present to her clan as a leader? He didn't seem to have a serious bone in his body.

When she did sleep, she had bloody dreams. She saw the men of her clan following an English flag, and one by one they were slaughtered. Stephen Montgomery stood holding the banner, ignoring the Scots' death as he kept trying to thrust his hand down Bronwyn's dress.

In the morning her mood wasn't lightened by an invitation from Stephen asking her to go riding with him. She'd crumbled the note and told Morag she wouldn't go. But Morag had a way of nagging that always made anyone do what she wanted. The old woman had already gotten Bronwyn to tell her why she was so angry at Stephen.

Morag snorted. "He's a healthy young man, and he asked ye to spend the night with him. I remember some other men asking, and ye certainly weren't insulted then."

Bronwyn was silent, thinking that the English had ended her days of freedom and laughter.

Morag didn't allow Bronwyn's silence to disturb her. She wanted something, and she wouldn't stop until she got it. "He asks ye to spend the day with him. After all, yer wedding is set for tomorrow."

"How do you know so much? I haven't heard of the new date."

"Stephen told me this morning," Morag said impatiently.

"So! You've seen him again! What is it about him that interests you? There are other men, even Englishmen, who are better."

Morag sniffed. "Not any I've met."

"Roger Chatworth is a kind, intelligent man, and he has a strong strain of Scots blood."

"Did he tell ye that?" Morag snapped. "Perhaps he meant he liked the Scots' land. I think Roger Chatworth would love to have the land ye possess."

Bronwyn's eyes flashed angrily. "Isn't that what all these Englishmen want? If I were fat and old, they'd still want me."

Morag shook her head in disgust. "One moment ye decry Stephen for his hotness, the next ye complain that the men want only yer wealth and not yer person. Give him a chance to redeem himself. Talk to him, spend the day with him, ask him why he was late."

Bronwyn frowned. She didn't want to see Stephen again, ever, if that were possible. She could imagine Roger riding beside her, but she couldn't imagine Stephen doing anything but what he wanted, regardless of her wants. She looked up at Morag. "I'll try to talk to him . . . if he can keep his hands still long enough to talk."

Morag cackled. "I think there's hope in yer voice."

Chapter Three

IN SPITE OF HER RELUCTANCE TO SPEND THE DAY WITH HER betrothed, Bronwyn dressed carefully. She wore a simple wool dress the color of dark wine. It was trimmed with a border of seed pearls around the deep, square neckline. The sleeves were tight, showing the curve of her arm.

As she walked down the stairs, Rab close at her heels, she held her head high. She planned to give Stephen Montgomery a chance to show that he meant well toward her and her people. Perhaps she had hastily judged him and he wanted what was best for her clan. She could forgive him for being late for their wedding. After all, what did her personal inconvenience matter? What was important was Stephen's attitude toward her clan, whether they could accept him or not. She wanted peace between the Scots and the English as much as King Henry did—more, since it was her family members who had been slaughtered.

She stopped at the foot of the stairs and stared out

into the sunlit garden. Stephen was leaning against a low stone wall, waiting for her. She had to admit he was a handsome man, and her attraction to him was extraordinary, but she couldn't let her personal feelings— either love or hate—stand before the needs of her clan.

"Good morning," she said quietly as she walked up to him. He stared down at her with a burning intensity. He familiarly took a curl of hair from her shoulder.

"Is this the Scots' custom, to not cover the hair?" He wrapped the silken stuff about his fingers.

"Until a woman has a child, she usually leaves her hair uncovered. Except when wearing a tartan," she added, watching him to see if he'd make any comment or show any sign of recognition.

"A child." Stephen smiled. "We'll see what we can do about that." He nodded toward the far end of the garden. "I have a couple of horses waiting. Are you ready?"

She twisted her head so that he dropped her hair. "A Scotswoman is always ready to ride." She lifted her long skirts and strode ahead of him, ignoring his amused chuckle.

A pretty black mare waited beside Stephen's roan stallion. The mare pranced, lifting her feet high in excitement to be away. Before Stephen could help her, Bronwyn vaulted into the saddle. The heavy, full skirts were awkward, and she cursed the English manner of dress for the hundredth time. She was glad Stephen had not given her one of those absurd sidesaddles like Roger had.

Before Stephen had even mounted his horse, she urged the mare forward. It was a spirited animal, as anxious to run as Bronwyn was. She guided the horse, full speed, toward the path Roger had shown her. She leaned forward in the saddle, delighting in the wind on her face and throat.

Suddenly she saw a movement out of the corner of her eye. Twisting around, she saw that Stephen was close behind her, gaining on her. She laughed aloud. No Englishman born could beat a Scotswoman on a horse! She talked to the mare and applied the crop to her flank. The horse sprang forward as if it had wings. A feeling of power and exultation coursed through Bronwyn.

Glancing over her shoulder, she frowned at seeing Stephen still gaining on her. Ahead the path narrowed, too narrow for two horses side by side. If he wanted to pass her, he'd have to leave the path, go into the forest, and risk running his horse's legs into a rabbit hole or hitting a tree. She guided the mare to the middle of the path. She knew what a Scotsman would do if she blocked his path, but these Englishmen were soft things, lacking guts and stamina.

The mare ran at a hard run. Stephen was nearly on her now, and Bronwyn smiled in triumph at his confusion. It was when her mare reared slightly and screamed that Bronwyn had her hands full keeping her seat. Stephen's war-trained stallion had nipped the mare's rump as it crowded the smaller horse.

Bronwyn worked hard at controlling the mare and cursed the English for taking her own horse from her. This animal was a stranger to her and not as receptive to her commands.

The mare screamed again as the stallion bit it a second time, then, against Bronwyn's commands, it pulled aside and Stephen went thundering by. The look he threw Bronwyn made her utter a horrendous Gaelic oath. She jerked the reins and led the mare back to the center of the path.

Through all of the race Bronwyn had never allowed the mare to slow down. It was only through her extraordinary affinity with horses that she was able to control the animal as it jumped into the forest, away from the charging stallion.

When she came to the stream and jumped it, Stephen

was there, waiting for her. He'd dismounted and was standing calmly by his horse as it drank. "Not bad." He grinned up at her. "You have a tendency to pull the right rein harder than the left, but you could be quite good with a little training."

Bronwyn's eyes shot blue fire at him. Training! She'd had her own pony when she was four, had ridden with her father in cattle raids since she was eight. She'd ridden at night across the moors, up the rocks by the sea coast . . . and he said she needed training!

Stephen laughed. "Don't look so stricken. If it'll make you feel any better, you're the best woman rider I've ever seen. You could give most Englishwomen lessons."

"Women!" she managed to gasp. "I could give all English*men* lessons!"

"From where I stand, you just lost a race to an Englishman. Now get off that horse and rub it down. You can't let a horse stand in its own sweat."

Now he dared tell her how to tend to her horse. She sneered at him, raised her riding whip, and bent forward to strike him. Stephen easily sidestepped the lash, then gave her wrist one sharp, painful turn, and the crop fell to the ground. Bronwyn was caught off balance by the unexpected movement. The heavy English dress had wrapped around her leg in such a way that she lost her footing in the stirrup and pitched forward.

She grabbed the pommel and would have recovered herself but Stephen's hands were already on her waist. He pulled her toward him and she pulled away from him. For a moment it was a struggle of strength, but what infuriated Bronwyn was that Stephen seemed to be thoroughly enjoying her humiliation. He was playing with her, letting her seem to win before he pulled her down again.

He laughed and gave one powerful tug and lifted her

from the saddle, lifting her high above his head. "Did you know that that hole in your chin gets deeper when you're angry?"

"Hole!" she gasped and drew her foot back to strike him.

Considering that her feet were a yard above the ground and her sole support was Stephen's hands on her waist, it was not a wise move. He laughed at her again, tossed her in the air, then, as she struggled for balance, he caught her in his arms. He hugged her to him and kissed her ear loudly. "Are you always so entertaining?" he laughed.

She refused to look at him even though he held her aloft. Her arms were pinned to her sides or she would have struck him. "Are you always so flippant?" she retorted. "Do you never have a thought besides that of pawing women?"

He rubbed his face on her soft cheek. "You smell good." He looked back at her. "I'll admit you're the first woman who's affected me like this. But then you're the first wife I've had, a woman who was completely and totally mine."

She stiffened even more in his arms, if that were physically possible. "Is that all a woman is to you? Something to own?"

He smiled, shook his head, and set her down, his hands on her shoulders. "Of course. What else are women good for? Now pull some grass and get that sweat off your horse."

She turned away from him gratefully. They didn't speak while they unsaddled their horses and began rubbing them down. Stephen made no attempt to help her with the heavy saddle, pleasing Bronwyn because she would have refused him. She might be a woman, but she was far from helpless as he seemed to think.

When the animals were tethered, she looked back at him.

"At least you know something about horses," he

said. He laughed at her expression, then went to stand beside her. He ran his hand down her arm, and his face became serious.

"Please don't start that again," she snapped and jerked away from him. "Do you never think of anything else?"

His eyes sparkled. "Not when you're around. I think you've bewitched me. I'd make you another proposition, but the last one made you too angry."

Mentioning the scene in the garden made Bronwyn look about her. Rab lay quietly by the stream. It was odd that he'd not threatened Stephen when he'd touched her. The dog still growled whenever Roger got too near. "Where are your men?"

"With Sir Thomas, I assume."

"You don't need them for protection? What about my Scots? Didn't you know they wait in the forest, ready to rescue me?"

Stephen took her hand and pulled her toward some rocks. She tried to free herself but he wouldn't allow it. He pulled her down to sit beside him, then stretched out beside her, his head cradled in his hands. Apparently he didn't seem to think her questions deserved an answer. Instead, he stared up through the trees at the brilliant blue sky. "Why did your father name you chief of his clan?"

Bronwyn stared at him for a moment, then smiled. This was what she wanted, to talk to him about what was most important in the world—her people. "I was to marry one of three men, any one of whom would have made an excellent laird. But none of the young men was within the nine degrees of kinship from which a chief can be chosen. My father named me the next MacArran, understanding that I'd marry one of those men."

"And the men?"

Bronwyn's mouth twisted angrily. "They were killed with my father. By the English!"

Stephen didn't seem to respond except for a slight knitting of his brows. "So now whoever marries you must become the laird?"

"*I* am the laird of MacArran," she stated firmly and started to rise.

He grabbed her hand and pulled her back to the ground. "I wish you'd stop being angry with me for longer than a breath. How am I supposed to understand you if you run away?"

"I don't run away from you!" She snatched her hand away because he'd begun to kiss her fingertips. Bronwyn made herself ignore the sensations running along her arm all the way to her earlobe.

Stephen sighed and lay back down. "I'm afraid I can't look at you and talk at the same time." He paused. "Surely your father must have had another relative who could inherit."

Bronwyn calmed herself. She knew exactly what this stupid Englishman was saying. He meant that surely *any* man would have been better than a female. She did not mention her older brother, Davey. "The Scots believe women have intelligence and strength of character. They do not expect us to be only bearers of children and nothing else."

Stephen grunted in reply, and Bronwyn had a delicious vision of smashing his head with a large rock. She smiled at the thought. As if understanding her, Rab lifted his big head and looked at her in question.

Stephen seemed unaware of the exchange near him. "What would be my duties as laird?"

She gritted her teeth and tried to be patient. "I am the MacArran, and my men answer to me. They would have to accept you before they obeyed you."

"Accept me?" he asked and turned toward her, but her breasts above the pearl-bordered neckline distracted him so badly that he had to look away in order to keep his composure. "I would think it would be more whether I accepted them."

"Spoken like a true Englishman!" she sneered. "You think that the circumstances of your birth place you above everyone else. You think your ways and ideas make you better than the poor Scots. No doubt you think us cruel and savage compared to you. But we do not capture your women and force them to marry our Scotsmen, though they'd make better husbands than any Englishman."

Stephen didn't take offense at her outburst. He merely shrugged. "I'm sure every man thinks his homeland is the best. Truthfully, I know very little about Scotland or the people there. I spent some time in the Lowlands, but I don't believe that's like the Highlands."

"The Lowlanders are more English than Scots!"

He was quiet for a moment. "It seems that being the chief of a clan—pardon me," he said with an amused little chuckle, "being the husband of a chief entails some responsibility. What must I do to be accepted?"

Bronwyn relaxed her shoulders. Since he looked away from her, she had leisure to look at him. He was so tall, taller than most of the men she'd met. His long body stretched out before her, and she was well aware of his nearness. In spite of his words she wanted to sit beside him, enjoyed gazing at him, at his strong legs, at the thickness of his chest, at the dark blond curls along his collar. She liked that his dress was subdued, not gaudy like so many of the Englishmen's. She wondered how he'd look in a Scots tartan, his legs bare from mid-thigh to just below his knees.

"You must dress as a Scot," she said quietly. "The men will always be aware that you're one of the enemy if you do not wear a plaid."

Stephen frowned. "You mean run around bare-legged? I heard the Highlands get quite cold."

"Of course, if you aren't man enough—" His arrogant look stopped her.

"What else?"

"You must become a MacArran, be a MacArran.
The MacGregors will be your enemies, your name will
become MacArran. You will—"

"What!" Stephen said as he jumped to his feet and
towered over her. "Change my name! You mean to say
I, a man, am to take my wife's name?" He turned away
from her. "That's the most absurd thing I've ever
heard. Do you know who I am? I am a Montgomery!
The Montgomerys have lasted through hundreds of
wars, through many kings. Other families have risen
and fallen, but the Montgomerys have survived. My
family has owned the same land for over four hundred
years."

He turned back to her and ran his hand through his
hair. "And now you expect me to give up the Montgomery name for that of my wife?" He paused, then
chuckled. "My brothers would laugh me to hell and
back if I were to consider such a thing."

Bronwyn rose slowly, letting his words sink in. "You
have brothers to carry on your family name. Do you
know what would happen if I were to take an Englishman home who does not even attempt to understand
our ways? First my men would kill him, then I would
need to choose a new husband. Do you know what
conflict that would cause? There are several young men
who'd like to become my husband. They would fight."

"So! I'm to give up my name so you can control your
men? And what if they still didn't accept me? Perhaps I
should dye my hair or cut off an arm to please them.
No! They'll obey me or they'll feel this!" He quickly
drew his long sword from the sheath at his side.

Bronwyn stared at him. He was speaking of murdering her people, her friends, her relatives, the people
whose lives she held in her hands. She could *not* return
to Scotland with this madman.

"I cannot marry you," she said quietly, her eyes hard
and deadly serious.

"I don't believe you have a choice," Stephen said as

he resheathed his weapon. He hadn't meant to get so angry, but the woman needed to know from the start who was in control . . . as did the Scots she called "her" men. "I am an Englishman," he said quietly, "and I will remain English wherever I go. You should understand that, as I don't believe you're willing to change your Scots ways."

Her body was feeling quite cold in spite of the warm autumn day. "It is not the same. You'd be living with my people, day in and day out, year after year. Can't you see that they could *not* accept you if you strut about in your fine English clothes with your old English name? Every time they saw you, they'd remember their children the English had killed, they'd see my father, slain while he was a young man."

Her plea reached Stephen. "I will wear the Scots' garb. I'll agree to that."

Sudden, red-hot anger replaced the coldness in Bronwyn's body. "So you'll agree to wear the plaid and saffron shirt! No doubt you like the image of showing your fine, strong legs to my women."

Stephen's mouth dropped open slightly, then he grinned so broadly he threatened to split his face in half. "I hadn't thought of that, no, but it's nice to know you have." He stuck his leg out, flexed the big muscle running from the top of his knee. "Do you think your women will agree with you?" His eyes sparkled. "Will you be jealous?"

Bronwyn could only stare in astonishment. This man could not be serious for a moment. He teased her and laughed at her when she talked of life and death. She grabbed her skirts and started toward the stream.

"Bronwyn!" Stephen called. "Wait! I didn't mean to make light of what you said." He'd instantly understood his mistake. He grabbed her wrist, whirled her to face him. "Please," he begged, his heart in his eyes. "I didn't mean to offend you. It's just that you're so beautiful that I can't think. I look at your hair and I want to touch it. I want to kiss your eyes. That damned dress is so low you're about to fall out of it, and it's driving me insane. How do you expect me to talk seriously about the disputes between the Scots and the Englishmen?"

"Disputes!" she spat. "'Tis more like war!"

"War, whatever," he said, his focus on her breasts, his hands running up her arms. "God! I can't stand so near you and not have you. I've been in this condition so long I'm in pain."

Involuntarily she looked down, then her face turned red.

Stephen smiled at her with hooded eyes, a knowing smile.

She curled her lip back and snarled at him. He was a low-minded man, and he obviously thought she shared his lack of character. She twisted away from his searching hands, and when he refused to release her, she gave him a sharp shove. Stephen didn't budge, but the impact against his hard chest made Bronwyn lose her balance. She had no idea she was so near the edge of the stream.

She fell backward as she frantically tried to grab hold of something. Stephen put out his hand to catch her, but even as it touched her wrist, she slapped at it. He gave a slight shrug and stepped back, since he had no desire to wet his own clothes from the splash she was going to make.

The water from the stream must have come from the mountains of the Highlands. There was no other way it could have been so cold. Bronwyn sat down hard in the water, and the heavy wool dress soaked up the liquid ice as if it'd been waiting for such a chance.

She sat still for a moment, slightly dazed, and looked up at Stephen. He was grinning at her as a cold drop of water clung to the tip of her nose. Rab stood beside Stephen and began to bark at her, his tail wagging in delight at her game.

"Could I offer you assistance?" Stephen asked cheer-fully.

Bronwyn brushed a wet black curl off her cheek. Any moment her teeth would begin chattering, but she would yank them from her mouth before she'd let him see. "No, thank you," she said as loftily as she could manage.

She looked around her for something to use as balance, but there was nothing unless she crawled to a rock some feet away. She would never crawl before him! "Come, Rab!" she commanded, and the large dog quickly splashed into the water after his mistress.

Bronwyn wiped more water from her face, studiously avoiding Stephen's grinning face. Placing her hands on the dog's back, she started to lift herself up. The wool dress was extremely heavy to begin with, but thorough-ly soaked with water, it was impossible. This in addition to the slippery stones under her feet were too much.

She was in a half-crouch, a position that had taken her minutes to achieve, when her feet flew out from under her. Rab jumped away as Bronwyn fell again, this time flat on her back, her face going under the water. She came up gasping.

The first sound she heard was Stephen's laughter, then with a sense of betrayal she heard Rab's bark—a bark that sounded suspiciously like a canine laugh.

"Damn both of you!" she hissed and grabbed the cold, clinging, offending skirt.

Stephen shook his head at her, then entered the water. Before she could speak he'd bent and picked her up in his arms. She would have given a lot then to be able to pull him into the water with her, but his footing was too sure. When he bent to lift her, he kept his legs straight, using only his back and avoiding most of the contact with the water.

"I would like you to release me," she said as primly as possible.

Stephen gave a one-shoulder shrug, then dropped his

arms. In a reflex motion, to keep from falling back into the icy water, she gasped and threw her arms about his neck.

"Much better!" he laughed and hugged her to him so tightly she couldn't remove her arms.

He waded ashore with her and then stopped, still holding her. "I don't believe I've ever seen blue eyes with black hair before," he whispered, his eyes devouring her face. "I'm more than sorry I missed our wedding."

She knew exactly why he was sorry, and his reasons didn't help her mood any. "I am cold. Please release me," she said flatly.

"I could warm you," he said as he drew her earlobe between his teeth.

Bronwyn felt a chill run along her arm, a chill that had nothing to do with the wet dress she wore. The sensation frightened her; she didn't want it. "Please let me go," she said softly.

Stephen's head came up quickly, and he looked at her with concern. "You are cold. Take that dress off and you can wear my jacket. Should I build a fire?"

"I'd prefer that you released me and we rode back to the house."

Reluctantly, Stephen stood her in front of him. "You're shivering," he said as he moved his hands along her arms. "You'll be ill if you don't get out of that dress."

She backed away from him. The sodden gown slapped about her legs, the sleeves dragged her arms down.

Stephen gave her a look of disgust. "That damned thing is so heavy you can scarcely walk. Why in the world you women wear such fashions is beyond me. It's so heavy now I doubt if your horse could carry you."

Bronwyn straightened her shoulders even though the dress threatened to drag them down again. "Women!

It's you Englishmen who impose these fashions on your women. It is an attempt to keep them immobile since you aren't men enough to deal with free women. I had this dress made so I wouldn't shame my clan. The English too often judge a person by her clothes."

She held the fabric out. "Do you know how much this cost me? I could have purchased a hundred head of cattle for what this one garment cost me. Yet you have ruined it."

"I? It was your stubbornness that ruined it. Just as now. You stand there shivering because you'd rather freeze than do what I say."

She gave him a mocking smile. "At least you are not completely stupid. You do understand some things."

Stephen chuckled. "I understand much more than you imagine." He removed his jacket and held it out to her. "If you're so afraid of me, go into the woods and change."

"Afraid!" Bronwyn snorted and ignored the offered clothing. She walked slowly, kicking the skirt as she moved, to the saddle on the ground. She withdrew a Highland tartan from the attached bag. She didn't bother looking back at Stephen as she went into the woods, Rab following her.

She had a great deal of difficulty with the catches that ran down the back of the dress. By the time she got to the last one, her skin was nearly blue. She grabbed the dress and pulled it from her shoulders, the last hooks snapping apart. She let the dress fall in a heap at her feet.

The thin linen of her undertunic and the once-stiff petticoat were dyed pink from the burgundy wool. She longed to remove her underwear but didn't dare with someone like Stephen Montgomery near. At the thought, she looked around her to make sure he wasn't spying on her, then lifted the petticoat and removed her silk stockings. When she'd removed as much clothing as she dared, she wrapped herself in her plaid and walked back to the stream.

Stephen was nowhere in sight.

"Looking for me?" he asked from behind her.

When she turned, he was grinning at her, her wet dress thrown over his arm. It was obvious he'd hidden and watched her undress.

Her eyes were cold as she stared at him. "You think you've won, don't you? You're so confident that soon I will be at your feet that you treat me like a toy of yours. I'm not a toy, and most especially, I am not yours. For all your English vanity, I am a Scotswoman and I have some power."

She turned to where the black mare was tied; then stopped and looked back at him. "What power I have, I will use." Ignoring his presence, she pulled the tartan up to her knees, grabbed the horse's mane, and swung onto its back. She kicked it forward, already in a gallop by the time she reached Stephen.

He didn't try to stop her but mounted his stallion bareback and followed her. He would send someone later for the saddles.

It seemed a long way back to the manor house, and the horse's sharp backbone hitting him seemed just punishment for his behavior. She was a proud woman, and he had treated her badly. It was just that she did things to him. He looked at her, and he had difficulty thinking. She tried to talk to him, and all he could think about was getting her in bed. Later, he thought, after they were married and he'd bedded her a few times, he'd be able to look at her without his blood boiling.

Bronwyn stood before the mirror in her room. She felt much better now that she'd had a hot bath and some time to think. Stephen Montgomery was not the man to become her husband. If he antagonized her people as he did her, he would be killed instantly, and then the English would come down upon their heads.

She'd not marry a man who would surely cause war as well as strife within her clan.

She adjusted her hair again. She'd pulled the top of it back from her forehead, allowing the rest of it to hang freely down her back. A servant girl had brought her freshly cut autumn daisies, and Bronwyn had made a band of these across the back of her head.

Her gown was of emerald-green silk. The trailing sleeves were lined with gray squirrel fur, accenting the gray silk revealed by the part in the front of the bell-shaped skirt.

"I want to look my best," Bronwyn said, catching a glimpse of Morag in the mirror.

Morag snorted. "I'd like to think ye were dressin' to please Sir Stephen, but I don't think so."

"I will *never* dress for him!"

"As far as I can tell, the man only wants ye undressed," Morag mumbled.

Bronwyn didn't bother to answer, nor would she allow herself to become upset. What she needed to do would affect the lives of hundreds of people, and she couldn't enter upon it when she was angry.

Sir Thomas was waiting for her in the library. His smile of greeting was cordial but reserved. He heartily wished he could get rid of the beautiful woman so his men would stop snapping over her.

When Bronwyn was seated, a glass of wine refused, she began. She knew the real reason that she couldn't accept Stephen: because he refused to accept the Scots' ways. But she'd planned a more English reason to give Sir Thomas.

"But my dear," he said in exasperation, "Stephen was chosen for you by King Henry."

Bronwyn lowered her head in shy submission. "And I'm willing to accept a husband chosen for me by the English king, but I am chief of Clan MacArran, and Stephen Montgomery is merely a knight. I would have trouble with my men if I were to marry him."

"But you think they'd accept Lord Roger?"

"Since his brother's recent death, he is an earl, more nearly my rank as chief."

Sir Thomas grimaced. He was getting too old for this sort of thing. Damn those Scots anyway for allowing a woman to think for herself. None of this would be happening if Jamie MacArran hadn't named his daughter his successor.

He walked to the door and asked for Stephen and Roger to be brought to him.

When the young men were seated, one on each side of Lady Bronwyn, Sir Thomas told them of her plan. He watched the men's faces carefully. He saw the light come into Roger's eyes, and Sir Thomas turned away from him. Stephen sat quietly; the only sign he gave that he heard was a slight darkening of his eyes. Bronwyn never moved, the green of her dress giving her eyes a new depth, the daisies in her hair making her appear sweet and innocent.

Roger was the first to speak when Sir Thomas finished. "The Lady Bronwyn is right. Her title should be honored."

Stephen's eyes flashed. "Of course you'd think that, since you plan to gain a great deal by such a decision." He turned to Sir Thomas. "The king spent a year choosing a bride for me. He wanted to reward my family for helping patrol the Lowlands borders."

Bronwyn whirled on him. "Kill and rape, you mean!"

"I meant what I said: patrol. We did very little killing." His eyes went to her breasts and his voice lowered. "And almost no raping."

Bronwyn stood. "Sir Thomas, you've been to the Highlands." She ignored his shudder of unpleasant memory. "My people would be dishonored if I were to bring back a lowly knight who was to be their laird. King Henry wants peace. This man," she pointed at

Stephen, "would only cause more trouble if he entered the Highlands."

Stephen laughed as he stepped behind Bronwyn and put a strong arm around her waist. He held her tightly against him. "This isn't a matter of diplomacy but a girl's anger. I asked her to come early to my bed, before the wedding, and she thought I'd insulted her."

Sir Thomas smiled, relieved. He started to speak.

Roger stepped forward. "I protest! Lady Bronwyn is not a woman to be put aside so easily. What she says makes sense." He turned to Stephen. "Are you afraid to put the winning of her to a test?"

Stephen raised one eyebrow. "I don't believe the Montgomery name has 'coward' attached to it. What did you have in mind?"

"Gentlemen! Please!" Sir Thomas fairly shouted. "King Henry sent Lady Bronwyn here for a wedding, a happy occasion."

Bronwyn jerked from Stephen's grasp. "Happy! How can you say the word when I am to be married to this greedy, insufferable lowling? I swear I'll murder him in his sleep the first opportunity I get."

Stephen smiled at her. "So long as it's after the wedding night, I might be content."

Bronwyn sneered.

"Lady Bronwyn!" Sir Thomas commanded. "Would you leave us?"

She took a deep breath. She'd said what she wanted, and now she could no longer bear being near Stephen. With great grace Bronwyn lifted her skirts and stepped from the room.

"Stephen," Sir Thomas began. "I wouldn't like to be the cause of your murder."

"I'm not threatened by the words of a woman."

Sir Thomas frowned. "You say that from innocence. You've never been north to the Highlands. There is no government there, not like we have. The lairds rule their clans, and no one rules the lairds. All Lady Bronwyn has to do is murmur discontent, and every man, or woman for that matter, in her clan would be ready to end your life."

"I am willing to take that chance."

Sir Thomas stepped forward and put a hand on Stephen's shoulder. "I knew your father, and I feel he wouldn't want me to send his son into sure death."

Stephen stepped back from the friendly hand. His face changed into one of furor. "I want that woman! You have no right to take her from me." He whirled on Roger, who had begun to smile. "I'll meet you on a battlefield, and then we'll see who is most worthy to claim chiefship."

"Accepted!" Roger snapped. "Tomorrow morning. The winner will wed her in the afternoon, bed her at night."

"Done!"

"No," Sir Thomas murmured, but he knew he'd lost. They were two hot-blooded young men. He sighed heavily. "Leave me, both of you. Prepare your own battlefield. I want nothing to do with it."

Chapter Four

STEPHEN STOOD BESIDE HIS STALLION, COVERED IN STEEL from head to foot, the sun beating down on his armor. It was weighing him down, but he'd long ago learned to handle its weight.

"My lord," his squire said, "the sun will be in your eyes."

Stephen nodded curtly. He was well aware of the fact. "Let Chatworth have what advantage he can. He'll need it."

The boy smiled in pride at his master. It had taken a long while to dress Sir Stephen in the layers of padded cotton and leather that went under the steel plates.

Stephen mounted his horse with ease, then reached to take his lance and shield from the boy. He didn't bother to look to his right. He knew Bronwyn stood there with a face as white as the gold-trimmed ivory dress she wore. It didn't help his spirit any to know the woman would like to see him lose or perhaps even be killed.

He adjusted the long wooden lance against his armor. He and Roger had not spoken since last night, and Sir Thomas had been true to his word; he was ignoring the fight. Thus no rules had been established. It was a joust, a fight to see who could stay on his horse longest.

Stephen's war-horse, a massive black stallion with heavy feathering on its feet, pranced once in impatience. The animals were bred for power and stamina rather than swiftness.

Stephen's men surrounded him, then pulled back as Roger appeared at the far end of the sand-covered field. A low wooden fence ran down the center.

Stephen lowered his helmet plate, leaving only a slit for his eyes, his head completely covered. A young man raised a banner, and when he lowered it, the two noble men charged at each other, lances raised. It was not a test of speed, but of strength. Only a man in the peak of condition could withstand the lance shattering against his shield.

Stephen gripped his horse hard with his powerful thighs when Roger's lance squarely hit his shield. The lance shattered, as did Stephen's. Stephen reined his horse back to his end of the field.

"He's good, my lord," one of Stephen's men said as he handed his master a new lance. "Watch the tip this time. I think he means to run it under your shield."

Stephen nodded curtly and shut his helmet again.

The banner was lowered to begin the second charge. All Stephen had to do was knock his opponent from his horse, and by all rules of jousting, he'd win. When Roger charged again, Stephen dipped his shield lower and effectively kept Roger from hitting him. Taken aback, Roger didn't see Stephen's lance as it struck his side. He reeled in the saddle and nearly fell from the mighty blow, but he managed to keep his seat.

"He's dazed," the man at Stephen's side said. "Hit him this time and he'll go down."

Again Stephen nodded and slammed his helmet shut.

Roger concentrated on his attack and didn't take care of defending himself. As he dipped his lance Stephen hit him again, this time much harder than before. Roger fell backward then toward the side, landing hard in the dirt at the feet of Stephen's horse.

Stephen glanced briefly at his opponent lying in the dust and then looked away toward Bronwyn.

But Roger Chatworth was not a man to turn one's back on. He grabbed a spike-headed club from his horse's saddle and ran with it aloft.

"Stephen!" someone screamed.

Stephen reacted instantly but not quite quickly enough. Roger's club came down hard on Stephen's left thigh. The steel armor bent and jammed into his flesh. The unexpected impact sent him reeling, and he fell from his stallion, clutching at the pommel.

Stephen righted himself and saw that Roger was again advancing on him, prepared to attack again. He rolled away, steel hinges creaking in protest.

Stephen was thrown a club just as Roger's club hit his shoulder. Stephen grunted and slammed his club into Roger's side. As Roger staggered sideways Stephen pursued him. Stephen meant to win this battle.

His second blow, on Roger's right shoulder blade, sent Roger sprawling. The armor protected the men from cut flesh, but the immense force of each blow was stunning.

Roger lay still, obviously dazed. Stephen withdrew his sword, straddled Roger's shoulders, and kicked open his face plate. Then Stephen, with both hands on the hilt, held the sword over him.

Roger glared up at the victor. "Kill me and be done with it! I would've killed you."

Stephen stared down at him. "I've won. It's enough for me." He stepped to one side of Roger's inert form and removed his gauntlet. He held out his bare hand, palm up to his prostrate opponent.

"You insult me!" Roger hissed, lifting his head and spitting on Stephen's offered hand. "I'll remember this."

Stephen raked his hand across his armor. "I'm not likely to forget it." He resheathed his sword and turned away.

He walked straight to Bronwyn, who was standing beside Morag. Bronwyn was rigid as Stephen approached. He stopped before her and slowly removed his helmet, tossing it to Morag, who caught it with a grin.

Bronwyn retreated a step.

"You cannot escape me again," Stephen said as he grasped her upper arm with his uncovered hand. He pulled her to him, his one arm stronger than her whole body.

He pulled her soft body against the steel of his armor. The coldness of it, the hardness of it, made Bronwyn gasp. More steel struck her back as his arms encircled her.

"You're mine now," Stephen murmured as his lips touched hers.

It was not the first time Bronwyn had kissed a man. There had been several stolen moments during fast cattle raids across the heather.

But it was the first time she'd experienced anything like this kiss. It was soft and sweet, but at the same time it was taking from her things she'd never given before. His mouth played with hers, touching it, caressing it, yet plundering it. She stood on tiptoe to reach him better, turned her head to more of a slant. He seemed to want her to part her lips, and she did so. The cold-hot touch of the tip of his tongue on hers sent little shivers down her spine. Her body seemed to go limp, and when her head moved back, his followed hers, holding her captive more than any chains could.

Abruptly Stephen pulled away, and when Bronwyn opened her eyes, he was grinning insolently at her. She realized that she was held entirely by his grip, that his kiss had made her surrender her entire body weight to him. She straightened, letting her own feet support her again.

Stephen chuckled. "You are mine more than you know." He released her and pushed her toward Morag. "Go and ready yourself for our wedding . . . if you can wait that long."

Bronwyn turned away quickly. She did not want him or anyone else to see her brilliantly red face or the tears that were forming. What none of his insults could do, his kiss was accomplishing in making her cry.

"What are ye greeting about?" Morag snapped as soon as they were alone in the room. "He's a fine, handsome man ye're to marry. Ye got your way, and he had to fight for ye. He proved himself to be a strong, aggressive fighter. What more do ye want?"

"He treats me like a tavern wench!"

"He treats ye like a *woman*. That other one, that Roger, can't see ye for yer lands. I doubt he even knows ye're a woman."

"That's not true! He's like . . . Ian!"

Morag frowned as she thought of the young man, killed when he was only twenty-five. "Ian was like a brother to ye. Ye grew up with him. Had he lived to marry ye he'd probably have felt guilty about bedding ye, felt like he was taking his sister to bed."

Bronwyn grimaced. "There's certainly no guilt in this Stephen Montgomery. He wouldn't know the meaning of the word."

"What's upsetting ye?" Morag demanded so loudly that Rab gave a little bark of concern. She stopped, and the wrinkles in her face rearranged themselves. Her voice became quieter. "Is it tonight?"

Bronwyn looked at Morag with such a bleak expression that Morag gave a snort of laughter.

"So ye are a virgin! I was never sure what with the way the laird let ye run wild with the young men."

"I was always protected. You know that."

"Sometimes a young man isn't the best protector of a young woman's virtue." She smiled. "Now stop yer frettin'. 'Tis an enjoyable experience ahead of ye; and unless I miss my guess, this Stephen knows how to make a woman's first time easier."

Bronwyn walked to the window. "I imagine he does. If I believed the way he acts, I'd think he's bedded half of England."

Morag looked at Bronwyn's back. "Are ye afraid yer inexperience will displease him?"

Bronwyn whirled about. "No pale Englishwoman can compete with a Scotswoman!"

Morag chuckled. "Yer color's comin' back. Now out of that dress, and let's get ye in yer weddin' dress. It's only a few more hours before ye go to the kirk."

Bronwyn's face lost its color again, and with resignation she set about the long process of changing.

Stephen sat buried up to his neck in a tub of very hot water. His leg and shoulder burned from the blows Roger had given him. His eyes were closed as he heard the door open and shut. "Go away!" he growled. "I'll call when I need you."

"And what will you call?" came an amused, familiar voice.

Stephen's eyes flew open, and the next minute he was bounding across the room, nude, dripping water. "Chris!" he laughed as he clasped his friend to him.

Christopher Audley returned the greeting briefly, then pushed Stephen away. "You're soaking me, and I don't want to have to change again for your wedding. I haven't missed it, have I?"

Stephen stepped back into the tub. "Sit over there so I can see you. You've lost weight again. Didn't France agree with you?"

"It agreed too well. The women nearly wore me

away with their demands." He set a chair by the tub. He was a short, thin, dark man with a small nose and chin and a short, well-trimmed beard. His eyes were brown and large, rather like a doe's. He used his soft, expressive eyes to their best advantage in bringing women to him.

He nodded toward Stephen's shoulder and the bruise. "Is that a new wound? I didn't know you'd been fighting lately."

Stephen dipped a handful of water over the injury. "I had to fight Roger Chatworth for the woman I'm to wed."

"Fight?" Chris said in astonishment. "I spoke to Gavin before I left, and he said you were almost sick at the prospect of the marriage." He smiled. "I saw that wife of Gavin's. She's a beauty, but from what I hear she's a hellion. She had the whole court agog with her escapades."

Stephen waved his hand in dismissal. "Judith's calm compared to Bronwyn."

"Is Bronwyn the heiress you're to marry? Gavin said she was fat and ugly."

Stephen chuckled as he soaped his legs. "You won't believe Bronwyn when you see her. She has hair so black that it almost makes a mirror. The sun flashes off of it. She has blue eyes and a chin that juts out in defiance every time I speak to her."

"And the rest of her?"

Stephen sighed. "Magnificent!"

Chris laughed at Stephen's tone. "Two brothers couldn't be as fortunate as you and Gavin. But why did you have to fight for her? I thought King Henry gave her to you."

Stephen stood up and caught the towel Chris tossed him. "I was four days late to the wedding, and I'm afraid Bronwyn has taken a . . . disliking to me. She has some absurd idea that if I marry her I must become a

Scot, even change my name. I don't know for sure, but I think Chatworth may have hinted that he'd do anything she wanted if she married him."

Chris snorted. "And no doubt she believed him. Roger always could charm the women, but I've never trusted him."

"We jousted for her, but when I tossed him in the dirt, he came at my back with a war club."

"The bastard! I always wondered how much of his brother was in him. Edmund was a vile man. I guess you won the fight."

"I was so damn mad that he'd attack me that I was close to killing him. Actually he begged me to do so, said I'd insult him if I didn't."

Chris was thoughtful for a moment. "You've made an enemy of him. That could be bad."

Stephen walked to the bed, where his wedding clothes lay. "I don't blame the man for trying for Bronwyn. She'd make any man fight for her."

Chris grinned. "I've never seen you act this way toward a woman before."

"I've never seen a woman like Bronwyn before." He stopped, then yelled "Come in" to a knock on the door.

A young maidservant stood there, her arms outstretched, a shimmering gown of silver cloth across them. She stared at the bare-chested Stephen.

"What is it?" he demanded. "Why didn't you give the dress to the Lady Bronwyn?"

The girl's lower lip trembled.

Stephen pulled his shirt on, then took the dress from the girl. "You can tell me," he said quietly. "I know the Lady Bronwyn has a sharp tongue. I won't beat you for repeating what she said."

The girl looked up. "She was in the hall, my lord, when I found her, and there were several people about. I gave her the dress, and she seemed to like it."

"Yes! Go on!"

The girl finished in a rush. "But when I said it was from you, to be worn for the wedding, she threw it back at me. She said she had a wedding dress, and she'd never wear yours. Oh, my lord, it was awful. She was very loud, and all the people laughed."

Stephen took the gown from the girl and gave her a copper penny.

As soon as the girl was gone, Chris began to laugh. "A sharp tongue did you say? It sounds to me like it's more like a knife blade."

Angrily Stephen thrust his arms through his doublet. "I've had about enough of this. It's time someone taught that young lady some manners."

He tossed the dress over his shoulder and left the room, taking long strides toward the Great Hall. He'd gone to a lot of trouble to get the exquisite garment. Bronwyn had complained about her ruined dress after she'd fallen in the stream, and so Stephen had made an attempt to repay her—not that he'd done anything to cause her to fall in the water, of course. He'd ridden into town and found the silver fabric, then paid four women to sit up all night sewing it. The material was a soft, fine wool with every other weft-thread a hair-thin piece of silver wire. It was heavy and luxurious. It shimmered and glowed even in the darkness of the hallways. In all likelihood it had cost more than all the gowns Bronwyn owned.

Yet she refused to wear it.

He saw her as soon as he entered the Great Hall. She sat on a cushioned chair wearing a dress of ivory satin. A young man sat close to her strumming a psaltery.

Stephen planted himself between them.

She gave one startled glance at him, then turned away.

"I would like you to wear this dress," he said quietly.

She didn't look up at him. "I have a wedding dress."

Someone near Stephen gave a low chuckle. "Having women problems again, Stephen?"

Stephen stood still a moment, then jerked Bronwyn to her feet. He didn't say a word, but the black look on his face was more than enough to keep her quiet. He locked his fingers about her wrist and pulled her after him. Her feet tangled in her skirts, and once she nearly fell before she could lift the fabric with her free hand. She knew Stephen would drag her if she fell behind.

He fairly tossed her inside her empty chamber, then slammed the door shut. He threw the dress on the bed. "Put it on!" he ordered.

Bronwyn held her ground. "I am not now, nor will I ever be, yours to command."

His eyes were hard and dark. "I've done everything humanly possible to make up for being late."

"Late!" she snarled. "Do you think that's why I hate you? Do you really know so little about me that you think I'm so vain as to hate you just because you have the manners of a boor? I wanted you to lose today because Roger Chatworth would have been better for my clan. They'll hate you as I do because of your arrogance, because of the way you think you own everything. You even believe you can dictate the dress I wear to be married in."

Stephen took one step forward, then grabbed her jaw in his hand, his thumb and fingers digging into her cheeks. "I'm sick of hearing of your clan, and I'm even more sick of hearing Chatworth's name from your lips. I had the dress made for you as a gift, but you're too stubborn, too hot-headed to take it as such."

She tried to free her head but couldn't. He tightened his grasp, causing tears to come to her eyes.

"You are my wife," he said, "and as such you will obey me. I know nothing about your people, and I can only deal with them when I meet them. But I do know how wives should act. I went to a great deal of trouble to have this dress made for you, and you are going to wear it."

"No! I will not obey you! I am the MacArran!"

"Damn you!" he said, grabbing her shoulders and beginning to shake her. "This is not between England and Scotland nor between a laird and a clansman. This is between *us*—a man and a woman! You are going to wear that dress because I am your husband and I say you will!"

He stopped shaking her and saw that his words had made no impression on her. He bent and flung her over his shoulder.

"Release me!"

He didn't bother to answer her as he tossed her on the bed, face down.

"Stop it! You're hurting me!"

"You've done more than hurt me," he retorted as his big fingers fumbled at the tiny buttons down the back of her dress. His legs straddled her. "Tonight I'll show you the wounds Roger made on me. Hold still or I'll tear this damn dress to pieces."

Instantly Bronwyn lay still.

Stephen gave the back of her a look of disgust. "It seems that I get the most response out of you when I threaten to cost you some money."

"We're a poor country and can't afford the waste that I see here in England." She was quiet while Stephen worked on the buttons. "You . . . fought well this morning."

He paused for a moment before he started again on the buttons. "That must have been hard for you to say, considering that you were hoping I was killed."

"I wanted no one killed! All I wanted was—"

"Don't tell me! I already know what you wanted! Roger Chatworth."

It was an odd moment. Bronwyn felt strangely intimate with Stephen, as if they'd known each other for many years. She knew she couldn't explain to him why she wanted Roger. She'd certainly tried often enough! Now it was almost pleasant to hear the note of jealousy in his voice. Let him think that she burned for Roger. It might do him good.

"There! Now get up and let's get that dress off."

When she didn't move, he leaned over her and ran his lips along her neck. "Let's not wait until tonight."

His words as well as his actions made Bronwyn come alive. She quickly rolled out from under him. She grabbed the front of her dress as it fell forward. "I'll put the dress on, but first you must leave."

Stephen lay back on his elbow. "I have no intention of leaving."

Bronwyn started to argue, but she knew it was no use. Besides, he'd seen her in wet underclothes twice before. At least this time she'd be hidden more completely by their dryness. She stepped out of the gown and carefully laid it across a wooden chest.

Stephen's eyes watched her hungrily, and when she went to get the silver dress, he held it away from her so that she had to step very close to him to get it. He had time to plant one quick kiss on her shoulder before she moved away.

The heavy silver fabric was beautiful, and she ran her hand admiringly over the skirt before she slipped it over her head. It fit perfectly, hugging her small waist, flaring gracefully over her hips. As it settled about her body she looked up at Stephen in astonishment. The neckline was not the deep square that was fashionable but was high, all the way to the base of her throat, where a tiny collar of lace rested.

Stephen shrugged at her puzzlement. "I'd prefer that not so much of what's mine be shown to the other men."

"Yours!" she gasped. "Do you plan to always choose all in my life? Am I no longer to even select my own clothes?"

He groaned. "I knew your sweetness wouldn't last for long. Now come over here so I may fasten it."

"I can do it myself."

He watched her struggle for a few moments before he pulled her to him. "Do you think you will ever learn that I am not your enemy?"

"But you are my enemy. All Englishmen are enemies to my clan and me."

He pulled her between his legs and began to fasten the tiny buttons. When they were done, he turned her around, holding her fast between his knees. "I hope to someday teach you that I am more than an Englishman." He ran his hands up her arms. "I am looking forward to tonight."

Bronwyn tried to twist away from him. Stephen sighed and released her. He stood beside her, then took her hand in his. "The priest and our guests are waiting below."

Bronwyn reluctantly took his hand. His palm was warm and dry, callused from years of training. Stephen's squire waited outside the door, holding out a heavy velvet jacket to his master. Bronwyn watched as Stephen thanked the boy, who looked up proudly at his master and wished him luck and happiness.

Stephen smiled and raised Bronwyn's hand to his lips. "Happiness," he said. "Do you think that for us happiness is possible?"

She looked away and didn't answer as they started down the stairs together, hand in hand. The silver dress weighed on her, and with each step she was reminded of this stranger's domination of her.

Many people waited at the foot of the stairs, all men, all friends of Sir Thomas's, men who'd fought against the Highlanders. They made no effort to conceal their animosity toward the Scots. They laughingly talked of Stephen's "conquering" of the enemy that night. They laughed at the way Bronwyn had fought them after they killed her father. They said that if Bronwyn were half as wild in bed, Stephen was in for a treat.

She lifted her head high, telling herself that she was

the MacArran and she must make her clan proud of
her. The English were a crude, bragging lot of men,
and she wouldn't lower herself to their level by replying
to their disgusting comments.

Stephen's hand tightened on hers, and she looked up
at him in surprise. His face was solemn, his mouth set in
a grim line; a muscle worked in his jaw. She would have
thought he would enjoy the comments of his countrymen since they were proof that he'd won a prize of war.
He turned and looked down at her, and his eyes were
almost sad, as if he meant to apologize to her.

The wedding was over very quickly. Truthfully, it
didn't seem much like a wedding at all. Bronwyn stood
before the priest, and in that moment she realized how
alone she was. When she'd imagined her marriage, it
had been in the Highlands, in the spring, when the
earth was just beginning to come alive. She would be
surrounded by her family and all the members of her
clan. Her husband would have been someone she
knew.

She turned and looked at Stephen. They knelt side by
side inside the little chapel in Sir Thomas's house.
Stephen's head was reverently bowed. How far away he
seemed, how remote. And how very little she knew of
him. They had grown up in two different worlds, in
completely separate ways of life. All her life she'd been
taught that she had rights and powers, that her people
would turn to her for help. Yet this Englishman had
known only a society where women were taught to sew
and to be extensions of their husbands.

Yet Bronwyn was condemned to sharing her life with
this man. He'd already made it clear that he believed
her to be his property, something he owned and could
command at will.

And tonight . . . Her thoughts stopped because she
could not bear to think of tonight. This man was a
stranger to her—a total stranger. She knew nothing
about him. She didn't know what he liked to eat, if he

could read or sing, what sort of family he had. Nothing!
Yet she was to climb into bed with him and share the
most intimate experience of life, and everyone seemed
to think she should enjoy it!

Stephen turned and looked at her. He'd been aware
of her staring at him, and it pleased him. There was
puzzlement and perplexity on her lovely brow. He gave
her a slight smile that he meant to be reassuring, but
she looked away from him and again closed her eyes
over her clasped hands.

For Bronwyn the day seemed to wear on endlessly.
The men who were the wedding guests made no
attempt to hide the fact that their only interest was in
the wedding night. They sat about the great trestle
tables and ate and drank for hours. And the more they
drank, the cruder their jests became. With each statement, each drunken jibe, Bronwyn's hatred for the
English increased. They cared nothing for the fact that
she was a woman; to them she was only a trophy to be
enjoyed.

When Stephen reached for her hand, she drew back
from him, and this action caused a new round of
raucous laughter. She didn't look at Stephen, but she
saw that he drank deeply of the strong red wine.

The rays of sun lengthened across the room, and a
couple of the men, drunk, began a quarrel and proceeded to wrestle with each other. No one tried to stop
them, as they were too drunk to do much harm.

Bronwyn ate very little and drank even less. As the
night approached she could feel her insides tightening.
Morag had been right: what bothered her was the
thought of tonight. She tried to reason with herself that
she was a woman of courage. Several times she'd led
cattle raids on the MacGregors. She'd rolled up in a
plaid and slept through a snowstorm. She'd even fought
the English beside her father. But nothing had ever
frightened her like the idea of tonight. She knew about
the physical act of mating, but what accompanied it?

Would she change? Would this Stephen Montgomery own her after mating, as he seemed to believe? Morag said the bedding was a pleasant experience, but Bronwyn had seen young men turned to jelly because they believed they were in love. She'd seen happy, exciting women become plump, complaisant housewives after a man slipped a ring on their finger. Something more than just mating happened in a marriage bed, and she was afraid of that unknown thing.

When Morag came from behind and told Bronwyn it was time to ready herself for bed, Bronwyn's face turned white and her hands gripped the carved lions' heads of the chair.

Stephen held her arm for a moment. "They are jealous. Please ignore them. Soon we'll be able to close the door and shut them out."

"I'd rather stay here," Bronwyn snarled at him, then followed Morag out of the Great Hall.

Morag didn't speak as she unfastened the silver dress. Bronwyn was like an obedient doll as she slipped nude beneath the covers of the bed. Rab lay down on the floor, close to his mistress.

"Come, Rab," Morag called. The dog didn't budge. "Bronwyn! Send Rab out. He won't like being with you tonight."

Bronwyn glared at her. "You fear for the dog but not for me? Has everyone left me? Stay, Rab!"

"Ye're feelin' sorry for yerself, 'tis all. Once it's over and done with ye won't feel so sad." She stopped as the door suddenly burst open.

Stephen rushed in and slammed the door behind him. "Here, Morag," he said. "Go quickly. They'll be angry when they see I've escaped them. But I can't stand another moment of them, and I'll not subject Bronwyn to any more of their crudities. Damn them!"

Morag grinned and put her hand on his arm. "Ye are a good lad." She leaned forward. "Beware of the dog."

She gave his arm a final pat. He opened the door for her and then closed it behind her.

Stephen turned to Bronwyn and smiled at her. She sat up in the bed, her black hair cascading over the sheets. Her face was white, her eyes large and frightened in her face. Her knuckles, which clutched the sheet to her chin, were white from her hard clasp.

Stephen sat down heavily on the edge of the bed and pulled off his shoes, then removed his jacket and doublet. As he was unbuttoning his shirt he spoke. "I'm sorry there wasn't a more festive atmosphere for our wedding. What with Sir Thomas's house so near the border, many of the men's wives are afraid to visit."

He stopped as he heard the men pounding on the door.

"No fair, Stephen!" they yelled. "We want to see the bride. You have her all your life."

Stephen stood up and turned to face his wife as he unbuckled his sword and small knife. "They'll go away. They're too drunk to do much harm."

When he was nude, he slipped beneath the sheet beside her. He smiled at her glassy, straightforward stare. He put his hand out to touch her cheek. "Am I so formidable that you can't look at me?"

Suddenly Bronwyn came alive. She jumped out of the bed and pulled the sheet with her. She backed against the wall, and a startled Rab came to stand before her. She stared at Stephen as he lay in the bed. His nude body, his muscular legs covered with pale blond hair, looked strangely vulnerable. His chest was even thicker than it seemed when clothed. She pressed her body closer to the wall. "Do not touch me," she said under her breath.

Slowly, and with great patience, Stephen threw his legs over the side of the bed. She kept her eyes on his face and could see that he considered her outburst little more than a nuisance. He walked past her to the table where a goblet and glasses sat beside a bowl of fruit. He poured her some wine. "Here, drink this and calm down."

She knocked the glass from his hand, sending it flying across the room where it fell into pieces. "I will not allow you to touch me," she repeated.

"Bronwyn, you're only nervous. Every bride is scared her first time."

"First time!" she said in a high pitch. "Do you think this is my first time? I have lain with half the men of my clan. I just don't wany any filthy Englishman touching me, that's all."

Stephen did not lose his patient smile. "I know as well as you do that that's a lie. You wouldn't be so frightened if you'd been with a man before. Now please relax. You're only making things worse. Besides, what can you do?"

She hated his smug self-assurance that she was helpless against him. She hated everything about him. He stood there so confident. Even nude he emanated a feeling of power. Bronwyn returned his smile, for she had something that would take that smile from his face.

"Rab!" she commanded. "Attack!"

The huge dog hesitated only a moment, then it sprang off its feet and headed directly for Stephen's head.

Stephen moved to one side, his reactions even faster than the dog's. As Rab flew toward him, a mass of snarls and long, pointed teeth, Stephen doubled his fist and slammed it into the side of the dog's great square head. Rab's flight immediately changed direction, and he hit the wall with force, then slid to a heap on the floor.

"Rab!" Bronwyn screamed and dropped her sheet as she ran to him.

The dog tried to stand but weaved about in a stunned way.

"You've hurt him," Bronwyn cried as she looked up at Stephen standing over them.

Stephen had given the dog only a brief glimpse to see that it was unhurt, then his eyes were on Bronwyn alone. He stared, open-mouthed, at her rosy-tipped breasts, her round hips covered with skin like ivory satin.

"I'll kill you for this!" Bronwyn screamed.

Stephen was too dazed with the beauty of her to see that she was reaching for the knife that lay by the fruit on the table. It was a dull knife, but the little point was sharp. He saw the flash of it only an instant before it would have sunk into his shoulder. He moved to one side, and it cut his skin.

"Damn!" he said as he put his hand over the wound. Suddenly he was very tired. Blood oozed between his fingers. He sat down on the bed, moved his hand, and looked at his shoulder. "Tear off a piece of that sheet so I can tie this."

Bronwyn stood still, the knife still in her hand.

Stephen looked back at her, his eyes raking her body. "Do it!" he commanded, then watched as she knelt and tore a long strip of linen from the sheet. She wrapped the rest of the sheet around her.

Stephen didn't ask for her help in bandaging his arm. When he'd tied it, using one hand and his teeth, he turned to the dog. "Rab, come here," he said quietly. The dog obeyed instantly. Stephen carefully examined the dog's head but saw nothing hurt. He patted the animal, and Rab rubbed his head on Stephen's hand. "Good boy. Now go over there and sleep." Rab went to where Stephen pointed and lay down.

"Now, Bronwyn," he said in the same tone, "come to bed."

"I'm not Rab to change loyalties so quickly."

"Damn you!" Stephen said, then took one long stride toward her and grabbed her wrist. He pulled the sheet away from her and tossed it to the floor. "You're going to obey me if I have to beat you." He threw her over his bare thighs, bottom end up, and applied several hard, painful smacks to her firm, round buttocks.

When he finished, when each cheek bore the prints of his fingers, he threw her to the far side of the bed. He ignored the tears of pain in her eyes. He stretched out beside her, threw one arm around her waist, one heavy thigh over hers.

Stephen lay still for a moment, feeling Bronwyn's delicious skin next to his, and he wanted very much to make love to her. But he was also very, very tired. He'd fought Roger that morning, and Bronwyn, as well as her dog, the rest of the day. A sudden feeling of contentment washed over him. He had her and she was his to enjoy for the rest of his life. His muscles began to relax.

Bronwyn lay under Stephen in a rigid position, braced for what was to come. Her backside burned from his spanking, and she sniffed once through her tears. When she felt him relax, then heard the even breathing that unmistakably said he was asleep, she felt relieved—then she was insulted. She started to move away from him, but he held her in a grip that threatened to break her ribs. When she saw there was nothing else she could do, she began to relax. And when she did, she found she rather liked his skin next to hers. His shoulder was hard and firm, and she rested her cheek against it. The candles in the room guttered, and she smiled dreamily as Stephen buried his face deeper in her hair.

Chapter Five

STEPHEN WOKE VERY EARLY THE NEXT MORNING. AT FIRST he was only aware of the pain and stiffness of his bruised shoulder and his gashed upper arm. The room was dark and quiet, with only the faintest pink light coming through the tall window.

Stephen first became aware of the smell of Bronwyn. Her thick black hair was wrapped around his arm. Her thigh rested between his. He forgot any feelings of discomfort in an instant. He took a deep, slow breath and looked at her. Asleep and relaxed, her eyes didn't shout hatred at him; her chin was lowered and defenseless, soft and womanly.

Cautiously he moved his hand to touch the side of her face. Her cheek was as smooth as a baby's, softly rounded, sleep-pinked. He buried his fingers in her hair, watched the curls grab at his forearm like a rose bush climbing a trellis. It seemed as though he'd wanted her all his life. She was the woman he'd dreamed about. He had no desire to rush his pleasure of her. He'd waited so long, and now he wanted to take his time and savor her.

He was aware when she first opened her eyes. He made no quick movements, did nothing that would startle her. Her eyes, large and blue, swallowing her face, reminded him of the deer in the Montgomery parkland. As a boy Stephen had been able to creep up on them; then he'd just sit and watch, and after a while the animals would lose their fear of him.

He touched her arm, ran his hand down it to catch her hand. Slowly he raised it to his lips, and as he put one finger in his mouth he looked into her eyes and smiled. She looked at him with a worried expression, as if she were afraid he'd take something more from her than her virginity. He wanted to reassure her but he knew no words could, that the only way to make her understand was to awaken her response to him.

He shifted so that both of his arms were free, and he felt her stiffen beside him. With one hand he held her fingertips to his mouth, touching the soft pads with his teeth and tongue. He ran his other hand across her ribs, hugging her waist, caressing her hip. Her body was firm, the muscles under her soft skin shapely and hard from use. He felt her draw in her breath sharply when he touched her breast. Very gently he let his thumb touch the pink tip. Even as he felt the crest grow firm under his touch, she did not relax. Stephen frowned slightly, realizing he was getting nowhere. All his gentleness had only made her more rigid.

His hand moved from her breast to her thigh. He bent his head and touched his mouth to her neck, then moved his lips down her shoulder to her breast while his hand played with the delicate shape of her knee. He felt her give a tiny shudder of pleasure, and he smiled as he moved to her left breast, his hands on her waist. He frowned as he felt her tense again.

He moved away from her. She lay on her back, staring up at him in wonder. He ran his fingertips along the line of her hair by her temple. Her hair was spread about her like a waterfall of liquid black pearls.

She's different, he thought, different from other women. Special, unique.

He grinned at her, and with a quick jerk he tossed aside the sheet that covered her legs from the knee down.

"No," Bronwyn whispered. "Please."

Her legs were magnificent: long, slim, curvaceous. She'd ridden all her life, learned to run long distances up hills and through valleys. Her legs were sensitive. Stephen realized it wasn't his touch on her breast that had caused that little tremor of pleasure but his hand on her knee.

He moved to the foot of the bed, looking at her, enjoying the beauty of her. He bent forward and put his hands on her ankles, then slowly ran them upward over her knees and thighs. Bronwyn jumped like someone had just touched her with a hot coal.

Stephen laughed deep within his throat and moved his hands down again. He took one of her feet in his hand, then his lips moved to her legs. He kissed them, ran his tongue over the sculpture of her knee.

Bronwyn moved restlessly under him. Little chills of pleasure shot through her body, running down her arms, across her shoulders. She'd never felt like this before. Her body was trembling, and her breath was rapid and uneven.

Stephen roughly turned her over on her stomach and put his mouth to the back of her knee. Bronwyn nearly went off the bed, but Stephen's hand on the small of her back kept her in place. She put her face in the pillow and moaned like someone in pain. Stephen kept torturing her. His hands and mouth explored every inch of her sensitive legs.

He wanted her so badly he couldn't resist her any longer. He turned her over again, and this time his mouth sought hers. He wasn't prepared for the force of her passion. She clung to him, her arms holding him in a viselike grip. Her mouth seemed to want to take the essence out of him. He knew what she wanted, but he also knew that she did not know.

When she started to push him down in the bed, her hands frantically running along his back and arms, he pushed her back. He mounted her, her legs opening naturally for him. She was ready for him. Her eyes opened wide, and she gasped when he first entered her. Then she closed her eyes, tilted her head back, and smiled. "Yes," she whispered. "Oh, yes."

Stephen thought his heart would stop. The look of her, her words uttered in a guttural tone, were more enticing than any love poem. Here was a woman! A woman unafraid of a man, one who could match him in passion.

He began to move atop her, and she didn't hesitate to follow his lead. Her hands caressed his body, rubbed his inner thighs until Stephen though he might be blinded by the force of the mounting desire within him. Yet Bronwyn met him thrust for thrust, giving and receiving. When he finally did explode within her, he shuddered violently, the force threatening to tear him apart.

He collapsed on Bronwyn, sweaty, limp, and held her so tightly he nearly crushed her.

Bronwyn didn't mind not breathing. For a moment she thought she must be dead. No one could go through what she'd just experienced and live. Her whole body throbbed, and she felt as if she couldn't have walked if her life depended on it. She drifted to sleep with her arms and legs still wrapped around Stephen.

When she awoke, she stared up into his amused blue eyes. Sunlight poured into the room, and in a flash she remembered everything that had happened between them. She could feel her face filling with hot blood. It was odd that now she couldn't seem to remember the feelings that had made her act in such an embarrassing way.

He touched her cheek, his eyes full of laughter. "I knew you'd be worth a fight," he said.

She moved away from him. She felt good. Actually she felt the best that she had in a long time. Of course! she thought. It was because she knew she was the same. She'd spent the night with a man and she hadn't changed. She still hated him; he was still the enemy. He was still an insufferable, arrogant braggart. "That's all I am to you, isn't it? To you I'm a wench to warm your bed."

Stephen smiled lazily. "You near set it on fire." He ran his hand over her arm.

"Release me!" she said firmly, then jumped from the bed and grabbed her green velvet chamber robe.

One quick knock sounded on the door, and Morag entered, carrying a ewer of hot water. "I heard yer quarrels all the way down the stairs," she snapped.

"There must have been other sounds you heard," Stephen said as he propped his hands behind his head.

Morag turned and grinned at him, her old face folding into so many wrinkles that her eyes disappeared. "Ye look well pleased with yerself." She gave an appreciative look at the sight of him, his sun-bronzed skin against the sheet, the heavy muscles of his chest and arms hard even when they were relaxed.

"More than pleased, I should say. No wonder you Highlanders never come south." His eyes roamed to Bronwyn, who was glaring at him with hatred.

Chris Audley appeared at the door.

"Are we allowed no privacy?" Bronwyn snapped as she turned toward the window, Rab at her side. She didn't touch the dog, as she felt betrayed by him, too, both last night and this morning when he'd allowed Stephen to . . . to . . . Her face began to feel warm again.

Stephen smiled at Chris. "She likes being alone with me."

"What happened to your arm?" Chris asked, nodding toward the bandage crusted with dried blood.

Stephen shrugged. "A mishap. Now if the two of you are satisfied that we didn't kill each other, perhaps you'd leave my wife and me alone so she could tend to my wound."

Morag and Chris smiled at him, gave one brief glance to Bronwyn's rigid back, and left.

Bronwyn whirled to face Stephen. "I hope you bleed to death," she spat at him.

"Come here," he said patiently, sweetly, and held out his hands to her.

In spite of her thoughts she obeyed him. He caught her hand and pulled her down to sit on the edge of the bed beside him. He rolled toward her, and the sheet slipped down, exposing more of his hip and waist. Bronwyn looked away, back to his face. She had to control an urge to touch his skin.

He held both her hands in one of his, then touched her cheek with his free hand. "Perhaps I tease you too much. You pleased me greatly this morning."

He watched the slow flush stain her cheeks. "Now what may I do to please you, short of throwing myself from the window?"

"I would like to go home," she said quietly, all of her longing sounding in her soft voice. "I want to go home to the Highlands, to my clan."

He bent forward and kissed her lips as softly and as sweetly as a spring rain. "Then we shall go today."

She smiled at him and then started to move away, but he held her hands firmly. Her face turned to coldness in an instant.

"You certainly distrust me, don't you?" He looked at the bloody bandage on his arm. "This needs to be cleaned and dressed properly."

She twisted away from him. "Morag can do it, and I'm sure it'd give her great pleasure, as she seems to lust after you as it is."

Stephen tossed the sheet aside and stood before her. He pulled her into his arms. "I wish that were jealousy in your voice. I don't want Morag to change the bandage. You made the wound, you must dress it."

Bronwyn couldn't move, could hardly think when he held her so close. She was remembering the feel of his lips on the back of her knees. She pushed him away from her. "All right, I'll do it. I'm sure it will be faster if I get it done with than argue with you. Then we can go home."

He sat down on the window seat, leaned back against the cushions, seemingly oblivious to the fact that he was nude. He held his arm out to her, smiling as she avoided looking at him.

Bronwyn didn't like his smugness, his easy self-assurance that his nearness had any effect on her. And worse, she hated the way his beautiful body kept drawing her eyes to it. She smiled wickedly as she ripped the bandage from his arm. Bits of raw skin and newly formed scab came away from the cut.

"Damn you!" Stephen yelled as he came up off the seat. He thrust his hand behind her neck and drew her to him. "You'll regret that! Someday you'll know that one drop of my blood is more precious than any angry feelings you carry."

"Is that your fondest wish? I tell you now that you'll not get it. I married you because it saved warfare within my clan. I do not kill you now because your old king would cause my clan grief."

Stephen pushed her away so violently that she slammed against the bed. "You do not kill me!" he sneered. Blood was running down his arm from the reopened wound. He stood and grabbed his clothes from the floor. "You think too much of yourself," he said as he thrust his legs into hose and breeches. He tossed his shirt and doublet over his arm. "Be ready in an hour," he said flatly as he slammed from the room.

The room seemed unnaturally silent when Stephen was gone, and somehow it seemed too big and too empty. She was glad, of course, that he was gone. For one brief moment she wondered who he'd get to dress the wound on his arm, then she shrugged. What did she care? She went to the door and called Morag. There was a great deal to be done in an hour.

They rode hard all that day and into the night. Bronwyn felt her heart and mind lighten the farther north they rode. She hated the noise and the many baggage wagons that followed them. To her Scots' sense of economy, the wagonloads of goods were needless. A Scotsman would take what he wore on his back, what food he could carry in a pack. The Englishmen stopped at midday for a cooked meal. Bronwyn had been too impatient to eat much.

"Sit down!" Stephen commanded. "You'll make my men nervous with your constant jumping about."

"Your men! What of my men who wait for me?"

"I can only take care of one group of men at a time."

"You can—!" she began, then stopped. Several of Stephen's men were watching them with interest. Christopher Audley smiled at her, his eyes twinkling. Bronwyn knew he was a pleasant young man, but now no one pleased her. She wanted to get out of these cursed Lowlands as soon as possible.

They crossed the Grampians at night. They were low mountains interspersed with wide valleys. As soon as they crossed, the air seemed to grow cooler, the landscape wilder, and Bronwyn began to breathe easier. Her shoulders relaxed, the muscles in her face untightened.

"Bronwyn!" Stephen said from beside her. "We must stop for the night."

"Stop! But—" She knew it was no use to go on. Only Morag felt as she did; the others needed their rest before they could continue. She took a deep breath and knew that being this close to home would help her sleep tonight. She dismounted her horse and unfastened her saddlebag. At least she could get out of the confining English clothes.

"What's this?" Stephen asked, touching the plaid over her arm. "Is this what you wore the first night I met you?" he asked, his eyes bright with memory.

She snatched it from his grasp and walked into the darkness of the trees. It wasn't easy to unfasten the English dress by herself, but she was determined to be rid of it. Once the heavy velvet dress was carefully placed on a rock, she stripped down to her skin. The Scots' way of dress was simple and gave the people freedom. She slipped a soft cotton chemise over her head, then a saffron-colored, long-sleeved shirt. The sleeves were gathered at the shoulder, tight at the cuffs. The skirt was cut of wide gores, small at the hips but free-flowing enough to allow her to run or ride a horse. It was of a soft blue heather plaid. A wide belt with a big silver belt buckle went around her small waist. Another plaid, a six-yard cloak, she deftly threw about her shoulders, then pinned it with a big, hinged brooch. The heavy silver brooch had been handed from daughter to daughter for generations.

"Here, let me see," came a voice from behind her.

She whirled about to face Stephen. "Were you spying on me again?" she asked coldly.

"I prefer to think of it as protecting you. There's no telling what could happen to a pretty lady alone in the woods."

She backed away from him. "I think the worst has already happened." She didn't want him near her, didn't want a repeat of the power he'd had over her last night. She turned and ran back to camp.

"Didn't you forget these?" Stephen called after her, holding up her shoes. He laughed when she didn't look back.

Bronwyn limped into the tent that she'd been told was Stephen's. His men were efficient at making a camp that resembled a small town. She winced even as her foot touched the edge of the carpet spread over the good Scots soil. She'd forgotten that it'd been months since she'd run barefoot across the open ground. Her feet had grown soft, and after her short run she'd cut and bruised them.

She sat down on the edge of the wide cot and bent to inspect them. When the tent flap opened and Stephen entered, she stood up quickly even though her hurt feet brought tears of pain to her eyes.

Stephen tossed her shoes into a corner. He sat down on the cot. "Let me see them."

"I have no idea what you're talking about," she said haughtily, walking away from him.

"Bronwyn, why must you always be so stubborn? You hurt your feet, I know you did, so come over here and let me look at them."

She knew that sooner or later they'd have to be tended. Reluctantly she sat down on the cot beside him.

With a sigh of exasperation, he bent and pulled her feet into his lap. Bronwyn fell back onto her arms. Stephen frowned as he inspected the cuts, one of them quite deep. He bellowed for his squire to bring him a basin of hot water and clean bandages.

"Now put your feet in here," he said when he'd set the water on the floor.

She watched as he tenderly washed and rinsed her

feet and then put them into his lap to dry and bandage them. "Why do you do this for me?" she asked quietly. "I am your enemy."

"No you're not. You're the one who fights me, not the other way around. I'd be only too willing to live in peace with you."

"How can there be peace when my father's blood is a wall between us?"

"Bronwyn—" he began, then stopped. It was no use arguing with her. Only his actions would be able to persuade her that he meant only good for her and her clan. He patted the bandage on her left foot. "That should hold you for a while." When she started to move away, he held her feet in his lap. His eyes turned darker as he ran a hand up her calf. "You have beautiful legs," he whispered.

Bronwyn wanted to pull away from him because she recognized the look in his eyes, but he hypnotized her, kept her still even though he held her lightly. Both of his hands went under her long skirt, and she lay back against the pillows, still as he caressed her legs and buttocks.

He lay beside her, pulled her into his arms, and began to kiss her face, her ears, her mouth. His hands expertly unfastened her brooch, her belt buckle. Her clothes slipped from her body before she knew they were even unfastened. Stephen moved away from her for only seconds while he discarded his own clothes. He laughed low in his throat as Bronwyn's hands sought his body and pulled him back close to her.

He fastened his mouth onto hers, tasting the sweetness of her tongue. "Who am I?" he whispered as he ran his teeth along her neck.

She didn't answer him but rubbed her thighs along his. Her heart was racing, and in spite of the cool night a slight sheen of sweat was beginning to form on her skin.

He grabbed her hair, the thickness of it swallowing his hand. "Who am I? I want to hear you say my name."

"Stephen," she whispered. "And I am the MacArran."

He laughed, his eyes brilliant. Even in her passion she didn't lose any of that incredible pride of hers. "And I am the conqueror of the MacArran," he laughed.

"Never!" she said in a throaty whisper as she grabbed his hair and pulled back hard. His head jerked backward, and she put her teeth to his throat. "Who is the conqueror now?"

Stephen pulled her on top of him, ran his hands up and down her firmly. "We English would lose all our wars 'twere such as you the enemy." Suddenly he lifted her, then slowly lowered her so that she sat on his shaft.

Bronwyn gasped in surprise, then gave a deep moan of pleasure as she bent over him and began to move up and down. Stephen stayed very still, allowing her to control their pleasure. When he felt her excitement begin to peak, he rolled her to her back, and she clasped at him with her strong arms and legs. They exploded together in a blinding flash.

Exhausted, they fell asleep as they were, wrapped together, their skin glued together by sweat and passion.

An owl woke Bronwyn. She awoke with her eyes wide and her senses alert. Stephen was sprawled half on top of her, pinning her beneath him. She frowned as she remembered their previous passion. It was gone now, and her head ruled her disobedient body.

The sound of the owl was very familiar. She'd heard that signal all her life. "Tam!" she half whispered. Slowly and with more gentleness than she felt, she pushed Stephen's sleep-heavy limbs off her body.

She dressed quickly in the dark, making almost no noise. She found her shoes where Stephen had tossed them and made her way outside the tent. She stood still for a few moments and listened as Rab stood beside her. Stephen had planted guards, and they walked about the edge of the camp. Bronwyn gave them a look of disgust as she slipped past them and into the forest. The heathery blend of her plaid and her dark hair made her nearly invisible.

She walked quickly and surely through the forest, her passage making little noise. Suddenly she stood very still. She sensed that someone was near.

"Jamie taught ye well," came a deep voice from behind her.

She turned, a brilliant smile on her face. "Tam!" she gasped an instant before she flew into his arms.

He held her very close, her feet off the ground as she gave over her whole weight to him. "Did they treat ye well? Are ye unhurt?"

She moved away from him. "Let me look at ye." The moonlight made Tam's hair even more silver than it actually was. He was a man of average height, no taller than Bronwyn, but he was powerfully built with arms and a chest an oak would envy. Tam was her father's cousin, and he'd been her friend all her life. One of Tam's sons had been one of the three men she would have chosen to be her husband.

Tam gave a deep laugh. "Yer eyes are better than my old ones. I can't tell if ye're well or not. We wanted to come for ye, but we were afraid for yer safety."

"Let's sit down."

"Ye have time? I hear ye have a husband now."

She could see the concern in his face, could even see that there were more lines about his eyes. "Aye, I have a husband," she said when they were seated side by side on a boulder. "He's an Englishman."

"What is he like? Does he plan to stay in Scotland with ye or go back to his England?"

"What do I know? He's an arrogant man. I've tried to speak to him of my clan, but he never listens. He is sure that there is no way of anything except the English way."

Tam touched her cheek. For so many years he'd thought of this girl as his daughter. "Has he hurt ye?" he asked quietly.

Bronwyn was glad for the darkness and the cover of her blushes. Stephen hurt her pride by making her writhe under him and above him. She could keep her head as long as he did not touch her. But that wasn't something you could say to a man who was like a second father. "No, he hasn't hurt me. Tell me, how is my clan? Have you had much trouble with the Mac-Gregors?"

"Nay. It's been quiet while ye were gone. We've all been greatly worried. The English king promised ye wouldna' be harmed." He put out his hand as Rab came to his side. He patted the big head absently. "There are things ye aren't telling me. What of this husband of yers?"

Bronwyn stood. "I hate him! He will cause more problems than I need. He laughed at me when I told him he must try to be accepted by my clan. He travels with an army of men and baggage."

"We heard ye days ago."

"I worry that his ignorance and his stupidity will harm my men. He will no doubt try to force my men to conform to his ways. Someone will slip a dirk between his ribs, and the English king will bring his soldiers down upon my clan's heads."

Tam stood and put his hands on Bronwyn's shoulders. They were small shoulders to bear the weight of the responsibility she carried. "Perhaps not. Perhaps some small pieces of his skin can be removed, and that will help him to learn our ways."

Bronwyn turned and smiled up at him. "You are good for me. The English say we are a savage, crude lot. They'd believe so for sure if they could hear you."

"Savage, are we?" Tam asked, teasing her.

"Aye, and they say the women are as bad as the men."

"Hmph!" Tam grunted. "Here, let's see if ye remember any of what I taught you."

Before she could blink, he'd drawn his dirk and had it aimed at her throat. He'd spent years teaching her ways to protect herself from strong men. She moved to one side in a quick, fluid movement, but it wasn't quick enough. The knife pressed against her throat.

Suddenly, from out of the trees, a man flew, literally off his feet, as he sailed through the air and slammed against the side of Tam. Bronwyn leaped to one side, and Tam struggled to keep his balance. He was a massive, thick man, and his strength was in his ability to stand firm against all comers. Bronwyn had seen four strong, grown men leap at him, and Tam had remained standing.

Tam shrugged, and the man fell off him as Tam blinked at him in curiosity.

Bronwyn smiled when she saw Stephen lying on his back. It would be a pleasure to see him laid low. He'd beaten Roger Chatworth, but Roger was an Englishman, trained in rules of chivalry and sportsmanship. Tam was a real fighter.

Stephen lost no time contemplating his assailant. All he knew was that he'd seen this man hold a knife to his wife's throat. To him, it was their lives to Tam's. He grabbed a piece of a log from the ground, and as Tam turned in puzzlement to Bronwyn, Stephen slammed the wood into the back of the big man's knee.

Tam gave a deep grunt and fell forward. Stephen, on his knees, plowed his fist into Tam's face and felt the man's nose crunch.

Tam knew that Stephen was not an unknown or Rab would have given warning, but when he felt his nose break, he no longer cared who his attacker was. He opened his big hands and went for Stephen's throat. Stephen knew he had no chance against the man's

strength, but his youth and agility were more than a
match. He sidestepped Tam's hands, then ducked and
pummeled both fists into the rock-hard stomach. Tam
didn't seem to notice Stephen's blows. He grabbed
Stephen by the shoulders, picked him up, and bashed
him against a tree—once, twice. Stephen was dazed as
his body hit the tree, but he lifted his legs and used all
his strength to push against Tam's chest. The strength in
Stephen's legs was enough to make Tam pause in his
squashing of Stephen.

Stephen brought his arms up under Tam's wrists, and
the suddenness of his action made Tam release him.
Instantly Tam was after Stephen again, his giant hands
going after the younger man's throat. Stephen had only
seconds to escape. He threw his legs into the air and did
a perfect backward flip.

Tam stood in a crouch for a moment. One second his
enemy was there and the next he was gone. Before he
could blink he felt a cold, steel blade at his throat.

"Don't move," Stephen said, panting, "or I'll cut
your throat."

"Stop it!" Bronwyn screamed. "Stephen! Release
him this instant!"

"Release him?" Stephen asked. "He tried to kill
you." He frowned when he felt Tam's deep laughter.

"Kill me!" Bronwyn said. "You are the stupidest
man I ever met. Rab would have been after him if
there'd been any danger. Now put down that knife
before you hurt someone."

Slowly Stephen resheathed his knife. "The damn dog
was so still he could have been dead for all I knew." He
rubbed the back of his head. His spine felt like it'd been
broken.

"He's right, Bronwyn," Tam said. "He did what he
should have done. My name's Tam MacArran," he said
as he held out his hand to Stephen. "Where did ye learn
to fight like that?"

Stephen hesitated for a moment before he took the

man's hand. What he really wanted to do was turn Bronwyn over his knee for calling him stupid when he'd been trying to protect her. "Stephen Montgomery," he said, shaking Tam's hand. "I have a brother built like you. I found the only way to beat him was to be faster. An acrobat taught me a few tricks, and they've come in handy."

"I should say so!" Tam said, rubbing his nose. "I think it may be broken."

"Oh, Tam!" Bronwyn cried, giving Stephen a look of hate. "Come back to camp and let me look at it."

Tam didn't move. "I think ye should ask yer husband's permission. I take it ye are her husband?"

Stephen felt himself warming to the man. "I already have scars to prove it."

Tam chuckled.

"Let's go and see if we can find some beer. And I'd like to talk to those guards of mine. How in the world they didn't hear Bronwyn leaving camp I'll never know. A man in full armor could have made less noise."

"Less noise!" Bronwyn said. "You Englishmen are—"

Tam put his hand on her shoulder and stopped her. "Even if the others didn't hear you, your husband did. Now go ahead and get me some warm water for washing. I think there's dried blood all over me." He looked at Stephen fondly. "You have some strength in your fists."

Stephen grinned. "Another blow on that tree and my back would have broken."

"Aye," Tam said. "Ye have no meat on ye for padding."

"Ha!" Stephen snorted. "If I got as heavy as you I wouldn't be able to move."

The men grinned at each other and followed Bronwyn and Rab back to camp.

"Stephen!" Chris said when they reached camp. "We heard the noise, but it took us a while to see that you were gone. God's teeth! What happened to you, and who's this?"

Torches were being lit as the men began to wake, disturbed by the commotion. "Go back to sleep, Chris," Stephen said. "Just get someone to send us some hot water and open a keg of beer, will you? Come inside, Tam."

Tam looked about the inside of the tent. The walls were lined with pale blue silk, the ground covered with carpets from the Orient. He sat down in a carved oak chair. "Fine place ye have here," he said.

"It's a waste of money!" Bronwyn snapped. "There are people going hungry and—"

"I paid people to make this tent, and I assume they bought food with the money," Stephen retorted.

Tam looked from one to the other. He saw anger and hostility coming from Bronwyn, but from Stephen he saw tolerance and maybe even affection. And Stephen had attacked him when he thought Tam was threatening Bronwyn.

The hot water was brought, and the two men stripped to the waist and began to wash. Bronwyn felt Tam's nose and assured him it wasn't broken. Stephen's back was a mass of bloody places where the tree bark had pierced his skin.

"I think your husband's back needs attention," Tam said quietly.

Bronwyn gave Stephen a look of disdain and left the tent, Rab behind her.

Tam picked up a cloth. "Sit down, boy, and I'll see to yer back."

Stephen was obedient. As Tam gently washed the young man's back, Stephen began to speak. "Perhaps I should apologize for my wife's manners."

"No need to. I think I should apologize to ye, since I was one of the ones who helped make her the way she is."

Stephen laughed. "I had more reason to fight you

than I knew. Tell me, do you think she'll ever get over being angry at me?"

Tam wrung out the bloody cloth. "It's hard to say. She and Davey have a lot of reasons to hate the English."

"Davey?"

"Bronwyn's older brother."

Stephen whirled about. "Brother! Bronwyn has a brother, yet her father named her his successor?"

Tam chuckled and pushed Stephen back around so he could finish cleaning his back. "The Scots' ways must seem strange to ye."

Stephen snorted. "Strange is a mild word for your actions. What kind of man was Bronwyn's father?"

"It's better that ye ask about her brother. Davey was a wild boy, never quite right from the day of his birth. He's a handsome lad and has some winning ways about him, and he could always get people to do what he wanted. The problem was that he never seemed to do what was best for the clan."

"But Bronwyn did? All she cares about is her clan—and that damned dog of hers."

Tam smiled at the back of Stephen's head. "Her father, Jamie, never had any illusions about his daughter. She has a hot temper, and sometimes she's a wee bit unforgiving." He ignored the look Stephen gave him. "But, as ye say, she loves the clan. She puts them first, above all else."

"So she was named laird over her brother."

"Aye, she was, but it wasn't as simple as all that. She had an agreement with her father that she was to marry a man he chose. He gave her a choice of three young men, all of them strong and stable, what Bronwyn needed to counteract her quick temper." Tam tossed the cloth in the basin and sat down again in the chair.

"And the men?" Stephen asked as he put his shirt back on.

"They were killed, all of them, along with Jamie."

Stephen was quiet for a moment. He knew the four men had been killed by the English. "And was Bronwyn in love with one of them? Had she made her choice?" He looked up when Tam took so long to answer. The man seemed to have aged in the last few minutes.

Tam lifted his head. He tried to move his strong features into a smile. "I like to think she had chosen, that there was one man she loved best." He took a deep breath and met Stephen's eyes squarely. "One of the young men killed was my eldest son."

Stephen stared at the man. They'd only met a few hours ago and now his body ached from Tam's beating, but he felt he'd known the man for years. The strong jaw, the wide nose, the dark eyes and long gray hair, seemed familiar. He felt Tam's sorrow at the loss of his son.

"And what of David?" Stephen asked. "Did he step aside gracefully for his little sister?"

Tam snorted, his eyes clearing. "No Scot ever did anything without passion. Davey threatened to divide the clan against his father when Jamie first declared Bronwyn his heir."

"Did he? What did Bronwyn say?"

Tam put his hand up and laughed. "She told me ye were a stupid man. Ye don't seem so to me."

Stephen gave him a look that said what he thought of Bronwyn's opinion of him.

Tam continued. "Davey did raise some men to follow him, but they wouldn't fight their own clan members, so they retreated to the hills, where they live in exile."

"And Bronwyn?"

"The poor darlin'. She adored Davey. I told ye he was a persuasive young man. She told her father she refused to take what was Davey's by right. But Jamie only laughed at her and asked if she wanted to stand aside and see war within her own clan."

Stephen stood. "And of course Bronwyn would do what was best for her clan," he said with a hint of sarcasm.

"Aye, that she would. The girl'd kill herself if she thought the clan could benefit by her death."

"Or she'd keep herself alive and suffer a fate worse than death."

Tam gave him a shrewd look. "Aye, she'd do that too."

Stephen smiled. "You'll ride with us to Bronwyn's home?"

Tam stood, moving his great bulk slowly. "I would be honored."

"Then could I offer you a space in my tent?"

Tam raised one eyebrow. "This is too fancy for me. I need no spoilin' at this stage in my life. I have my plaid but I thank ye just the same."

For the first time Stephen became aware of Tam's dress. He wore a shirt with big, gathered sleeves, and a long, quilted doublet that hung to mid-thigh. On his feet he wore crude, thick shoes over heavy wool hose that reached only to below his knee. His muscular knees were bare. About his shoulders was thrown a long, wide piece of tartan cloth. A thick, wide belt was around the doublet, a dirk at his side.

Tam stood quietly during Stephen's examination, waiting for the usual English comments.

"You might get cold," Stephen said.

Tam grinned. "We're no weak men, we Scots. I'll be seein' ye in the mornin'." He left the tent.

Stephen stood still for a moment, then went to the flap. He gave a low, quiet whistle, and after a moment Rab came to him. "Bronwyn," he commanded in a quiet voice.

The dog gave a quick lick to Stephen's hand, then walked toward the dark woods with Stephen following.

Bronwyn was asleep, wrapped tightly and snugly in

her plaid. He smiled down at her, pleased with her ability to sleep on the cold, hard, damp ground. He bent and picked her up. Her eyes opened briefly, but he kissed the corner of her mouth and this seemed to reassure her. She snuggled against him as he carried her back to his tent and his bed.

Chapter Six

IT WAS LATE AFTERNOON THE NEXT DAY WHEN THEY reached Larenston Castle. Bronwyn, too impatient to wait any longer, spurred her horse forward.

"Go with her," Tam urged Stephen. "I'll wager ye've never seen anything like Larenston."

Curious to see the place that was to become his home, Stephen urged his horse up the grassy hill.

Tam was right: nothing could have prepared him for Larenston. The hill he was on fell away sharply to a wide, deep valley where shaggy cattle grazed and crofters' cottages rested. A narrow road led through the valley and up the wall on the far side. At the top of the valley wall was a high, flat, red-stone peninsula that jutted out into the sea like a huge armored fist. The peninsula was connected to the mainland by a piece of rock only the width of the narrow road. The sides fell away in sheer drops to the sea. Guarding the entrance to the peninsula were two massive gatehouses, each three stories high.

The castle complex itself consisted of several stone
buildings and one enormous hall in the center. There
was no surrounding wall. There was no need for one.
The sheer cliffs rising out of the sea could be guarded
by a few men with bows and arrows.

Bronwyn turned to him, a light in her eyes that he'd
never seen before. "It has never been taken," she said
flatly before she started down to the valley below.

Stephen had no idea how they knew she was arriv-
ing, but suddenly every door to every cottage opened
and people came running toward her, their arms
open.

Stephen put his horse to a gallop to keep up with her,
then he stood back as she hastily dismounted and began
hugging people—men, women, children, even a child's
fat pet goose. He was touched by the scene. He'd seen
her only as an angry young woman. She'd told him her
clan meant her life to her, but he hadn't visualized the
individuals of the clan. She seemed to know them all
personally, called each person's name, asked after their
children, their illnesses, if they had everything they
needed.

He lifted himself in the saddle and looked around.
The ground was poor. His horse pawed it and turned up
little more than peat moss. Yet he saw fields. The
barley growing was stunted but it was making an effort.
The cottages were small, very poor looking.

It came to Stephen that these people were akin to the
serfs on his brother's estates. Bronwyn owned the land
and they farmed it. The very same as the serfs.

He looked back at her as she accepted a piece of
cheese from a woman. These people were her serfs, yet
she treated them as part of her family. He couldn't
imagine any lady he knew touching a serf much less
hugging one. They were calling her Bronwyn, not Lady
Bronwyn as was her right.

"Ye are frownin', lad," Tam said from beside him.
"What of our ways displeases ye?"

Stephen removed his hat and ran his hand through his thick hair. "I think I have some things to learn. I don't think I understand what a clan is. I thought her clan members were like my men. They're all from noble houses."

Tam watched him for a moment. "Clan is a Gaelic word which means children." His eyes twinkled. "And as for nobility, ye can ask any Scot and he can trace his ancestry back to a Scots king."

"But the poverty . . ." Stephen began, then stopped, afraid he'd offended Tam.

Tam's jaw hardened. "The English and the soil God gave us have made us poor. But ye'd best learn that in Scotland a man's worth is based on what he is inside and not the gold he has in his pocket."

"Thank you for the advice. I'll remember it." He urged his horse forward until he was beside Bronwyn. She gave only a brief look up at him, then turned away to continue listening to an old woman's talk of some new cloth dyes.

One by one the people began to quieten as they stared up at him. His clothes were very different. Most of the Scotsmen wore nothing on their legs, neither shoes nor hose, while some wore the short hose like Tam's.

But Stephen's eyes were on the women. They didn't have the pale, protected complexions of an English lady but a golden tan from their days out-of-doors. Their eyes sparkled, and their glorious hair hung free to their small, belted waists.

Stephen swung down from his horse, took Bronwyn's hand tightly in his left one, and extended his right. "Allow me to introduce myself. I'm Stephen Montgomery."

"An Englishman!" a man near Stephen said, his voice virulent with hatred.

"Aye, an Englishman!" Stephen said with emphasis, his blue eyes hard as he held the Scotsman's.

"Here!" Tam said. "Leave him be. He attacked me when he thought I meant to harm Bronwyn."

Several people smiled at the absurdity of this statement. It was obvious who'd won, since Tam weighed at least sixty pounds more than the slim Stephen.

"He won," Tam said slowly. "He near broke my nose, then took a knife to my throat."

The people were silent for a moment, as if they didn't believe Tam.

"Welcome, Stephen," one of the pretty young women said as she shook his outstretched hand.

Stephen blinked several times at being called by his first name, then he smiled and began shaking more hands.

"It won't be so easy with my men," Bronwyn was saying as they rode side by side down the road that connected the peninsula to the mainland. The road was so narrow that only two could ride together. Stephen gave a nervous look at the sheer wall to his left. One wrong move and he could be over the side. Bronwyn didn't seem to notice their danger, since she'd traveled the narrow road all her life.

"My men are not so easily won as my women," she said haughtily. She looked at him, saw the way he kept glancing down toward the sea. She smiled and reined her horse sharply toward his.

Stephen's horse shied away from Bronwyn's; then when it felt one foot step into the nothing beside the road, it panicked and reared. Stephen fought desperately for a moment to bring the horse under control and keep it from falling off the road and into the nothingness to the side.

"Damn you!" Stephen yelled when he once again had control of the horse.

Bronwyn laughed at him as she looked back over her shoulder. "Are our Scots' ways too fierce for you?" she taunted.

Stephen dug his spurs into his horse's side. Bronwyn saw him coming at her but didn't react fast enough. Stephen grabbed her about the waist and pulled her into the saddle before him.

"Release me!" she demanded. "My men are watching!"

"Good! Then they saw you try to make a fool of me. Or were you hoping I'd fall over the side?"

"And have King Henry's troops down on us? No, I don't wish your death on Scots' soil."

Stephen gasped at her honesty. "Perhaps I asked for that." He put a finger to her lips when she started to speak. "But I didn't ask to be made to look like a fool, so you'll pay for it. How many other men have ridden into Larenston with the MacArran across their saddle?"

"We have brought back many dead, usually killed by—"

He stopped her words with a kiss.

In spite of herself Bronwyn clung to him, her arms going about his neck, her lips fastening hungrily on his. He pulled her close to him, his hands caressing her back. He could feel her skin, warm through the linen of her shirt. He decided he liked the Scots fashion. The heavy English fabrics hid the feel of a woman's skin.

Stephen was the first to come out of the trance. He felt they were being watched. He opened his eyes, lifted his head slightly, his lips still on Bronwyn's. He hadn't realized that his horse had kept moving up the trail toward the gatehouses. Several men surrounded them, all solemn, serious men, their faces closed, showing no emotion.

"Bronwyn, love," Stephen said quietly.

Bronwyn reacted immediately. She jerked away from him and looked down at her men. "Douglas," she whispered and slid down into the man's waiting arms. One by one she greeted the men.

Stephen dismounted slowly and led his horse as he

followed her through the gate. The spiked, iron portcullis was drawn up. The men did not speak to him or look at him, but Stephen was very aware of the way they surrounded him, solemnly, distrustfully. Bronwyn walked ahead of him, laughing with her men, asking questions and receiving answers.

Stephen felt very much the alien, the outsider. The men who walked beside him were wary of him, and he felt their hostility. These men were dressed differently from the men in the valley. Some wore short hose and shoes like Tam, others wore tall boots reaching to their knees. Yet all of them were bare-legged from knee to thigh.

Once through the gate the land was open, and they went past several small buildings to the great house. Stephen recognized the outbuildings as a dairy, a blacksmith's, stables. There was even a small kitchen garden in one area. A place such as this could withstand a long siege.

The inside of the house was simple and unadorned. The stone walls were damp, unpainted, unpaneled. The small windows let in little light. It was cold inside the castle, colder even than the outside autumn chill, but there was no fire burning.

Bronwyn sat down in an uncushioned chair. "Now, Douglas, tell me of what has been happening."

Stephen stood to one side, watching. No one asked after her comfort or suggested she should rest.

"The MacGregors have been raiding again. They took six head of cattle two nights ago."

Bronwyn frowned. She'd deal with the MacGregors later. "What problems inside the clan?"

The man called Douglas tugged absently at a long lock of hair. "The land by the loch is in dispute again. Robert says the salmon are his while Desmond demands he be paid for them."

"Have they drawn swords yet?" Bronwyn asked.

"No, but they are close. Shall I send some men in to

settle this thing? A little blood shed in the right places will stop their quarrels."

Stephen started to rise. He was used to making decisions of this sort. Tam's hand on his arm stopped him.

"Can you think of nothing else but your sword arm, Douglas?" she asked angrily. "Did it never occur to you that the men have a reason for their quarrels? Robert has seven children to feed, and Desmond has an ailing wife and no children. Surely there must be a way to solve their problems."

The men gave her blank looks.

She sighed. "Tell Robert to send his oldest and youngest children to Desmond to foster. Robert will not demand fish that are going to feed his own children, and Desmond's wife will stop feeling sorry for herself for having no children of her own. Now, what else has happened?"

Stephen smiled at her wisdom. It had come from her love and knowledge of her clan. It was a wonder to see her in her home surroundings. With each passing moment she seemed to come more alive. Her chin no longer jutted forward in anger as she looked at the people around her. Her shoulders were still straight but not as if she meant to ward off blows and angry words.

He watched the faces of the men around her. They respected her, listened to her, and each decision she made was wise and in the best interests of her clan.

"Jamie taught her well," Tam said quietly.

Stephen nodded. This was a completely different side of her, one he'd never imagined existed. He knew her to be angry, impulsive, filled with hatred, given to using a knife and making impossible demands. He remembered laughing at her when she fell into the stream.

Suddenly he felt a swift wave of jealousy. He'd never seen this woman who sat so calmly before these men and made decisions that affected their lives. They knew a side of her that he'd never even guessed at.

Bronwyn rose and walked toward the stairway at the far end of the hall. Stephen followed her. It suddenly occurred to him that the men knew nothing about the backs of her knees. He smiled to himself and felt somewhat reassured.

"Look at him," Bronwyn said in disgust. It was early morning, the late-autumn air nippy. She looked down at Stephen from the window of their third-story chamber. He was in the courtyard below, he and Chris wearing full armor. The Scotsmen around them stood and stared in sullen silence.

They had been married for two weeks, and during that time Stephen had made a strong effort to train her men in the English way of fighting. She'd stood by while he lectured the men on the importance of protecting themselves. He'd offered to purchase armor for the men who trained the longest and hardest. But the Scotsmen had said little and didn't seem the least interested in the valuable prize of a suit of hot, heavy armor. They seemed to prefer their own wild costumes, which left half their bodies bare. The only concession toward war Stephen could get them to make was to wear a shirt of chain mail beneath their plaids.

Bronwyn turned away from the window, smiling to herself.

"Ye needn't be so pleased with yerself," Morag snapped. "Those men of yers could do with a little work. They sit about too much. Stephen makes them work."

Bronwyn kept smiling. "He's an obstinate man. Yesterday he dared to lecture my men that Scotland is a land of unrest, that he is trying to teach them to protect themselves. As if we didn't know! It's because of the English that—"

Morag put up her hand in defense. "Ye can try to drive him insane with yer constant lectures, but not me. What is it that upsets ye about him? Is it the way he makes ye cry out at night? Are ye ashamed of yer passion for the enemy?"

"I have no—" Bronwyn began but stopped when she heard the soft click of the door behind Morag. She turned and looked back at Stephen. She had to admit to herself that it upset her the way her body reacted to his touch. Quite often she found herself trembling as soon as the sun began to set. She was careful never to allow Stephen to see the way she felt. She never made an advance toward him or gave a word of affection to him; after all, he was her enemy, he was of the race that killed her father. It was easy to remember that he was her enemy during the day. He dressed as an Englishman, talked as one, thought as one. His difference screamed at her and her men. It was only at night when he touched her that she forgot who he was and who she was.

"Stephen!" Chris said as they walked across the sand-covered field. They stopped by the edge of the peninsula, gazing out at the sea. "You've got to stop working like this. Can't you see that they're not interested in what you're trying to do for them?"

Stephen removed his helmet. The cool wind rushed at his sweat-dampened hair. Each day he was increasingly frustrated at his attempts to work with Bronwyn's men. His own men trained each day, learning to handle their heavy armor and weapons. But Bronwyn's men stood on the outskirts and watched the Englishmen as if they were animals in King Henry's menagerie.

"There must be a way to reach them!" he said under his breath.

Suddenly he heard a man running toward them.

"My lord," one of Stephen's men said. "There's been an attack on some of the MacArran cattle in the north. The men are already saddling."

Stephen nodded once. Now he'd have a chance to show these Scotsmen what fighters his English knights were. He was used to protecting lands from poachers and thieves.

The heavy steel armor made quick movement impossible. His squire waited with his horse, it too wearing armor. The horse was a heavy one, bred through hundreds of years to be able to bear the weight of a man in full armor. The horse would never be called upon for speed but must stand steady through the thickest of battles, obeying its master's knee commands.

By the time Stephen and his armored men mounted, the Scotsmen were gone. Stephen grimaced and thought of the necessary discipline he'd have to enforce for punishment.

It wasn't until years later that Stephen could remember the events of that night on the Scots moors without once again experiencing a sense of shame and bewilderment.

It was dark when he and his men reached the place where the MacGregors had stolen the cattle. The noise they made as they rode echoed through the countryside. Their armor clanked; their heavy horses' hoofs thundered.

Stephen thought he must have expected the MacGregors to meet him like Englishmen in hand-to-hand combat. It was with consternation that he and his men sat atop their horses and watched the ensuing battle. It was like nothing Stephen had ever seen or imagined.

The Scots left their horses and melted into the woods. They discarded their plaids from their shoulders, leaving them free to run in their loose shirts. There were great shouts from the trees, then the sounds of the Scots' Claymores striking steel.

Stephen motioned for his men to dismount, and they followed the sound of the Scots into the trees. But the Scots had already moved elsewhere. The heavy armor made the Englishmen too slow, too unsteady.

Stephen was looking about in a confused manner

when one of Bronwyn's men stepped from the shadows.

"We routed them," the Scotsman said, his mouth in a slight smirk.

"How many were hurt?"

"Three injured, none killed," he said flatly, then smiled. "The MacArrans are too fast for any MacGregor." The man was flushed from the excitement of the battle. "Shall I get some men together to lift you onto your horse?" he said as he smiled openly at Stephen in his armor.

"Why you—!" Chris began. "I'll take a sword to you here and now."

"Come on, English dog," the Scotsman taunted. "I can have your throat cut before you can move the hinges on that steel coffin."

"Cease!" Stephen commanded. "Chris, put your sword away. And you, Douglas, see to the wounded." Stephen's voice was heavy.

"You can't let him get away with such insolence," Chris said. "How do you plan to teach them to respect you?"

"Teach them!" Stephen snapped. "A man cannot teach another to respect him. He must earn respect. Come, let's go back to Larenston. I have some thinking to do."

Bronwyn tossed in the bed, slamming her fist into the pillow. She kept telling herself that she didn't care that Stephen preferred to spend the night somewhere else. She didn't care if he chose someone else to spend it with. She thought of her clan members. Margaret's daughter was a pretty thing, and she'd heard a couple of the men laughing about what a good time they'd had with her. She must speak to Margaret in the morning! It wasn't good to have a girl like that around.

"Damn!" she said aloud, and Rab growled. She sat up in bed, the covers falling away from her lovely breasts. It was cold in the bed alone. Morag had told her of the cattle raid. She had a few choice words to say about the MacGregors. Morag hissed when Bronwyn said she hoped Stephen wasn't killed because his death would bring the English king down on their heads.

Now she kept looking at the door, frowning once in a while.

When the door began to open, she held her breath. It could be Morag with news. Her breath escaped when she saw Stephen enter, his hair as well as his shirt-front wet from dousing himself at the well.

Stephen barely looked at her. His blue eyes were dark, a crease between his brows. He sat down heavily on the edge of the bed and began to remove his clothes. He couldn't seem to put his mind on the task but kept pausing for long periods of time.

Bronwyn searched for something to say. "Are you hungry?" He didn't answer, so she moved across the bed to sit closer to him. The sheet was wrapped about her lower body, the upper bare. "I asked if you were hungry," she said loudly.

"Oh?" Stephen mumbled as he removed a boot. "I don't know. I don't think so."

Bronwyn had an urge to ask him what was wrong, but of course she'd never do anything like that. She didn't care what was wrong with the Englishman. "Were any of my men hurt in the cattle raid?"

When Stephen again didn't answer, she pushed his shoulder. "Are you deaf? I asked you a question."

Stephen turned to her as if he'd just realized she was there. His eyes raked her nude body, but he showed no interest as he stood and unfastened his belt. "No one was seriously hurt. A few stitches in one man's arm, but nothing else."

"Who? Whose arm needed stitches?"

Stephen waved his hand and stepped nude into the bed. He put his arms behind his head and stared at the ceiling. He didn't attempt to touch her. "Francis, I think," he said finally.

Bronwyn was still sitting, frowning at him. What was wrong with him? "Did our Scots' ways frighten you, Englishman? Were my men too strong for you or too fast?"

To her amazement Stephen did not take the bait.

"Too fast," he said quite seriously, still watching the ceiling. "They moved quickly and freely. Of course, they'd never last in England, because a few armed knights could cut fifty of them apart. But here—"

"Fifty!" Bronwyn breathed. The next instant she brought both her fists down against Stephen's broad, bare chest. "You'll never see the day when one Englishman can harm fifty Scots," she fairly yelled as she beat her fists against his hard chest.

"Here! Stop that!" Stephen said, grabbing her fists in his hands. "I have enough bruises without your adding to them."

"I'll give you more than bruises," she said as she struggled against his grip.

Stephen's eyes lightened. He pulled on her hands and drew her forward; her breasts pressed against him. "I'd like more than bruises," he said huskily, his full attention at last on her. He released one of her hands and touched her hair. "Will you always bring me back to reality?" he asked as he touched her temple. "I think I could be worried about the greatest problem in the universe, and you would contrive to turn my thoughts to your lovely skin, your eyes," he said, moving his fingers, "your lips."

Bronwyn felt her heart begin to pound. His breath was so soft and warm. His hair was still damp, and a curl stuck by his ear. She had an urge to touch that curl, but she was always careful to make no advances toward him. "And were you worried about some great problem?" she asked nonchalantly, as if it didn't matter.

He stilled his fingers and his eyes captured hers. "Do I hear concern in your voice?" he asked quietly.

"Never!" she spat and rolled away from him. She expected to hear his amused laughter, but when he was silent, she had an urge to turn and look at him, keeping her back to him. He was very still, and after a while she heard the quiet, even tone of his breathing that meant he was asleep. She lay very, very still, and after a while she felt tears forming in the corners of her eyes. There were times when she felt so alone that she didn't know what to do. Her idea of marriage was of two people who shared their lives and their love. But she was married to an Englishman!

Stephen turned suddenly and threw a heavy arm around her, then drew her close to him. She tried to remain stiff and aloof from him, but in spite of herself she wiggled her bottom against him, snuggling closer.

"That's not the way to help a man sleep," Stephen whispered, then raised his head and kissed her temple. "What's this?" he said. "Tears?"

"Of course not. I merely had something in my eye, 'tis all."

He turned her about in his arms so that she faced him. "You are lying," he said flatly. He searched her face with his eyes, touched the cleft in her chin. "You and I are strangers," he whispered. "When will we become friends? When will you share yourself with me? When will you tell me the cause of your tears?"

"When you become a Scotsman!" she said as fiercely as she could. But Stephen's nearness made the words come out oddly, as if they were a plea instead of an impossible demand.

"Done!" he said with great confidence, almost as if he could actually change into a Scotsman.

She wanted to laugh at him, to tell him that he could never become a Scotsman—or her friend. But he pulled her even closer and began to kiss her. He kissed her as if he had all the time in the world, lazily, slowly.

Bronwyn felt the blood pounding through her veins. She wanted to pull Stephen to her, but he held her off. He held her slightly away from his body so he could touch her breasts, stroke her ribs and stomach.

She arched away from him, her legs entwined with his, her thighs clasping one of his. Stephen's hand strayed downward to her legs, and he smiled when he felt her sharply indrawn breath.

"My beautiful, beautiful wife," he whispered as he ran his nails lightly along the tendon in the back of her knee. "I wish I knew how to please you out of bed."

She moved back to him, sought his lips, then ran her mouth down his neck. His skin tasted good, slightly salty with sweat, firm yet soft. She touched her tongue to his ear, and she felt a shiver run through him. A low rumble of laughter ran through her.

Stephen grabbed her shoulders fiercely. "Come here, laird of Clan MacArran." He pushed her down in the bed and lowered himself on top of her.

She arched up to meet him, lifting her hips high. She was a Scotswoman, and she was equal to him. Now she did not wait for his advances but met him evenly, with as much passion as his.

Later they lay together, so close they were as one. Bronwyn sleepily opened her eyes and saw the curl by Stephen's ear. It was the one she'd wanted to touch earlier. She moved her head and kissed that curl, feeling the soft hair between her lips. Then she pulled away, her face flushing. Somehow that kiss seemed more intimate than their lovemaking.

Stephen smiled slightly, his eyes closed, more asleep than awake, and pulled her even closer, more under him than beside him. Bronwyn could hardly breathe but it didn't matter. No, breathing was the last of her thoughts.

Stephen stood in the little crofter's cottage, warming his hands before the peat fire. A raw wind was blowing outside, and the fire was needed. Tam was visiting his sister, leaving Bronwyn's house for a few days. The thick older man sat on the far side of the stone-walled room, a fisherman's net spread across his bare knees. He was working the knots, his big hands pulling at the coarse ropes.

"So you want me to help ye to look less like a fool," Tam said seriously.

Stephen turned. He still wasn't quite used to the way the Scotsmen sat or stood, according to their own wishes, in his presence. He was perhaps too used to being "my lorded." "I wouldn't quite put it that way," he said. Thinking back over the events of the cattle raid, he shook his head. "I did look like a fool, both to my own men and to the Scots. I did feel as if I were standing in a steel coffin as Douglas said."

Tam paused for a moment as he tightened a knot. "Douglas always thought he should have been one of the men chosen by Jamie to be Bronwyn's husband." He chuckled at the expression on Stephen's face. "Don't worry, boy, Jamie knew what he was doing. Douglas is a follower, not a leader. He's too awed of Bronwyn to ever be her master."

Stephen laughed. "No man is strong enough to be her master."

Tam didn't comment on that statement, but he smiled to himself. Morag kept a close watch on the couple and reported to Tam. Tam wanted to make sure Bronwyn was in no danger of being harmed by the Englishman. From what Morag said, Stephen was the one in danger—of exhaustion.

Tam looked up. "The first thing ye must do is rid yerself of those English clothes."

Stephen nodded; he'd expected this.

"And then ye must learn to run, both for distance and speed."

"Run! But a soldier must stand and fight."

Tam snorted. "Our ways are different. I thought ye

knew that already. Unless ye're willin' to learn, I'll be no use to ye."

With an air of resignation Stephen agreed.

An hour later he began to wish he hadn't agreed. He and Tam stood outside in the cold autumn wind, and Stephen had never felt so bare in his life. Instead of the heavy, padded, warm English clothes, he wore only a thin shirt, a belted plaid over it. He wore wool socks and high boots, but he still felt as if he were bare from the waist down.

Tam slapped him on the shoulder. "Come on, boy, ye'll get used to it. A little more hair and ye'll be nearer a Scot than ever."

"This is a damned cold country to be running about bareassed," Stephen muttered as he flipped up the plaid and shirt to show one bare cheek.

Tam laughed. "Now you know what a Scotsman wears under his plaid." His face turned serious. "There's a reason for our dress. The plaid makes a man disappear in the heather. The dress is easy to remove, easy and fast to put on. Scotland's a wet country, and a man can't afford to have wet, clinging garments on his skin; he'd die of lung sickness if he did. The plaid is cool in summer, and the constant chafing of yer knees'll make ye warm in winter." His eyes twinkled. "And it allows free air circulation to all yer most vital parts."

"That it does," Stephen said.

"Ah! now ye look to be a man!" Morag said from behind him. She openly stared at his legs. "Wearin' all that armor has put some muscle on ye."

Stephen grinned at her. "If I weren't already married, I think I might consider asking you."

"And I might consider acceptin'. Though I wouldn't like to fight Bronwyn for ye."

Stephen gave her a bleak look. "She'd give me away to anyone if she could."

"As long as she could have ye in bed, is that it?" Morag cackled before turning away.

Stephen blinked once. The familiarity within a clan always startled him. Everyone seemed to know everyone else's business.

"We're wastin' time," Tam said. "Try runnin' to that pole down there," he pointed.

Stephen thought that running would be easy. After all, even children ran, and he was in good condition. But he felt his lungs were about to burst after his first short sprint. It took several minutes to calm his racing heart and regain his breath. His heart sounded as if it were about to break his eardrums.

"Here, drink some water," Tam said as he held out a dipper. "Now that ye have yer breath, run it again."

Stephen raised one eyebrow in disbelief.

"Come on, boy," Tam said. "I'll run it with ye. You wouldn't let an old man beat ye, would ye?"

Stephen gasped for air. "The last thing I'd call you is old." He tossed the dipper aside. "Come on, let's go."

Chapter Seven

BRONWYN WAS STANDING ALONE AT THE FOOT OF THE stairs leading to the top of the old tower. Her eyes were dry and burning, almost swollen from the tears she hadn't shed. Clutched tightly in her hand was a heavy silver belt buckle. On the back was engraved: "To Ennis from James MacArran."

An hour ago one of the crofters had brought the buckle to her. Bronwyn remembered when her father had given the buckles to the three young men he'd chosen to succeed him. It had almost been a ceremony. There'd been food and wine, dancing, and much, much laughter. Everyone was teasing Bronwyn about which man she'd choose for her husband. Bronwyn had flirted and laughed and pretended that all of them were worthless compared to her father.

There'd been Ian, Tam's son. Ian was only as tall as she was but thick like his father. Ramsey was blond, broad-shouldered, with a mouth that sometimes made

Bronwyn nervous. Ennis had freckles and green eyes, and he could sing so sweetly he could make you cry.

She squeezed the belt buckle until it cut into her palm. Now they were all dead. Strong Ian, handsome Ramsey, sweet Ennis—all dead and buried. Killed by the English!

She turned and hurried up the stairs to the top floor. From the bunch of keys at her side, she took one and unlocked an oak door. The heavy door creaked in protest as it swung on its unoiled hinges.

She thought she was braced for the sight of the room, but she wasn't. She almost expected her father to look up at her and smile. She hadn't been in the room since his death; she'd been afraid to see it again.

She stepped inside the room and looked about her. There was a plaid thrown across a chair, the bottom of it worn and ragged. Weapons hung on the stone walls, axes, Claymores, bows. She touched the worn place on her father's favorite bow. Slowly she walked to the chair near the one window in the room. The leather held the imprint of Jamie's body.

Bronwyn sat down in the chair, the dust whirling about her. Her father came often to this room to think and be alone. He allowed no one to enter it except himself and his two children. Bronwyn had teethed on an arrow from her father's pack.

She looked from one familiar, loved object to another and felt her head begin to ache. It was all gone now. Her father was dead, her brother had turned away from her with hatred in his heart, and the beautiful young men she would have chosen were rotting in a grave somewhere.

Now there was no laughter or love at Larenston. The English king had married her to one of his killers, and all happiness was gone.

The English! she thought. They thought they owned the world. She hated the way Stephen's men stood off from him, the way they bowed and scraped and called him "my lord." The English were a cold lot. She'd tried hundreds of times to tell him about the ways of the Scots, but he was too vain to listen.

She smiled to herself. At least her men knew who was laird. They laughed at Stephen behind his back. All morning she'd heard stories of the aborted cattle raid the night before. How ridiculous Stephen must have looked standing there in his foolish armor.

A noise in the courtyard below drew her attention. She went to the window to look down.

At first she didn't recognize Stephen. She thought only that he was a well-built man with an exceptional look of self-confidence. His belted plaid swung about his legs with a jaunty air. She gasped in indignation when she realized it was Stephen who walked so arrogantly and wore the Scots' dress as if he had a right to wear it.

Several of her men stood about the courtyard, and she was glad to see that they made no effort to greet him. They certainly knew an impostor when they saw one.

The smile left her face as first one man then another walked toward Stephen. She saw him smile and say something, then flip the tail of his plaid up. She heard laughter echoing.

Douglas—*her* Douglas!—stepped forward and put out an arm to Stephen. Stephen grabbed it, and the two of them hooked ankles and forearms and began a standing wrestle. It wasn't a minute later that Douglas went sprawling in the dirt.

She watched in disgust while Stephen challenged the men, one after another. She drew her breath in sharply when Margaret's daughter stepped forward, her hips swaying provocatively. She lifted her skirt to expose trim ankles and proceeded to show Stephen a few Highlands dance steps.

Bronwyn turned away from the window and left the room, locking the door behind her. There was anger in every step she took down the stairs.

Stephen was standing there. His hair was tousled, his cheeks pink from his day's exercise in the cold air. His eyes were flashing and bright. Behind him stood several of his men as well as Bronwyn's, and several pretty young women.

He looked at her like a boy trying to please. He held out his leg to her. "Will I pass?" he teased.

She glared at him for a moment, ignoring his muscular leg. "You may fool some of them, but you're an Englishman to me and will always be. Because you've changed your clothes doesn't mean you've changed inside." She turned and walked away from all of them.

Stephen stood still for a moment, frowning. Perhaps he did want them to forget he was an Englishman. Perhaps . . .

Tam slapped him on the shoulder. "Don't look so grieved."

Stephen turned to see that the Scotsmen behind him were smiling.

"For all she's a good laird, she's still a woman," Tam continued. "No doubt she was upset because ye were dancin' with the women."

Stephen tried to smile. "I wish you were right."

"Why don't ye go to her and soothe her?"

Stephen started to reply, then stopped. There was no use telling Tam that Bronwyn wouldn't welcome anything about him. He followed her up the stairs. She was standing over a weaver, directing the arrangement of the weft threads of a new plaid.

"Stephen," called one of the women, "but don't you look good." The pretty young woman almost leered at him in his short clothes.

Stephen turned to smile at the woman, but he caught sight of Bronwyn as she fairly snarled at him before she left the room. He caught her at the head of the stairs. "What's wrong with you? I thought you'd be pleased with my clothes. You said I must become a Scot."

"Dressing as one doesn't make you a Scot." She turned away from him.

Stephen caught her arm. "What's wrong? Are you angry because of something else?"

"Why should I be angry?" she asked, her voice heavy with sarcasm. "I'm married to my enemy. I'm—"

Stephen put his fingers to her lips. "Something is bothering you," he said quietly. He watched her face, but she lowered her eyes so he couldn't see the pain registering there. He took both her arms then ran his hands downward until they touched hers. Her left hand was clutched tightly over something. "What's this?" he asked softly.

She tried to pull away from him, but he forced her hand open. He stared at the buckle, read the inscription. "Did someone give this to you today?"

She nodded silently.

"Did it belong to your father?"

She kept her eyes lowered, and again she could only nod.

"Bronwyn," he said, his voice rich and deep. "Look at me." He put his hand gently under her chin and lifted her face. "I'm sorry, truly sorry."

"How can you know?" she snapped, jerking away from him. She silently cursed herself for almost believing in him, for letting his voice and his nearness affect her.

"I know what it's like to lose a father as well as a mother," he said patiently. "I'm sure it hurt me as badly as you've been hurt."

"But I did not kill your father!"

"Nor did I, personally, kill yours!" he said fiercely. "Listen to me, just once, listen to me as a man, not as a political pawn. We're married. It's done. There's no more stopping it. We could be happy, I know we could, if only you'd be willing to give us a chance."

Her face hardened, her eyes turning cold. "And will you brag to your men that you have a Scotswoman eating from your hand? Will you try to win my men, as well as my women, to your side as you did today?"

"Win!" Stephen began. "Damn you! I've spent all day running, literally, in this cold climate bare-legged and bare-assed too, if the truth be known, all to please you and those men you care about so much." He pushed her away from him. "Go and wallow in your hatred. It will keep you cold company at night." He turned away and left her.

Bronwyn stood very still for a moment before slowly going down the stairs. She wanted to trust him. She needed a husband to trust. But how could she? What would happen if her lands were attacked by raiding Englishmen? Could Stephen be expected to fight against his own people?

She knew how she reacted to him. It would be easy to forget their differences and succumb to his sweet touches, his rich voice. But when she needed to be wary and alert, her senses would be dulled. She couldn't afford that. She wouldn't risk her people's lives merely because she enjoyed a lusty time in bed with a man who could be a spy.

She sat in the little garden behind the tall stone house. She couldn't trust him. For all she knew, his entreaties for her to believe in him were a means to use her. She knew he had brothers. Perhaps he'd call them to his side once he made an opening in Bronwyn's defenses. Would he boast to his brothers that she would do what he wanted, that to make her pliable, he had only to kiss the back of her knees?

She stood and began to walk quickly to the edge of the peninsula. The sea beat against the rocks, and she could see for miles. It was a great responsibility to be laird of a clan. Many, many people looked to her for protection and, if need be, even for food. She worked hard at knowing her people and understanding them. She could not let her defenses down for even a moment. So when Stephen caressed her, held her, she had to protect herself against him, against allowing her emotions to rule her head. If ever she knew she could trust him, then she could ask what was in her heart.

"Bronwyn."

She turned. "What is it, Douglas?" She looked into the young man's brown eyes. She could see the unasked question in his eyes, as it was in all her men's eyes. They didn't know whether or not to trust Stephen and were waiting for her judgment. And she was to be judged also. If she was in error about him, they would no longer trust her.

"I have received word that the MacGregors plan another cattle raid tonight."

Bronwyn nodded. She knew Douglas had access to an informer. "Have you told anyone else of this?"

Douglas paused, reading her thoughts correctly, knowing she meant Stephen. "No one."

She looked back at the sea. "I will lead my men tonight, and we will show the MacGregors who is the MacArran. I'll not be laughed at again."

Douglas smiled. "It will be good to ride with you again."

She looked back at him. "Tell no one of our plans. No one! Do you understand?"

"Aye, I understand." He turned and left her.

The long dinner table was spread heavily with food. Stephen was at first suspicious of the abundance because Bronwyn's Scots sense of thrift made her set a more modest table. At dinner she'd smiled at him. This had surprised him, since he'd assumed she'd be angry after what had happened that afternoon. But perhaps she'd listened to his words, perhaps she was willing to give him a chance.

He sat back in his chair and ran his hand along her thigh. He smiled when he felt her jump.

She turned to him, her eyes soft and warm, her lips parted, and Stephen felt his body grow hot. He leaned toward her.

"This is not the time or place," she said, a note of sadness in her voice.

"Come above stairs with me then."

She smiled seductively. "In a moment. Perhaps you'd like to try a new drink I had made. It is of wine and fruit juices with a little spice." She handed him a silver goblet.

Stephen hardly noticed what he drank. Bronwyn had never looked at him as she was doing now, and his blood was beginning to boil. Her thick lashes lowered over her eyes, which had turned to a luster like a blue pearl. The tip of her pink tongue touched her lower lip, and Stephen felt chills run up his spine. So this is what she looked like when she was willing!

He put his hand over hers and had to control himself from squeezing it hard enough to break her fingers. "Come with me," he whispered huskily.

Before he'd finished climbing the stairs, he began to feel sleepy. By the time he reached the door to their bedroom, he could hardly keep his eyes open.

"Something's wrong with me," he whispered, the words an effort to get out.

"You're tired, that's all," Bronwyn said sympathetically. "You spent most of the day in training with Tam, and he can wear a man out. Here, let me help you." She put her arm around his waist and led him to the bed.

Stephen collapsed onto the bed's softness. His limbs felt heavy and useless. "I'm sorry, I . . . ."

"Quiet," Bronwyn said softly. "Just rest. You'll feel better after a little sleep."

Stephen had no choice but to obey her as he easily slipped off into sleep.

Bronwyn stood over him for a moment, frowning. She hoped she hadn't put too much of the sleeping drug in his drink. She had a sudden pang of conscience as he lay there so quietly. But she had to make sure he didn't interfere tonight. She had to show the MacGregors they couldn't steal her cattle and get away with it.

She turned to leave the room, then looked back. With a sigh she pulled Stephen's boots off. He didn't move but lay still, so still, not watching her, not asking anything of her. She bent and touched his hair, then on impulse she gently kissed his forehead. She backed away from him, her face pink, cursing herself for being so foolish. What did she care about the Englishman?

Her men were already saddled and waiting for her. She pulled her long skirt up and slung her legs into the saddle. The men needed no verbal command as they followed her down the narrow path onto the mainland.

Douglas's informer had been right about the proposed cattle raid. Bronwyn and her men rode hard for two hours, then abandoned their horses and walked stealthily into the dark woods.

Bronwyn was the first to hear a man's footsteps. She put up her hand to halt her men, then signaled them to spread out, Douglas to stay with her. The men of Clan MacArran were silent as they slipped through the trees and surrounded the cattle thieves.

When she was satisfied that her men had had time to get to their places, she opened her mouth and gave a high-pitched cry that set the cattle to nervous prancing. The MacGregors dropped the ropes they held and grabbed their Claymores. But it was too late, for Bronwyn's men were upon them. They'd discarded their plaids so they were free to fight in their loose shirts. Their savage war cries echoed through the countryside. Bronwyn threw off her skirt and wore only her shirt and plaid, which reached just to her knees. She stayed in the background to direct the men and not hamper them with her frail strength. At times like this she cursed her lack of strength.

"Jarl!" she screamed in time to save one of her men from a Claymore across his head. She rushed across the grass just in time to thwart a MacGregor from jumping onto another man.

The moonlight caught the flash of a dirk as it poised above Douglas's head. She saw that Douglas had lost his weapon. "Douglas!" she called, then tossed him her weapon. The MacGregor behind him turned to look at her, and in that instant Douglas caught him under the ribs with the dirk. The man fell slowly.

The fighting seemed to come to a halt instantly. Bronwyn, sensing a change in the men, looked down at the man at her feet. "The MacGregor," she whispered. "Is he dead?"

"No," Douglas answered, "only wounded. He'll come to in a minute."

She looked about her. The other MacGregors had faded into the trees now that their leader was down. She knelt beside the fallen man. "Give me my dirk," she said.

Douglas obeyed her without hesitation.

"I'd like the MacGregor to remember me after tonight. How do you think he'd like my initial carved into his flesh?"

"Perhaps in his cheek?" Douglas said avidly.

Bronwyn gave him a cold look, her eyes made silver by the moonlight. "I don't want to cause more war, only a memory. Besides, I've heard the MacGregor is a handsome man." She pulled his shirt open.

"You seem taken with handsome men lately," Douglas said bitterly.

"Perhaps it is you who are worried about my men. Is

it your jealousy or your greed that eats at you? See to my men and stop your childish tantrums."

Douglas turned away from her.

Bronwyn had heard tales of the MacGregor and knew he'd prize a scar made by a woman who had beaten him. She used the tip of her dirk and barely broke the skin as she carved a small B in his shoulder. She'd make sure he remembered her the next time he tried to steal her cattle.

When she'd finished, she ran back to her men, and together they ran to their horses. It was a heady experience: her first victory as laird of her clan.

"To Tam!" she cried when she was on her horse. "Let's rouse him from his bed. He'll want to hear how the MacGregor wears the brand of the MacArran." She laughed as she thought of the rage of the man when he saw the present she'd given him.

But they weren't destined to get home so easily. Suddenly the skies opened, and a deluge of very cold rain poured down on them. All of them wrapped their plaids over their heads, and Bronwyn thought with longing of the warm skirt she'd left on the ground. Lightning flashed and the horses jumped about, skittish at the light and sound.

They rode back to Larenston along the cliff edge of the sea. It was not the safest way but the quickest, and they knew the MacGregors would not pursue them on unknown, dangerous pathways.

Suddenly a stupendous bolt of lightning tore through the skies and hit the ground directly in front of Alexander. The horse reared, pawing the ground frantically with its forefeet. The next instant a roar of thunder threatened to bring the rocks down about their heads. Alexander's horse changed direction, and its feet came down in midair, hanging over the edge of the cliff. For an instant horse and rider hung suspended, half on land, half in the air. Then suddenly they fell, Alex coming out of the horse's saddle.

Bronwyn was the first one to dismount. The cold rain pelted against her face. Her legs were blue with cold.

"He's gone!" Douglas shouted. "The sea has him now."

Bronwyn strained to see through the darkness and rain to look at the sea below. A flash of lightning showed her the horse's body below, still as it lay against the rocks. But there was no sign of Alex.

"Let's go!" Douglas shouted. "You can't help him."

Bronwyn stood. She was as tall as Douglas, on an equal level with him. "Do you give me orders?" she demanded, then looked back toward the water. "Hold my ankles so I can see farther over the edge."

Bronwyn stretched out on her stomach as Douglas grabbed her ankles. Immediately two men came to her side to steady her arms. Another man put his hands on Douglas's shoulders.

Inch by inch Bronwyn eased herself over the side until she could see down the side of the sheer rock wall. It was frightening hanging over the edge, trusting her life to the strong hands about her ankles. Her first impulse was to say she saw nothing but she couldn't leave Alex if there was a chance he was still alive. She had to wait patiently for the next burst of lightning, then scan the area. Slowly she moved her head to see another part of the cliff. Her half upside-down position was making her dizzy, and the fear was making a knot in her stomach.

It was when she turned her head the third time that she thought she saw something. It seemed like an eternity before lightning illuminated the wall again. Her neck felt as if it would break from holding her head up.

The lightning flashed, and suddenly all her pain left her. There, to her left, about halfway down, was a familiar flash of the red plaid Alex favored.

She waved her hand, and the men pulled her up.

"Alex! Down there!" she gasped, her mouth filling with rainwater. She impatiently wiped her forearm across her eyes. "He's on a narrow ledge. We'll tie a rope around me. I think I can get to him."

"Let me go!" Francis said.

"You're too big. There's not enough room on the ledge. Get me some rope and I'll put it over my shoulder. Understand?" Her shouts were accompanied by hand gestures.

The men nodded, and almost immediately she was coiling a rope to put around her shoulder. She gave one end to Douglas. "When I jerk twice, pull him up." Next she tied another rope about her waist. "When Alex is safe, get me."

She walked to the edge of the cliff. She wouldn't look down at the hard nothingness below her. She paused for a moment. "Tam is my successor," she said, without adding that he would be only if she died.

The heavy rope cut into her waist, and although the men eased her down as slowly and gently as they could, she slammed against the rock wall several times. Her knees and shoulders ached painfully, and she could feel the skin coming off her hands as she clutched the rope. Think of Alex, she thought, think of Alex.

It was a long time before she reached the narrow ledge. There was barely room for her to put her feet beside Alex's big body. After some careful maneuvering, she managed to straddle his hips.

"Alex!" she shouted above the lashing rain.

The young man slowly opened his eyes, then looked at Bronwyn as if she were an angel on earth. "Chief," he whispered while closing his eyes, the sound of his words lost in the storm.

"Damn you, Alex, wake up!" Bronwyn screamed.

Alex opened his eyes again.

"Are you hurt? Can you help me with the rope?"

Alex suddenly became aware of his surroundings.

"My leg's broken, but I think I can still move. How did you get here?"

"Don't talk! Just tie knots!"

She was standing in a precarious position, and there was very little room for moving about. She bent forward, keeping her legs straight, not changing the placement of her feet, as she and Alex fastened the rope around his body. They made a crude sort of sling, the rope going between his legs and around his back.

"Are you ready?" she shouted.

"You go first. I'll wait."

"Don't argue with me, Alex. This is an order." She gave two hard tugs on the rope, then felt it tighten as the men above pulled it up. She frowned as Alex slammed against the wall, further injuring his leg.

When he was just above her head, she plastered herself against the rock. The rain slashed at her; the sheer wall of the cliff was hard and menacing against her back. Suddenly she felt very alone—and very frightened. Her concern for Alex had motivated her early courage, but now she had nothing. Alex was safe, and she was so alone and so frightened. It flashed through her mind that where she wanted to be right now was in Stephen's lap, sitting before a fire, his arms around her.

The rope about her waist tightened, and she had no more time for thought. Yet even as she held on to the rope, her hands tight, her feet wrapped about the cord to relieve the pressure on her waist, the image of Stephen stayed with her.

Somehow it was no surprise at all when she reached the top of the cliff to find Tam and Stephen pulling her up. Stephen put out his hands and caught her under the arms, then lifted her onto the land. He caught her close to him in an embrace that nearly crushed her, but she enjoyed the pressure, was glad she was no longer alone. He held her away from him, her face between his hands, and studied her. His eyes were dark and shadowed. She wanted to say something, that she was glad to see him, glad she was safe again, but his expression didn't allow for words.

Abruptly he moved his hands to her arms, then began an impersonal inspection of her. He tossed her back against his arm and ran his hand over her legs, frowning at the bloody places on her knees. All her soft feelings left her. How dare he inspect her in such a way in front of her men!

"Release me!" she commanded.

Stephen ignored her as he looked up at Tam, who hovered over them. "Several cuts and a few bruises, but it looks like nothing serious."

Tam stood up from his half-crouch and nodded. About ten years seemed to leave him.

Bronwyn kicked once and struggled against Stephen. "If you are quite finished with me," she said haughtily, "I'd like to go home."

Stephen turned to look at her, and she understood the expression on his face. He was angry—very, very angry. The rain was beginning to lessen somewhat and dawn was lighting the sky. She sat up and attempted to pull away from him. "I need to see to Alex."

"Alex is being cared for," Stephen said flatly, his teeth clenched. His hand firmly clasped her wrist, and as he stood he pulled her with him. He started toward his horse, dragging her behind him.

"I demand that you release me," she said as quietly as possible, since all her men were standing near them.

He whirled on her, jerked her close to him. "If you say one more word, I just may throw that bit of shirttail over your head and beat your backside black and blue. Alex is safe—safer than you are at the moment, so don't tempt me further. Is that clear?"

She put her chin in the air and glared at him. But she gave him no cause to carry out his threat. He turned and pulled her toward a waiting horse. He gave her no time to mount but picked her up and slammed her into the saddle so hard her teeth jarred together. Instantly he was on his own horse.

He held the reins to her horse. "Will you follow me, or must I lead your horse?"

She couldn't bear being led away like some naughty child. "I'll follow," she said, her back straight, her chin high.

They rode away from the men on the narrow cliff path, and Bronwyn didn't look back. Her humiliation was too complete. Her men respected her, obeyed her, but Stephen tried to reduce her to a child. Rab ran along beside the horses, following his mistress as he always did.

They rode for over three hours, and Bronwyn knew they were headed for her northernmost estates. The country was hilly, wild, with many streams to cross. Stephen kept a slow, steady pace, never looking at her but sensing when he needed to slow down to wait for her.

Bronwyn was very tired. She hadn't eaten since before the cattle raid during the night, and now that seemed like days ago. She was so hungry her stomach felt as if it were eating itself. The rain had slowed to a cold, wet drizzle, and she was chilled to the bone. She shivered often and sneezed a few times. Her legs were cut and bruised, and no matter which way she turned, the saddle rubbed on a sore place.

But she would have died before she asked Stephen to stop and rest.

Toward midday he halted, and Bronwyn couldn't help but breathe a sigh of relief. Before she could dismount, he was beside her, pulling her down from her horse. She was too weary, too cold, too hungry, to even remember the happenings of the night.

He stood her on the ground, then walked away from her. When he looked back, she saw that none of his anger had gone away. "Why?" he asked, and the word showed how much control he was using to keep from lashing out at her. "Why did you drug me?"

She tried to hold her shoulders straight. "The Mac-Gregors were planning another raid, and I had to protect my people's property."

His eyes were cold and hard. "Has no one ever told you that it is a *man's* duty to lead a war party?"

She shrugged. "That is how you're taught in England. We're different in Scotland. I was fostered when I was seven, just as my brother was. I was taught how to ride and, if need be, how to use a sword."

"And you thought I wasn't capable of leading the men, so you threw off your clothes"—he sneered at the short skirt she wore—"and led them yourself. Do you consider me so little a man that you believe yourself to be a better one?"

"Being a man!" she said in disgust. "That's all you concern yourself with. On the last raid you went in your armor. Do you know the MacGregors *laughed* at me! They said the MacArrans had a woman for a laird and a steel pillar for a leader. Well, last night I made them stop laughing. I carved a B on the MacGregor's shoulder."

"You what!" Stephen spluttered.

"You heard what I said," she said arrogantly.

"Oh, God!" Stephen said, running his hand through his wet hair. "Don't you understand anything about a man's pride? All his life he'll bear the mark a woman put on him. He'll hate you—and your clan."

"You're wrong! Besides, the MacGregors and the MacArrans already hate each other."

"Not as far as I can see. You seem to tease each other. It's more a game than a true war."

"You know nothing about it. You're an Englishman," she said as she turned back to her horse and began to unbuckle the saddle.

He put his hand across hers. "I want your word that you'll never drug me again."

She jerked away from his touch. "There are times when—"

He grabbed her shoulders and turned her to face him. "There is never a time when you can control my life as well as my reason. What would have happened if there'd been trouble and I was needed? I was asleep so hard someone could have torn down the castle and I wouldn't have known. I cannot live with someone I cannot trust. I want your promise."

She gave him a little smile. "I cannot give it."

He pushed her away from him. "I'll not endanger my men because of the whims of a foolish girl," he said quietly.

"Girl!" she said. "I am the MacArran. I have hundreds of men and women who obey me and respect me."

"And let you have your own way too often. You're an intelligent woman and your judgment is good. But you don't have the experience to lead fighting men. That I will do."

"My men won't follow you."

"They will as long as I am awake enough to lead them." He stared at her when she didn't answer. "I have asked you for your promise, now I will take it. If you ever drug me again I will take that dog away from you."

Bronwyn opened her mouth in astonishment. "Rab would always return to me."

"Not if he's several feet under the ground, he wouldn't."

She was slow in understanding his words. "You'd kill him? You'd kill a dog to get what you want?"

"I'd kill a hundred dogs, or horses, to save one man, either mine or yours. Their lives are in danger if I'm not there to protect them, and I can't spend my life worrying that my own wife will decide whether or not she wants me conscious on any given night. Do I make myself clear?"

"Very clear. You would no doubt enjoy killing my dog. After all, you've taken nearly everything else away from me."

Stephen gave her a look of exasperation. "It's obvious that you're going to see only what you want to. Just remember that if you love that animal, you'll think twice before tampering with my food again."

Suddenly it was all too much for Bronwyn. The long, wet night, the horror of being lowered down a cliff, and now the thought of losing Rab were all too much for her. She sank to her knees in the soggy ground, and Rab came to her. She put her arms around the big dog and buried her face in his rough, damp coat. "Yes, I love him," she whispered. "You English have taken away everything else, you might as well take Rab too. You killed my father and his three favorite men. You killed all my chances for happiness with a husband I could love." She lifted her head, her eyes bright with unshed tears. "Why don't you take Rab? And Tam too? And burn my house down while you're at it?"

Stephen shook his head at her, then offered her his hand. "You're tired and hungry and don't know what you're saying."

She ignored his hand and stood up.

Stephen suddenly grabbed her and pulled her into his arms. He didn't seem to notice her struggles to push him away. "Has it ever occurred to you that you could love me? If you did, it would save the both of us an awful lot of quarreling."

"How could I ever love a man I couldn't trust?" she asked simply.

Stephen didn't say a word but kept holding her to

him, his cheek against her wet hair. "Come on," he said after a while. "It's about to rain again. We have several more miles before we reach shelter." He didn't look at her after he released her, and Bronwyn had a passing thought that he was sad. She dismissed it immediately and mounted her horse.

Chapter Eight

It was late afternoon before Stephen stopped in front of an old stone house. The back of the cottage was buried into the side of a little hill, the roof covered with grassy sod. Rain was beginning again, just when Bronwyn's clothes had begun to dry.

She stopped her horse but didn't dismount. She was too tired and weary to move.

Stephen put his hands to her waist and half dragged her to the ground. "Hungry?" he murmured just before he tossed her into his arms and carried her into the cottage.

The dirt-floored room was warm from a peat fire. There was a stool against the wall. He put her on it. "Stay here while I see to the horses."

She hardly noticed when he returned, she was so tired.

"I thought you Scots were a stout bunch," he teased, then laughed when she wearily sat upright, no longer leaning against the wall. "Come here and look what I have." He opened a chest along one wall and began withdrawing food. There was a warm pot of a heavenly smelling stew. Thick dark bread came next. There was fish and soup, fruit and vegetables.

Bronwyn felt as if she were in a dream. Slowly she left the stool and went to Stephen's side. Her eyes hungrily looked at each dish, then followed it to where he set it on the far side of him.

When she reached for a succulent piece of roast pork, Stephen pulled the dish away from her.

"There's a price for all this," he said quietly.

She moved away from him, her eyes glassy-hard. She started to rise.

Stephen set the dish down. "Here!" he said, grabbing her shoulders. "Is there no humor about you?"

"Not when it concerns a murdering Englishman," she said stiffly.

He suddenly pulled her close to him. "At least you are consistent." He held her away from him, caressed her cheek with the back of his knuckles. "And what do you think I would charge for the food?"

"That I and my men swear allegiance to you, that we would fight for you even if you bade us fight against our own people," she said flatly.

"Good God!" Stephen half yelled. "What a monster you must think I am." He stared at her, frowning for a moment, then he smiled. "The payment I want will cost you much more. I want a kiss from you. One kiss, freely given. One kiss that I don't have to fight you for."

Bronwyn's first reaction was to tell him what he could do with his food and his kisses, in Gaelic of course, but she was sure he'd understand. Then she paused. If nothing else, a Scotsman was practical. She couldn't very well let all that food go to waste.

"Aye," she whispered. "I'll kiss you."

She leaned forward, on her knees, and touched her lips to his. He started to grab her to him but she pushed his arms away. "Mine!" she said possessively. Stephen smiled and leaned back on his elbows, allowing her to take charge of him.

Her lips played with his ever so gently, touching them, moving on them. She used the very edge of her teeth, the tip of her tongue, to explore and search his mouth.

She moved away just enough to look at him. It was raining outside, and the soft sound made them feel isolated and especially alone. The soft gold of the flickering fire cast gentle shadows on his handsome face. With his eyes closed, his lips slightly parted, Bronwyn could feel her heart begin to pound. Was it her imagination or had he grown better-looking since she'd first met him? He suddenly seemed perfection in a male.

Yet he lay still, waiting quietly. There was no sign of the excitement that she was feeling. No sense of humor! she thought and smiled. Let's see how much humor you have, Englishman!

Stephen briefly opened his eyes before Bronwyn's lips descended on his again. This time she wasn't sweet or gentle but hungry. She bit at his lips, sucked at them.

Stephen lost his easy position of relaxation and fell against the hard floor. His hands closed about Bronwyn's waist, pulling her closer to him. She laughed deep within her throat and again pushed his hands away. Obediently he let them fall to his side.

She pulled her head away, her lips still fastened to his, and his head followed her. With one hand behind his head, her fingers twisted in his hair, she moved her other hand to his knee. As she began to move it slowly upward, she felt his body tremble. He wore the Scots' dress, and he was bare under the shirt and plaid. Inch by slow inch she caressed his inner thigh, higher and higher. When she touched him between his legs, Stephen's eyes flew open, and the next minute he'd thrown Bronwyn to her back and had one leg across her.

"No!" she said, pushing against him. "One kiss, that was your price." She was breathing so hard she could hardly talk, as if she'd been running for miles.

Stephen did not come to his senses quickly. He stared at her quite stupidly.

Both of her hands were against his chest. "You promised I could eat if I gave you one kiss. I believe I did that," she said in all seriousness.

"Bronwyn," Stephen said as if he were a dying man.

She smiled quite merrily and gave him a sharp push, then scrambled away from him. "Never let it be said that a Scotsman doesn't keep his word."

Stephen groaned and closed his eyes for a moment. "I must have aged twenty years since I met you. Drugs this morning, then you climbing a rock wall, and now you try to finish me. What more can I expect? The rack, or do you prefer the water torture?"

She laughed at him, then handed him a juicy piece of roast pork. She was already eating, her lips red from the kiss, glossy from the meat. She grabbed a piece of meat pie when Stephen took the pork. "How did you come to this place? Who brought the food? How did you hear about the cliff?"

It was Stephen's turn to laugh as he began to eat, but without Bronwyn's gusto. He still hadn't recovered from Bronwyn's hand between his legs. Tam had been more than right about the convenience of the Scots' dress.

"Douglas went to Tam," he said after a while, then frowned. "I wish I could teach your men to come to me," he said in disgust. "I seem to hear everything second-hand."

Bronwyn had her mouth and both hands full of food. "Douglas was merely being an obedient son."

"Son? What are you talking about?"

She blinked at him. "Douglas is Tam's son."

"But I thought Tam's son was killed."

She gave him a look of disgust as she buttered a piece

of black bread. "A man may have more than one son.
My father said Tam was trying to make his own clan.
He has an even dozen sons, or did have until you
English killed one."

Stephen put his hand up in defense. "Who are they?"

"Douglas, Alex, Jarl, Francis, are the oldest. Then
he has some boys who are too young to fight, and his
new wife is about to bear him a new one any day."

Stephen chuckled. It was always the quiet ones you
needed to watch.

"You haven't answered my questions," Bronwyn
said, not anywhere near to slowing down her eating.
"And why did you bring me here?"

"I thought the ride might cool my temper, and I
didn't want your men interfering," he said before
answering her other questions.

"Tam tried to wake me but he couldn't." He gave
Bronwyn a chastising look, but she ignored him.
"Morag made me drink some disgusting concoction
that nearly killed me. Before I could recover, I was on a
horse and we were running along the cliff path. We got
there just as Alex was being pulled up."

He put down the chicken leg he was eating and gave
her a searching look. "Why did you have to go over the
side? Why the hell did those men of yours *allow* you to
do that?"

She set down the scone she was eating. "Can't you
ever understand? *I* am the MacArran. It is I who allows
or disallows. My men follow my orders, not the other
way around."

Stephen rose to put more peat on the fire. His
English upbringing warred within him. "But you're not
strong. What if Alex had been unconscious and
couldn't have helped you? You haven't the muscle to
lift the dead weight of a man."

She was patient with him, realizing that he was trying
to understand. "I went myself because I'm small. There
was very little room on the ledge, and I felt I could

move about more easily than a large man. As for lifting
Alex, I can't lift his entire body but I knew I could get a
rope under enough parts of him so that he could be
pulled up. If I thought there'd been a better chance for
Alex by sending someone else, I wouldn't have hesitated. I always try to do what is best for my people."

"Damn!" Stephen said fiercely, then jerked her to
her feet. "I don't like hearing words of wisdom from a
woman."

She blinked, then smiled at his honesty. "Don't you
know some good leaders who use their heads instead of
their muscles?"

He stared at her, then pulled her into his arms, his
hand buried in her hair. "I was so angry," he whispered, "I didn't at first believe the men when they told
me where you were. I don't think I breathed until I saw
that you were all right."

She lifted her head and looked at him, her eyes
searching his face. "If I had been killed, I'm sure Tam
would have given some of my estates to you."

"Estates!" he gasped, then pushed her head back to
his shoulder. "Sometimes you are a stupid woman. I
should punish you for that insult." He wouldn't let her
move when she tried to. "I think maybe I will delay
your eating," he said huskily. He lifted her face and
kissed her greedily, laughing at the grease on her lips.
"You're an earthy thing," he said, then said no more as
she slipped her arms around his neck.

It took only moments to renew his passion. Recalling
the events of the morning, his fear for her while she'd
been suspended against a sheer rock wall, made him
kiss her almost in desperation. He held her face in his
hands, his tongue sweetly drawing on her nectar.

He put his arms beneath her knees and carefully laid
her by the fire. He took his time undressing her,
unbuckling her belt, then kissing her stomach. He slid
her plaid away from her hips, then kissed her legs, the
whole golden length of them.

"Come to me," she whispered.

But it was his turn to be the torturer. He pushed her pleading hands away, then began unbuttoning her blouse. He kissed each patch of skin at it was bared and smiled when she arched toward him.

He only laughed when she pulled on his hair, demanding that he come to her. He shook his head vigorously, his face buried in her breasts, and her hands fell away. He sat back on his heels and looked at her. Her body was so beautiful.

She opened her eyes to stare up at him and wondered what he was thinking. She watched as he threw off his clothes and came to lay beside her. She gasped as his skin touched hers.

It was warm in the room, but their hot skin touching made it an inferno. "Stephen," she whispered, the word sounding almost like an endearment.

"Yes," he murmured before pulling her under him.

In spite of their passion their lovemaking was slow. They took their time with each other. Bronwyn pushed Stephen to his back once and controlled their movements. Then, as their desire rose, faster and higher, Stephen shoved Bronwyn to the floor for the last few deep, hard thrusts.

Weak, he collapsed on top of her, his lips against her neck. Within minutes they both fell asleep.

Two weeks later Stephen's prediction that the Mac-Gregor would hate Bronwyn came true.

Stephen had spent that two weeks learning from Bronwyn's men. That one disastrous cattle raid had shown him the need for learning to fight in the Scots manner. He learned to run, to use the heavy Claymore. He could slip in and out of his plaid in seconds. His legs grew brown and weathered, and he didn't even mind the cold when the first snows arrived.

As for Bronwyn, she watched him suspiciously, only relaxing her guard at night when she was in his arms.

Stephen had changed so much in the last few weeks that it seemed a long time since that cattle raid when Bronwyn had scratched her initial on her enemy's shoulder. The first sign Lachlan MacGregor gave of his anger was when he burned three crofters' houses on the northern estates.

"Was anyone hurt?" Bronwyn asked weakly when she heard the news.

Tam pointed to a young man standing amid the ruins. He turned, and on his cheek was branded an *L*.

Bronwyn put her hand to her mouth in horror.

"The MacGregor said he'd brand all the clan before he's finished. He said he nearly died from blood poisoning from the wound ye gave him," Tam continued.

She turned away and walked back to her horse. Stephen stopped her.

"You needn't worry that I'll lecture you," he said flatly when he saw her face. "Perhaps you've learned something from this. Now it's my turn to settle the matter."

"What are you planning to do?" she asked.

"I'm going to try to meet with the MacGregor and settle this once and for all."

"Meet with him!" she gasped. "He'll kill you! He hates the English more than I do."

"That's impossible," he said sarcastically as he mounted his horse and rode away from the smoldering ruins of the houses.

An hour later Chris was agreeing with Bronwyn. The two men, who had come to Scotland looking so much alike, were now very different in appearance. Chris still wore the English dress—a heavy velvet jacket lined in mink, satin breeches, and tight, fine woolen hose. But Stephen had changed completely; even his skin had darkened. His hair hung past his ears, curling around them in a becoming manner. If anything, his legs were even more muscular from his daily sprints with the Scotsmen.

"She's right," Chris said. "You can't go knocking on the door and ask to see the MacGregor. I've heard some of the tales of what he's done. You'd be lucky if he killed you right away."

"What am I supposed to do then? Sit back and watch my people branded, burned out?"

Chris stared at his friend. "Your people?" he asked quietly. "When did you become a Scotsman?"

Stephen grinned and ran his hand through his hair. "They're good people, and I'd be proud to be one of them. It was just Bronwyn's temper that caused this mess. I'm sure it can be straightened out."

"Did you know this feud has been going on for hundreds of years? Every one of these clans is at war with one of the others. It's a barbaric place!"

Stephen merely smiled at his friend. A few months ago he'd have said the same thing. "Come on inside and let's have a drink. I got a letter from Gavin yesterday, and he wants me to bring Bronwyn home for Christmas."

"Will she go?"

Stephen laughed. "She'll go whether she wants to or not. What about you? Will you come with us?"

"I'd *love* to. I've had about all I can take of this cold country. I don't understand how you can move about when half of you is bare."

"Chris, you should try it. It gives a man a great deal of freedom."

Chris snorted. "The freedom to freeze off my finer parts isn't exactly what I want. Maybe you can tell me where to do some hunting. I thought I'd take some of your men and mine and see if I could get a deer."

"Only if you promise to take some of Bronwyn's men too."

Chris gave a little snort of derision. "I don't know

whether I should be insulted by that or not." He stopped at Stephen's expression. "All right, I'll do as you say. If there is any trouble, I guess it would be better if I had a few of your bare-legged men near me." He smiled and put his hand on Stephen's shoulder. "I'll see you tomorrow, and we'll have fresh venison."

Stephen never saw Chris alive again.

The winter sun was just setting when four of Bronwyn's men rode through the gates at the mouth of the peninsula. Their clothes were torn and bloody. One man bore a long, jagged gash across his cheek.

Stephen was on the training field, listening to Tam instruct him in the use of the lochaber axe. Bronwyn stood close by, watching the men.

Tam was the first one to see the disheveled and wounded men. He dropped the axe and ran forward, Stephen and Bronwyn close behind him. "What is it, Francis?" he gasped, pulling the young man from his horse.

"MacGregor," he said. "The hunting party was attacked."

Stephen was on his horse before Francis had dismounted. The boy looked up at Stephen. "Two miles past the loch on the East Road." Stephen nodded once before he rode away. He didn't seem to be aware that both Bronwyn and Tam were trying to keep up with him.

The fading sunlight flashed off Chris's armor as he lay so still on the cold Scots ground. Stephen leaped from his horse and knelt beside his friend. He tenderly pushed back the face plate.

He didn't look up when he heard the voice of one of Chris's men over his shoulder. "Lord Chris wanted to show the Scots how the English could fight," the man said. "He put on his armor and planned to meet the MacGregor face to face."

Stephen glanced down at Chris's quiet form. He

knew the heavy armor had made his friend immobile, and the MacGregor had been free to hack at Chris at will. There were places unprotected by the armor, and now there were dents and mutilations in the steel.

"They tried to save him."

Stephen noticed for the first time the three Scotsmen who lay beside Chris. Their strong young bodies were bloody and ugly.

Stephen felt rage well up inside him. His friend! His friend was dead. He stood, then grabbed Bronwyn, turned her so she faced the four dead men.

"This is what has happened because of your escapade. Look at them! Do you know them?"

"Yes," she managed to whisper as she stared at them. She'd known the young men all her life, for all their short lives. She looked away.

Stephen buried his hands in her hair, pulling her head painfully back. "Do you remember the sound of their voices? Can you hear their laughter? Do they have any family?" He moved her head so she looked at Chris. "Chris and I were fostered together. We spent our childhoods together."

"Let me go!" she said desperately.

Abruptly Stephen released her. "You drugged me and led your men in a cattle raid, and you carved your initial on the MacGregor. Stupid, childish actions! And now we have paid for your actions, haven't we?"

She tried to hold her head high. She wouldn't believe he was right.

Douglas held his Claymore aloft. He'd ridden to the scene behind Bronwyn and his father. "We must revenge this act," he said loudly. "We must ride now and fight the MacGregor."

"Yes!" Bronwyn shouted. "We must repay him *now!*"

Stephen took one step forward and sank his fist into Douglas's face. He grabbed the Claymore just before Douglas fell.

"Hear me and hear me well," Stephen said in a quiet voice that carried to all the men. "This will be settled, but not by more blood being shed. This is a useless feud, and I'll not retaliate by drawing more blood. More deaths will not bring these men back." He gestured to the four bloody corpses at his feet.

"You're a coward," Douglas said in a low voice as he stood, rubbing his bruised jaw.

Before Stephen could speak, Tam stood next to his son. In his hand was his dirk. He held it low, aimed at his son's ribs. "Ye may disagree with the man, but ye'll not call him a coward," he said in his deep, rumbling voice.

Douglas locked eyes with his father, then he nodded once before he turned to Stephen. "We'll be willin' to follow ye," he said after a while.

"Follow him!" Bronwyn fairly shouted. "*I* am the MacArran. Are you forgetting that he's an Englishman?"

Tam spoke for his son. "I don't think we've forgotten so much as we've learned," he said quietly.

Bronwyn didn't ask what he'd learned. She looked at the faces of one man after another, and she could see they were changing toward her. Had it been a gradual thing, or did they too blame her for the men's deaths? She took a step backward from them, feeling as if she should put her hands up in protection. "No," she whispered before she turned and ran for her horse.

She didn't care where she went or how far. Tears blurred her vision so badly she could barely see. She rode for miles, across the hills and lochs. She never even noticed when she left the MacArran land.

"Bronwyn!" someone from behind her screamed.

At first she only spurred her horse faster, urging it away from the familiar voice. It wasn't until he was beside her that she realized it was her brother who called to her.

"Davey," she whispered and reined in her horse sharply.

Davey grinned at her. He was tall like Bronwyn, with their father's black hair, but he had inherited their mother's brown eyes. He was thinner than Bronwyn remembered, and his eyes seemed to have a wild inner glow. "You've been crying," he said. "Because of the men the MacGregor killed?"

"You knew?" she said, wiping her tears away with the back of her hand.

"It's still my clan, in spite of what Father said." For an instant his eyes were hard and cold, then they changed. "I haven't seen you in a long time. Sit with me and let your horse rest."

Suddenly her brother seemed like an old friend, and she pushed from her mind the last time she'd seen him—the night Jamie MacArran had named her laird. It had been an unexpected announcement and therefore more painful. All the clan had gathered and was waiting for the proclamation that Davey would be the next laird. James MacArran was always honest about himself and especially about his children. He told the clan about his children. He said Davey liked war too much, that he cared more for battle than for protecting his clan. He said Bronwyn had too much temper and too often acted before she thought. Both of his children felt deeply humiliated at their father's complaints. Jamie went on to say that Bronwyn could be controlled if she had a level-headed husband such as Ian, Ramsey or Ennis. Even after that statement no one guessed what Jamie had in mind. When he announced Bronwyn as his successor, provided she marry one of the young men, the hall was silent. Then, one by one, the clan raised cups to salute her. It took Davey a few moments to realize what was happening. When he did, he rose and cursed his father, called him a traitor, and declared himself no longer his son. He asked for men to follow him, to forever leave the clan. Twelve young men walked out of the hall behind Davey that night.

Bronwyn had not seen her brother since that night. Since then several men had been killed, her father included; she had been married to an Englishman. Suddenly all that Davey'd said so long ago seemed unimportant.

She dismounted her horse and put her arms around him. "Oh, Davey, everything has turned out so badly," she cried.

"The Englishman?"

She nodded against his bony shoulder. "He's changed everything. Today my men looked at me as if I were the intruder. I saw it in their eyes that they thought he was right and I was wrong."

"Do you mean he's turning the men against you?" Davey snapped, moving away from her. "How could they be so blind? He must be a good actor to overcome the horror of our father's death. How can the men forget that it was the English who killed the MacArran? And what of Ian? Has even Tam forgotten his son's death?"

"I don't know," Bronwyn said as she sat down on a fallen log. "They all seem to trust him. He dresses as a Scotsman. He trains with my men. He even spends time with the crofters. I see them together, laughing, and I know they like him."

"But has he ever done anything to gain their trust? I mean something besides kissing babies?"

She put her hands to her temples. All she could see was the four dead men on the ground. Had she caused their deaths? "He hasn't done anything to make them distrust him either."

Davey snorted. "He would be careful not to. He will wait until he gets their confidence before he brings his Englishmen here."

"Englishmen? What are you talking about?"

"Don't you see?" Davey said with great patience. "Tell me, is he planning to return to England soon?"

"Yes," she said, surprised. "I believe he plans us to leave in a few weeks."

"That's when he'll bring his Englishmen back here. He'll teach them all he's learned about fighting like a Scotsman, and we'll have very little defense against them."

"No!" she said as she rose. "Davey, you can't mean this. He's not like this. He can be kind, and I know he's concerned about my men."

He gave her a look of disgust. "I've heard how he makes you howl in bed. You're afraid of losing him. You'd sacrifice your clan for an Englishman's hands on your body."

"That's not true! The clan always comes first with me." She stopped abruptly. "I had forgotten how much we quarrel. I must go back now."

"No," Davey said quietly, his hand on her arm. "Forgive me for upsetting you. Sit here with me for a while. I've missed you. Tell me how Larenston is. Did you get the leak in the roof fixed? How many sons does Tam have now?"

She smiled as she sat down again. They talked for several minutes as the night closed about them, about the everyday happenings within the clan. She found out that Davey was living somewhere in the hills, but he was evasive about his life and so she respected his privacy.

"And do you enjoy being laird?" he asked amiably. "Do the men obey you?"

She smiled. "Yes. They treat me with great respect."

"Until this morning when they turned to your husband."

"Don't start again."

Davey leaned back against a tree. "It just seems a shame that centuries of MacArrans are now ruled by an

Englishman. If you'd had time, you could have established your own authority, but you can't expect the men to follow a woman when a man is there pushing her behind him."

"I don't know what you mean."

"I was just daydreaming. What if this Stephen is a spy sent by King Henry? When he has the trust of your men, he could do a great deal of damage to Scotland. Of course, you'd be there and you'd try to get your men to follow you, but by then they would be so used to disobeying your orders that you'd never even get their attention."

She couldn't answer him. She was remembering all the times lately that her men had gone to Stephen, whereas when they'd first returned from England, her clan had asked only her opinion.

Davey continued. "Too bad you haven't had time alone with your clan. If you had, they'd see you had sense enough to lead them. When—or if—Montgomery betrayed you, you could lead the clan to safety."

She didn't like to think about his words. She had caused her men's deaths today. Her stupidity and arrogance had caused four deaths, and Stephen was right to blame her. Her men were right to turn to him. But what if Stephen were a spy? What if he did decide to use her men's trust against them? For generations the Scots had hated the English. Surely there was a reason for that hatred. For all she knew there could be a hundred tragedies in Stephen's life that would cause him to hate the Scots. Perhaps Davey was right and Stephen wanted to lead them all into slaughter.

She put her hands to her head. "I can't think," she whispered. "I don't know what he is or whether he can be trusted."

"Bronwyn," Davey said as he took her hands. "You may not believe this, but I want what is best for the clan. I've had months to come to terms with myself—and with you. I know you're the one who should be laird, not me." He put a finger to her lips. "No, let me finish. I want to help. I want to be sure he isn't a spy, that he won't turn on our clan."

"Sure? What do you mean?"

"I'll take him to my camp, that's all. He won't be harmed, and while he's gone you can reestablish yourself as the true head of Clan MacArran."

"Take him!" She rose, her eyes flashing even in the darkness of the night.

"He wouldn't be harmed. I'd be foolish to harm him. King Henry would declare war on Clan MacArran. All I want to do is buy you a little time."

She pulled away from him. "And what do you get out of it?" she asked coldly.

"I want to come home," he said heavily. "If I do this good deed for you, then I hope to come home with honor. My men and I are starving, Bronwyn. We aren't farmers, and we have no crofters to farm for us."

"You're welcome at home, you should know that," she said quietly.

He jumped up. "And have the men laugh at me, saying I came home with my tail between my legs? No!" He calmed somewhat. "It would save our dignity if we could return in triumph. We'll ride back into Larenston with your English husband, and everyone, from King Henry down, would be grateful to us."

"I . . . no, it's not possible. Stephen is—"

"Think about it. You'd have control of your people. I could return home in honor. Or maybe you care more about this Englishman than your own brother," he sneered.

"No! Of course not! But if he were harmed—"

"You insult me! Do you think I have no brain? If I were to harm him, think what King Henry would do to us! Oh, Bronwyn, please consider it. It would be so good for the clan. Don't confuse them any more than they already are. Don't wait until you see them standing on a battlefield trying to choose between England

and Scotland. Let them know they're Scotsmen. Don't make them divide their loyalties."

"Davey, I must go, please."

"You should go. Think about it. In three days I'll meet you along the cliff wall. Where Alex fell."

She looked up, startled.

"I know a lot about my clan," he said as he threw a leg into his saddle and rode away.

Bronwyn stared after him for a few minutes until the darkness swallowed him. She dreaded returning to Larenston, dreaded facing the deaths of her men, as well as Stephen's anger. But the MacArran couldn't afford to be a coward. She straightened her shoulders and mounted her horse.

Chapter Nine

BRONWYN WALKED SLOWLY ACROSS THE COURTYARD. She'd had three days since her men were killed to think. Davey's words haunted her. Every minute she became more aware of the way her men were turning to Stephen. It was natural that they'd look to a man for leadership, since it'd been only months ago that they'd followed Jamie MacArran. But Bronwyn didn't trust any Englishman. She knew what foul, crude, greedy people they were. Hadn't she met several Englishmen when she was held captive at Sir Thomas Crichton's?

As for Stephen, the death of his friend affected him greatly. He didn't talk much, and Bronwyn often caught him staring into space. Immediately after the killings he ordered the packing for the trip to England to begin. He said that he wanted to take Chris's body back to his family.

At night, when they were alone, they lay side by side without touching, without speaking. Bronwyn was haunted by the sight of the three dead men. She wondered how her father came to terms with himself when he made a mistake that cost the lives of men he loved. She felt the knot forming in her throat. The laird of a clan shouldn't cry. She must be strong and not be afraid of being alone.

Besides the heaviness of her guilt, she had Davey's pleas to consider. She knew of the pride of her brother, knew that it had been difficult for him to ask anything of her. Yet how could she turn Stephen over to him?

She put her hands to her ears. She wanted to do what was right for everyone, but she felt so alone and so powerless. What *was* right?

She saddled her horse herself and left the peninsula to meet Davey.

Davey stared at her for some moments, his eyes hot and piercing. When Bronwyn looked down at her hands, trying to put her thoughts into words, he knew her decision.

"So!" he said, his eyes changing to an unforgiving look. "You're going to put your lover before the clan."

She looked at him without blinking. "You know that isn't true."

He snorted. "Then I can assume that it's me you don't believe in. I hoped you'd let me prove myself, prove that I've matured over that horrible boy who cursed his father."

"I want to, Davey," she said quietly. "I want to do what is right for everyone."

"Like hell you do!" he exploded. "You only care for yourself. You're *afraid* for me to return. You're afraid the men will follow me, the true MacArran." He turned toward his horse.

"Davey, please, I don't want us to part like this. Come home, at least for a while."

"And stand by and see my sister," he sneered the word, "take my rightful place in the clan? No thank you. I'd rather be king of my own poor kingdom than a servant in another." He nearly jumped into his saddle and thundered away.

Bronwyn had no idea how long she stood there alone, staring at the ground, feeling stupid and helpless.

"Who was that?" Stephen asked quietly.

She looked up at him, not surprised to see him there. So often he seemed to be near her even though she wasn't aware of his presence. "My brother," she said quietly.

"David?" he asked with interest as he looked in the direction of the galloping horse.

She didn't answer him.

"Did you ask him to come to Larenston?" he continued. "Did you tell him the gates are always open?"

"I don't need you to tell me what to say to my own brother." She turned away, tears in her eyes.

He grabbed her arm. "I'm sorry. I didn't mean it like it sounded."

She jerked away from him, but he drew her back, pulled her into his arms.

"I was wrong to curse you when I found Chris dead," he said quietly. "I was just so angry I wanted to lash out at someone. I was wrong."

She kept her face pressed to his chest. She longed for him to hold her in his arms. "No! You were right! I did kill my men and your friend."

He pulled her closer, felt the trembling in her body. Her shoulders were so small and delicate. "No, that's too much responsibility for you to assume." He lifted her chin. "Here, look at me. Whether you believe this or not, we're in this together, and I share the burden of the men's deaths."

"But I was the one," she said desperately.

He put his finger to her lips, then his eyes searched her face. "You're so young, not even twenty, but you're trying to take care of hundreds of people, even to protect them from me, a man who you think could be a spy."

He laughed at the expression on her face. "I'm beginning to understand you. Right now you're thinking that I have an ulterior motive for talking this way. You're thinking that I'm planning some treacherous act, and I want you quietly dazed by my honeyed words."

She pulled away from him. "Let me go!" His words were so close to what she'd been thinking that she was almost frightened.

He gave a low laugh. "Am I too close to home? You want me to remain a stranger, don't you? Someone you can easily hate. But I don't plan to leave you alone long enough to forget that I'm a man before I'm an Englishman."

"You—you're not making sense. I need to get back to Larenston."

He ignored her as he sat down on the grass and pulled her down beside him. "Tomorrow we start for England. How do you feel about meeting my family?"

She stared at him. "I haven't thought of it." Her eyes flashed blue fire as she remembered her time at Sir Thomas Crichton's house. "I don't like the English people."

"You don't know them!" Stephen retorted. "You've met only the scum. I was embarrassed by my own people at the way they treated you at Sir Thomas's."

"None of them left me standing at the altar in my wedding dress."

He chuckled. "You're not about to forget that, are you? When you meet my sister-in-law Judith, perhaps you'll forgive me."

"What . . . what's she like?" Bronwyn asked tentatively.

"Beautiful! Kind and sweet-tempered and smart. She runs Gavin's estates with one eye closed. King Henry was quite taken with her and more than once asked her opinion."

Bronwyn sighed heavily, her breath catching in her throat. "It's good to hear of someone who is competent and doesn't mishandle her responsibilities. I wish my father had a daughter who was worthy of the title of laird."

He laughed and pulled her back against him, stretched out on the cold, damp ground. "For a woman, you're quite capable as a laird."

She blinked. "For a woman? Does that mean you think no woman is capable of being chief of a clan?"

He shrugged. "At least not one so young and pretty or so ill-trained."

"Ill-trained! I have trained all my life. You know I can read better than you as well as add a column of figures."

He laughed. "There's more to ruling men than adding numbers." He looked at her for a moment. "You're so beautiful," he said quietly as he bent forward to kiss her.

"Let me go! You are an insufferable, narrow-minded, ignorant—" She stopped because his hands were on her legs, caressing them.

"Yes," he whispered against her mouth. "What am I?"

"I do not know and I do not care," she said as if from a long way away. She arched her neck backward as he touched it with his lips.

In spite of the seeming privacy Bronwyn and Stephen were not alone. David MacArran stood on the hill above them, watching them. "The whore!" he whispered. She put her own lust before the needs of her brother. And to think Jamie MacArran thought she was more worthy to be laird.

He raised his fist toward the couple below him. He'd show them! He'd show all of Scotland who was the most powerful man, the true laird of Clan MacArran.

He sharply reined his horse away and headed back toward his secret camp in the hills.

The sun was barely up as the wagons rolled down the steep path to the mainland. Stephen's men, now so brown, hardly distinguishable from Bronwyn's Scots, rode beside him. They were a quiet group, apprehensive about the outcome of the journey. The wagons were loaded with English clothes, and Bronwyn's men wondered if they'd be able to function in English society.

Bronwyn had her own worries. Morag had lectured her for a long time when the old woman heard about Davey's plan. "Don't ye be atrustin' him," she said, pointing a short bony finger at Bronwyn. "He always was a sly one, even as a boy. He wants Larenston, and he'll stop at nothin' to get it."

Bronwyn had defended her brother, but now she remembered Morag's warnings. She looked about her for the hundredth time.

"Nervous?" Stephen said from beside her. "You needn't be. I'm sure my family will like you."

It took her a full minute to understand what he was talking about. She put her nose haughtily in the air. "You should worry whether the MacArran will like them," she said as she spurred her horse forward.

It was sundown when the first arrow whizzed past Bronwyn's left ear. She'd just begun to relax and forget her apprehensions. At first she didn't realize what was happening.

"Attack!" Stephen yelled, and within seconds his men had formed a circle of defense, their weapons ready. Bronwyn's men slipped off their horses, out of their plaids, and into the woods.

She sat stupidly on her horse as she saw one man after another go down.

"Bronwyn!" Stephen yelled. "Ride!"

She obeyed him instinctively. The arrows flew about her. One grazed her thigh, and her horse screamed as the shaft burned the animal's skin. It suddenly came to her why she was so stunned. The arrows were all directed at her! And one of the archers she'd seen in a tree was one of the men who'd left the clan to join Davey. Her brother was trying to kill her!

She put her head down and urged her horse forward. There was no need to turn around; she could feel the pounding of the horses' hoofs behind her. She followed Stephen's horse as he led her away from the flying arrows. For once there was no thought of whether she trusted him or not.

She screamed once when her horse was shot from under her. Before the animal could even go to its knees, Stephen had circled back, and his arm was about her waist as he pulled her to the front of his saddle. She twisted until she was astraddle, then bent low over the animal's neck.

They rode hard across unknown, wild country. Bronwyn could feel Stephen's big stallion beginning to tire.

Suddenly Stephen slumped forward onto Bronwyn's back. She didn't have time to think before she grabbed the reins and jerked sharply. The horse left the bit of a road and plunged into the woods. She knew she had to get Stephen off the horse before he fell. They couldn't move quickly in the woods, but perhaps she could find a few moments of cover.

She stopped the horse suddenly, the bit tearing its mouth. Stephen's inert body fell to the ground before Bronwyn could dismount. She gasped as she jumped beside him. There was a bloody place along the back of his head where an arrow had creased the skin. She didn't have much time to think, as she could already hear the other riders approaching. The forest floor was covered with dried leaves, and an idea came to her.

Quietly, so she wouldn't be heard, she led the horse

away from Stephen. She couldn't risk the sound of a slap, so she unfastened her brooch and jammed the sharp end into the horse's rump. It began running almost instantly. She ran back to Stephen, fell to her hands and knees, and pushed him against a fallen log. She covered him with armfuls of leaves. The heathery plaids he wore blended with the leaves. She lay beside him and dug herself in.

Seconds later they were surrounded by angry, stomping men. She held Stephen close to her, her hand over his mouth in case he should waken and make a sound.

"Damn her."

She held her breath; she'd recognize Davey's voice anywhere.

"She always did have seven lives! All of which I mean to take," he added viciously. "And that English husband of hers! I'll show King Henry the Scots rule Scotland."

"There goes her horse!" said another voice.

"Let's go!" Davey said. "She can't have gone too far."

It was a long time before Bronwyn moved. She was too stunned, too upset at first, to move. When her brain cleared a bit, she turned cautious. She wanted to be sure that Davey left no one behind in the area. She hoped to hear the sound of approaching horses, her own men, but when they did not appear in an hour, she stopped hoping.

It was full dark when Stephen groaned and made his first movement.

"Quiet!" she said, running her fingers along his cheek. Her right arm was dead from his weight on it for so long.

Slowly, listening for each sound of the forest around her, she moved the leaves away. Her eyes were keen in the dark, and she'd had some time to listen to her surroundings. There was a stream not far from them at the bottom of a steep ridge. She ran down to it, then knelt and tore away a large square of linen from her underskirt and wet it.

She knelt by Stephen, placed a few drops of water on his lips, then wiped the gash on the back of his head. The gash was not bad on his forehead, but she knew that sometimes such wounds had more serious consequences. It was quite possible that his brain could be addled.

He opened his eyes and stared up at her. The moonlight made his eyes silver. She leaned over him with concern. "Who am I?" she asked quietly.

His face was very serious, as if he puzzled over her question. "A blue-eyed angel who makes my life heaven and hell at the same time."

She groaned in disgust, then dropped the bloody cloth in his face. "You are, unfortunately, the same."

Stephen made a sorry attempt at a grin, then tried to sit up. He raised one eyebrow when Bronwyn quite naturally slipped her arm around him and helped him. "Is the news that bad?" he asked, his fingers rubbing his temple.

"What do you mean?" she asked suspiciously.

"If you're helping me, the news must be worse than I thought."

She stiffened. "I shouldn't have covered you but left you exposed for them to find."

"My head is killing me, and I don't feel like arguing. And what the hell did you do to my back? Drive steel pins into it?"

"You fell off your horse," she said with a certain amount of satisfaction. Even in the darkness she could see his look of warning. "I guess I should start at the beginning."

"It would please me greatly if you did," he said, one hand on his head, the other rubbing his back.

She told him as succinctly as possible about Davey's plan to kidnap Stephen.

"And no doubt you agreed," he said flatly.

"Of course not!"

"But getting rid of me would have solved many of your problems. Why didn't you agree to his plan?"

"I don't know," she said quietly.

"His arguments were quite logical, and it was a perfect way to get rid of me."

"I don't know!" she repeated. "I guess that I really didn't trust him. Here, while we were under the leaves, I heard him say . . . that he meant to kill both of us."

"I guessed as much."

"How could you?"

He touched a curl of her black hair. "Just a guess based upon the number of arrows aimed directly at you. And the way they tried to separate us from the men. It's upset you, hasn't it?"

Her head snapped up. "What if you heard one of your brothers say he'd just tried to kill you?"

Even in the darkness she could see Stephen's face turn white. He looked at her in horror. "It is an impossible idea," he said flatly, finishing the subject. He looked around. "Where are we?"

"I have no idea."

"What about the men? Are they around here?"

"I'm only a woman, remember? How would I know about war strategy?"

"Bronwyn!" he warned.

"I don't know where we are. If the men don't find us soon, they'll return to Larenston, where we must go as soon as possible." She put her head to one side. "Quiet!" she whispered fiercely. "Someone's coming. We must hide!"

Stephen's first impulse was to meet whoever it was head on, but he had no weapon besides the little dirk at his side, and he had no idea how many people there were.

Bronwyn took his hand and pulled him forward. She led him to the crest of the steep ridge, then over the side. They quietly snuggled down into the thick bed of leaves and watched the two men who approached. They were obviously hunters, looking for game instead of the missing laird and her husband.

Stephen made a gesture as if he meant to say something to the men, but Bronwyn stopped him. He looked at her in surprise, but he didn't make a sound.

When the men were out of hearing distance, he turned to her. "They weren't David's men."

"Worse," she said. "They were MacGregors."

"Don't tell me you know each of the MacGregors personally."

She shook her head at his stupidity. "The cockades on their hats bore the MacGregor colors and insignia."

He gave her a brief look of admiration for her extraordinary night vision.

"I think I know where we are now."

He turned over, leaned back against the bank, and sighed. "Don't tell me," he said sarcastically. "Let me guess. We're in the middle of the MacGregor's land. We're weaponless, horseless, no food or gold. We're hunted by your brother, and the MacGregor would just love our heads on a platter."

Bronwyn turned to look at his profile, and suddenly a little giggle escaped her.

Stephen looked at her in astonishment, then he too smiled. "Hopeless, isn't it?"

"Yes," she agreed, her eyes dancing.

"Of course, this is no time to laugh."

"None whatever."

"But it is almost funny, isn't it?" he laughed.

She joined his laughter. "We'll probably be dead tomorrow, one way or another."

"So what do you want to do on your last night on earth?" he asked, his blue eyes picking up rays of moonlight.

"Someone could stumble on us at any moment," she said quite seriously.

"Hmmm. Shall we give them something to see?"

"Such as?"

"A couple of sublimely happy, totally nude wood-spirits."

She pulled her plaid close about her. "It's awfully cold, don't you think?" she said coyly.

"I'll wager we can find a way to get warm. In fact, it makes a great deal of sense to combine our warmth."

"In that case—" She launched herself from the ground and jumped on him.

Stephen gave a gasp of surprise, then laughed. "I think I should have brought you to the MacGregor's land before."

"Quiet, Englishman!" she commanded as she lowered her head and began to kiss him.

Neither of them seemed to remember that they were perched on the side of a very steep ridge. Their passion, intensified by the danger of their predicament, made them oblivious to even more immediate dangers.

Bronwyn was the first one to lose her footing. She'd just moved to Stephen's side, slipped her skirt off while he removed his clothing, when the next instant she was rolling down the side of the hill.

Stephen made a grab for her, but his senses were dulled by his passion and he missed her. But he'd extended himself too far and tumbled down just after her.

They landed together in a tangle of nude, moonlit skin and a flurry of leaves.

"Are you all right?" Stephen asked.

"I will be as soon as you get off me. You're breaking my leg."

Instead of moving off her, he moved his body more fully onto her. "You never complained before that I was too heavy for you," he said as he began to nibble her ear.

She smiled as she closed her eyes. "There are times when you don't weigh much at all."

He moved his lips to her throat.

Suddenly something enormous and heavy landed smack on Stephen's back. He collapsed onto Bronwyn for a moment, then quickly lifted himself with his arms, protecting her. "What the hell!"

"Rab!" Bronwyn said, then squirmed out from under Stephen. "Oh, Rab," she said with great, deep joy. "Rab, sweet Rab." She buried her face in the dog's coarse fur.

Stephen sat back on his heels. "That's all I needed," he said sarcastically. "As if my back weren't sore enough already."

Rab moved away from Bronwyn to leap at Stephen. In spite of his words Stephen hugged the big dog while it licked his face and tried to smother him with affection.

"Now, aren't you ashamed," Bronwyn laughed. "He loves you and is quite glad to see you."

"I wish he'd paid more attention to *my* loving. Down, Rab! You're going to drown me. Here, boy, fetch." Stephen threw an imaginary stick, and the dog happily ran after it.

"That was terrible! You know he'll spend hours looking for it. He so wants to please."

Stephen reached out and grabbed her wrist. "I hope he spends the rest of the night. Do you know how delicious you look in the moonlight?"

She looked at him, his broad chest, his shoulders. "You're not exactly an unpleasant sight yourself."

He pulled her to him. "You keep this up and I may never return you to Larenston. Now where were we?"

"Your back was killing you and—"

His mouth on hers made her stop talking.

"Come here, wench," he whispered as he pulled her down into the leaves.

It was quite cold, but neither of them felt it. The leaves came up around them and sheltered them, hid them, warmed them. Bronwyn felt Stephen's thighs against hers, and she pulled him closer and closer to her.

They wrestled together, laughing. There were sticks and rocks poking their skin, but neither of them minded. Once Stephen began tickling Bronwyn, and the sound of her laughter, so unusual a sound to him, fired his passion to white-hot.

"Bronwyn," he whispered before pulling her under him and becoming serious.

When they came together, it was somehow different from the other times. In spite of their differences, their impossible situation, they made love as if they were free for the first time. There was not only passion but a sense of joy and fun too.

"I had no idea you were ticklish," Stephen whispered sleepily as he held Bronwyn close to him.

Rab snuggled on her other side. "Neither did I. Shouldn't we get our clothes?"

"In a minute," Stephen whispered. "In a min—"

They were awakened very early by Rab's growling. Stephen's reflexes were instant. He sat up and pushed Bronwyn behind him. He stared at a man who was some twenty feet away. He was a short, wiry man with brown hair and eyes. And he wore the MacGregor cockade.

"Good mornin'," he called heartily. "I didna' mean to disturb you. I came to get some water, but your dog wouldn't let me pass."

Stephen heard Bronwyn take in breath to speak. He turned and gave her a look of warning. She was half buried in the leaves, only her head and bare shoulders visible.

"Mornin'," Stephen called just as heartily, his voice heavy with the Scots burr. "Rab, come away, let the fine gentleman pass."

"I thank ye, sir," the man said as he walked the few feet to the stream.

"Rab, fetch our clothes," Stephen said, then watched as the dog obeyed. He looked back at the man at the edge of the stream, who was looking at the nude pair with curiosity. "A bit of Adam and Eve, aren't we?" Stephen laughed.

The man laughed also. "Just what I was thinkin'." He stood. "I didn't see your wagon or horses, so I had no idea anyone was here."

Stephen put on his shirt, then deftly threw his plaid about him and buckled his wide belt. Both men discreetly turned away as Bronwyn dressed. She didn't speak but was fascinated by Stephen's newly acquired accent.

"To tell the truth," Stephen said, "we have only what we have on our backs."

Bronwyn watched as he put his cap behind his back and tore the MacArran cockade from it.

"We were set upon by thieves."

"Thieves!" the man said. "In the MacGregor's land? He won't like that."

"Aye, that he won't," Stephen agreed. "Especially since it was some of those thievin' MacArrans. Oh! I'm sorry, my dear, I didn't mean to pull your hair," he said when Bronwyn gave a little gasp of horror.

"Ah, the MacArrans," the man said. "There's never been a more dishonest, treacherous, cowardly lot ever put on the face of the earth. Did you know that not long ago they nearly killed the MacGregor, merely because the man was riding across the woman's land? The hag took her knife to him and nearly mutilated him. I heard she tried to cut his manhood off. Probably jealous."

Stephen whirled Bronwyn to face him so the man couldn't see her face. "Let me help you with the brooch," he said pleasantly in his heavy burr.

"I barely scratched him," she said in disgust.

"What?" the man asked.

Stephen smiled. "My wife is warning me that I scratched her last time I fastened her brooch."

The man chuckled. "I'm Donald Farquhar of Clan MacGregor."

Stephen smiled happily. "I'm Stephen Graham, and this is my wife, Bronwyn." He smiled at the face she pulled at him.

"Bronwyn!" Donald said. "'Tis an ill-favored name that one. Did ye know it was that witch the MacArran's name?"

Stephen held Bronwyn's shoulders firmly. "One can't help the name one was born with."

"No, ye canna." He looked at Bronwyn's long thick hair falling down her back, a few leaves stuck in it. "Anyone can see your Bronwyn isn't like that other one."

Bronwyn bent her head and acted as if she were kissing Stephen's hand, but in truth she applied her teeth sharply to the back of it. He released her, and she turned to smile at Donald. "And of course you've seen the MacArran many times," she said sweetly.

"No, not close, but I've seen her from a distance."

"And ugly is she?"

"Oh, aye. Great shoulders like a man and taller than most of her men. And a face so ugly she must keep it covered."

Stephen's fingers bit into her shoulders in warning. She nodded. "That's what I've always heard. It's nice to meet someone who knows her, so to speak," she said seriously.

Stephen bent forward to kiss her ear. "Behave yourself or you'll get us killed," he whispered.

Donald beamed at the two of them. "Ye must be newlyweds," he said happily. "I can't miss the way ye can't keep from touchin' one another."

"You miss little, do you, Donald?" Bronwyn said.

"I like to think I'm an observant man. Our wagon is on the ridge above. Perhaps you'd like to take a meal with us and meet my wife, Kirsty."

"No—" Bronwyn began, but Stephen stepped in front of her.

"We'd like that very much," he said. "We haven't eaten since yesterday noon. Perhaps you can give us directions. I'm afraid that after we were robbed, we wandered for quite some time and lost our way."

"But ye made good use of the time," Donald laughed, looking at the leaves with meaning.

"That we did!" Stephen said jovially, his arm firmly around Bronwyn's shoulders.

"Well, come on then. A MacGregor always welcomes a MacGregor." He turned and started up the hill.

"Don't do anything to endanger us," Stephen warned as they followed him.

"A MacGregor!" she muttered angrily.

"And an Englishman!" he added in the same tone.

"I don't know which is the lesser evil."

Stephen grinned. "Hate me but not him. He has the food."

At the top of the ridge all three of the people stopped and stared at the little woman bending over the fire. She was a delicate thing, no larger than a child, and her profile showed a little nose, a fragile mouth. But what was so unusual was that she was heavily, heavily pregnant. Her big belly stuck out in front of her like some massive monument. It was against all forces to reason that she was able to stand up and not let the weight of her burden pull her forward.

She did stand, quite easily, and turned to look at the three people watching her. For a moment she looked only at Donald, and a smile of pure adoration lit her face. When she turned and saw Bronwyn, her face changed. It seemed to go through several emotions· bewilderment, fear, disbelief, until finally she smiled.

Stephen and Bronwyn stood still, not breathing, expecting any moment that she'd announce who they were.

"Kirsty!" Donald said as he ran to his wife's side. "Are you all right?"

She put her hand on the side of her big belly and looked up in apology. "I'm sorry to greet ye like that, but I had a very strong kick."

Donald looked up and smiled. "He's a strong lad," he laughed. "Come and sit by the fire."

Stephen was the first to relax his muscles and walk toward the fire. Bronwyn followed him slowly. She still wasn't sure there hadn't been recognition on Kirsty's face. Perhaps she planned to tell Donald later and the MacGregors would attack them at night.

Donald introduced them to his wife, and even when the name Bronwyn was said, she only smiled. It wasn't a Scots name but a Welsh one, and it should have caused comment.

"Do you think we have enough food?" Donald asked.

Kirsty smiled. She had dark blonde hair and innocent brown eyes. It was difficult for anyone to mistrust her. "We always have enough to share," she said quietly.

They sat down to a meal of oatcakes baked on a griddle, and a savory rabbit stew. A cold wind blew around them. Donald's wagon stood at the edge of the road. It was small, with a wooden shelter built on top of it; a comfortable place but not meant for long-distance travel.

After breakfast Stephen proposed that he and Donald do some hunting.

Bronwyn immediately stood, brushed the crumbs off her skirt, and obviously meant to go with them.

Stephen turned to her. "Perhaps you should stay with Kirsty," he said quietly, with meaning. "A woman's place is by the fire."

Bronwyn felt anger flush through her. What did she

know of cooking? She could help on the hunt. It was when she saw approval in Donald's face that she understood Stephen. Donald might begin to be suspicious of a woman who could hunt but couldn't cook. She sighed in resignation. "At least we'll have Rab for protection."

"No," Stephen said. "I think we'll need him on the hunt."

"Rab!" she commanded. "Stay with me."

"Come, Rab," Stephen said patiently. "Let's go hunting."

The big dog didn't even seem to consider moving from Bronwyn's side.

Donald chuckled. "That's a well-trained dog you have there."

"My father gave him to me," she said proudly.

"Your father?" Donald began.

"We'd better go," Stephen said quickly as he gave Bronwyn a look of warning.

She turned away from them and went to sit by the fire, close to Kirsty—her enemy.

Chapter Ten

BRONWYN TWISTED A PIECE OF GRASS ABOUT IN HER
hands. Stephen's warning had made her realize how
easily she could give herself away. She knew very little
about being a wife and how the ordinary wife acted. All
her life had been spent with men. She could ride and
shoot, but cooking was a mystery to her. The everyday
talk between women was also unknown to her.

"Have you been married long?" Kirsty asked.

"No," Bronwyn answered. "And you?"

"About nine months," Kirsty smiled as she rubbed
her big stomach.

Bronwyn suddenly realized that someday her stomach could look like that. It had never occurred to her
that she'd have to bear pregnancy. "Does the child hurt
very much?" she asked quietly.

"Only now and then." Suddenly a look of pain
crossed her face. "Tonight seems to be worse than
usual," she said breathlessly.

"Could I get you something? Water? A pillow? Anything?"

Kirsty stared at her, her eyes blinking rapidly. "No, just talk to me. I haven't had a woman to talk to in a long time. Tell me, what's your husband like?"

"Stephen?" Bronwyn asked blankly.

Kirsty laughed. "Don't mind me. I'm just curious. You never seem to know a man until you live with him."

Bronwyn was cautious. "Were you disappointed in Donald?"

"Not at all. He was quite shy before we married, and now he's very kind, considerate. Your Stephen seems like a good man."

Bronwyn realized she'd never thought of Stephen as anything except an Englishman before. "He . . . he makes me laugh," she said after a while. "He makes me laugh at myself when I tend to be too serious."

Kirsty smiled, then she put her hand to her stomach and bent forward.

"What is it?" Bronwyn cried and went to her.

Kirsty sat up slowly, her breathing deep and difficult.

"Please let me help you," Bronwyn pleaded, her hands on Kirsty's arm.

Kirsty looked into Bronwyn's eyes. "You're very kind, aren't you?"

Bronwyn smiled. "I'm not a kind person in the least. I'm—" She broke off as she started to say she was the MacArran. But what was she away from her clan?

Kirsty put her hand over Bronwyn's. "I think you try to hide it. Tell me more about yourself. It keeps my mind off my own problems."

"I think I should call someone. I think you're about to have the baby."

"Please," Kirsty said desperately. "Don't frighten Donald. My baby isn't due yet. I can't have it now. Donald and I are going home to my parents'. My mother will deliver my child. It's just something I ate. I've had these pains before."

Bronwyn frowned as she sat back down on the ground.

"Tell me about yourself," Kirsty urged again. Her eyes were glazed. "What's it like to be married to an—"

Bronwyn's head came up sharply, but Kirsty didn't finish the sentence. She doubled over in pain, and the next minute Bronwyn caught the little woman in her arms.

"It's the baby," Kirsty whispered. "The baby is coming. You're the only one who can help me."

Bronwyn could only stare in horror. They were in the middle of nowhere, so who was going to be the midwife? She hugged Kirsty as another pain swept her. "Rab," she called quietly. "Go get Stephen. Get Stephen and bring him back here immediately."

Rab was away before Bronwyn finished speaking.

"Come inside the wagon, Kirsty," she said gently. Bronwyn was strong, and it was easy for her to get the small woman into the wagon. Kirsty lay down, and another pain made her double over.

Bronwyn looked out into the woods. No sign of the men. She went back to Kirsty, gave her a drink of water. Stephen would know what to do, she kept thinking. She didn't realize that for the first time she was depending on him.

She smiled when she heard Stephen's angry bellow.

"Bronwyn!"

She stepped down from the wagon.

"What the hell is this Satan-spawned dog of yours trying to do?" he demanded. "He jumped on me just as I was aiming at a deer. Then he nearly tore my leg off dragging me here."

She just smiled at him. "Kirsty is going to have her baby."

"Oh my God!" Donald breathed, then ran to the wagon.

"How soon?" Stephen asked.

"I think right away."

"Think!" Stephen said angrily. "Don't you know?"

"How would I know?"

He sputtered. "Women are supposed to know these things."

"And are they told them during reading lessons or sword play?" she asked sarcastically.

"Damned inadequate education for a girl if you ask me. There must have been some time when your family wasn't leading cattle raids."

"Damn you!" she began, then stopped when Donald stepped down from the wagon.

He was obviously worried. "She wants you," he said, his brow creased into a frown. There was a white line on each side of his lips. He reached for a piece of wood for the fire, but his hand shook so badly he dropped it.

"Me?" Bronwyn began, but Stephen gave her a sharp push forward.

"There's no one else," he said.

Her face lost all its color. "Stephen, I don't know the first thing about birthing a baby."

He put his hand to her cheek. "You're frightened, aren't you?"

She looked down at her hands.

"It couldn't be much different from a mare or a cow," he said helpfully.

"A cow!" Her eyes flashed at him, then she relaxed. "Stay with me," she said quietly. "Help me."

Stephen had never seen her look so soft, so in need of help. "How can I? A man can't attend a birth. Maybe if she were a relative of mine . . ."

"Look at him!" Bronwyn said, nodding toward Donald. "He only cares that his wife gets well. He doesn't care about anything else."

"Bronwyn!" Kirsty suddenly screamed from inside the wagon.

"Please," she said, her hand on Stephen's chest. "I've never asked you for anything before."

"Except to change my name, my nationality, my—"

She turned away from him, but he caught her arm. "Together," he whispered. "For once, let's do something together."

It wasn't an easy birth. Kirsty was very small, and the baby was large. None of the three of them knew much about having a baby, and they all agreed it was a wonderful experience. Bronwyn and Stephen sweated as much as Kirsty. When the head appeared, they looked at each other with pride. Stephen held Kirsty up so she could see while Bronwyn held the little head and gently guided the shoulders out.

The last part of the baby seemed to pop out, and Bronwyn held him in her arms.

"We did it!" she whispered.

Stephen grinned at her, then gave Kirsty a smacking kiss.

"Thank you," Kirsty smiled as she lay back against Stephen's arm, thoroughly exhausted but very happy.

It took them some minutes to clean the baby and Kirsty. Stephen and Bronwyn looked down at the mother and child, the baby already nosing around Kirsty's breast.

"Let's tell Donald he has a son," Stephen whispered.

Donald stood just outside the wagon, waiting, his face full of fear.

"Cheer up!" Stephen said, laughing. "Go have a look at the boy."

"A boy," Donald said in a very shaky voice before he climbed into the wagon.

It had grown dark while they were inside with Kirsty. The bright, cold day had turned to dark, even colder night.

Bronwyn stretched and drank deeply of the fresh,

clear air. For some reason she had a feeling of freedom. She suddenly threw back her head, extended her arms, and twirled round and round.

Stephen laughed and grabbed her in his arms, lifting her feet off the ground. "You were wonderful," he said enthusiastically. "You were so strong and calm, and you helped make things easier for Kirsty." He braced himself as he realized he'd made an opening for Bronwyn to tell him of her training to become the MacArran.

Bronwyn smiled up at him, put her arms around his neck, and snuggled her face into his shoulder. "Thank you. But it was your knowing what to do that was the most help. If it'd been me alone, I think I would have just stopped and stared when the baby's head came."

Stephen didn't believe her for a moment, but it helped his pride to hear her say he was of some use to her. "Are you tired?" he asked quietly as he held her close and ran his hand over her hair.

"Very," she said, feeling quite comfortable and relaxed.

He bent and put his arm under her knees. "Let's go find some place to sleep." He carried her over the side of the ridge, then put her down as he deftly unfastened his plaid and spread it on the ground. Within minutes they were snuggled together, close for warmth, Rab against Bronwyn's back.

"Stephen?" Bronwyn asked quietly. "What are we going to do now? We still have no way to get to England, and alone we'll be recognized."

Stephen lay very still while his thoughts raced. Bronwyn had never asked his opinion before, nor had she lain beside him in just such a way before, with trust. He smiled, kissed the top of her head, and pulled her closer, and he knew his chest swelled several inches. "I haven't given it much thought, but I think that if we can, we should stay with Kirsty and Donald." He paused a moment. "What do you think?" As soon as the words were out, he realized how he'd changed. A few months ago he would have ordered his wife about what to do. Now he was asking her opinion.

Bronwyn nodded against him. "They're heading south to her parents. If we could travel there with them, maybe we could buy some horses."

"Buy? With our good looks?" Stephen asked. "We don't have anything worth a pence. We can't even repay Donald for his hospitality."

"A Scot won't need to be repaid."

"Even a MacGregor?" Stephen teased.

She gave a soft laugh. "As long as he believes we're not MacArrans. As for food, you're a good hunter, a better one than Donald, I'm sure. Now we just need a way to pay for some horses." She sighed. "Too bad Davey didn't attack us closer to the border."

"Why?"

"I would have had on one of those English dresses. The damned things are covered with jewels, and we could have sold them."

"If you'd been dressed as an Englishwoman we probably wouldn't be alive, and besides, we wouldn't have a warm plaid to roll about us."

She looked up at him. "I thought you hated our Scots dress. You said, if I remember correctly, that it left the whole bottom half of you bare."

"Don't be impertinent," he said in mock seriousness. "There's something to be said for quick access. A man can get out of a plaid in the time it takes an Englishman to think about undressing."

She smiled up at him. "Do I hear pride in your voice?" she teased. "And where in the world did you get that accent?"

"I have no idea what ye mean," he teased. "And if the truth were known, I think I put it on with the plaid."

"I like it," she said softly as she moved her knee up his bare leg and under the shirt he still wore. "How would you like to make love to a midwife? Or do you insist upon having the laird of a clan?"

He put his hand in her hair. "Right now I'll take you whatever you are. You're Bronwyn, a sweet, delicious bit of a thing who can ride like a demon, save her husband's life, and deliver a baby all in a few hours."

"I had a bit of help," she whispered before she lifted her mouth to his for his kiss.

Bronwyn too felt the strangeness of the place and time. She should be worried about her clan, but she knew Tam was there to guide them, and maybe her men would be better off if they didn't have to deal with the war that constantly raged between her and Stephen. Right now she didn't feel at all like being at war with him. She felt like she'd never felt before: soft and feminine. There were no decisions to make, no anger, no worry that Stephen was on the other side. Right now they were hunted equally.

"You have a faraway look," he said. "Will you share your thoughts with me?"

"I was thinking that right now I'm happy. I haven't had a happy or even a quiet thought since before my father died."

Stephen smiled because for the first time, she didn't accuse him of murder. "Come here, sweet, and see if I can't make you happier."

He took his time in undressing her. They twisted together under the swaddling plaid and laughed when an elbow punctured any delicate spot. It was an intimate wrestle, rolling, laughing, enjoying each other and their freedom.

Stephen's hands on Bronwyn's skin made her quieten. She was learning about the pleasures of his lovemaking. She kissed his face, his neck, watched the play of moonlight on his skin.

He ran his lips across her shoulder, then down to her breast. She felt chills run through her. "Stephen," she whispered. He ran his hands over her waist and ribs. The strength of him excited her, made her feel small and in his power.

"You are so beautiful," he whispered.

She smiled and knew that he made her feel beautiful. He ran his hands down the inside of her thighs, and when he felt her tremble, the same emotion ran through him.

He moved on top of her slowly. She gave herself to him freely and eagerly, pulling his mouth down to hers. When she groaned aloud in her pleasure, Stephen kissed her deeply. The sounds she made, her abandonment to his lovemaking, were exciting to him.

They made love slowly, until Bronwyn clawed at Stephen, demanding more of him. She arched up to meet him, and he exploded in one massive thrust. She clasped him to her, not letting him go, wanting all of him.

They fell asleep that way, joined together, wrapped in each other's arms.

It was Bronwyn who woke first. Stephen held her so close to him that she could scarcely breathe. She watched him for a moment. There was a curl along his ear. She noticed how much he'd changed over the last few months. Gone was the pale English skin and the short, neat English hair. Yes, she thought, hardly anyone would recognize him as an Englishman now. She moved so she could kiss the curl of hair. She remembered that once she'd been afraid to make advances of such a nature toward him. This morning it seemed right that she'd kiss him awake.

He smiled before he opened his eyes.

"Good morning," she whispered.

"I'm afraid to look," he said dreamily. "Has someone changed my Bronwyn for a woodsprite?"

She bit his earlobe.

"Ow!" His eyes flew open, then he chuckled. "I don't think I'll trade you for a sprite of any kind," he said as he moved toward her.

"Oh no you don't!" She pushed him away. "I want to see our baby."

"Our baby? I'd rather stay here and make one of our own."

She rolled away from him. "I'm not sure I want to go through what Kirsty did yesterday. Come on, I'll race you up the hill."

Stephen hurriedly dressed, and it wasn't until Bronwyn was already on the top of the ridge that her laughter caused him to turn. She held his boots aloft. He yelled to Rab to fetch his boots, and the tussle between dog and mistress gave him time to get up the hill. He wrestled the boots away from Bronwyn, then ran in his short wool hose to the wagon. He was sitting there calmly when she returned. "Good morning," he called as if he'd not seen her for days. "Did you sleep well?"

She laughed at him and went inside the wagon to see to Kirsty.

During the rest of the day there was little time for laughter or play. The men went hunting, and Bronwyn was left to care for Kirsty and the camp. She was appalled at the small amount of food the couple had. There were two small bags of oatmeal and little else. She didn't want to insult Kirsty by asking for more supplies, but she hoped there were more somewhere.

The men returned at sundown with only two small rabbits in their hands, hardly enough for one meal.

"Stephen," Bronwyn said as she drew him aside, "we can't keep taking from them. They have little enough as it is."

He leaned back against a tree. "I know, but at the same time I hate to leave them alone. Donald hardly knows which end of a bow to use. And the game in this area is wary of all hunters. I hate to leave them and I hate to stay."

"I wish we could help them some way. Here, drink this." She held out a mug.

"What is it?"

"Kirsty had me make it. It's made from some lichens with a little ale. She says it cures everything. All day she worried about you and Donald working in the cold."

Stephen sipped the hot liquid. "And did you worry about us?"

She smiled. "Maybe about Donald, but I knew you could take care of the both of you."

He started to answer, but the drink drew his attention. "This is really good. I think it's making my head stop hurting."

She frowned. "I didn't know your head was hurting."

"It hasn't stopped since your brother's arrow creased it." He dismissed the subject. "I just had an idea. Were these lichens hard to find?"

"Not at all," she said, curious.

Stephen's eyes began to glow. "Today Donald told me about a town near here. He wants to take his son to be baptized. If you and I could make up a tub of this stuff, maybe we could sell it."

"What a clever idea!" she agreed, already making plans.

They spent the evening hunting lichens. Donald took what money there was and used one of the wagon horses to go into town and buy more ale.

It was late when they rolled their plaids on the ground near the dying fire and went to sleep. Bronwyn stayed close to Stephen, happy enough to be near him without needing to make love. This feeling of closeness was new to her and made her feel warm and content.

Very early the next morning they hitched the wagon and rolled into the little walled town. There seemed to be hundreds of shops as well as tiny houses inside the walls, and the air was heavy and hardly worth breathing. The whole place made Bronwyn long for the out-of-doors.

She'd been to few towns in her life. Instead the merchants had traveled to Larenston to sell their goods.

Donald pulled the wagon off the narrow main street, just in front of an alleyway, and unhitched the horses. They set up a pot of the drink they'd made, then started to call to people to buy. Kirsty and Bronwyn sat inside the wagon and listened. Stephen's deep voice boomed out over all the noise of the town. He made some rather extraordinary promises for the drink, talking about his own slight experience with it as if it'd cured him from leprosy.

But no one bought from them.

People paused and listened, but they offered no pennies to buy the miracle liquid.

"Perhaps you should do some of those body flips like you did for Tam," Bronwyn teased.

Stephen ignored her taunts as he tried to coax a young man to buy by telling him the drink would improve his love life.

"Maybe you need some help, but I don't," the young man replied. The crowd laughed and began to move away.

"I think it's time I gave this a try," Bronwyn said as she began unbuttoning her shirt.

"Bronwyn!" Kirsty protested. "Are you planning to do something that'll make Stephen angry?"

She smiled. "Probably. Is this low enough?" She glanced down at the generous curve of her breasts exposed by the unbuttoned shirt.

"More than enough. Donald would have my hair if I walked about like that."

"The Englishwomen wear dresses cut as low as decently possible," Bronwyn replied.

"But you're not English!"

Bronwyn only smiled in answer as she climbed down the front of the wagon, on the far side of where Stephen stood.

Stephen smiled in surprise when he first heard Bronwyn call out. "This will cure anything from boils to the sweating sickness," she was saying. He watched as the crowd began to move to the side of the wagon.

"Is your wife unhappy?" Bronwyn called. "Maybe it's your fault. This drink will make you the most powerful of men. And as a love potion it's unsurpassed."

"Do you think it'll get me something like you?" a man shouted.

"Only if you were to drink a whole hogshead of it," Bronwyn replied instantly.

The crowd laughed.

"I think I'll try it," another man shouted.

"I'm going to buy some for my husband," a woman cried before she hurried to the end of the wagon, where Donald and Stephen waited.

For a while Stephen was too busy filling the townspeople's containers and taking pennies to really listen to Bronwyn. He was proud of the way she was selling and pleased that the people liked her. He chuckled once at the idea of an English lady acting as a barker with so much success.

It was when he began to hear the low, suggestive laughter of the men that she really got his attention.

One of the men holding out a cup turned to his companion. "She half as much promised to meet me by the town well."

Stephen's face turned cold. "Did she tell you that I'd be there too?" he asked in a deadly voice.

The man looked up at Stephen, at the challenge in

the handsome face. The man backed away. "Don't blame me, 'twas her that gave me the idea."

"Damn her!" Stephen said viciously and threw the ladle into the drink. Just what the hell did she think she was doing?

He stopped when he rounded the corner of the wagon. Her shirt was unbuttoned, exposing a great deal of her high, firm breasts. She'd removed her concealing plaid, and her skirt clung to her hips. She walked back and forth in front of the ever increasing crowd of people. And the way she walked! Her hands were on her hips, and her hips swayed seductively.

For a moment he was shocked, too stunned to move; then he took two long strides toward her. He grabbed her arm, pulled her into the alleyway behind the wagon. "Just what the hell do you think you're doing?" he said between clenched teeth.

"Selling the tonic," she said quite calmly. "You and Donald didn't seem to be doing such a good job, so I thought I'd help."

He released her arm, then angrily began to button her blouse. "You were certainly enjoying yourself, weren't you? Parading yourself like a joywoman!"

She looked up at him and smiled happily. "You're jealous, aren't you?"

"Of course not!" he snapped, then stopped. "You're damn right I'm jealous. Those dirty old men have no right to see what's mine."

"Oh, Stephen, that's . . . that's, I don't know, but I find I'm quite pleased by your jealousy."

"Pleased?" he asked in bewilderment. "Next time I hope you depend on your memory and don't try to provoke the feeling afresh." He grabbed her in his arms and kissed her fiercely, hungrily, possessively.

Bronwyn responded, pushing her body against his, letting herself go to his possession of her.

Suddenly a bellowing voice that fairly shook the

houses around them interrupted their kiss. "Where's the wench selling the tonic?"

Bronwyn reluctantly broke away, looking in puzzlement at Stephen.

"Where is she?" the voice boomed again.

"That's the MacGregor," she whispered. "I heard him once before."

She turned toward the voice, but Stephen caught her arm. "You can't go out there to meet the MacGregor."

"Why not? He's never seen me. He won't know who I am, and besides, how can I refuse? This is the MacGregor's land."

Stephen frowned but he released her. A refusal would make them seem suspicious.

"Here I am," she called as she left the alleyway, Stephen close behind her. The MacGregor sat on his horse, looking down at her in an amused way. He was a big, thick man, his hair gray at the temples, his jaw especially strong. His eyes were green and alive above a prominent nose. "And who wants me?" she asked arrogantly.

The MacGregor threw back his head and bellowed laughter. "As if you didn't know your own laird," he said, his eyes deepening to a shade of emerald.

She smiled up at him sweetly. "Is that the same laird who doesn't know his own clan members?"

He didn't lose his smile. "You're a saucy wench. What's your name?"

"Bronwyn," she said proudly as if the name were a challenge. "The same as the laird of Clan MacArran."

Stephen's hand clamped on her shoulder in warning.

The MacGregor's eyes turned hard. "Don't mention that woman to me."

Bronwyn put her hands on her hips. "Is that because you still bear her mark on your person?"

Suddenly there was dead silence around them. The crowd stilled, its breath held.

"Bronwyn," Stephen began, aghast at what she'd said.

The MacGregor put his hand up. "You're not only saucy but you have courage. No one else has dared mention that night to me."

"Tell me, what made you so angry about such a small mark?"

The MacGregor was quiet as he seemed to consider both her and her question. "You seem to know a lot about it." The tension seemed to suddenly leave him, and he smiled. "I think it was a matter of the woman herself. Had she looked a bit like you, I think I'd have born the mark proudly, but no witch-ugly woman is about to mark the MacGregor."

Bronwyn started to speak, but Stephen put both hands on her waist until she couldn't breathe. "Forgive my wife," he said. "She tends to be a bit outspoken."

"That she is," the MacGregor agreed enthusiastically. "I hope you keep her firmly in hand."

"All that I can reach," Stephen laughed.

"I like a woman with spirit," the MacGregor said. "This one's beautiful and has a head on her too."

"It's just that I'd like her to keep her thoughts to herself once in a while."

"Not many women can do that. Good day to you both," he said as he reined his horse away.

"Damn you!" Bronwyn said fiercely as she whirled to face Stephen.

Before she could speak, he gave her a teeth-jarring shake. "You could have gotten us in trouble!" he began, then looked up at the crowd that still stared at them. He grabbed her arm and pulled her to the side of the wagon. "Bronwyn," he said patiently, "don't you know what you could have done? I could see you announcing yourself as laird of Clan Mac-Arran."

"And if I did?" she asked stubbornly. "You heard him say—"

He cut her off. "What a man boasts of to a pretty girl and what he must do when faced with a crowd are two different things. Did you consider Kirsty and Donald? They've been giving us shelter."

To his astonishment Bronwyn relaxed, or rather deflated. The spirit seemed to leave her. She leaned forward into his arms. "You're so right, Stephen. Will I ever learn?"

He held her tightly to him, stroking her hair. He liked having her lean on him, mentally as well as physically.

"Will I ever be smart enough to deserve being the MacArran?"

"You will, love," he whispered. "The desire's within you, and you'll make it soon."

"Bronwyn?"

They both looked up to see Donald standing close to them. "Kirsty wanted me to ask if you were ready to see the priest. We thought we'd have the baby christened before nightfall. Neither of us likes being inside walls all night."

Stephen smiled. "Of course we're ready." He watched Donald, noticing that something was bothering the quiet young man. And why had he addressed Bronwyn first? It occurred to Stephen that if Donald had been inside the wagon, he could have heard them talk of Bronwyn being the MacArran. If he did know, Stephen could see that Donald didn't mean to turn them over to the MacGregor.

The church was the largest building in the town, tall, awe-inspiring. Inside they were quiet, the baby asleep in Kirsty's arms.

"Could I speak to you?" she asked quietly before they reached the altar. "Will you be godparents to our son?"

Bronwyn stared for a moment. "You know so little of us," she whispered.

"I know more than enough. I know you'll take the responsibility of being godparents seriously."

Stephen took Bronwyn's hand. "Yes, we'll be godparents, and we'll abide by all that it means. The boy will never want for anything as long as we're alive," he said.

Kirsty smiled at both of them and went forward to the waiting priest. The baby was christened Rory Stephen. Stephen, after a startled look, grinned broadly. There was no protest from Bronwyn when he gave the surname of Montgomery to the priest.

As they left the church, he carried the child back to the wagon. He looked at Bronwyn. "Why don't we make one of these? I'd like a little boy with black hair and blue eyes and a hole in his chin."

"Are you saying my looks are more suited to a male?" she teased.

He laughed. "You know, I'm beginning to like you now that you're not always screaming that I'm an Englishman."

She looked at his long hair, the way he wore a plaid so easily. "You don't look much like an Englishman. What are your brothers going to say when they see their brother's become half Scots?"

He snorted. "They'll accept me as I am, and if they have any brains they'll learn a few things from us Scots."

"Us?" she asked sharply as she stopped walking.

"Come on and quit looking at me as if I'd grown two heads," he said.

She followed, watching him, and suddenly realized that he now used the Scots burr all the time, even when they were alone. His plaid hit his knees at just the right angle, and he walked as if he'd always been a Scotsman. She smiled and hastened her step. He looked good, carrying the baby easily in one arm, and she liked the way he slipped his other arm around her shoulders.

They walked back to the wagon together, laughing, happy.

Chapter Eleven

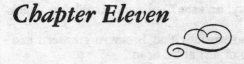

THEY TRAVELED VERY SLOWLY FOR TWO DAYS. BRONWYN tried to get Kirsty to stay in the wagon, but she only laughed. Stephen said Kirsty came out in self-defense after trying some of Bronwyn's cooking.

"This is the worst rabbit stew I ever tasted," Stephen said in disgust one evening. "It has no flavor at all."

"Rabbit?" Bronwyn said absently. She was holding the baby, watching its eyes follow the movement of the dying sunlight on her brooch. "Oh, no!" she said as she finally realized what Stephen had said. Her face turned a becoming shade of pink. "The rabbits are still hanging on the side of the wagon. I—"

Stephen's laughter cut her off. "What happened to that smart woman I married?"

Bronwyn smiled at him with great confidence. "She's still here. Anyone can cook. I can—" She stopped and looked up in bewilderment.

"We're waiting," Stephen said.

"Stop teasing her," Kirsty said quietly. "Bronwyn,

as beautiful as you are, you don't need to cook. And besides, you are courageous, fearless, have great practical sense and—"

Bronwyn laughed. "See!" she said to Stephen. "I'm glad someone appreciates me."

"Oh, Stephen appreciates you," Kirsty smiled. "In fact, I don't believe I've ever seen two people more in love than you two."

Bronwyn looked up from the baby, startled. Stephen was staring at her in an idiotic way, rather like the first time she'd seen him.

"She is pretty, isn't she?" he said. "If only she could cook."

He said it so wistfully that Bronwyn grimaced and threw a clump of dirt at his head.

He laughed and seemed to come back to the present. "Let me hold my godson, will you? He spends too much time with women." He laughed again at the reply Bronwyn made.

Late the next evening they rolled into sight of Kirsty's parents' home. It was a typical crofter's cottage, whitewashed stone with a thatched roof. There were a few fields of barley near it and some sheep as well as cattle. A steep rock formation ran along the back of the land not far from the cottage.

Kirsty's parents came out to meet them. Her father, Harben, was a short, gnarled little man, his right arm gone from his shoulder. His face was obscured by gray hair and a voluminous beard. But what could be seen looked to be forever angry.

Nesta, Kirsty's mother, was a tiny little thing, her gray hair pulled back tightly. She was as warm as Harben was cold. She hugged the baby, Kirsty, and Bronwyn all at once. She thanked Stephen and Bronwyn repeatedly for delivering her only grandchild. She kissed Stephen as enthusiastically as she did Donald.

Stephen asked if they could stay the night and be on their way in the morning.

Harben's face looked as if he'd just been insulted. "Stay only one night?" he growled. "What kind of man are ye? That wife of yers is too skinny, and where are yer children?" He didn't wait for Stephen to answer. "My home brew will put a baby in that flat belly of hers."

Stephen nodded his head as if he'd just heard a great piece of wisdom. "And here I always thought that it was what I did that'd make her pregnant, and all along it was the home brew."

Harben made a sound that could have been a laugh. "Come inside and welcome."

It was after a simple supper of milk, butter, cheese, and oatcakes that they all sat around a peat fire inside the single room. Stephen sat on a stool whittling a toy for Rory Stephen. Bronwyn sat on the dirt floor, leaning against his knee. Kirsty and her mother were on the other side, Donald and Harben facing the fire.

Donald, who'd already shown he was a good story-teller, had just given a hilarious account of Bronwyn selling the drink and Stephen's reaction to her enticing movements. He finished with the story of Bronwyn meeting the MacGregor.

Bronwyn laughed at herself along with the others.

Suddenly Harben jumped up, overturning his stool.

"Father," Kirsty said quietly, looking worried, "is your arm hurting you?"

"Oh, aye," he said with great bitterness. "It never stops, not since the MacArrans took it off."

Stephen immediately put his hand on Bronwyn in warning.

"Now's not the time," Nesta began.

"Not the time!" Harben shouted. "When isn't it time to hate the MacArrans?" He turned to Bronwyn and Stephen. "See this?" he asked, indicating his empty sleeve. "What can a man do without a right arm? The MacArran himself took it off of me. Six years ago he raided my cattle and took my arm with him."

"Six years," Bronwyn whispered. "Didn't the Mac-Gregor do some raiding too, and didn't he kill four men then?"

Harben waved his hand. "Served them right for stealin' from us."

"Should the MacArran have sat still while you killed his men? He shouldn't have revenged himself?"

"Bronwyn—" Stephen warned.

"Leave her alone," Harben snapped. "Ye got yerself a good one there. What do ye know of the MacArran?"

"He—"

Kirsty cut her off. "Bronwyn lives next to the border of MacArran land."

"Ah, you must have a lot of trouble with them," Harben said with sympathy.

"Actually, none at all," Bronwyn smiled.

"Ye must tell me how—" Harben began.

Kirsty stood. "I think it's time we all went to bed. We have to see to the milking in the morning."

"Aye," Harben said. "Mornings come earlier with every year."

It was later, when Bronwyn and Stephen were snuggled together under their plaids on a straw pallet, that she spoke. "Don't give me any lecture," she whispered with resignation in her voice.

He pulled her closer to him. "I wasn't planning to. I like to see you and old Harben argue. I think that for once you've met your match. Neither of you can believe anything good about the other's clan."

He kissed her when she started to reply, then they settled peacefully into sleep.

A rider brought news the next morning that changed Stephen's plans to leave Harben's cottage. It was known that the MacArran was missing as well as her

English husband. The MacGregor had offered a generous reward for their capture.

Stephen grinned when Harben said he'd like to turn the ugly witch-woman over to the MacGregor. He stopped grinning when Harben referred to the Englishman as a worthless peacock who wasn't worth the dirt to bury him in. Stephen scowled as Bronwyn began to agree heartily with Harben's opinion of the English. She egged him on until Kirsty made her father stop his tirade.

"I'll repay you for that," Stephen whispered as they went to the leanto, where the milk cows waited.

"By subjecting me to your greedy English ways?" she teased, then walked ahead of him, her hips swaying seductively.

Stephen started to reply but he suddenly felt very greedy. He smiled at her and went to a cow.

Bronwyn had spent her life around the MacArran crofters, and she was at least familiar with farm work. Stephen knew only how to direct fighting men. He sat on a stool beside the cow and stared in bewilderment.

"Here," Kirsty said quietly and showed him how to squeeze milk from the cow. She ignored his cursing when he managed to get more milk on himself than in the bucket.

Later they pooled their milk so that Stephen's pail was as full as theirs. Nesta looked puzzled at the unusually low milk production, but she smiled fondly at all of them and sent them to the fields.

There were winter vegetables to be gathered and fences to be repaired. Donald and Bronwyn had a good laugh when they saw Stephen's face at the sight of the stone fence. He was as pleased as a child that here at last was something he could do. He carried more rocks than the rest of them put together. He was putting his back to what was more a boulder when Kirsty nudged Bronwyn. Harben was looking at Stephen with adoration in his eyes. "I think you have a home as long as you want," Kirsty said quietly.

"Thank you," Bronwyn said, and again she had the feeling that Kirsty knew a great deal about her.

That night it was a very tired group who returned to the warm little cottage. But they were a happy group. Harben watched them as they teased each other and laughed, recounting the day's events. He lit a pipe, put his elbow on his knee, and for the first time in years he didn't think of the day he'd lost his arm.

It was two days later when Kirsty and Bronwyn went to look for lichens on the other side of the rock ridge behind the cottage. Rory Stephen was snuggled warmly in a plaid, sleeping in a basket beside the stream. It had snowed lightly during the night, and the women were taking their time with their foraging. They were laughing, talking about the farm, their husbands. Bronwyn had never felt freer in her life. She had no responsibilities, no worries.

Suddenly she froze where she was. She hadn't really heard a sound, but something in the air made her know that danger was near. She'd had too many years of training to forget them for an instant.

"Kirsty," she said quietly—it was the voice of command.

Kirsty's head came up sharply.

"Be very still. Do you understand me?" She was no longer a laughing woman but the MacArran.

"Rory," Kirsty whispered, her eyes wide.

"Listen to me and obey me." Bronwyn spoke clearly and deliberately. "I want you to go through those high weeds and hide."

"Rory," Kirsty repeated.

"You must trust me!" Bronwyn said firmly.

Their eyes locked. "Yes," Kirsty said. She knew she could trust this woman who'd become her friend. Bronwyn was stronger, faster than she, and Rory meant more to her than to risk him to a mother's vanity. She turned and walked away through the weeds, then crouched where she could see Rory's basket. She knew Bronwyn would have a better chance of escaping with the baby—the men could catch the weaker Kirsty in seconds.

Bronwyn stood quietly, waiting for she knew not what.

The rushing water was loud, and it covered the sound of the horses' hoofs. Four riders came into sight around the rock ridge almost before Kirsty could hide. They were English, dressed in the heavy padded clothes. Their doublets were frayed, their hose patched, and their eyes had a hungry look.

They saw Bronwyn immediately, and she recognized the light that came into their eyes. Rory began to cry, and Bronwyn ran to the baby, clasped it against her breast.

"What do we have here?" said a blond-haired man as he led his horse directly in front of her.

"A beauty on the Scots moor," laughed a second man as he led his horse behind her.

"Look at that hair!" said the first man.

"The women of Scotland are all whores," said a third man. He and the fourth one closed the circle around Bronwyn.

The man in front urged his horse forward until she had to step backward. "She doesn't look too frightened to me," he said. "In fact, she looks like she's just begging us to wipe that look off her face. Women should not have cleft chins," he laughed. "It isn't fitting."

"Black hair and blue eyes," said the second man. "Where have I seen that before?"

"I think I'd remember her if I'd seen her before," said the third man. He drew his sword and held it out toward Bronwyn, put the tip of it under her chin.

She looked up at him, her eyes glassy and hard, steady as she assessed the situation.

"God in Heaven!" said the second man. "I just remembered who she is."

"Who cares who she is," said the first man, dismounting. "She's something I plan to taste, and that's all I care about."

"Wait!" the second man cried. "She's the MacArran. I saw her at Sir Thomas Crichton's. Remember that she was wed to one of the Montgomerys?"

The man standing by Bronwyn stepped away. "Is that true?" he asked quietly in a voice of awe.

She only stared at him, her hands trying to soothe the child she held.

One of the men on horseback laughed. "Just look at her! She's the MacArran all right. Did you ever see a woman with such a proud look? I heard she made Montgomery fight for her even after King Henry promised her to him."

"She did," the second man confirmed. "But you can see why Montgomery was willing to draw his sword for her."

"Lady Bronwyn," said the first man, for her name was known in the higher circles of England, "where is Lord Stephen?"

Bronwyn didn't answer him. Her eyes flickered once in the direction of the rocks that separated her from Harben's cottage. The baby whimpered, and she put her cheek against its head.

"What a prize!" said the fourth man, who'd been very quiet. He said the words under his breath, wistfully. "What should we do with her?"

"Turn her over to the Montgomerys. I'm sure Stephen must be looking for her," said the first man.

"And no doubt will pay handsomely for her return," laughed another.

The fourth man moved his horse closer, forcing Bronwyn to step backward. "What of her clan?" he asked seriously. "Did you know the MacArrans are at war with the MacGregors? This is MacGregor land, you know."

"Charles," said the first man slowly, "I think you're beginning to have some good ideas. She's obviously hiding. Whose child is that?" he asked, directing the question at Bronwyn.

"It's too old to be Montgomery's. Maybe she ran away from him to have another man's child."

The second man laughed. "He'd probably pay a lot to have her back then, maybe just so he can boil her in oil."

"What about asking ransom from all three: her clan, the MacGregor, and Montgomery?"

"And enjoying her ourselves while we wait," laughed the third man.

Kirsty watched from the weeds beside the stream. There were tears in her eyes and blood on her lower lip where she'd bitten it. She knew that Bronwyn could have gotten away. The rocks behind her were too steep for the men's horses, and Bronwyn could possibly have escaped from them. But not with the child. It would take the use of both hands to climb those rocks. Bronwyn couldn't get away as long as she held the child.

"I like the idea," said the first man. He stepped closer to Bronwyn. "You won't be harmed if you cooperate. Now give me that child." He talked to her as if she were dull-witted. When Bronwyn stepped backward, he frowned. "We know the babe isn't Montgomery's, so wouldn't it be better if we got rid of it now?"

Bronwyn stood firmly. "You harm me or my child, and all my clan, as well as the Montgomerys, will be down on your head," she said quietly.

The man looked at her in surprise for a moment, then he recovered himself. "Are you trying to frighten us?" He took a step nearer. "Give me the child!"

"Do not come any nearer," Bronwyn said flatly.

One of the men laughed. "I think you should watch out for her. She looks dangerous to me."

The man behind her slid to the ground. "Need some help?" he asked quietly.

The other two men stayed on their horses and moved closer.

Bronwyn did not panic. She could not put the child down and could not get to her knife. Her only chance was to be able to outrun the Englishmen, who were used to life on a horse. She easily sidestepped the man in front of her, nestled Rory against her, and began to run.

But even a Scotswoman was no match for a horse.

One of the men on horseback cut her off. His insidious laughter rang through the air. Rory began to cry as Bronwyn held him closer to her. She knew the men would kill the child if she put him down.

The men circled her once again. One of them grabbed her shoulder, then pushed her back toward the other man.

Suddenly an arrow appeared out of nowhere and sank into the breast of the first man just as he reached out to touch Bronwyn again.

The other three men were stunned. They stood and stared at their companion, silent, lifeless, at their feet.

Bronwyn lost no time wondering who shot the arrow. She used the few seconds of time to run for the rocks.

The men looked around them to find the source of the arrow. Before they could think, a lone Scotsman stood from the rocks and fired another arrow. The third man, also on foot, fell.

The two men on horses turned sharply and started back the way they came.

Stephen came over the rocks agilely and quickly, Rab behind him. The dog had given him the alarm. He ran after the men on horseback, loading his bow as he ran. One of the men went down as his horse kept running, his dead master's foot caught in the stirrup, the body dragging across the rough ground. Stephen kept running after the fourth man.

Slowly Kirsty came out of her hiding place. She was too frightened to move quickly. Bronwyn met her more than halfway. Kirsty took her child, held him tenderly, then looked up to see Donald coming toward her. She handed the baby to his father, then she clasped Bronwyn. Her body was trembling. "You saved him," she whispered shakily. "You could have gotten away but you didn't. You risked your life to save my baby."

But Bronwyn was hardly listening. She was looking at the space where Stephen had been. "He killed Englishmen!" she whispered again and again, feeling both happy and astonished. Stephen killed Englishmen to protect her and a Scots baby.

Donald put his hand on Bronwyn's shoulder. "You and Stephen will have to leave," he said sadly.

"Oh, Donald, please—" Kirsty began.

"No, it must be. The men—" He stopped when he saw Stephen appear.

Bronwyn walked toward him as if she were in a daze. She looked at him carefully, but she saw no sign of blood. He was sweaty from his run, and she wanted to wipe his brow. "Did they harm you?" she asked quietly.

He stared at her, then grabbed her to him. "That was a brave thing you did, the way you protected the baby."

Before she could speak, Donald was there. "Stephen? What of the other man?"

"He got away," Stephen said as he held Bronwyn close to him, running his hands over her back as if to assure himself she was safe.

Kirsty and Donald exchanged looks. "He'll go to the MacGregor, I'm sure," Donald said.

Bronwyn pushed away from Stephen's embrace. "How long have you known that I'm the MacArran?" she asked.

"Since I first saw you," Kirsty answered. "I saw you a year ago, one day when you were riding with your father. My mother and I were picking berries."

"So your mother knows too," Bronwyn said. She still held Stephen's hand and was glad for his reassurance. "And your father?"

Kirsty frowned. "He's too angry to be forgiving. I wanted more time. I wanted him to get to know both of you, then after you'd gone we would tell him. We knew he'd have trouble hating you."

"But there's been too little time," Donald added. "That Englishman will tell people."

"Stephen," Bronwyn said. "We must go. We can't endanger Kirsty and her family."

He nodded. "Donald, Kirsty—" he began.

"No," Kirsty said, interrupting him. "You don't need to say a word. You're my son's godparents, and I plan to hold you to it."

Stephen smiled at her. "He can foster with one of my brothers."

"An Englishman!" Bronwyn snapped. "No, Kirsty, he can come to the MacArrans."

Donald grinned. "Stop it, both of you. We'll make more boys for you. Now take the English horses and go home. There's time before Christmas for you to get to Stephen's brother's."

"Kirsty," Bronwyn began, and Kirsty hugged her fiercely. "What will people say when I tell them my best friend is a MacGregor?" Bronwyn laughed.

Kirsty was serious. "You must return to us and talk to the MacGregor. He's a good man, and he has an eye for a pretty woman. You must try to settle this feud. I wouldn't want our sons to have to fight each other."

"Nor would I," Bronwyn said, breaking away. "I give you my word that I'll return to you."

Stephen put his arm around her. "We have to come back so I can get more of Harben's home brew."

Donald laughed. "And Bronwyn, I believe I owe you

something for laughing at me when we first met. When I think of all the things I said about the MacArran!"

"They're all true," Stephen laughed. "She is the most headstrong, disobedient—"

"Magnificent woman ever," Donald finished, then grabbed Bronwyn and hugged her. "I can never repay you for my son's life. Thank you." He set her aside, then hugged Stephen. "Go now, both of you. Take the Englishmen's horses and go." He pulled away from Stephen. "When Kirsty told me you were an Englishman, I didn't believe her. I still don't."

Stephen laughed. "I'm sure that was meant as a compliment. Kirsty, it's been an honor to meet you. I wish we could have stayed longer so my wife could learn more of your gentle ways."

Before Bronwyn could make a retort, Donald burst out laughing.

"That's just the way she appears, friend. She gets her way just as much as Bronwyn does, she just goes about it differently."

Bronwyn narrowed her eyes at Stephen. "Think before you reply," she warned.

Stephen pulled her to him. "I'm thinking we must go." He touched Rory's hand, felt the little fingers wrap around his for a moment, then grabbed Bronwyn's hand and walked toward the horses.

Neither of them could look back as they rode away. The short time in the crofter's cottage had been a time of peace, and it was too painful to think of leaving it.

They rode at a steady pace for several hours. They did not want to attract attention to themselves by proceeding at a quick run. Stephen stopped once and removed some of the more English trappings on the horses and threw them into the gorse. Bronwyn persuaded a crofter's wife to give her a pot of dark dye, and she dyed the white markings of the horses. If one looked closely, it could be seen that the forelegs were slightly purple instead of the deep chestnut of the rest of the horse.

Stephen was worried about food and wanted to spend the few coins they found in the saddlebags. But Bronwyn only laughed at him and reminded him that they were still in Scotland. Everywhere they went, they were received with hospitality and generosity. Sometimes a crofter had little enough for his own family, but he was always willing to share what he had with another Scot—or anyone who wasn't English. Bronwyn laughed at the way Stephen quite often joined the abuse against the English. One Scot after another showed Stephen fields burned by the English. One man introduced his grandchild, the product of an English rape on his young daughter. Stephen listened and replied in his soft, rolling burr that was now as natural to him as breathing.

At night they rolled together in their plaids and made love. Sometimes, during the day, they'd look at each other from atop their horses, and the next moment they'd be on the ground, their clothes scattered and abandoned.

Stephen had merely to look at Bronwyn and she knew what he was thinking. Her eyes would catch fire and her body would grow warm. She smiled at him as his arm slid around her waist and pulled her into the saddle in front of him.

"I don't think I can get enough of you," Stephen whispered as he nibbled on her earlobe.

"It's not for lack of trying," she said impudently, but she closed her eyes and moved her head so he had access to her neck. "Stephen!" she said suddenly and sat upright because several people were staring at them from the roadside.

"Mornin'," Stephen said, then returned to Bronwyn's neck.

She pulled away from him. "Have you no modesty? We should at least—" She stopped as she saw the light in his eyes. "There're a few trees over there," she whispered.

Rab kept guard as Stephen and Bronwyn lay side by side in the little copse of trees. It seemed to Bronwyn that the more often they made love, the more Stephen's body fascinated her. The dappled light through the trees played on the dark skin over his muscles. She was fascinated by the strength and power of him, his ability to move her body with one hand. She teased him, rolled away from him, yet he had only to put one hand to her waist and pull her back to him.

They made love in every position imaginable. They had been away from her clan long enough to remove her sense of heavy responsibility, and she felt free and happy. She sought Stephen as eagerly as he sought her. She experimented, her body taking over her mind. She lay on her back, her legs thrown over Stephen as he lay on his side. She clutched at him, pulled him closer, groaned as his hands caressed her legs. Her whole body shuddered when they exploded together.

They lay still for a long while, wrapped about each other, neither of them noticing the cold winter air or the damp, nearly frozen ground.

"What's your family like?" Bronwyn asked huskily.

Stephen smiled and looked at her body, perpendicular to his. He was pleased that she looked weak and exhausted, exactly how he felt. He gave a little shiver as a gust of wind sent little needles through his body. "Get dressed and we'll make some oatcakes."

After they were dressed, Stephen went to his horse, took a broad metal plate from under the saddle flap, and got a bag of oatmeal. The disk had been their only purchase. Bronwyn had a fire going by the time he returned. They mixed the meal with water while the plate heated, then spread the paste thinly over the hot griddle. Stephen turned the cake with his fingers.

"You haven't answered me," Bronwyn said as she ate the first oatcake.

Stephen knew what she meant, but he didn't want her to see how pleased he was that she asked him about his family. He had a sudden feeling that he didn't ever want to reach the Montgomery estates, that he always wanted her to himself. The firelight flickered on her hair and flashed off the brooch at her shoulder. He didn't want to share her with anyone.

"Stephen? You're looking at me strangely."

He smiled and looked back at the oatcake on the griddle. "Just thinking. Let's see. You wanted to know about my family." He rolled a hotcake and began to eat it. "Gavin is the oldest, then me, then Raine and Miles."

"What are they like? Are they like you?"

"It's difficult to judge one's self. Gavin is tall and extremely stubborn. He's dedicated to the Montgomery lands and spends most of his time there."

"And he's the only one who's married."

"Are you forgetting me?" he laughed. "Gavin and Judith were married nearly a year ago."

"What's she like?"

"Beautiful! Kind, sweet, forgiving." He chuckled. "She'd have to be to live with Gavin. He doesn't know much about women, and as a result he gets in a lot of trouble with them."

"I'm glad he's the only one of you four who knows little about women."

Stephen missed the sarcasm in her words. He was beginning to remember his family with longing. "Then there's Raine. He's the one who's like Tam, heavy and thick, like our father. Raine is the . . . I don't know how to explain him. He is good, deep-down good inside. He can't stand any injustice. He'll put his own life in danger before he'd ever harm a serf or let anyone else harm one."

"And Miles?"

"Miles," Stephen said and smiled. "Miles is quiet and no one knows much about him. He keeps to himself, but every once in a while he explodes with the most horrible temper imaginable. Once when we were children he got angry at one of my father's squires, and it took all three of us to hold him back."

"What was the squire doing?" she asked curiously, accepting another oatcake.

Stephen's eyes danced with memory. "The boy was teasing a little girl. Miles loves women."

"All women?"

"All!" Stephen said. "And they follow him around as if he had the key to all happiness. I never met a female who didn't like Miles."

"He sounds quite interesting," she said, licking her fingers.

"If you ever!" he began, then stopped because Bronwyn was looking at him with such interest. He turned his attention to the oatcakes. "And then there's Mary."

"Mary?"

"Our sister."

Something about the way he said the words made her stare at him. "I've never heard you mention a sister. What's she like? Will she be there at Christmas?"

"Mary is like the Madonna," he said reverently. "Even as children we knew she was different. She's the oldest child, and she always knew how to keep her younger brothers out of trouble. Sometimes Gavin and Raine were at each other's throats. Gavin was always aware that the land would be his someday, and he was always angry when Raine forgave a serf for causing any destruction to the land, even when it was clearly caused by an accident. Mary would come between them and in her soft voice soothe them."

"How?" Bronwyn asked, thinking of her own responsibilities with her clan.

"I never understood how she did it. That time when Miles tried to kill the squire, it was Mary who was able to calm him."

"And what of her now? Is her husband kind to her?"

"She has no husband. She asked to be allowed never to marry, and since we'd never met a man who we thought would ever be kind enough to her, we granted her wish. She lives in a convent not far from the Montgomery estates."

"It was kind of you to grant her wish. I've heard that Englishwomen usually have little choice about their futures."

Stephen didn't take offense at her words. "I think you're right. Perhaps they should learn from the Scots."

"They?" she said smoothly.

He laughed at her meaning. "Do you know, I am almost beginning to feel that I *am* a Scot." He stood up, stuck his bare leg out. "Do you think my own brothers will recognize me?"

"Probably," she said. "But I doubt if anyone else would." There was pride in her voice.

"I'd like to see if you were right."

"Are you planning something?" she asked suspiciously, because at that moment he looked like a mischievous little boy. "Stephen, we already have the MacGregors searching for us, my brother and his men, and no doubt some Englishmen since you did kill three of them. I would like to get to your brother's in one piece."

"We will," Stephen said, a faraway look in his eyes. "We might just pay a visit on the way though."

Bronwyn sighed, then stood and dusted her skirt. As she walked back to her horse, her mind was full of thoughts about little boys who never grew up.

Chapter Twelve

As they entered England, Stephen could feel a difference in the air. Even on the border of Scotland, the people were not used to seeing the Highlanders. Some people stared openly at their dress; some shouted angry words because their land and property had been attacked by the Scots. Bronwyn rode with her back rigid and her head held high. She refused to answer anything the Englishmen said. Only once did she show any emotion. Stephen stopped at a farmer's well to replenish their water jugs, and the farmer ran after them with a haying fork. Stephen, the blood flushing his body, started after the little man who was cursing the Scots so vividly. Bronwyn grabbed her husband's arm and pulled him back to the horses. For hours afterward Stephen muttered about the stupidity of the English. Bronwyn only smiled at his words; there wasn't one she hadn't already thought or said.

Now they were arguing about something else. Two

nights ago Stephen had told Bronwyn of a plan he had to fool a boyhood friend.

"No, I do not understand!" Bronwyn said for, she was sure, the hundredth time.

"It's a feud," Stephen said patiently. "You, above anyone else, should understand what a feud is."

"What is between the MacGregors and the MacArrans is real, based upon many years of anger and hostility. They've killed my men as well as stolen my cattle. Some of my women care for MacGregor bastards." She gave him a pleading look. "Please, Stephen, this is a child's game, and it will only cause trouble. What does it matter whether this man recognizes you or not?"

Stephen refused to answer her, especially since she'd already asked the question several times. He couldn't explain to her about Hugh. He couldn't even remember the time with Hugh without embarrassment and no little pain.

They'd been together, patroling the Lowlands borders for King Henry, when word reached them that King Henry had chosen Stephen as a husband for the laird of Clan MacArran. Hugh had exploded with laughter. For days he did little else but conjure hideous pictures of Stephen's new bride. Before long the entire camp was talking of the ugly creature Lord Stephen would have to marry.

The decree was especially unpleasant because at the time Stephen thought he was in love. Her name was Margaret, Meg for short. She was a plump, pink-and-white blonde, the daughter of a Lowlands merchant. She had great blue eyes and a tiny little mouth that always seemed to be puckered for kissing. She was shy and quiet and she adored Stephen—or so he thought. At night Stephen would hold her in his arms, feel her soft white body, and imagine the hideous life ahead of him with a woman who was chief of a clan.

After several nights with no sleep, he began to think

of refusing the king's offer. He thought of marrying the merchant's daughter. She wasn't rich but her father was comfortable, and Stephen had an income from a small estate of his own. The more he thought of the idea, the more he liked it. He tried to forget the wrath of the king when Stephen refused him.

But it was Hugh who shattered Stephen's dreams. Hugh told Meg of Stephen's forthcoming marriage, and the poor girl, distraught and helpless, had flung herself into Hugh's willing arms. Hugh didn't think twice about helping her into his bed, or so Meg had told Stephen.

Stephen was bewildered when he found his friend and the woman he loved together in bed. But oddly enough his bewilderment never turned to anger, and because of this he realized he hadn't really loved Meg or she him if she could so easily turn to another. His only thought had been how to repay Hugh with some of his own medicine. Before he could make a plan, a messenger arrived saying Gavin needed help, and Stephen went to his brother without another thought of Hugh.

Now Stephen saw a way to repay his friend, and Hugh was still his friend. If he, Stephen, could get inside Hugh's estate and out again, undetected, yet leave a message that he'd been there, then he felt he'd have accomplished something. Hugh didn't like to feel there were strangers around him; he rarely went anywhere without a full guard. Yes, Stephen smiled, there were ways to repay Hugh Lasco.

They arrived at the Lasco estate just before sundown. It was a tall, stone house, the windows covered with ironwork shutters. The entrance courtyard was filled with people who walked about in an orderly manner, as if they had a task and were hurrying to do it. There were no groups of servants standing about and gossiping.

Stephen and Bronwyn were challenged by guards as soon as they were within sight of the house. Stephen, in a heavy Scots burr, asked if he could sing for his supper. They waited patiently while one of the guards returned to the house and got permission from Sir Hugh.

Stephen knew Hugh considered himself an exceptional lute player and wouldn't miss an opportunity to judge someone else's playing. He smiled when the guard told them to take their horses to the stable, then go to the kitchen.

It was later, when they sat before a hearty meal at the enormous oak table in the kitchen, that Bronwyn began to resign herself to Stephen's plans. Not that he'd even told her much about them! All she'd been able to find out was that Stephen planned some boyish prank on his friend.

"What is Sir Hugh like?" she asked, her mouth full of freshly baked bread.

Stephen snorted in derision. "He's handsome enough, I guess, if that's what you mean, but he's short and thick, very dark. And he is damned infuriating to be around. He moves slower than anyone else alive. In the Lowlands I was always worried that we'd be attacked and Hugh would be killed before he could even open his eyes, much less put his armor on."

"Married?"

He gave her a sharp look. He studied her for a moment in speculation. He could never see it himself, but for some reason women found Hugh quite attractive. To Stephen, Hugh's plodding, overly cautious ways were infuriating. But the women . . .

"I want you to keep your head down at all times," he said firmly. "Just this once I want you to try and act like an obedient, respectful wife."

She raised one eyebrow at him. "When have I ever been anything else?"

"Bronwyn, I'm warning you! This is between Hugh and me, and I don't want you involved."

"You sound almost as if you were afraid of him," she teased. "Is there something about him that makes women throw themselves at his feet?"

She meant her words lightly, but the look on Stephen's face told her she was closer to the mark than she realized. Suddenly she wanted to reassure him that it was highly unlikely that she'd ever throw herself at any man's feet. Of course, there had been a few times, a few positions, where she'd found her head against Stephen's feet. She smiled warmly in memory.

"I see nothing to laugh about!" Stephen said stiffly. "If you don't obey me, I'll—" He stopped as one of Hugh's guards approached and said Stephen was to come and entertain now.

The trestle tables had already been set in the Great Hall and the meal begun. Stephen half pushed Bronwyn onto a low stool against a far wall. She smiled impishly at his behavior and even smothered a giggle when he gave her such a black look of warning. She hoped she made him regret this whole childish scheme.

Stephen took the lute that was handed him, then sat several feet from the head table. He played quite well; his voice was rich and deep, and he carried the melody beautifully.

For a while Bronwyn looked about the room. The dark man at the head of the table never looked up at the singer. She watched without interest as he ate, as Stephen had said, very slowly. Each movement seemed to be planned and thought out.

She quickly lost interest in watching Hugh Lasco and leaned her head against the stone wall, closed her eyes, and gave her mind over to Stephen's music. She felt as if he played for her alone; once she opened her eyes and saw that he was watching her, and his look was as startling as a touch. She felt chills race across her body as she saw the expression in his eyes. She smiled in answer, the ' closed her eyes again. He sang a Gaelic song, and she was pleased that he'd taken the time to learn the words, probably from Tam. The sweet music, the words of love sung in her own language, made her forget she was in England, surrounded by Englishmen, married to an Englishman. Instead she was at home in Larenston, and she was with the man she loved.

She smiled dreamily at the thought, but even as she smiled she was aware of a change in Stephen's song. She opened her eyes quickly. He wasn't looking at her but across the room at Hugh. Slowly she turned her head. She knew before she looked that Hugh was watching her.

He was quite handsome in an earthy sort of way. He was dark-haired, dark-eyed. His mouth had lips a little too large for a man, but they only drew Bronwyn's attention. As she watched, Hugh blotted his lips in his slow manner, and it flashed across her mind to wonder if he moved that slowly and lingeringly in bed.

She smiled at her own thoughts. So that was Hugh's attraction! Of course, Stephen wouldn't be able to see it, but as a woman, she found his ways quite interesting. She smiled again as she thought of telling Stephen of her discovery.

She turned to her husband and saw him scowling at her, his brows drawn together, his blue eyes turned a dark sapphire. For a moment she wondered what she'd done to anger him, then she nearly laughed aloud. He's jealous, she thought with a sense of wonder, and that thought gave her more of a thrill than any of Hugh's hot looks.

She looked down at her skirt, traced her finger along the plaid. She shouldn't be, of course, but she was extraordinarily pleased that Stephen was jealous. She wouldn't dare tell him that Hugh had no more interest for her than . . . than the gardener, because it made her feel warm all over to think Stephen cared enough to be jealous.

Hugh said something to one of the two guards behind him, and the guard went to Stephen. Stephen listened to the man, handed him the lute, then strode angrily across the room, grabbed Bronwyn's arm, and half dragged her with him.

He spun her around once they were outside in the moonlit courtyard. "You certainly enjoyed yourself!" he hissed, his teeth clenched.

"You are hurting me," she said quite calmly, trying to pry his fingers from her upper arms.

"I ought to beat you!"

She glared at him. He was really going too far! "That is truly a man's logic! You were the one who wanted to come here. You were the one who insisted upon acting like a child. And now, to cover your own stupidity and childishness, you wish to beat *me!*"

He dug his fingers deeper into her arms. "I told you to sit quietly, out of sight, but there you were giving Hugh those enticing little smiles. You were telling him that anything he wanted from you he could have."

Her mouth dropped open in surprise. "That may be the most absurd thing I ever heard."

"You're lying! I saw you!"

Her eyes opened even wider, and she was very calm when she spoke. "Stephen, what in the world is wrong with you? I looked at the man as I would any man. I was curious because you talked of how slow he was, yet you seemed to think he had a lot of women."

"Were you trying to add yourself to his stable?"

"You are being crude and insulting," she said flatly. "And you are still hurting me."

He didn't release her. "Perhaps you wish the king had given you him for a husband, along with Roger Chatworth. If I can beat one, I can certainly beat the other."

The statement was so childish that Bronwyn could do nothing except laugh. "That is an irrational statement. I did nothing but look at the man. If I smiled it was because I was thinking of something else. I will remind you again that I never wanted to come here in the first place."

Suddenly all of Stephen's anger left him, and he grabbed her to him in a bone-crushing embrace. "Don't do that again," he said fiercely.

She started to reply that she hadn't done anything, but the way Stephen held her was almost comforting. Her arms hurt and she could feel the imprint of each of his fingers, but somehow she rather liked the idea that he was jealous of another man looking at her.

He held her away. "I almost wish you weren't so damned pretty," he whispered, then put his arm around her shoulders. "I'm hungry again. Let's see if there's anything left in the kitchen."

Bronwyn felt especially close to Stephen as they went back to the kitchen. It was almost as if they were in love and not just physical lovers. The kitchen people grumbled that they were back again, but Stephen winked at the cook, and Bronwyn saw the fat old woman melt under his warm blue eyes. She had her own pang of jealousy and realized she wanted all of Stephen's looks for her own.

They stood to one side for a moment, eating juicy apple-filled fried pies. "There's too much waste in here," Bronwyn said.

Stephen started to retort in defense of the English kitchen, but he'd been in Scotland too long. He'd lived with Kirsty's parents, seen their poverty. Even in Larenston the people were frugal, always aware of the value of food and that tomorrow it might all be gone. "Aye, it is," he said firmly. "We could use some of this food at home."

Bronwyn looked up at him with great warmth. She reached up and moved a curl from off his neck. The long hair and deep tan suited him. She glanced across the room and saw a buxom young cook's helper staring with interest at Stephen's bare, muscular thigh, which was exposed as he put one leg on the seat of a chair. She grabbed his hand. "I've had enough of this place. Shall we go outside?"

Stephen agreed with her and left before he noticed the kitchen maid.

It was the storm that kept them from leaving Hugh's estate. It came suddenly, raining violently. One minute the skies seemed to be clear, and the next there threatened to be a repeat of Noah's flood.

Bronwyn begged Stephen not to stay. She told him a little rain never hurt a Scotswoman, but he wouldn't listen. He didn't want to risk her to lung fever, not when he could possibly prevent it. So they prepared to spend the night at Hugh's house.

The Great Hall floor was covered with straw pallets, ready for the many retainers and guests. Stephen tried to find a private corner but there was no such thing. When he was settled beside Bronwyn, he slipped his hand under her skirt and touched her knee. She hissed at him and told him in no uncertain terms that she'd not perform in such a public place. He sighed and eventually agreed with her. She snuggled next to him and was asleep in minutes.

But Stephen couldn't sleep. He'd been in the open too long, and now all the walls seemed to be closing in on him. He shifted his position again and again, but the straw still felt too soft. Rab even growled at him once because he was so restless. He put his hands behind his head and stared up at the beamed ceiling. He kept remembering the way Hugh had looked at Bronwyn. Damn the man! Hugh thought he could get any woman he wanted. No doubt he was encouraged by the way Meg had gone to him.

The more he thought about the trick Hugh had played on him, the angrier he became. In spite of

Bronwyn's warnings he knew he wanted to let Hugh know he'd been there.

He quietly slipped off the pallet, commanded Rab to stay with Bronwyn, and silently went toward the eastern door to the Great Hall.

As children he and his brothers had often visited the Lasco estate. One day, when they were very young, he and Hugh had discovered a secret passage leading upstairs. They were trembling with excitement when they reached the door at the top of the stairs. They were surprised to find the door well oiled and silent as they slipped into the room behind a heavy tapestry. They weren't even sure where they were until they heard sounds coming from the bed. But it was too late then. Hugh's grandfather was in bed with a very young housemaid, and both of them seemed to be having a marvelous time. The old man found no humor in looking up and seeing two seven-year-old boys watching him with wide-eyed interest. Stephen still winced when he remembered the beating Hugh's grandfather gave them and the one he promised if they revealed their knowledge of the secret passage. Four years ago, when the old man died, Stephen cried at his funeral. He hoped he could pleasure young girls at the same age. Stephen laughed and was glad Bronwyn hadn't heard that thought.

He slipped behind a screen in the anteroom off the Great Hall. He went to the window seat and took his knife and pried off the linen-fold paneling behind the cushions. It had been a particularly violent pillow fight that had knocked the panel away the first time so long ago. He had to stick his arm through an inch of cobwebs before he could even see the outline of the stone staircase. Once inside, he pulled the panel back into place.

It was black inside the stairwell, and tiny feet scurried back and forth. More cobwebs hit his face, and he wished he had his sword to clear them away. The passage had been in constant use and had been kept clean when Hugh's grandfather was alive. Since Hugh lived alone, Stephen guessed he had no reason to hide his trysts from anyone.

The door at the top of the stairs opened with only a slight creak, but Stephen had no time to wonder at this. His eyes were used to the black stairwell, and so the room, lit by a single fat night candle, seemed to blaze with light. Stephen smiled at his extraordinary luck, for Hugh lay asleep on the bed. Stephen smiled at the quiet, unsuspecting man, then removed his knife from its sheath at his side.

Even as a child Hugh had a fear of being unguarded. There had been a kidnap attempt on him when he was only five. He'd said very little about it then or since, but he never went anywhere without a guard. To wake in the morning and find a knife beside his head would more than repay him for the girl he'd taken from Stephen.

Stephen wrapped a bit of plaid around the hilt, then attached the MacArran cockade. Silently he placed the knife beside his friend. Grinning broadly, he turned toward the tapestry and the secret door.

"Seize him!" Hugh's deep voice rang out.

Four men jumped from the dark corners of the room and ran at Stephen. He ducked the first one, and his fist slammed into the face of the second. The man staggered backward. Stephen's reactions were faster than those of the other two men. He was at the door before he felt the tip of Hugh's sword on the back of his neck.

"Well done!" Hugh said with admiration. "I can see you didn't neglect your training in Scotland." He drew back his sword so Stephen could turn around.

Hugh was fully dressed. He held the sword at Stephen's throat, motioned his guards to surround his friend, then picked up the knife on his pillow. "Mac-

Arran, isn't it?" He tossed the knife in his left hand. "It's good to see you again, Stephen."

Stephen grinned broadly. "Damn you! How did you know?"

"Gavin came by a couple of days ago and said he was expecting you. He'd heard some tale of your getting into trouble in Scotland, and he was beginning to worry. He thought perhaps you'd stop here first."

Stephen shook his head. "Betrayed by my own brother." He looked up in surprise. "But even expecting me, how . . . ?" He knew he looked quite different from the English Stephen he had been.

Hugh smiled, his eyes lighting warmly. "One of the songs you sang was one we learned together in the Lowlands, remember? How could you forget the time it took us to learn that chord?"

"Of course!" Stephen said, realizing he'd been over-confident in his disguise. "Bronwyn said it'd never work, that I'd give myself away."

"I must say that that accent of yours is well done, but you can drop it now."

"Accent?" Stephen asked, genuinely bewildered. "I stopped using the accent when we left the MacGregor's land."

Hugh laughed deeply. "Stephen, you really have become a Scot. Tell me what happened in Scotland. Did you marry that awful woman? What was she, the laird of some clan? And who was that delicious creature who kept staring at you with such lust while you played?"

Stephen frowned. "She is Bronwyn," he said flatly.

"Bronwyn? A Welsh name, isn't it? Did you find her in Scotland? And how did you escape your wife?"

"Bronwyn is the laird of Clan MacArran, and she is my wife." Stephen was very stiff, his lips hardly moving as he spoke.

Hugh's mouth dropped open. "You mean that blue-eyed angel is the chief of some clan, and you have the good fortune to be married to her?"

Stephen didn't answer but glared at Hugh. Why was he still standing surrounded by guards? "What's going on here?" he asked quietly.

Hugh smiled, his dark eyes sparkling. "Nothing at all. Just a little game, like the one you wanted to play on me." He rubbed the knife between his fingers. "Bronwyn, is it?" he asked quietly. He had lowered his sword point but it was still at the ready. "Remember when we first heard the news? You kept groaning and saying you wouldn't marry such an ugly woman. You wanted . . . what was her name? Elizabeth?"

"Margaret," Stephen snapped. "Hugh, I don't know what you have in mind, but—"

"I have in mind exactly what I had before."

Stephen stared at him, remembering all too well seeing Meg and him in bed together. The idea that he'd even touch Bronwyn . . . "You touch her and I'll kill you," he said in deadly earnest.

Hugh blinked in surprise. "You almost sound serious."

"I am more than serious."

Hugh smiled. "But we're friends. We've shared women before."

"Bronwyn is my wife!" Stephen shouted before he lunged at Hugh.

All four of the guards were on him at once, but even they couldn't hold him. Hugh moved away as quickly as he could, but Stephen still came for him. The chamber door suddenly flew open, and three more guards entered and seized Stephen.

"Take him to the tower room," Hugh said, looking at his friend in admiration, the seven guards holding him.

"Don't do it!" Stephen warned even as he was being dragged from the room.

"I won't force her if that's what you mean," Hugh

laughed. "All I want is one full day, and if I haven't gotten her by then you'll know you have a faithful wife."

"Damn you!" Stephen cursed and made another lunge before he was forcibly pulled from the room.

Bronwyn stood before the long mirror and studied herself critically. It had taken over an hour to dress in the English gown. The skirt and sleeves were of a shimmering, muted orange brocade. Tied with ribbons at the shoulders, then drawn over her arms, was a small cloak of ermine. The skirt parted in front to show cinnamon velvet. The square neck was very low.

Her hair hung down her back in thick, fat curls with elf locks before her ears.

"You look lovely, my lady," said the timid little maid behind her. "Sir Hugh has never had a lady here who was so pretty."

Bronwyn looked at the woman and started to speak, but then she stopped. It hadn't taken her long to learn how useless questions were in the Lasco household. This morning she'd had to restrain Rab from attacking Hugh as he came to her pallet in the Great Hall. For some reason Rab took an extraordinary dislike to the man.

Hugh embarked on a long explanation of Stephen's absence before Bronwyn could ask a single question. When he'd finished his tale—that Stephen had gone to see to one of Hugh's estates as a favor to his old friend—he stood back and smiled at Bronwyn with great confidence.

She began firing questions at him. Why had Stephen left without speaking to her? What business couldn't Hugh handle on his own? How was Stephen more suited? If Hugh needed help, why didn't he ask Stephen's brothers earlier?

She watched as Hugh sputtered and seemed to trip over his words. He was looking at her oddly, sometimes not able to meet her forthright stare. After a moment he smiled, and she had the impression that an idea had just come to him. He began another story about how Stephen had wanted to prepare a surprise for her and he wanted Hugh to entertain her for the day.

Bronwyn closed her mouth on her questions. For now it would be better to act as if she believed Hugh's obviously false words. She smiled sweetly at the man who was an inch or two shorter than she was. "A surprise!" she said in what she hoped was a girlish and innocent voice. "Oh, what do you think it could be?"

Hugh smiled at her in a benevolent way. "We'll just have to wait and see, won't we? But in the meantime I have some entertainment planned. Pavilions are being erected and bonfires lit."

"Oh! How nice!" she said, clapping her hands together in childish glee and at the same time ordering Rab to keep away from the man's throat.

Hugh led her upstairs to a clean, warm room where the brocade dress had been readied for her. The hem had been let down to accommodate her height. Bronwyn realized someone had worked on the dress all night. Hugh gave her one of his slow, seductive smiles just as he left the room, and Bronwyn had to work hard to give him the simpering little smile he seemed to expect in return.

Once alone, she ran to the window. On the grounds below carpenters worked quickly on a platform. There were six fires already lit and an enormous charcoal brazier set under an open canopy. She frowned in consternation. Why in the world would an Englishman plan an outdoor entertainment in December? Last night's rain had turned to snow, and the ground was lightly powdered. From what she'd seen of the English, they were weak creatures who liked to stay indoors.

The maid came and helped her dress, but Bronwyn could get little information from her. She said Sir Hugh had been up all night ordering the day's festivities.

Bronwyn wondered if she was making too much of everything. Perhaps Stephen had been called away and Hugh merely wanted to honor his friend's bride. But would Stephen leave her to prepare some sort of surprise for her? Stephen was too much of a realist. More likely, he'd make her help him with her own gift.

Before she could sort out her thoughts, Hugh came to the door. He looked at her in awe, his eyes slowly running the length of her. "You are magnificent," he whispered. "Stephen is a very lucky man."

She thanked him and took the arm he offered her as they descended the stairs.

"You must tell me all about this clan of yours," he said, his eyes on her lips. "I imagine you were glad to get an English husband. Perhaps you can meet King Henry and thank him someday."

Bronwyn nearly exploded with the force of her reaction. She thought Stephen's vanity was the limit, but this man surpassed anything she'd ever imagined. "Oh, yes," she said in a gentle voice. "Stephen has been very good to me, and we've learned so much from him." She nearly choked as she thought how Stephen had changed but not her men.

"Of course," Hugh smiled. "We English are superior fighters, and you Scots could learn a great deal." He stopped. "I must apologize. I hadn't meant to say such things. After all, you are, what is it? The laird of a clan."

He said the words as if they were a token thrown to a beggar. She didn't dare reply because if he said one more word, she would probably let Rab have the worthless peacock. "Oh, look!" she exclaimed happily. "Isn't that pretty?" she cried, referring to the gaily colored pavilion.

Hugh stopped, glanced briefly up at the walls of his house, then took her hand and kissed it. "Nothing is too good for you, nothing is too beautiful for you."

She watched him with detached interest. When she'd

first seen him, she thought his slow movements, his unusual mouth, were interesting, but now she found him rather tedious. For some reason he seemed to think, to assume, that she would like having her hand kissed by him.

She used all the control she could muster to keep from drawing away from him. Did all men consider themselves so appealing to women? She suddenly realized how little experience she'd had. The men of her clan never tried to touch her, probably out of fear of her father's wrath. In England she'd only spent time with Roger Chatworth, who wanted to talk of his plans for her people. Stephen was the only man who'd ever touched her and, it would seem, the only man to whom she could respond. At least it felt that way, since Hugh Lasco's touch made her want to pull away from him.

He seemed satisfied with her response, or lack of it, and led her to a gilded chair under the pavilion. Hugh clapped his hands once, and three jugglers appeared on the wooden platform before them. She gave a little smile to Hugh and pretended to watch the performers. But the truth was she was more interested in her surroundings. With each passing moment she grew more suspicious. Something was not quite right. Why were they being entertained outside?

Some dancing girls joined the jugglers, and Bronwyn could see that their shoulders were blue with cold. A raw wind began to blow in their faces. One of Hugh's retainers suggested the pavilion be turned to block the wind. Hugh's response was almost violent, refusing to turn the canvas another direction.

"You must pardon me, Sir Hugh," Bronwyn said in her sweetest voice. She had to have time to look about his house. Perhaps she could find a clue to the mystery. Perhaps Stephen hadn't really gone away.

"Oh, but you can't leave yet. Here. I'll have the fire made hotter. Or another brazier brought."

"I'm not cold," she said honestly as she kept herself

from smiling at Hugh's blue nose. "I merely wish to . . ." She looked down at her hands in confusion.

"Of course!" he said in embarrassment. "I will send a guard—"

"No! I have Rab, and I'm sure I can find my way."

"Your wish is my command," he smiled, then kissed her hand again.

Bronwyn had to control herself from running inside the house. She wanted to do nothing to make Hugh suspicious. Once inside, though, she knew the need to hurry. "Rab," she commanded, "find Stephen."

Rab raced up the stairs in a spurt of joy. All morning he'd been straining against Bronwyn's commands. The dog stopped before a door she suspected was Hugh's. He sniffed and danced about until he took off up some stairs, Bronwyn lifting her heavy skirts and running after him.

At the top of the third flight of stairs was a heavy oak door, its window set with iron bars. Rab jumped up, his forefeet at the window. He barked twice in recognition.

"Rab!" came Stephen's voice.

"Get down!" Bronwyn commanded. "Stephen, are you all right? Why are you being held prisoner?" She held her hand out to him, grabbed his through the bars.

He took her hand in both of his, stared at her. "Is this the hand you've let Hugh kiss so often?" he asked coldly.

"This is no time for one of your jealousy attacks. Why are you being held prisoner? And what is that absurd celebration about?"

"Absurd?" Stephen sputtered, tossing her hand back through the bars. "You didn't look like you weren't enjoying yourself. Tell me, do you find Hugh attractive? A lot of women do."

She stared at him, patted Rab who was nervous because his master was being held captive. Her mind was racing. "This isn't serious at all, is it?" she asked quietly. "This is some sort of game between you and your friend."

"It's not a game when my wife is involved," he said fiercely.

"Damn you, Stephen Montgomery!" she hissed. "I told you not to come here. No, you think you're so superior. Now I want to know what's going on and how to get you out of here, though I have no idea why I want you out."

Stephen narrowed his eyes at her. "If you give in to Hugh and let him win, I'll break your neck."

She was beginning to understand. "Do you mean that I am being used in some sort of wager? What is he supposed to win?"

When Stephen didn't speak, she answered for him. "I think I can guess. Hugh thinks he can woo me to his bed, and you believe him. Did it ever enter that swollen, vain, pea brain of yours that *I* might have some say in this? Do you think I am so mindless that any man who smiles at me and kisses my hand can have me in his bed? You should know I'd take a knife to him at the least. Rab growls every time Hugh touches me."

"Which seems to be often from what I can see."

Bronwyn noticed the window in the far side of the cell. So that's why Hugh refused to turn the pavilion. He wanted Stephen to be able to see them together. She looked at Stephen's cold, angry face, and she began to get angry too. Those two men were using her in some childish prank that was more suited to ten-year-olds. Hugh had said he could win Bronwyn to his bed, and Stephen obviously thought so little of her morals and integrity that he believed she could be won by any man who set himself to the task. And Hugh! He insulted her, treated her as if she were stupid, yet had every confidence that she'd succumb to his charms.

"Damn both of you!" she whispered before turning away.

"Bronwyn! Come back here!" Stephen commanded. "Tell Hugh you know of the plot and get the key from him."

She looked back at him and gave him her sweetest smile. "And miss the entertainment Sir Hugh has planned for me?" she asked, wiggling her eyebrows. She started down the stairs, her mouth set against the string of curses Stephen yelled after her. "Damn the both of them," she repeated to herself.

Chapter Thirteen

BRONWYN WAS STILL FUMING WHEN SHE REACHED THE foot of the stairs. Sir Hugh waited for her, an impatient look on his face. He looked as if he might chastise her for tarrying too long. Her first impulse was to lecture him about what he was trying to do, but the thought vanished as quickly as it came. Englishmen! she thought. When she'd first met Stephen, he knew there was no way but the English way. He laughed at her when she asked him to wear the Scots dress instead of the heavy English armor. Now she doubted if she could get him into one of Sir Hugh's heavy, padded jackets. But Stephen had had to go through a battle before he was willing to change.

Perhaps she could wage her own battle, and both of these Englishmen could learn something that every Scotsman knew—that women were quite capable of thinking on their own.

"I was beginning to worry about you," Sir Hugh said, extending his hand.

Bronwyn widened her eyes innocently. "I hope you don't mind but I was looking about your house. It is magnificent! Tell me, is all this yours?"

Sir Hugh took her arm and tucked it under his. His chest expanded visibly. "All of it and about seven hundred acres. Of course, I have another estate in the south."

She sighed heavily. "Stephen," she began shyly, "Stephen doesn't have a place such as this, does he?"

Hugh frowned. "Why, no. He does own some land somewhere, I believe, and it has an old tower on it but not a house. But surely your own estates . . ."

Again she sighed. "But they're in Scotland."

"Oh, yes, of course. I understand. It's a cold, wet country, isn't it? No wonder you want to live here. Well, perhaps Stephen—" He broke off.

She smiled to herself. It was just as she thought. Hugh wasn't really interested in her, or at least he wouldn't actually dishonor his friend; he was merely bored and wanted to see Stephen fume. He mentioned his friend too often to be a true enemy. Stephen thought she could be enticed into any attractive man's bed, and Hugh merely used her as a means to antagonize his friend. Neither man considered her wants or thoughts.

She smiled more broadly as she began to wonder what would happen if she upset their plans somewhat. What would Sir Hugh say if she told him she was discontent with Stephen and that she would love to stay in England with a fine, handsome man like Hugh?

As they approached the pavilion she looked skyward. "I think the sun is about to shine. Perhaps we could move our chairs from under the canopy."

Sir Hugh smiled at her suggestion, then ordered the chairs brought forth.

Bronwyn ordered them set closer together, then smiled at Hugh's frown. She wasted no time once they were seated. Musicians played a sweet love song, but she never looked at them; she had eyes only for Hugh. "You have no wife, my lord?" she asked quietly.

"No . . . not as yet. I have not been as fortunate as my friend Stephen."

"Is he really your friend? Could you possibly be my friend also?"

Hugh looked deeply into her eyes, fearing that he'd lose himself in them. Stephen was indeed fortunate. "Of course, you are my friend," he said in a fatherly manner.

She sighed, moistened her lips and parted them. "I can tell you are a sensitive, intelligent man. I wish I had a husband such as you." She smiled becomingly at the way his jaw dropped. "You must know about my marriage. I had no choice in the matter. I tried to choose someone else but . . . Lord Stephen . . ."

Hugh stiffened his back. "I heard that Stephen had to fight for you, and he did a damn good job of it too. I heard that Chatworth came at his back."

"Oh, yes, Stephen is a good fighter, but he isn't . . . how can I say it? He doesn't content me."

Hugh's eyes widened. "Are you saying that Stephen Montgomery is lacking in some way? Let me tell you that we've been friends all our lives. And as for his women!" He was starting to get angry now. "When we were in Scotland together, Stephen was half in love with a little whore, and he was blind to the fact that she was sleeping with half the troops. I paid her to go to bed with me at a time when I knew he'd see us together."

"Is that why he is so angry with you?" she asked, forgetting for a moment to use her honey-coated voice.

"He never would have believed me if I'd told him what she was. He couldn't see past her dimples."

Bronwyn drew back as she digested this news. So! Stephen was using her in a scheme to repay a man for taking one of his women. A woman he was half in love with! She felt a sharp pain through her breast, and burning tears gathered behind her eyes. He hadn't wanted to marry her because he'd been in love with a dimpled whore.

"Lady Bronwyn, are you all right?"

She touched her eye with her knuckle. "Something in my eye, I think."

"Here, let me see." He took her face in his large, strong hands, and Bronwyn looked up at him.

She knew Stephen was watching, and it crossed her mind to wonder if he was thinking of the woman he had wanted.

"I see nothing," Sir Hugh said, his hands never leaving her face. "You are an incredibly beautiful woman," he whispered. "Stephen is—"

She twisted away from him. "I don't want to hear that name again," she said angrily. "Today I'm free of him, and I want to remain so. Perhaps the musicians could spare some room for us and we could dance. I could show you some Scottish dances."

He gave a nervous look upward toward his house, then allowed himself to be pulled toward the wooden platform.

Sir Hugh didn't know when he'd been so entertained. He wasn't used to seeing a woman's hair flowing freely about her lithe body. Bronwyn's eyes flashed and laughed as he awkwardly tried to copy her intricate steps. The cold day seemed to grow warmer, and he forgot about her husband watching from above.

"Bronwyn," he laughed, having dropped the formal "Lady" an hour before, "I have to stop! I fear I have a stitch in my side."

She laughed at him. "You'd no' make a good Scotsman if you can stand so little exercise."

He took her arm. "I haven't worked so hard since I spent a week in training with the Montgomery brothers."

"Yes," she said as she sat down. "Stephen does train hard." Her expression became serious.

"He's a good man," Hugh said as he took a piece of cheese from a tray a servant held for him.

"Perhaps," she said, drinking deeply of warm, spiced wine.

"I envy him."

"Do you?" she asked, her eyes searching his. "Mayhaps you could replace him . . . in some ways." She watched with interest as Hugh began to take her meaning. The vain peacock! she thought. It never occurred to him—to any man—that he wasn't God's gift to women.

"Lady Bronwyn," he said formally. "I must talk seriously with you. About Stephen—"

"What was he like as a child?" she asked, cutting him off.

Hugh was obviously startled. "Serious, like Gavin. All the brothers grew up in a world of men. Perhaps if Stephen is awkward, it's because he knows very little about women."

"So unlike you," she purred.

Hugh smiled in a confident way. "I have had some experience, and I'm sure that's why you're . . . attracted to me. You've been married to Stephen so short a time. I'm sure that in years to come you'll grow . . . fond of one another."

"Is that what you want from life? Fondness?"

"I am a different man than Stephen," he said smugly.

Bronwyn smiled at him as a plan began to form in her mind. "Not long ago, while we were in Scotland, Stephen and I stayed with some farmers. One of the women made a delicious drink from some lichens. When we rode into your estate, I saw some growing near the rocks. I thought perhaps we could take a walk and collect them. I'd like to make the drink for you."

Hugh looked worried for a moment, then nodded in agreement. He didn't like the way the events were happening. It almost looked as if Stephen's wife wanted to betray her husband. Hugh wanted to report that Bronwyn could not be won by another man, but she seemed to be showing a preference for Hugh.

As they walked Hugh began to talk of Stephen, what an honorable man he was, how worthy he was of a woman of Bronwyn's standing. He spoke of how generous Stephen was in wearing that ridiculous Scots dress.

Bronwyn said very little as she gathered lichens and the dried heads of flowers in the little basket Hugh had given her. She listened carefully and said nothing.

It began to rain again when they returned to the house. Sir Hugh was very formal as he led her upstairs to a private solar. A servant brought hot wine and mugs so Bronwyn could prepare the drinks. As she carefully mixed and stirred the ingredients she watched Hugh, his thick chest puffed out, his mouth smug in his belief that he was being noble in refusing Bronwyn's advances.

"My lord," she said quietly, handing him the warm mug. Her hand touched his caressingly for a moment. She smiled as he declared the drink delicious and drained his cup then asked for more.

"I need to talk to you," he said seriously, sipping from the second mug of the hot liquid. "I mustn't let you leave here believing as you do."

"And what do I believe?" she asked sweetly.

"Stephen is my friend, has always been my friend. I just hope he will be my friend after this."

"And why should he not?"

"I guess that depends upon you. You must never mention your . . . your attraction to me."

"My attraction to you?" she asked innocently. She took a chair across from him. "Whatever do you mean?"

"Oh, come now, my lady. You and I both know what's been happening between us today. All women know about affairs of the heart."

She raised her eyebrows. "All women? Pray tell me what else all women know?"

"Don't turn coy on me!" he snapped. "I'm not so innocent about women as Stephen Montgomery is. Perhaps you'll be able to persuade him that you don't look at other men, and since he is my friend I will back your story, but don't try to play innocent with me."

"I am caught!" she said, smiling. "You know so much about women and about your friend that I have no means of escape."

Hugh started to speak, but a sudden pain shot through his gut and he closed his mouth.

"Here, let me refill your cup. You look pale."

Hugh grabbed the cup, drained it. He was out of breath when he recovered. "The fish must have been bad," he said, then dismissed the subject. "Where was I?"

"You were telling me how I was ready to leave my husband for you."

"You stretch my words," he said. "I—"

Bronwyn slammed the empty pitcher down on a table, and the glaze on the pottery crackled. "No! Let me tell you!" She stood over him, hands on her hips. "You say you are Stephen's friend, yet you play a childish trick on him and lock him where he can see you play the fool over his wife."

"Fool! You did not think I was a fool today."

"You think you can read my thoughts? Are you so vain that you think I can spend months in Stephen Montgomery's bed and yet be unsatisfied?"

"You said—"

"You were certainly ripe for believing anything you wanted. You act as if you did something noble in paying that whore to go to bed with you. You think you did Stephen a favor, but I wonder if you were just jealous. Every man in camp had to pay for her—all except one: my Stephen!"

"Your Stephen!" Hugh began, starting to rise, but

another pain cut through him. He looked up in horror.
"You poisoned me."

She smiled. "Not poison really, but you'll be quite ill
for several days. I want you to remember today for a
long time."

"Why?" he whispered, grabbing his stomach. "What
have I done to you?"

"Nothing," she said seriously. "Absolutely nothing.
I have been used to Englishmen too long to stand it
another time. You used me to play a game with
Stephen. It never occurred to you that I might have
some thought in the matter. I could see it last night
while Stephen played the lute. You were so sure of
yourself, that any woman would want you."

Hugh doubled in pain. "You bitch!" he gasped.
"Stephen is welcome to you."

"I'm a bitch because I decided to be more than a
pawn in your little games? Remember, Sir Hugh,
there's only one female on the chessboard, and she is
the most versatile, most powerful piece." She bent and
slipped the key from his doublet pocket before she
turned away.

"Stephen saw you. He will never believe you weren't
hot for me."

Her back stiffened. "Contrary to your thoughts of
him, Stephen Montgomery is the most sane, intelligent
man I have ever met." She paused at the door. "Oh,
yes, and Sir Hugh, the next time you need help with
your women, I'd advise you to ask for Stephen's advice.
As far as I can tell, there's very little he doesn't know."
She left the room.

Rab was waiting for her outside Hugh's door, and
together they ran up the stairs to the room where
Stephen was held. She looked through the barred door
and saw Stephen glowering at her. The anger and
hatred in his eyes made a chill run along her spine. She
thrust the key into the lock and opened the door.

"You are free now," she said quietly. "It is still

daylight, and we can ride toward your brother's estate."

Stephen sat silently, his eyebrows drawn together.

She walked close to him, put out her hand, and touched a curl of hair along his collar. "It would be better if you spoke about your anger."

He pushed her hand away. "Do you dare come to me directly from him? You wear a gown he gave you, the one you flaunted yourself in in front of him. Did he enjoy it? Did he enjoy the sight of the upper half of you bare?"

She sighed and sat down on the window seat. "Hugh said you'd not believe me innocent after what you'd seen."

"Hugh, is it?" Stephen growled and raised both his fists toward her, but then he dropped then helplessly at his side. "You have repaid me in full for marrying you. You waited long enough to have your revenge." He sat down heavily on a stool, ignoring Rab who nuzzled against him. "On our wedding night that knife of yours should have found my heart."

Bronwyn moved so quickly that even Rab didn't see her. She slapped Stephen across the face so hard his neck snapped backward. "Damn you to hell, Stephen Montgomery!" she gasped. "I am sick of being insulted. First that so-called friend of yours treats me as a piece of property to make a claim on, then when I refuse him and repay him for his vanity, he calls me a bitch. Now I must stand by and listen to you accuse me of being a whore. I am not your dimpled camp woman!"

Stephen paused in rubbing his bruised jaw. "What are you talking about? What woman?"

"She means nothing," she said angrily. "What have I done to cause you to believe I am a whore? When have my actions shown me to be dishonest or that I don't keep my vows?"

"You're not making sense. What vows?"

She gave a sigh of exasperation. "Our marriage vows, you dunce! I agreed to them. I would not betray them."

"You agreed to obey me too," he said sullenly.

She turned away from him. "Come, Rab. Let's go home."

Stephen was on his feet instantly. He grabbed her arm. "What do you think you're doing? Are you returning to Hugh?"

She pulled her foot back to kick him, but he whirled her about and pulled her to him, her back to his front.

"I nearly went insane," he whispered. "How could you have done that to me? You knew I was watching."

His words made her skin glow. It seemed like an eternity since he'd held her. She put her cheek against his arm. "You made me angry. The two of you were using me as if I had no rights of my own."

He turned her to face him, his hands on her shoulders. "We forgot that you're the MacArran, didn't we? Bronwyn, I—"

"Hold me," she whispered, "just hold me."

He nearly crushed her in his embrace. "I couldn't stand for him to touch you. Every time he touched your hand . . . and when he held your face in his hands!"

"Stop it!" she commanded. "Stop it this minute." She pulled away from him. "Nothing happened between Hugh Lasco and me. He thought he could win any woman in the world, and I wanted to show him he couldn't."

Stephen's anger returned. "You certainly did a good job of it. From here you looked as if you'd been lovers for years."

"Is that what you think? Do you believe I'd let a man paw me as he did if it weren't for a reason?"

Stephen's eyes darkened to almost black. "There was a reason! I know what you're like in bed. Maybe you wanted to find out if other men could make you cry. Tell me, did he find your knees the first time?"

She glared at him. "Do you honestly believe I spent the afternoon in bed with him?"

"No," he said, defeated. "There wasn't enough time, and Hugh . . ."

"Let me finish for you," she said flatly. "Hugh is your friend and you know he's an honorable man and wouldn't, in truth, do something so dishonorable. On the other hand, I am only a woman and therefore without honor. I am a piece of plant fluff and will go where the wind blows me, is that right?"

"You're twisting my words!"

"I don't believe I am. This morning, when I first saw you in here, you assumed that Hugh could have me if he wanted. All he had to do was ask or speak sweetly to me. If you knew anything about me, you would have sat in this cell and calmly waited for me. Then we could have laughed together over the jest I played on your Sir Hugh."

"What jest?" Stephen asked sharply.

Bronwyn felt that all the breath had been knocked from her. She'd learned so much about Stephen in the last few months, had come to trust him, believe in him, even think she loved him. But he'd learned nothing about her! He thought she was an empty-headed, weak plaything.

Her voice was expressionless. "I gave him a drink with some herbs in it that Kirsty said causes severe stomach cramps. He will be ill for days."

Stephen stared at her for a moment. How much he wanted to trust her! It seemed as if half his life had passed as he watched her leaning toward Hugh, talking to him. He'd torn at the bars on the windows when they'd danced together. Bronwyn's ankles showed beneath her skirt; the sunlight flashed off her dress. How could she ask him to be reasonable when she'd nearly turned him into an animal? If he could have gotten free, he would have killed Hugh, torn his friend apart with his bare hands.

He wiped his hand across his eyes. How could she ask him to think rationally when he couldn't think at all? He stared at her in wonder. What had she done to him? He hadn't had a clear thought since he'd first seen her, tossed on the floor in a wet chemise. He'd fought for her, nearly died when she risked her life over the side of a cliff for one of her men, nearly killed her when her childishness had cost Chris his life. How could she talk to him of reason? Being near her took away all semblance of sanity.

"We should go," she said coldly, then turned away.

He watched her leave the room, Rab following her. He wanted to go to her, tell her he believed in her, knew she was honorable, but he couldn't. Hugh had proved once that he could take a woman from Stephen. Sweet Meg had loved Stephen, yet Hugh had been able to take her. Bronwyn made no secret of the fact that she considered Stephen her enemy. To her, one Englishman was as good as another. Perhaps Hugh had made promises concerning her clan. If her clan was involved . . .

He looked up as Rab gave a sharp bark at him. He came back to the present and ran down the stairs to Hugh's room.

Hugh lay on his bed, his knees drawn into his chest, four servants and three guards surrounding him. "Get out of here," he gasped through a well of pain. "I never want to see you or that bitch you married again."

Stephen backed away, but not before he began to smile. She'd been telling the truth!

"Get out, I say!" Hugh commanded. He grabbed at his stomach and fell back on the bed.

"Bested by a woman," Stephen laughed as he left the room. He hurried down the stairs to the Great Hall. Bronwyn waited for him, wearing her plaid skirt and white blouse. She was once more his Highlands lassie. He went to her, touched her arm, smiled at her.

She turned away coldly.

"Bronwyn," he began.

"If you're through here, I think we should ride. You are, of course, the master, and we will stay if that is your command."

He stared for a moment at the icy blueness of her eyes. "No, I don't want to stay," he said after a while. He turned away from her and walked toward the front door of the house.

Bronwyn followed him slowly. The whole episode had started as a game, a childish game of one-upmanship, but through it she'd learned something startling about her husband. For some reason she thought she was the one who had to learn to trust him. She'd watched him over the last few months, dispassionately observed the changes in him. She'd seen him go from being an arrogant Englishman to becoming almost a Scot. She'd seen a lot of the coldness toward his men leave him, and the men, who were Englishmen, changed almost as much as their master. One by one they began wearing a plaid and stopped spending hours a day polishing their armor. Then, just a few days ago, Stephen had killed three Englishmen in an effort to save Bronwyn and Kirsty's baby. To Bronwyn that act had been the final gesture she needed to make her believe in him.

But what had Stephen learned about her? He disapproved of everything she did. He cursed her if she led her men. He was angry if she risked her life to save someone else. What could she do to please him? Should she try to become someone else? Would he like her better if she were like . . . like his beautiful sister-in-law? She had a clear idea of what Judith was like: gentle, never raising her voice, always smiling sweetly at her husband, never arguing with him, always agreeable.

"That's what men really want!" she said under her breath. Stephen expected her to sit still and be quiet, to never contradict his words. Just like the Englishwomen! Damn him! she cursed. She was no milk-and-water Englishwoman! She was the MacArran, and the sooner Stephen Montgomery learned that the better for all of them.

She held her chin high as she walked toward the stables.

By a silent, mutual agreement they did not stop for the night. They rode at a steady pace, neither speaking, each with his own thoughts of the last two days. Stephen could think of little but the sight of Hugh's hands on Bronwyn. He knew she'd repaid Hugh, but he couldn't help wishing she'd not been so subtle and had taken a knife to the man.

As for Bronwyn, she had almost forgotten Hugh. What mattered to her was that Stephen hadn't trusted her, had accused her of being a liar.

In the early dawn the walls of the old Montgomery castle rose before them. She had not expected this dark, massive fortress but a house more on the order of Hugh Lasco's. She glanced at Stephen and saw his face was alight, much as she must look each time she saw Larenston.

"We'll enter by the river gate," he said as he spurred his horse forward.

The front of the tall walls were set with two massive gate towers protecting the closed gates. She followed Stephen to low walls that made a roofless tunnel leading to the smaller gate at the far side of the castle walls.

Stephen slowed and cautiously entered the mouth of the narrow, walled alley. Immediately an arrow flew though the air to land at the feet of Stephen's horse.

"Who goes there?" demanded a faceless voice from the top of the wall above them.

"Stephen Montgomery!" he declared loudly.

Bronwyn smiled because Stephen's voice held the burr of the Highlands.

"You're not Lord Stephen, for I know him well! Now turn those nags about and leave. No one enters these walls but friends. Return in an hour to the front gate and beg entrance from the gatekeeper."

"Matthew Greene!" Stephen shouted up. "Have you forgotten your own master?"

The man leaned over the wall and stared downward. "It is you!" he said after a moment. "Open the gate!" he shouted, his voice full of joy. "Lord Stephen is safe! Welcome home, my lord."

Stephen waved his hand at the man and proceeded. All along the way men called in greeting from the top of the wall. At the end of the passageway a gate opened, and they rode inside to a private courtyard, the house looming over them.

"My lord, it's good to see you," said an old man as he took Stephen's reins. "I wouldn't have known you if the men hadn't told me it was you."

"It's good to be home, James. Are my brothers here?"

"Lord Gavin returned no more than an hour ago."

"Returned?"

"Aye, my lord, all your brothers have been searching for you. We heard you'd been killed by that heathen wife of yours."

"Watch yourself, James!" Stephen commanded. He absently stepped backward and took Bronwyn's hand. "This is my wife, the lady Bronwyn."

"Oh, my lady," the old man gasped. "Forgive me. I thought you were one of Lord Stephen's . . . I mean, he's often brought home . . ."

"You've said quite enough. Come, Bronwyn," Stephen said.

He gave her no chance to prepare herself. She was to be presented to his family looking like a serving wench. Even his servant thought so. She knew how the English set such store by a person's clothes, and she thought wistfully of the beautiful gowns she'd worn at Sir

Thomas Crichton's. The best she could do was hold her head high and endure the English snubs. Except for the perfect Judith. No doubt she'd be kind and considerate, a soft-spoken pillow.

"You look scared to death," Stephen snapped, staring at her. "I assure you that Gavin rarely beats women, and Judith—"

She put up her hand. "Spare me. I've heard enough of this Judith." She straightened her back. "And the Scots will give up their plaids before you'll see the MacArran afraid of mere Englishmen."

He smiled at her, then pushed open the door to a room brilliant with early sunlight. Bronwyn only glanced at the beautifully paneled room before her attention was drawn to the two people standing in the middle of it.

"Goddamn you, Judith!" a tall man shouted. He had dark hair, gray eyes, and sharp cheekbones. An extraordinarily handsome man, and now his face was ablaze with anger. "I left exact orders as to how I wanted the dairy rebuilt. I even left drawings. As if I didn't have enough to worry about with Stephen and his new wife missing, I return to find the foundations laid and they have no resemblance to my plans."

Judith looked up at him quite calmly. She had rich auburn hair only partially concealed by a French hood. Her eyes flashed gold. "Because your plans were completely inefficient. Have you ever made butter or cheese? Even milked a cow for that matter?"

The man towered over her, but the small woman didn't flinch. "What the hell does it matter that I've never milked a goddamn cow?" He was so angry that his cheekbones seemed ready to cut through his skin. "The point is that you countermanded my orders. How does that make me look to my dairymen?"

Judith narrowed her eyes at him. "They'll only be grateful they don't have to work in that rabbit warren you designed."

"Judith!" he growled. "If I thought it'd do any good, I'd beat you black and blue for your insolence."

"It's remarkable how angry you get when I'm right."

The man ground his teeth together and took a step forward.

"Gavin!" Stephen shouted from beside Bronwyn as he grabbed an axe from an arrangement of weapons on the wall.

Gavin, war trained, his senses always alert, recognized the call. He turned quickly, then grabbed the war axe that Stephen tossed to him. For a moment Gavin looked in puzzlement from his brother, who wore such odd clothing, to the axe he held.

"To protect you from Judith," Stephen laughed.

Before Gavin could react, Judith ran across the room and threw herself into Stephen's arms. "Where have you been? We've been looking for you for days. We were so worried about you."

Stephen buried his face in his sister-in-law's neck. "You're well now? The fever . . . ?"

Gavin's snort interrupted him. "She's well enough to put her nose into all my affairs."

"Affairs?" Stephen laughed. "Haven't you learned your lesson yet?"

"Hush, both of you," Judith said as she disengaged herself from Stephen.

Gavin clasped his brother to him. "Where have you been? We heard you'd been killed and then that you'd been killed a second time. It was . . ." He couldn't finish or tell Stephen of the agony they'd gone through while searching for him.

"I'm all right now, as you can see," Stephen laughed and stepped back from his brother.

"I can see that you've grown even more handsome," Judith said, frankly appraising her brother-in-law's brown, muscular legs.

Gavin threw his arm around Judith in a possessive way. "Stop flirting with my brother, and I'll tell you right now that I'm not going to wear one of those things."

Judith laughed quietly and fitted herself against her husband.

Bronwyn stood in the shadow of a tall chair, an outsider watching the family. So this was the gentle Judith! She was shorter than Bronwyn, a tiny bit of a thing, as lovely as a jewel. Yet she stood up to her tall husband without fear. This was no woman who spent her days sewing!

Judith was the first to notice Bronwyn watching them. Her first impression was that Stephen had done what he once threatened: locked his wife in a tower and found a beautiful commoner to make him happy. But as she watched Bronwyn she realized that no commoner could carry herself as Bronwyn did. It wasn't just the pride of being startlingly lovely, but some inner pride that made her stand that way. This was a woman who knew that she was worth something.

Judith pushed away from her husband and walked toward Bronwyn. "Lady Bronwyn?" she asked quietly, her hand extended.

Bronwyn's eyes met Judith's, and there passed between them an understanding. They recognized each other as equals.

"How did you know?" Stephen laughed. "James thought she was one of my . . . well, certainly not my wife."

"James is a fool," Judith said flatly. She stepped away from Bronwyn, studied the taller woman's clothes. "That skirt would give you much freedom, wouldn't it? And it wouldn't be as heavy as this gown, would it?"

Bronwyn smiled warmly. "It's wonderfully light, but then yours is so beautiful."

"Come to my solar and let's talk," Judith said.

The men stared at their departing wives in open-mouthed astonishment.

"I've never seen Judith take to anyone like that," Gavin said. "And how did she know she was your wife? From the way she was dressed, I would have agreed with James."

"And Bronwyn!" Stephen said. "She hates the English clothes. You can't imagine how many sermons I've heard about the confining way the English dress their women."

Gavin began to smile. "Black hair and blue eyes! Did I really see her or was it my imagination? I thought you said she was ugly and fat. She couldn't really be the laird of a clan, could she?"

Stephen chuckled. "Let's sit down, and do you think I could have something to eat?" His eyes twinkled. "Or do the servants only obey Judith now?"

"If I weren't so glad you were safe, I'd repay you for that remark," Gavin said as he left the room to order food and send men to find Raine and Miles.

"How is Judith, really?" Stephen asked when the food was brought. "I know you said in your letters that she was fully recovered from the miscarriage, but . . ."

Gavin picked up a hard-boiled egg from Stephen's plate. "You saw her," he said heavily. "I have to fight for every inch of control I have over my own people."

Stephen looked up sharply. "And you love it," he said slowly.

Gavin grinned. "She certainly makes life interesting. Every time I see one of those prim, pink-and-white wives of other men, I'm thankful I have Judith. I think I'd go crazy if I couldn't have a good, rousing fight once a week. Enough about me! What's your Bronwyn like? Is she always so sweet and docile as a few minutes ago?"

Stephen didn't know whether to laugh or cry. "Docile? Bronwyn! She has no idea what the word means. She was standing to one side probably to judge whether to use a knife or that hell-hound dog of hers."

"Why should she do that?"

"She's a Scot, man! The Scots hate the English for burning their crops, raping their women, because the English are a damned, insufferable, arrogant lot of bastards who think they're better than the honest, generous Scots, and—"

"Wait a minute!" Gavin laughed. "The last I heard, you were an Englishman."

Stephen returned to his food, forcing himself to calm. "I guess I forgot for a moment."

Gavin leaned back in his chair and studied his brother. "From the length of your hair, I'd say you forgot some months ago."

"I wouldn't criticize the Scots' dress until you've tried it, if I were you," Stephen snapped.

Gavin put his hand on his brother's arm. "What's wrong? What is worrying you?"

Stephen rose and walked toward the fireplace. "Sometimes I don't know who I am anymore. When I went to Scotland, I knew I was a Montgomery, and I felt quite noble about my mission there. I was to teach the ignorant Scots our more civilized ways."

He ran his hand through his hair. "They aren't ignorant, Gavin. Far from it. Lord, but what we could learn from them! We don't even know the meaning of loyalty. That clan of Bronwyn's would die for her, and damned if she won't—and hasn't—jeopardized her life for them. Their women sit in on their decision-making councils, and I've heard the women make damn good decisions."

"Like Judith," Gavin said quietly.

"Yes!" Stephen said loudly. "But she has to fight you for every inch."

"Of course," Gavin answered firmly. "Women should—"

Stephen's laugh stopped him. "Somewhere along the way I stopped thinking 'women should.'"

"Tell me more about Scotland," Gavin said, wanting to change the subject.

Stephen sat down again, returned to the food. His voice sounded far away. "It's a beautiful place."

"I heard it does little but rain."

Stephen waved his hand. "What's a little rain to a Scot?"

Gavin was thoughtful, watching his brother, hearing beyond his words. "Christopher Audley came by some time ago. Did he find you before your wedding?"

Stephen pushed his food away. "Chris was killed in Scotland."

"How?"

Stephen wondered how he could explain that Chris was killed in what, to a knight like Gavin, would be a dishonorable fight. "A cattle raid. Some of Bronwyn's men were killed trying to protect him."

"Protect Chris? But he was an excellent fighter. His armor—"

"Damn his armor!" Stephen snapped. "The man couldn't run. He was, as Douglas said, trapped inside a steel coffin."

"I don't understand. How?"

Stephen was saved from answering by the door bursting open.

Raine and Miles exploded into the room. Raine bounded across the floor, his footsteps jarring the windows. He lifted his older, but lighter, brother into a crushing embrace. "Stephen! We heard you were dead."

"He will be if you don't release him," Miles said calmly.

Raine let up on some of the pressure he was exerting. "You're still a skinny little thing," he said smugly.

Stephen grinned at his brother, then proceeded to push his arms out against Raine's. He grinned more broadly as he felt Raine's arms move. Stephen pushed harder and Raine applied more pressure. Raine lost.

Stephen smiled at his brother in pure pleasure. There weren't many men who could overpower Raine's massive strength without resorting to a weapon. He offered silent thanks to Tam.

Raine stepped away and grinned at his brother with pride. "Scotland seems to agree with you."

"Or else you've neglected your training," Stephen said smugly.

Raine's dimples deepened. "Perhaps you'd like to test that."

"Here!" Miles said, stepping between his brothers. "Don't let Raine kill you before I can welcome you home." He embraced Stephen.

"You've grown, Miles," Stephen said, "and you've put on weight."

Gavin snorted. "It's the women. Two of the cook's helpers are trying to see which one can outcook the other."

"I see," Stephen laughed. "And the prize is our baby brother?"

Raine laughed. "What there is left of him after the other women have finished with him."

Miles ignored all of his brothers. He rarely smiled broadly, as his brothers did. He was a solemn man, and the emotion that he felt showed in his piercing gray eyes. Now he looked about the room. "James said your wife returned with you."

"Leave it to Miles," Gavin laughed. "At least now I can have Judith to myself once in a while. Every time I look up, she's with one of my worthless brothers."

"Gavin works her like a serf," Raine said half seriously.

Stephen smiled. It was good to be home again, to see Gavin and Raine arguing, to hear them teasing Miles. His brothers had changed little in the last few months. Raine, if anything, looked stronger and healthier, his love for the world carried openly. Miles still stood to one side, a part of the group yet separate. And Gavin drew them all together. Gavin was the solid one, the one who loved the earth. Where Gavin was, was home for the Montgomerys.

"I'm not sure I'm ready for you to meet Bronwyn," Stephen began.

"Shy, is she?" Raine asked, concerned. "I hope you didn't drag her all across England with you. Why didn't we see your baggage wagons? Where are your men?"

Stephen took a deep breath and laughed. They'd never believe him if he told the truth. "No, I wouldn't exactly call Bronwyn shy," he chuckled.

Chapter Fourteen

BRONWYN SAT UP TO HER NECK IN A TUB OF HOT, SOAPY water. A fire burned brightly in the big fireplace, making the room warm and fragrant. She relaxed in the tub and looked about her. The bedchamber was beautiful, from the beamed ceiling to the Spanish-tile floor. The walls were of white-painted wood with tiny rosebuds twining about the joints. The enormous canopied bed was hung with deep rose velvet. The chairs, benches, and cabinets in the room were all handsomely carved with tall, pointed arches.

Bronwyn smiled and leaned back in the tub. It was pleasant to be in such luxury, even if at the same time she felt the money could have been spent for something else. She and Stephen had seen great poverty as they rode toward the Montgomery estate. For herself, she would have used the money on her people, but she knew the English were different.

She closed her eyes and thought of the last few

minutes. She smiled as she thought of the Judith she'd expected and the Judith she met. She'd expected a soft, sweet woman, but there was nothing soft about Judith. There wasn't a servant who didn't jump to do her bidding. Before Bronwyn was fully aware of what was happening, she had found herself undressed and in a tub. She hadn't known it but the hot water was exactly what she needed.

The door opened softly, and Judith entered. "Feeling better?" she asked.

"Much. I had forgotten what it was like to be so pampered."

Judith grimaced and held out a large, warm towel for Bronwyn. "I'm afraid the Montgomery men are not ones for pampering their women. Gavin thinks nothing of asking me to ride with him through the worst of storms."

Bronwyn wrapped the towel around her body and looked at Judith carefully. "And what would you do if he bade you stay at home?" she asked quietly.

Judith laughed warmly. "I would not stay at home. Gavin too often overlooks what he considers unimportant details, such as a steward stealing grain from the storehouses."

Bronwyn sat down before the fire and sighed. "I wish you could look at my account books. I'm afraid I too often neglect them."

Judith picked up an ivory comb and began to untangle her sister-in-law's freshly washed hair. "But you have more to consider than just the beans in a storehouse. Tell me, what's it like to be the laird of a clan, to have all those handsome young men obey your every wish?"

Bronwyn exploded with laughter, both at Judith's wistful tone and at the absurdity of the idea. She stood, slipped on a robe of Judith's, and began to pull at the tangles in her hair. "It is a great responsibility," she said seriously. "And as for my men obeying me . . ." She sighed and pulled some hair from the comb.

"In Scotland we're not like you are in England. Here women are treated as if they were different."

"As if we have no minds!" Judith said.

"Yes, that's true, but when men believe women are intelligent, they expect more from them."

"I don't understand," Judith answered.

"My men do not obey me blindly. They question me every step of the way. In Scotland every man believes he is every other man's equal. Stephen tells his men to saddle their horses and be ready to ride in an hour. His men don't even question him."

"I'm beginning to understand," Judith said. "Would your men want to know where they are going and why? If so, that could be quite . . ."

"Infuriating at times," Bronwyn finished for her. "There is a man, an older man, Tam, who watches my every move and comments on every decision I make. Then there are all of Tam's sons, who contradict me at every opportunity. In truth, I make only the minor decisions. All the major ones are a joint effort."

"But what if you want something and they are against it? What do you do?"

Bronwyn smiled slowly. "There are ways of getting around men, even ones who hover like eagles."

It was Judith's turn to laugh. "Like the dairy! I couldn't let Gavin build that awful one he'd drawn. I had the men work all night to get the foundations dug before he returned. I knew he was too frugal to have them torn out and too proud to admit I was right."

Bronwyn sat down on the bench beside her sister-in-law. "And to think that I dreaded meeting you. Stephen said . . . well, the way he described you made me think you were nothing more than a pretty, but lifeless, idiot."

"Stephen!" Judith laughed, then took Bronwyn's

hand. "I was the one who caused him to be late for your wedding. I was appalled when I found out he hadn't even sent you a message to explain himself." She hesitated a moment. "I heard it caused you some problems."

"Stephen Montgomery caused his own problems," Bronwyn said flatly. "There are times when he can be the most arrogant, insufferable, infuriating—"

"Fascinating man alive," Judith said heavily. "Don't tell me. I know all too well, since I'm married to one. But I wouldn't trade Gavin for all the sweet-smelling, chivalrous men in the world. You must feel the same way about Stephen."

Bronwyn knew she needed to reply, but she had no idea what she meant to say.

Suddenly Rab was on his feet, his tail wagging as he barked excitedly at the chamber door.

Stephen entered and knelt as he scratched Rab's ears. "You two look happy about something," he said.

"A moment's peace and quiet has been a joy," Bronwyn retorted.

Stephen smiled at Judith. "While we're here, perhaps you can sweeten her tongue. By the way, there's a man downstairs raving something about some dresses."

"Wonderful!" Judith declared and practically ran from the room.

"What was that all about?" Stephen asked, rising and walking toward his wife. He lifted a damp curl from her breast. "You look as enticing as a fresh spring morning."

She pulled away from him and looked back at the fire.

"Bronwyn, you still aren't angry about what happened at Hugh's, are you?"

She turned to face him. "Angry?" she asked coldly. "No, I'm not angry. I was merely foolish, that's all."

"Foolish?" he asked, putting his hand on her shoulder. He didn't mind her rages or even when she took a knife to him nearly as much as he was distressed by this coldness of hers. "How were you foolish?"

She turned to face him. "I had begun to believe that there could be something between us."

"Love?" he asked, his eyes bright, a smile beginning to curve his lips. "It's not wrong to admit you love me."

She curled her lip at him and pushed his hand away. "Love!" she said angrily. "I'm talking about more important things than love between a man and a woman. I'm talking of trust and loyalty and the faith one person must have in another."

He frowned at her. "I have no idea what you're talking about. I thought love was what most women wanted."

She sighed in exasperation, and her voice was quiet when she spoke. "When are you going to learn that I am not 'most women'? I am Bronwyn, the MacArran, and I am unique. Perhaps most women do think love is the major goal of their lives, but I have love. My men love me, Tam loves me. I have friendships with the women of my clan and now even Kirsty, a MacGregor."

"And where do I fit into this?" Stephen asked, his jaw set.

"I'm sure we do love each other, in our own way. I cared for you when Davey's arrow wounded you, and you often exhibit that you care for me."

"Thank you for small favors," he said grimly. "And here I thought you'd be pleased to hear that I love you."

She looked at him sharply and felt her heart jump at his words, but she wouldn't tell him so. "I want more than love. I want something that will last past my smooth skin and my narrow waist." She paused for a moment. "I want respect. I want honor and trust. I do not want to be accused of being a liar, nor do I want your jealousy. As the MacArran, I must live in a world of men, and I do not want a husband who accuses me of all manner of dishonorable things when I am out of his sight."

A muscle in Stephen's jaw worked. "So! I am to stand by and watch man after man touch you and say nothing?"

"I do not believe there has been more than one man. You should have reasoned that there was a purpose behind my actions."

"Reasoned! Damn you, Bronwyn! How can I think when someone else touches you?"

Rab's bark kept her from replying.

The door opened a crack. "Is it safe?" Judith asked, watching Rab.

"Come, Rab," Bronwyn commanded as Judith entered. "He won't hurt you unless you come at me with a weapon."

"I'll remember that," Judith laughed and held out her arms. Across them lay a gown of deep, rich dark brown velvet, embroidered all over with heavy gold thread. "For you," she said. "Let's see if it fits."

"How . . .?" Bronwyn began as she held the luscious gown up to her.

Judith smiled secretly. "There's an awful little man who works for Gavin; Gavin was always locking him in the cellar for all manner of . . . indiscretions. I decided to use the man's talents. I gave him a bag of silver, told him how tall you were, and told him to get me a gown worthy of a lady."

"It's beautiful," Bronwyn whispered, running her hands over the velvet. "You've been so kind to me, made me feel so welcome."

Judith was staring at Stephen, who had his back to them. She put her hand on his shoulder. "Stephen, are you all right? You look tired."

He tried to smile at her and absently kissed her hand. "Perhaps I am." He turned to Bronwyn. "My brothers would like to meet you," he said formally. "I would be

honored if you'd visit with us." He turned and left the
room.

Judith didn't ask about what had happened between
the newlyweds. She only wanted to make their visit as
free of strife as possible. "Come and I'll help you dress.
Tomorrow you should be able to try on the new clothes
I've ordered for you."

"New . . .? You shouldn't have done that."

"But I did, so the least you can do is enjoy them.
Now let's see if this fits."

It was hours later when Bronwyn was dressed and
groomed to Judith's satisfaction. Judith said she'd
learned many tricks while she was at court, a place she
never cared to visit again. She liked Bronwyn's Scots
way of leaving her hair free so much that she discarded
her own hood and let her rich auburn hair flow down
her back. Judith wore a gown of violet satin, the sleeves
and hem trimmed in dark brown mink. A gold belt set
with purple amethysts was about her waist.

Bronwyn smoothed the velvet over her hips. The
dress was heavy and confining, but today she liked it.
The low, square neckline showed her full breasts to
advantage. The puffed sleeves were slashed to pull
through tissue-thin cloth of gold. She straightened her
shoulders and went down the stairs to meet her
brothers-in-law.

The four men stood side by side in front of the stone
fireplace in the winter parlor, and both Bronwyn and
Judith paused for a moment to look at them with pride.

Stephen had trimmed his long hair and discarded his
Scots clothes, and Bronwyn felt a sudden pang of loss
for the Highlander he'd been. He wore a coat of dark
blue velvet, collared with rich sable. His heavy, muscular legs were encased in dark blue wool hose.

Gavin dressed in gray, his coat lined with gray
squirrel fur. Raine wore black velvet, the collar embroidered with silver thread worked in an intricate

Spanish design. Miles's coat was of emerald-green velvet, the sleeves cut and slashed to reveal silver tissue beneath. There were pearls sewn onto his shirt sleeves.

Miles was the first to turn and see the women. He set his silver wine chalice on the mantelpiece and went forward. He stopped in front of Bronwyn, his eyes darkening almost to black—a hot black fire. He dropped to one knee before her. "I am honored," he whispered in great reverence, his head bowed.

Bronwyn looked at the others in consternation.

Judith smiled with pride at her sister-in-law. "May I introduce Miles?"

Bronwyn held out her hand, and Miles took it, and kissed it lingeringly.

"You've made your point, Miles," Stephen said sarcastically.

Gavin laughed and slapped Stephen on the shoulder so hard his wine sloshed onto his hand. "Now I have someone to help me with our baby brother," Gavin said. "Lady Bronwyn, may I introduce myself more formally? I am Gavin Montgomery."

Bronwyn took her hand from Miles's grasp, and only reluctantly did her eyes leave him. There was something extraordinarily intriguing about the young man. She gave her hand to Gavin, then turned toward the other brother. "And you must be Raine. I've heard quite a bit about you."

"Any of it good?" Raine asked, taking her hand, smiling so his dimples were quite deep.

"Very little of it," she answered honestly. "One of my men, Tam, a great oak of a man, was Stephen's trainer in Scotland. For weeks on end I heard your name used as a cry to goad Stephen whenever he tried to get away from Tam's rather strenuous demands."

Raine laughed loudly. "It must have worked, for he beat me in a short wrestle this morning." He eyed Stephen. "Though of course he has yet to accept my challenge to a longer match."

Bronwyn widened her eyes and studied the massiveness of Raine's wide shoulders and thick chest. "It seems to me that the first time would be the only necessary time to beat a man."

Raine grabbed her by the shoulders and exuberantly kissed her cheek. "Stephen, you should keep this one," he laughed.

"I am trying," he said as he took her hand just before Miles reached for it again. "Dinner is laid, shall we go?" he asked, his eyes searching hers.

She smiled at him sweetly, as if they'd never had a quarrel. "Yes, please," she said demurely.

It was while they sat at dinner, as course after course of food was brought, that Bronwyn realized how different these people were from the English people she'd met before. This laughing, happy family bore no resemblance to the men she'd met at Sir Thomas Crichton's. Judith had gone to great expense and trouble to make her welcome. Stephen's brothers accepted her, did not make sneering remarks because she was the laird of a clan.

Suddenly everything seemed to be spinning around and around. She'd grown up hating the MacGregors and the English. Now she was godmother to a MacGregor, and she found herself loving this warm, close English family. Yet the MacGregors had killed the MacArrans for centuries. The English had killed her father. How could she love people she should hate?

"Lady Bronwyn?" Gavin asked. "Is the wine too strong for you?"

"No," she smiled. "Everything is very nearly perfect. And that, I'm afraid, is my problem."

He studied her for a moment. "I want you to know that we're your family too. If you need any of us at any time, we'll be here."

"Thank you," she answered seriously. She knew he meant his words.

After dinner Judith took Bronwyn on a tour of the

area inside the castle walls. There were two sections to
the castle, the outer one where the castle retainers lived
and worked, and the more protected inner circle for the
family. Bronwyn listened and asked hundreds of questions about the incredibly efficient and well-organized
castle complex. The acres of land inside the tall, thick
walls were almost self-sustaining.

Stephen stopped them as they were speaking to the
blacksmith and Judith was showing her a new forging
technique.

"Bronwyn," Stephen said, "may I speak to you?"

She knew he had something serious to say, so she
followed him outside where they could be private.

"Gavin and I are returning to Larenston to get
Chris's body."

"Tam will have buried him by now."

He nodded. "I know, but I feel we owe it to Chris's
family. They don't even know yet that he's dead. It will
help some if he can be buried in his own land."

She nodded in agreement. "Chris didn't like Scotland," she said solemnly.

He ran his knuckles along her cheek. "It's the first
time we've been apart since we were married. I'd like
to think—" He stopped and dropped his hand.

"Stephen—" she began.

Suddenly he took her into his arms and held her
close to him. "I wish we could go back to the time we
spent with Kirsty and Donald. You seemed happy
there."

She clung to him. In spite of the danger they'd been
in, she too remembered the time as happy.

"You've come to mean so much to me," he whispered. "I hate to leave when you're so . . . cold to
me."

When she laughed, he pushed her away, frowning.
"Do I amuse you?" he asked angrily.

"I was thinking that I feel far from cold right now.
Tell me, how long do you have before you leave?"

"Minutes," he said in such a tone of regret that she laughed again.

"And how long before you return?"

He put his fingers under her chin. "Three long, long days, at least. Knowing Gavin, we'll ride hard." He smiled. "We won't stop every few hours as you and I did."

She slipped her arms up around his neck. "You will not forget me while you are gone?" she whispered, her lips against his.

"As easily as I could forget a thunderstorm," he said evenly, chuckling when she tried to move away. "Come here, wench," he commanded.

His mouth took possession of hers in such a way that she forgot all thoughts of honor and respect. She remembered only their romps on the Highlands moors. His hand moved her head to slant against his mouth, and she opened her lips under his, drinking in the sweetness of the tip of his tongue. She pressed her body closer to his and tightened her arms.

"Stephen—" she began.

He put two fingers on her lips. "We have much to talk of when I return. Are you willing?"

She smiled happily. "Yes, I am very willing."

He kissed her once again, with longing and promises of what was to come. When he turned away, it was with obvious reluctance.

It was at night that Bronwyn realized how much she missed Stephen. The big bed in the lovely tiled bedchamber seemed cold and unbearable. She thought of Stephen riding back into Scotland without so much as a night's rest. She cursed herself for not insisting she'd return with him.

The more she thought, the more restless she became. She tossed the covers aside and walked quickly across the cold floor to a chest in the corner. She withdrew her Highlands clothes, and within minutes she was fastening her plaid to her shoulder. She thought perhaps a walk in the cold courtyard below would help her sleep.

As soon as she was outside, the clatter of horses' hoofs on the bricked yard echoed against the buildings. "Stephen!" she gasped and began to run forward. She knew that only family would be allowed to enter at night.

"Lady Mary," someone said quietly. "It's good to see you again. Was your trip pleasant?"

"As good as I could wish, James," came a gentle, soft voice.

"Shall I fetch Lady Judith?"

"No, don't bother her. She needs her rest. I can find my own way."

Bronwyn stood in the shadows and watched as one of the castle retainers helped Lady Mary dismount. She remembered how Stephen had compared his sister to the Madonna, said she was the peacemaker and that she lived in a convent near the Montgomery estates.

"We expected you earlier," James said. "I hope nothing was wrong."

"One of the children was sick. I stayed to tend the child."

"You're too kind-hearted, Lady Mary. You shouldn't take in them beggars' children. Some of them have murderers for fathers. And mothers too if the truth be known."

Mary started to speak, then stopped and whirled to face Bronwyn. She smiled. "I had the oddest feeling I was being watched." She stepped forward. "You must be Stephen's Bronwyn."

The courtyard was very dim with only the moonlight and one lantern for light. Mary was short and plump with a perfectly oval face. It was a face anyone would trust.

"How did you know?" Bronwyn smiled. "I haven't been able to fool any of the Montgomerys."

"I've heard of the heartiness of the Scots. And to

withstand this wind when there is no need, it would take a great deal of stamina."

Bronwyn laughed. "Come inside to the winter parlor, and I'll have a roaring-hot fire for you in minutes."

"It sounds heavenly," Mary said, keeping her hands under her plain dark wool mantle.

Mary followed her sister-in-law into the large, paneled room, then stood quietly by as Bronwyn did indeed stoke and load the fire herself. She smiled, pleased that a lady of Bronwyn's rank felt secure enough to do humble work.

Bronwyn turned. "You must be tired. Perhaps you'd rather have the fire lit in your room."

Mary sat down in a cushioned chair and put her hands toward the fire. "I am tired, too tired to go to sleep. I'd just like to sit here a moment and get warm."

Bronwyn paused a moment before returning the iron fire tool to its holder. Mary did indeed look like the Madonna. Her oval face had a high, clear forehead above soft, expressive brown eyes. Her mouth was small, tender, delicate, and there was a dimple in one cheek. Raine's dimples, Bronwyn thought.

"It's good to be home again," Mary sighed, then looked back at Bronwyn. "Why are you awake?" she asked sharply. "Has Stephen . . .?"

Bronwyn laughed and took a chair beside Mary. "He and Gavin have returned to Scotland to . . . bring home the body of a friend."

"Christopher," Mary said and sighed as she leaned back in the chair.

"You know about him?" Bronwyn asked almost fearfully.

"Yes. Stephen wrote me about his death."

Bronwyn was very quiet. "Did he say how I was the one who caused Chris's death?"

"No! And you shouldn't even think that. He said that Chris's own arrogance caused his death. He said that all

Englishmen were committing suicide when they entered the Highlands."

"The English have killed many Highlanders!" Bronwyn said fiercely, then turned and looked quickly at Mary. "I apologize. I forget—"

"That we are English? That's a compliment, I'm sure." She studied Bronwyn in the soft glow of the firelight. "Stephen wrote me of your beauty, but he didn't tell me half of it."

Bronwyn grimaced. "He sets too much store by a woman's looks."

Mary laughed. "You've discovered what Judith has also. My brothers think all women are like me, without spirit or passion."

Bronwyn looked at her. "But surely—"

Mary put her hand up. "But surely a woman with brothers as passionate as mine must have some of her own? Is that what you meant to say?" She didn't wait for an answer. "No, I'm afraid I tend to run away from life. Women like Judith—and you if I guess correctly from Stephen's letters—grab life with both hands."

Bronwyn didn't know what to say. She thought about what an odd conversation they were having. They were talking as if they'd known each other for years instead of a few minutes. But somehow the quietness of the room, and the way the light of the fire seemed to isolate them from the dark corners, made everything seem quite ordinary.

"Tell me, are you lonely?" Mary asked. "Do you miss your Scots ways? What of your family and friends?"

It was a while before Bronwyn spoke. "Aye, I miss my friends." She thought of Tam and Douglas and all her people. "Yes, I miss them very much."

"And now it seems that Stephen is gone also. Perhaps tomorrow we could ride together. I'd like to hear some about Scotland."

Bronwyn smiled and leaned back in the chair. She'd very much like to spend the day with this woman. There was something quiet and peaceful about her, something Bronwyn felt she needed right now.

Bronwyn spent the next two days with Lady Mary, and it didn't take long to grow to love the woman. While Judith was busy with the account books and the worries of managing her own vast estates, as well as Gavin's, Mary and Bronwyn discovered their mutual love of people. Bronwyn had never been able to interest herself in numbers on paper, but she could tell more about the prosperity of a place by talking with the people than any other way. She and Mary rode across the acres and acres of land and talked with everyone. The serfs were timid at first, but they soon responded to Bronwyn's openness. She was used to speaking to underlings as equals, and one by one Mary saw the men and women straighten their shoulders in pride. Bronwyn sent people who were ill to bed. She asked for, and was happily given, extra supplies for some families' children.

But she wasn't always generous with her bounty. She considered the serfs people and so did not look at them with pity. She found several men who were stealing from their masters, and she saw that they were punished. Some quiet, hardworking, loyal families were put in places of responsibility and position.

On the evening of the first day Judith and Bronwyn spent hours together, Judith listening with admiration to all Bronwyn had to say. Judith realized her sister-in-law's wisdom immediately and took all her advice.

On the other hand Bronwyn learned a great deal about organization and efficiency, all of which knowledge she planned to take back to Larenston. She studied Judith's designs for buildings, her garden plans. Judith promised to send a wagonload of bedding plants to Larenston in the spring.

And Judith was a wonder with the breeding of animals. Bronwyn was fascinated by the way Judith had bred and cross-bred her sheep and cattle until she produced more meat, milk, and wool.

When Bronwyn retired for the night, she was too tired to stay awake. Charts and numbers swam before her eyes. A hundred faces and names floated through her dreams.

In the morning she was up early and in the stables before most of the castlefolk were awake. She wore her Highlands dress again, since she found the people responded enthusiastically to the simple clothes.

She swung a light saddle onto the back of a strawberry mare.

"My lady," came a strong young voice from beside her. "Allow me."

She turned to see a short, handsome blond man, one of Miles's men, who'd accompanied her and Mary the day before. "Thank you, Richard."

His eyes, a dark green, warmed as he looked at her. "I had no idea you knew my name. It is an honor for me."

She laughed. "Nonsense! In Scotland I know all my men's names, and they call me by mine."

He bent to fasten the cinch. "I've been talking to some of Lord Stephen's men who were with him in Scotland. They said you often traveled at night, alone, with your men."

"True," she said slowly. "I am the MacArran, and I am the leader of my men."

He smiled in a slow, provocative way. "May I say that I envy your Highlanders? In England we are seldom led by a woman and never one so beautiful."

She frowned and reached for the reins of her horse. "Thank you," she said stiffly and led the animal from the stables.

"What do you think you're doing?" snapped a man behind Richard.

Richard glanced at the door Bronwyn had used before turning to the man behind him. "Nothing that would interest you, George," he said, shoving his way past the knight.

George grabbed Richard's arm. "I saw you talking to her, and I want to know what you said."

"Why?" Richard snapped. "So you can have her all to yourself? I heard what you and the rest of Stephen's men said about her."

"*Lord* Stephen to you!"

"You're a hypocrite! You call her Bronwyn and talk to her as if she were your little sister, yet let someone else speak to her and you want to draw a sword. Let me tell you that I for one don't mean to treat her like anything but the Scots whore she is. No lady would talk to the men and the serfs like she does unless she was after what they carry between their legs. And I—"

George's fist smashed into Richard's mouth before he could say another word. "I'll kill you for that!" George yelled as he went for Richard's throat.

Richard was able to sidestep the second blow. He clasped his hands together and brought them down across the back of George's neck. George went sprawling forward, face first into the straw.

"What's going on here?" Bronwyn demanded from the doorway.

George sat up and rubbed his neck. Richard's nose was bleeding, and he wiped the blood away with the back of his hand.

"I asked a question," Bronwyn said quietly, watching the two men. "I will not ask the cause of your quarrel, as that is personal, but I want to know who struck the first blow."

Richard looked at George pointedly.

"I did, my lady," George said as he started to rise.

"You, George? But—" Bronwyn stopped herself. There must have been a good reason from someone of George's quiet, steady nature to strike a first blow. She didn't like Richard and she didn't trust him. Yesterday he'd too often leered at the young serf girls. But she couldn't leave George and Richard alone together, and she couldn't take George with her because he was the one who started the quarrel. It was better to keep Richard with her and protect Stephen's man.

"Richard," she said quietly, "you may go with Lady Mary and me today." She gave one look of regret to George and left the stables.

"Hot for me, the woman is," Richard laughed as he left the stables before George could attack him again.

Chapter Fifteen

MARY SWUNG INTO THE SADDLE AND GAVE HER SIS-
ter-in-law a sleepy look. She wondered if cold or
exhaustion were words Bronwyn knew. They'd ridden
all day yesterday until even the guards who followed
them were tired. Then Bronwyn had sat with Judith,
eagerly talking and asking questions until after midnight.

Mary stretched and yawned, then smiled. No wonder
Stephen wrote that he had to work hard to keep up with
his wife. She suddenly wondered if Stephen ever told
Bronwyn how much he admired her. Stephen's letters
were full of praise for his new people and his new life,
and especially his courageous wife.

Mary urged her horse forward to catch Bronwyn.
Already the Scotswoman was stopping at a serf's hut.

It was late morning when they finally stopped on the
side of a hill for a moment's rest. The men stretched out
on the grass, breathing deeply, eating hungrily of
bread, wine, and cheese.

Mary and Bronwyn sat on the crest of the hill at a place where Bronwyn could see across the countryside. It had taken all of Mary's strength to follow.

"What was that?" Bronwyn asked suddenly.

Mary listened for a moment, but all she heard was the soft sigh of the wind and the guards' voices.

"There it is again!" Bronwyn looked over her shoulder, and Rab came to nudge her. "Yes, boy," she whispered. She stood quickly. "Someone's hurt," she said to Mary as she began to run to the top of the hill, Rab beside her.

The guards looked up, but they gave the women privacy, thinking a call of nature took them over the crest of the hill.

Mary strained her eyes but saw nothing. Below them lay a pond, the edges half frozen, great thin sheets of ice floating in the water.

Bronwyn strained her eyes until suddenly Rab gave a sharp bark. "There!" Bronwyn yelled as she began to run.

Mary didn't see a thing but lifted her heavy skirts and followed. It was only when she was halfway to the pond that she saw the child's head and shoulders. The child was trapped in the icy water.

Mary felt a shiver run along her spine, and she began to run faster and faster. She didn't notice when she passed Bronwyn. She ran straight into the water and grabbed the child.

The little boy looked up at her with great, blank eyes. Only minutes were left if they were to keep the child from freezing.

"He's stuck!" Mary called to Bronwyn. "His foot seems to be caught on something. Can you throw me your knife?"

Bronwyn's mind worked quickly. She knew the child could stand little more of the icy water so time was of the essence. If she tossed Mary the knife and Mary didn't catch it, they'd probably lose the child.

There was only one way to make sure Mary got the knife.

"Rab!" Bronwyn said, and the dog recognized the sound of urgency in her voice. "Go to the men and get help. Bring someone here. We need help, Rab."

The dog shot away like an arrow from a bow. But he did not head toward the guards who waited just over the hill.

"Damn!" Bronwyn cursed, but it was already too late to call the dog back to her.

She took her knife from her side and plunged into the cold water. She moved as quickly as she could, hindered by the growth under the water. Mary was blue with cold, but she held on to the boy, whose face was turning gray.

Bronwyn knelt, the water smacking against her chest like a brick wall. She felt for the child's legs, felt the undergrowth that held him. Her teeth were beginning to chatter as she sawed away at the tough growth.

"He's free!" she whispered after a moment. She saw that Mary's face was beginning to lose its blueness, turning to the more dangerous gray. Bronwyn knelt and lifted the child. "Can you follow?" she called over her shoulder to Mary.

Mary didn't have the excess strength to reply. She concentrated all her energies on moving her legs and following Bronwyn's quickly moving form.

Bronwyn barely reached the edge of the pond before the child was taken from her arms. She looked into Raine's serious face.

"How . . .?" Bronwyn began.

"Miles and I were riding to meet you when your dog came to us. Rab was bounding like a demon." As Raine spoke he was constantly moving. He put the child into one of his men's arms, then wrapped his cloak around Bronwyn's cold, wet shoulders.

"Mary?" Bronwyn asked as she began to shiver.

"Miles has her," Raine said as he tossed his sister-in-law into his saddle and mounted behind her.

They went quickly back to the Montgomery castle. Raine held his horse under control with one hand while his other hand rubbed Bronwyn's shoulders and arms. She realized she was freezing, and she tried to make herself into a ball and snuggle against Raine's solid warmth.

Once inside the gates Raine carried Bronwyn upstairs to her bedchamber. He stood her in the middle of the floor while he opened a chest and pulled a heavy robe of golden wool from it. "Here, put this on," he commanded as he turned his back on her and began to stoke the fire.

Bronwyn's fingers trembled as she tried to unfasten her shirt. The wet, clammy fabric clung to her. She peeled it away from her skin, then took the robe Raine had tossed on the bed beside her. The wool was heavy and thick, but she couldn't yet feel any of its warmth.

Raine turned back to her, took one look at her colorless face, and swept her into his arms. He sat down in a large chair before the fireplace with her in his lap. He tucked the big robe, one of Stephen's, around her, held her closely as she drew her legs in to her chest and tucked her head into Raine's broad chest.

It took several minutes before she was able to stop shivering. "Mary?" she whispered after a moment.

"Miles is taking care of her, and by now Judith has her in a hot tub of water."

"And the child?"

Raine looked down at her, his eyes turning dark blue. "Did you know it was only a serf's child?" he asked quietly.

She pulled away from him. "What does it matter? The child needed help."

Raine smiled at her and pulled her back to his chest. "I didn't think it would matter to you. I know it wouldn't to Mary. You'll have trouble with Gavin, though. He wouldn't risk a hair on one of his family's heads for all the serfs in the world."

"I've dealt with Stephen for months, so I guess I can deal with Gavin." She gave a great sigh of resignation.

Raine gave a laugh that started in his flat belly. She felt it before she heard it. "Well said! I see you understand my elder brothers."

She smiled against his chest. "Raine, why haven't you ever married?"

"The universal question from women," he chuckled. "Did you consider that no one would have me?"

The question was so absurd she didn't even reply.

"Actually I've turned down six women in eight months."

"Why?" she asked. "Were they too ugly, too thin, too fat? Or didn't you meet them?"

"I met them," he said quietly. "I'm not like my brothers, who are willing to meet their brides on their wedding days. The fathers made the offers, and I spent three days with each woman."

"Yet you turned them all down."

"Aye, that I did."

She sighed. "What do you expect of a woman? Surely one of them must have been pretty enough."

"Pretty!" Raine snorted. "Three of them were beautiful! But I want more than a pretty woman. I want a woman who has a thought in her head besides the latest embroidery pattern." His eyes twinkled merrily. "I want a woman who'll walk into an icy pond and risk her life to save a serf child."

"But surely, had any woman seen the child—"

Raine looked away from her to the fire. "You and Mary are special, as is Judith. Did you know Judith once led Gavin's men when Gavin was held captive by some madman? She risked her own life to save his." He smiled down at her. "I'm waiting until I get someone like you or Judith."

Bronwyn considered this for a moment. "No, I can't see that we're what you want. Gavin is attached to the land, and so is Judith. They fit together. And Scotland is for me. Stephen is free to live there with me. But you . . . I feel you never stay in one place too long. You need someone as free as you are, someone who isn't tied to a piece of stone and earth somewhere."

Raine looked at her with his mouth agape, then closed it and smiled. "I won't ask how you know all that. I'm sure the answer would be that you're a witch. Now, since you seem to know so much about me, I'd like to ask you some personal questions."

He paused and looked into her eyes. "What is wrong between you and Stephen?" he asked quietly. "Why are you angry at him all the time?"

Bronwyn was slow to speak. She knew of the closeness between the brothers, and she wasn't sure how Raine would take to any criticism of his elder brother. But how could she lie?

She took a deep breath and spoke the truth. "Stephen thinks I have no honor or pride. He believes anyone before he believes me. In Scotland he thought everything I did was wrong, and in truth some of it was, but he had no right to treat me as if everything I did was wrong."

Raine nodded in understanding. It had taken Gavin a while to realize Judith was more than just a pretty body.

But before he could say a word, the door burst open and a tired, dirty Stephen stormed into the room.

"Miles said Bronwyn jumped into an icy lake!" he thundered. "Where is she?" Even as he said the words, he saw her in Raine's lap. He took two long steps across the room and snatched her from him.

"Damn you!" he bellowed. "I can't leave you for more than an hour without your getting into trouble."

"Release me!" she said coldly. He'd been away for days, the first time they'd ever been separated, and now all he did was curse her.

Stephen must have felt some of her thoughts. He set her on the floor before him. "Bronwyn," he said quietly, touching her cheek.

She gathered the bottom of the wool robe off the floor and walked toward the door. She was one of the few women in the world who could manage to look dignified while barefoot and wearing a robe hanging several inches past her hands.

She put her hand on the door latch and, without turning, said, "Someday you'll learn that I am neither a child nor an idiot." She opened the door and left the room.

Stephen took a step toward the closed door, but Raine's voice stopped him.

"Sit down and let her alone," Raine said with resignation.

Stephen looked toward the door for a moment longer, then turned and took a chair across from Raine's. He ran his hand wearily through his dirty hair. "Is she unhurt? Will she be all right?"

"Of course," Raine answered confidently. "She's strong and healthy, and from what you say of the Scots she's lived out-of-doors most of her life."

Stephen stared at the fire. "I know," he said heavily.

"What's eating you?" Raine demanded. "You're not the Stephen I know."

"Bronwyn," he whispered. "She's going to be the death of me. In Scotland one night she decided to lead her men on a raid against her clan's enemy. In order to assure herself that I'd be out of the way, she drugged me."

"She did what?" Raine exploded, realizing the full danger of Bronwyn's act.

Stephen grimaced. "One of her men found what she'd done and helped wake me. When I found her, she was down the side of a cliff, dangling by a rope about her waist."

"Good God!" Raine gasped.

"I didn't know whether to beat her or lock her away to protect her against herself."

"And which did you do?"

Stephen leaned back in the chair. His voice was full of disgust. "What I always end up doing: I made love to her."

Raine chuckled deeply. "It seems to me your problem would be if she were selfish and cared only about herself."

Stephen stood and walked to the fireplace. "She cares too little for herself. Sometimes she makes me ashamed of myself. When it comes to that clan of hers, she does whatever she thinks is best without regard to her own safety."

"And you worry about her?" Raine asked.

"Damned right! Why can't she stay at home and have babies and care for them—and me—as a wife should? Why does she have to lead cattle raids, carve her initials on a man's chest, roll in her plaid and sleep on the ground in perfect comfort? Why can't she be . . . be . . ."

"A simpering little mealy-mouthed wench who'd look at you with adoring eyes and embroider all your shirt collars?" Raine suggested.

Stephen sat down heavily. "I don't want that, but there has to be some compromise."

"Do you really want to change her?" Raine asked. "What is it about her that made you love her in the first place? And don't tell me it was her beauty. You've been to bed with several beautiful women, but you've not fallen in love with them."

"Is it so obvious?"

"To me and probably to Gavin and Miles, but I don't think it is to Bronwyn. She doesn't believe you care for her at all."

Stephen sighed. "I've never met anyone like her, male or female. She's so strong, so noble, almost like a man. You should see the way her clan treats her. The Scots aren't like us. The serf children run to her and hug her, and she kisses all the babies. She knows the name of every person on her land, and they all call her by her first name. She goes without food and clothes so her clan can have more. One night, about a month after we were married, I noticed her wrapping bread and cheese in her plaid. She ignored me but kept looking toward Tam. He's a man who often acts as her father. I realized she was doing something she didn't want Tam to see, so after supper I followed her off the peninsula. She was taking the food to one of her crofter's children, a sulking little boy who'd run away from home."

"And what did you say to her?" Raine asked.

Stephen shook his head in memory. "Me, the great wise one, I told her she had to send the boy back to his parents instead of encouraging him to run away from home."

"And what did Brownyn say?"

"She said the boy was as important to her as the parents, and she had no right to betray him just because he was a boy. She said he'd go home in a few days and accept his punishment as he should."

Raine gave a low whistle of admiration. "Sounds like you could learn something from her."

"You think I haven't? She's changed my whole life. When I went to Scotland, I was an Englishman, and now look at me. I can't abide these English clothes. I feel like Samson with my hair cut short. I find myself looking at the English countryside and thinking it's dry and hot compared to home. Home! I swear I'm homesick for a place that I never saw before a few months ago."

"Tell me," Raine said, "have you told Bronwyn how you feel? Have you told her you love her and are only concerned with her safety?"

"I've tried to. Once I tried to tell her that I loved her, and she said it didn't matter, that honor and respect were more important to her."

"But from what you say, you do have those feelings for her."

Stephen started to grin. "It's not easy telling Bronwyn anything. We had . . . I guess you could call it an argument before we arrived here." He told Raine briefly about the trick of Hugh Lasco's.

"Hugh!" Raine snorted. "I never much liked the man with his slow ways."

"Bronwyn didn't seem to mind them," Stephen said in disgust.

Raine laughed. "Don't tell me you are touched by Gavin's jealousy!"

Stephen whirled on his brother. "Just wait until you are obsessed by some woman! I'll wager you aren't so cool-headed then."

Raine put up his hand. "I hope I look on love as a joy and not as the disease you seem to be eaten with."

Stephen turned away and stared into the fire. Sometimes his love for Bronwyn did seem like a disease. He felt she'd taken his soul along with his heart.

When Bronwyn left her own bedchamber, she went to Mary's. Mary was in bed, Judith hovering over her, placing hot bricks throughout the bed.

"Judith," Mary said quietly. "I am not about to die of a little cold water." She looked across the room and smiled at Bronwyn. "Come and help me persuade Judith that our escapade was not of the killing sort."

Bronwyn smiled at the women and studied Mary. Her pale skin was even paler, and there were bright pink patches on her cheeks. "It was nothing," Bronwyn said. "But I envy you with the control of spirit so you can rest." Her eyes twinkled. "I'm so excited about the new dress Judith promised me that I cannot rest.

Perhaps we could see it now," she said suggestively to Judith.

Judith understood immediately, and the two women quietly left the room. "Do you think she will be all right?" Judith asked as soon as they were in the hall.

"Yes, she needs rest, I can tell. I don't believe our Mary is completely in this world. I think Heaven owns part of her. Perhaps that's why she's so weak."

"Yes," Judith agreed. "Now, about that gown—"

Bronwyn waved her hand. "It was only an excuse to give Mary a chance to rest."

Judith laughed. "As becoming as Stephen's robe is, it doesn't substitute for the gown you need. Now come with me, and I want no excuses."

An hour later Bronwyn stood arrayed in a gown of lush, deep green velvet. The color was of a forest just at sunset. The undersleeves were of brilliant green silk, and the loose, hanging oversleeves were banded with a wide border of red fox. Heavy gold cords were attached to the shoulders and hung below the deep, square neckline.

"It's beautiful, Judith," Bronwyn whispered. "I don't know how to thank you. All of you have been so generous."

Judith kissed her friend's cheek. "I must go now and do the day's work. Perhaps Stephen would like to see the new gown," she suggested.

Bronwyn turned away. Stephen would only complain that the neck was too low or some other such accusation.

After Judith was gone, Bronwyn went to the cold courtyard below. She threw a fox-lined mantle about her shoulders and walked toward the stables.

"Bronwyn," an unfamiliar voice said once she was inside the dark place.

She looked into the shadows and saw the man who'd fought Stephen's George that morning. "Yes," she said curtly. "What is it?"

The man's eyes sparkled even in the dimness. "The English gown becomes you." Before she could speak, his manner changed to a more formal one. "I've heard your Scotsmen are quite good with a bow. Perhaps you"—this seemed to amuse him—"could teach me a better way to handle a bow."

She ignored the undercurrent of laughter in the man's voice. Perhaps his laughter was meant as a defense in case she refused his request. But Bronwyn had spent many hours learning how to handle a bow, and she was used to training men. It was good that this Englishman wanted to learn the Scots' ways. "I would be happy to give you instruction," she said, then walked past the man—and straight into Stephen's hard chest. The man quickly left the stables.

"What were you saying to the man?" Stephen asked flatly.

She twisted out of his grip. "Do you never say anything to me except in anger? Why can't you be like other husbands and greet your wife in a friendly manner? I have not seen you in days, and all you have done is curse me."

He grabbed her into his arms. "Bronwyn," he whispered. "You will be the death of me. Why did you have to jump into an icy pond in the dead of winter?"

She pushed away from him. "I refuse to answer such questions."

He grabbed her again, pulled her mouth to his, bruising her, his teeth hard against her lips. He seemed as if he wanted more than just a kiss from her. "I missed you," he whispered. "Every minute I thought of you."

Her heart was pounding in her breast. She felt like she could melt against him. But his next words broke the spell.

"Was that one of Miles's men you were talking to when I entered?"

She tried to pull away from him. "Is this your jealousy again? I can hear it in your voice."

"Bronwyn, no. Listen to me. I only want to warn you. The Englishmen are not like your Highlanders. You can't talk to them as if they were your brothers as you do your own men. In England too often the ladies sleep with their husbands' men-at-arms."

Bronwyn's eyes widened. "Are you accusing me of sleeping with your men?" she gasped.

"No, of course not, but—"

"But you accused me of doing just that with Hugh Lasco."

"Hugh Lasco is a gentleman!" Stephen snapped.

Bronwyn nearly jumped away from him. "So!" she blazed. "At least you think I am a discriminating whore!" She whirled about and started toward the door.

Stephen grabbed her arm. "I am not accusing you of anything. I am trying to explain that things are different in England than in Scotland."

"Oh! So now I'm too stupid to be able to learn the difference between one country and another. You can adjust but I can't!"

He stared at her. "What's wrong with you? You aren't acting like yourself at all."

She turned away from him. "And what would you know of me? You've never done anything but curse at me since I met you. Nothing I do outside the bedroom pleases you. If I lead my men, that makes you angry. If I try to save one of your brother's serfs, that angers you. If I'm kind to your men, you accuse me of sleeping with them. Tell me, what can I do to please you?"

Stephen glared at her with cold eyes. "I had no idea you found me so unpleasant. I will leave you to your own company." He turned away stiffly and left her.

Bronwyn stared after him, tears beginning to form in her eyes. What *was* wrong with her? Stephen hadn't really accused her of sleeping with the man, and he had every right to warn her about what his men would think. Why couldn't she welcome him home like she wanted to? All she wanted was to be held by him, loved by him. Yet for some reason she started a quarrel every time he approached her.

Suddenly she felt as if her whole body ached. She put her hand to her forehead. She wasn't used to not feeling well, and now she realized she'd been ignoring the feeling for days. Of course, her late nights with Judith and this morning spent in a half-frozen pond hadn't helped her any. She cursed the disease-ridden English countryside and left the stables.

"Bronwyn," Judith called. "Would you like some fresh bread?"

Bronwyn leaned back against the stone wall of the stables. The quarrel was upsetting her stomach. The thought of food nauseated her. "No," she whispered, her hand to her stomach.

"Bronwyn, what is it?" Judith asked, setting the basket down. "Aren't you feeling well?" She put her hand on her sister-in-law's forehead. "Here, sit down." She urged her to a barrel set by the wall. "Breathe deeply and it will pass."

"What will?" Bronwyn asked sharply.

"The nausea."

"The what?" Bronwyn gasped. "What are you talking about?"

Judith paused. "Unless I miss my guess, you're going to have a baby." She smiled broadly at Bronwyn's look. "It is rather startling when you first realize it." She caressed her own stomach. "We'll deliver close together," she said proudly.

"You! You're going to have a baby too?"

Judith had a faraway smile on her face. "Yes. I . . . lost my first one, a miscarriage, so for this one I'm being so careful I'm not even telling anyone. Except Gavin, of course."

"Of course," Bronwyn said and looked away, then back again. "When is your baby due?"

"In seven months." She chuckled.

"What are you laughing at?" Bronwyn asked. "I need some humor right now."

"I was just thinking that my mother will be able to come to my lying-in." She paused, then began to explain. "I thought she would not be able to come, as she was to deliver at the same time."

"Your mother! How fortunate you are to have your parents alive."

"No," Judith smiled. "My father died several months ago."

"And the child is not his?" Bronwyn asked quietly.

"Oh, no, and I am pleased by that. My father often beat my mother. She was held captive by a young man, and her guard was Gavin's best man, John Bassett. I'm afraid my mother and he found an extraordinary means of entertainment."

Bronwyn laughed.

"Yes," Judith continued. "When Gavin found out there was to be a child, he allowed John and my mother to marry."

"And she's had her own babe now?"

"It's due in a couple of months, so she should be well enough to travel to me when I am due. I must get back to work now. Why don't you just sit there and rest?"

"Judith, you said your mother was being held captive. How did she escape?"

Judith's golden eyes darkened with memory. "I killed her captor, and Stephen's men brought down the wall of the old keep."

Bronwyn could see the pain in Judith's eyes. She asked no more questions before Judith turned away toward the gate that separated the two parts of the castle complex.

Bronwyn sat still for quite some time. A baby! she

thought. A soft, sweet thing like Kirsty's baby. Her mind seemed to leave her, and she hardly noticed when she stood and began to walk. She thought of Tam and how proud he'd be of her. She smiled dreamily when she thought of Stephen's reaction to the news. He'd be so happy! He'd grab her and toss her above his head and laugh with pleasure. Then they'd argue over whether the child would be named MacArran or Montgomery. There was no doubt, of course, that he'd be a MacArran.

She kept walking in a dreamlike trance, never noticing when she reached the open gate. The men on the wall guarding the entrance didn't challenge her or hinder her movements in any way.

What would she name her child? she thought. James for her father, and perhaps another name for Stephen's family. What if the babe was a girl? she thought and smiled warmly. Clan MacArran would have two female lairds in a row. She must teach her daughter all the things she'd need to know to be laird.

"My lady," someone said.

Bronwyn hardly heard the voice. She was in a trance, and very little penetrated it. In fact, she was hardly aware that she'd walked for quite some time and was now out of sight of the castle guards.

"My lady," the voice repeated. "Are you well?"

Bronwyn looked up at the man with an angelic smile of great warmth. "I am well," she said in a vague manner. "I am more than well."

The man dismounted and went to her side. "I can see that," he said in a low voice, his lips close to her ear.

Bronwyn still paid little attention to the man. All she could think of was her child. Morag would love another baby to care for, she was thinking as the man's lips touched her ear. The touch brought her out of her reverie.

She jumped away from him. "How dare you," she

gasped. No man except Stephen had ever touched her unless she allowed him. She gave a quick look about her and realized how far she was from the castle.

Richard misinterpreted her look. "There's no need to worry. We're quite alone, and Lord Gavin has just returned from Scotland, so everyone is busy at the moment. We have time."

She backed away from him. A thousand thoughts flew through her mind. Stephen's warnings screamed at her. And worry for her baby occupied most of her mind. Please don't let my child be hurt!

"There's no reason to fear me," Richard said in a honey-coated voice. "We could have fun, you and I."

Bronwyn straightened her shoulders. "I am Bronwyn MacArran, and you will return to the castle."

"MacArran!" he laughed. "The men said you were an independent woman, but they didn't say you'd go so far as to disown your husband."

"You are insulting. Now go and leave me alone."

Richard's smile left his face. "You think I'm going to leave you after the way you've been teasing me? You chose me to accompany you this morning. I'll wager you were sorry when we had no time to be alone."

She was aghast. "Is that what you thought? That I wanted to be alone with you?"

He touched her hair, his little finger grazing her breast.

Her eyes opened wide, then she looked for Rab. The dog was always with her.

"I took the precaution of locking your dog in a granary," Richard smiled. "Now, come and stop playing these games. You know you want me as much as I want you." He grabbed Bronwyn, his hand twisting in her hair. He ground his lips against hers.

Bronwyn felt waves of anger shoot through her. She relaxed in his arms, leaned backward, and as he bent forward to press against her, she brought her knee up.

Richard groaned and released her abruptly.

Bronwyn struggled to keep from falling, then tripped on the heavy velvet skirt. She cursed as she gathered handfuls of the fabric and began to run. But no matter how much she held, more fabric swirled about her legs and hindered her. She tripped once again, then slung the velvet over her arm. The third time she tripped, Richard was upon her. He grabbed her ankle, and she fell forward, face down into the cold, hard earth. She gasped for air.

Richard ran his hand up her legs. "Now, my fiery Scotswoman, we'll see if that fire can be put to use."

Bronwyn tried to kick out at him, but he held her to the ground. He grabbed her dress and tore it, exposing the skin of her back to the cold winter air.

"Now," he said as he placed his lips to the nape of her neck.

The next moment Richard screamed as a mass of gray fur and sharp teeth attacked him. Bronwyn rolled away as Richard tried to stand and fight Rab.

An arm pulled her up. Miles drew her to him, held her with one arm, his drawn sword in the other. "Call your dog off him," Miles said quietly.

Bronwyn's voice was shaking. "Rab!" she commanded.

The dog reluctantly left off his attack and went to her side.

Richard tried to stand. There was blood on his arm and his thigh. His clothes were torn in several places. "The damned dog attacked me for no reason!" he began. "Lady Bronwyn fell, and I stopped to help her."

Miles stepped away from his sister-in-law. His eyes were as hard as steel. "You do not touch the Montgomery women," he said in a deadly voice.

"She came at me!" the man said. "She asked—"

They were the last words he ever spoke. Miles's sword went straight through Richard's heart. Miles barely glanced at the dead man, one of his own men.

He turned to Bronwyn and seemed to sense what she felt—helpless and violated.

He put his arms around her gently and drew her to him. "You're safe now," he said quietly. "No one else will try to harm you."

Suddenly her body began to tremble, and Miles drew her closer. "He said I had encouraged him," she whispered.

"Hush," Miles said. "I've been watching him. He didn't understand your Scots ways."

Bronwyn pulled away to look at him. "That's what Stephen said. He warned me of talking to the men. He said the Englishmen didn't understand when I talked to them."

Miles smoothed the hair from her forehead. "There's a formality between an English lady and her husband's men that is not in your culture. Now let's return. I'm sure someone will have seen me leave following your dog."

She glanced at the dead man beside them. "He locked Rab away and I didn't even notice. I was—" She couldn't tell anyone about the baby before she told Stephen.

"I heard the dog yelping, and when I released him, he went crazy, barking at me, sniffing the earth." He looked with admiration at the big dog. "He knew you were in trouble."

She knelt and rubbed her face in Rab's rough coat.

They both turned at the sound of horses. Gavin and Stephen rode toward them quickly. Stephen slid from the saddle before the horse came to a full stop. "What happened here?" he demanded.

"The man tried to attack Bronwyn," Miles said.

Stephen glared at his wife, his eyes taking in the scraped place on her cheek, her torn gown. "I told you," he said through clenched teeth. "You wouldn't listen to me."

"Stephen," Gavin said, his hand on his brother's arm. "Now's not the time."

"Not the time!" Stephen exploded at his wife. "Not an hour ago you listed all my faults. Did you find someone else with fewer faults? Did you encourage him on purpose?"

Before anyone else could speak, Stephen turned away and mounted his horse. Bronwyn, Miles, and Gavin watched helplessly.

"He should be whipped for that!" Miles sneered.

"Quiet!" Gavin commanded. He turned to Bronwyn. "He's upset and confused. You have to forgive him."

"He's jealous!" Bronwyn whispered fiercely. "That empty jealousy of his changes him into a madman." She felt weak and defeated. He cared nothing for her but only for his own jealousy.

Gavin put his arm around her protectively. "Come home and let Judith get you something to drink. She makes a delicious apple drink."

Bronwyn nodded numbly and allowed herself to be put onto Miles's horse.

Chapter Sixteen

THE DRINK JUDITH GAVE BRONWYN PUT HER TO SLEEP
almost instantly. She'd had too much in one day—the
rescue of the child and the near rape. She dreamed of
being lost and of searching for Stephen, but he wasn't
there.

She woke suddenly, her body coated in sweat, and
reached for him. The bed was empty. She sat up and
looked about the dimly lit room, searching for him.

She felt unbearably lonely. Why did she quarrel with
Stephen all the time? When Miles had told her the
Scots' ways were different, she didn't get angry. It was
only when Stephen said the same thing that she flew
into a rage.

She threw the covers back and grabbed a robe Judith
had lent her. She must find Stephen and tell him that
she'd been wrong. She must tell him about the child
and ask that he forgive her for her foul mood.

Rab followed her as she went to a chest and withdrew
her plaid. The dog was afraid to let her out of his sight.

She dressed quickly and left her room. The house was silent and dark as she made her way downstairs. A single fat candle shown from the half-open winter parlor door. The fire was nearly dead.

She pushed the door open as she heard a woman giggle. Bronwyn halted as she realized she'd probably interrupted Raine or Miles with one of the house-maids. She turned to go as the woman's words stopped her.

"Oh, Stephen," the woman giggled. "I've missed you so much. No man has hands like yours."

Bronwyn heard the deep rumble of a familiar laugh.

She was not a timid woman to run crying from the room. She'd had one insult too many for the day. She pushed the heavy door open with a vicious shove and marched to the fireplace.

Stephen sat in a large chair, fully clothed, a plump young girl, bared from the waist up, sprawled across his lap. He disinterestedly had one hand on her breast; the other held a flagon of wine.

Rab bared his teeth at the girl, and she gave one look from Bronwyn to the dog, screamed, then fled the room.

Stephen only glanced at his wife. "Welcome," he slurred and held up his cup to her.

Bronwyn felt her heart pounding. To see Stephen touching another woman! Her skin felt as if it were on fire and her head throbbed.

Stephen looked up at her. "How does it feel, my dear wife?" His eyes were red, his movements slow. He was obviously drunk. "I've had to stand aside and watch you play with man after man. Do you know how I felt when you let Hugh touch you?"

"You did this on purpose," she whispered. "You did this to punish me." She held her shoulders back. She wanted to hurt him, to make him ache as she did. "I was right when I told Sir Thomas Crichton I couldn't marry you. You aren't fit to be married to a Scotswoman. I've stood by for months and watched you ape our ways. And I've seen you fail at everything."

In spite of his drunkenness he reacted swiftly. He threw his flagon to the floor, sprang to his feet, and grabbed her by the neckline of her dress. "And what have you given me?" he rasped. "I have made every effort to learn from you, but when have you listened to me? You've fought me at every moment. You've laughed at me before your men, even scorned my advice in front of my own brothers. Yet I've taken everything because I am fool enough to believe I loved you. How can anyone love someone as selfish as you? When are you going to grow up and stop hiding behind your clan? You aren't concerned with your clan; your only concern is what you want and what you need."

He pushed her away as if he were suddenly very tired of her. "I'm tired of trying to please some cold woman. I'm going to find one who can give me what I need."

He turned away and drunkenly left the room.

Bronwyn stood where she was for a long time. She had no idea he despised her so much. How many times had he been close to saying he loved her yet she'd ignored him? Oh, but she'd been fiery and proud when she told him that of course they cared for each other but that what she wanted was more important than love.

What meant more to her than Stephen's love? She could see now that there was nothing nearly as important. She'd had that love in the palm of her hand, and she'd thrown it right back in his face. In Scotland he'd worked hard to be fair and to learn how to live in her country. Yet what had she done to conform to his way of life? Her biggest concession was to dress in the luscious English fashions, and she'd even complained about that.

She clenched her hand. Stephen was right! She was selfish. She demanded he become a Scot, change every fiber of his being, yet she'd never done a thing for him.

From the moment they'd met, she'd made him pay for the privilege of marrying her.

"Privilege!" she gasped aloud. She'd made him fight for her on their wedding day. She'd taken a knife to him on their wedding night. What was it Stephen had said? "Someday you'll know that one drop of my blood is more precious than any angry feelings you carry."

How could she have hurt that beautiful body she knew so well? How could she have drawn blood from him?

Tears began to run down her face. He loved her no longer. He'd said that. She'd had his love and discarded it like so much rubbish.

She blinked at the tears and looked around her. Stephen was good and his family was good. She'd hated him for being an Englishman just as she'd hated all the MacGregors. But Stephen had shown her there were good MacGregors and warm, generous Englishmen.

Stephen had shown her! He'd taught her so much, yet she'd never so much as softened to him. When had she ever been kind to him? She drugged him, cursed him, defied him—anything to be spiteful.

Anything to keep from loving him, she realized. She hadn't wanted to love an Englishman. She was afraid her clan would think she was weak, unworthy of being laird. Yet Tam had loved him, and most of her men had even come to love him.

She turned toward the door and went quietly through the Great Hall and outside into the courtyard. She looked about for Stephen. Perhaps she could find him. Somehow she knew he hadn't gone upstairs.

"Stephen rode away a few minutes ago," Miles said softly from behind her.

She turned slowly. This man was also kind to her. He'd held her after she'd been attacked.

Suddenly a cold wind brushed past her, and she had a vision of Scotland. More than anything else in the world she wanted to go home. Perhaps at home she could think what to do to win Stephen's love again. Maybe she could imagine how to make him understand that she loved him too and that she was willing to bend as he had.

She looked at Miles as if she didn't really see him, then turned and walked toward the stables.

"Bronwyn," he said as he grabbed her arm. "What's happened?"

"I'm going home," she said quietly.

"To Scotland?" he asked, astonished.

"Aye," she whispered, rolling her words. "Home to Scotland." She smiled. "Would you give my regrets to Judith?"

Miles searched her face for a moment. "Judith understands things without being told. Come on, let's get started."

Bronwyn started to protest but then closed her mouth. She knew she couldn't prevent Miles from accompanying her any more than she could stop her urge to go home.

They rode through that long, awful night without saying a word to each other. Bronwyn felt only her pain at having lost Stephen. Perhaps he'd be happier in England where his family was, where he didn't have to struggle just to survive. She often held her hand to her stomach and wondered when it was going to begin to swell. She wanted an outward sign that she would soon have his child.

They crossed into Scotland in the early morning, and it suddenly occurred to her how selfish she'd been in allowing Miles to accompany her. There were too many Scotsmen who were like old Harben, who'd love to kill any Englishman on sight. She suggested to Miles that since they had no guard, they might be safer if he were to dress as a Highlander. Miles looked at her in an odd way that she didn't understand.

Later, as they traveled north, she began to understand. Miles would always be safe wherever there were women. Pretty girls stopped and offered them dippers of milk, and their eyes offered Miles much more. One woman, walking with her four-year-old daughter, stopped and spoke to them. The little girl ran and leaped into Miles's arms. Miles seemed to see nothing unusual about this action. He merely swung the child onto his shoulders and they walked quite some distance together.

Near sundown they came to an old crofter's cottage, and an ugly, old, toothless crone greeted them. She smiled delightedly at Miles and took his hand. She rubbed it warmly between her own, then held his palm up to the dying light.

"What do you see?" Miles asked gently.

"Angels," she cackled. "Two angels. A beautiful angel and a cherub."

Miles smiled sweetly, and the woman laughed harder. "They're angels to others but they're the devil's own to ye." A bright streak of lightning flashed in the sky. "Oh, aye, that's what they are. They're angels of rain and lightning to ye." She laughed again and turned to Bronwyn. "Now let me see yer palm."

Bronwyn backed away from her. "I'd rather not," she said flatly.

The old woman shrugged and invited them to spend the night with her.

In the morning she grabbed Bronwyn's palm and her face clouded. "Beware of a blond-haired man," she warned.

Bronwyn snatched her hand away. "I'm afraid your warnings are too late," she said, thinking of Stephen's sun-kissed hair, and left the little house.

They rode all day and stopped that evening in the roofless shelter of a destroyed castle.

Miles was the one who realized it was Christmas Eve. They made a celebration of sorts, but Miles recognized Bronwyn's sadness and left her to her own thoughts. It occurred to Bronwyn that part of Miles's fascination lay in the way he seemed to understand what a woman was feeling. He didn't demand anything of her as Stephen did or try to talk to her as Raine did. Miles quietly understood and left her alone. She had no doubt that if she wished to speak, Miles would make an excellent listener.

She smiled at him and took the oatcake he offered. "I'm afraid I've caused you to miss Christmas with your family."

"You're my family," he said pointedly. He looked at the black sky over the ruined walls around them. "I just hope that for once it doesn't rain."

Bronwyn laughed. "You're too used to your dry country." She smiled in memory. "Stephen never seemed to mind the rain. He—" She broke off and looked away.

"I think Stephen would live underwater to be with you."

She looked up, startled, and remembered the kitchen maid sprawled across her husband's lap. She blinked several times to clear her vision. "I think I'll go to sleep."

Miles watched in amazement as she curled up in her thin plaid and immediately relaxed. He sighed and wrapped his fur-lined mantle closer about his body. He didn't think he'd make a good Scot.

It was still morning when they reached the hill overlooking Larenston. Miles sat still in astonishment as he gaped at the fortress on the peninsula. Bronwyn spurred her horse forward, then leaped into a big man's arms.

"Tam!" she cried, burying her face in the familiar neck.

Tam held her away. "Ye put new gray hair on my head," he whispered. "How can someone so little get into so much trouble?" he asked, ignoring the fact that she was a bit taller than he. Indeed, she was small next to his great mass.

"Did ye know the MacGregor has asked to meet with ye? He sent a message about some drink and a saucy wench who'd laughed at him. Bronwyn, what have ye done?"

Bronwyn stared at him in astonishment for a moment. The MacGregor asked to meet with her! Perhaps now there would be a way to prove to Stephen she wasn't so selfish.

She hugged Tam again. "There's time to tell you all of it. I want to go home now. I'm afraid this trip has made me tired."

"Tired?" Tam asked, alarmed. He'd never heard her use the word before.

"Don't look at me like I was daft," she smiled. "It's not easy carrying another person all the time."

Tam understood instantly, and his face nearly split with his grin. "I knew that Englishman could do something right without any training. Where is he, anyway? And who is he?"

Bronwyn answered questions all the way across the narrow strip of land and up the trail to Larenston. Her men joined her and fired hundreds of questions at her. Miles stood back, staring in awe at the sight. Bronwyn's servants and retainers acted more like an enormous family than the classes of society that they were. The men greeted Miles affectionately, talking constantly of Stephen this and Stephen that.

Bronwyn left the men and went upstairs to her room. Morag greeted her.

"Did ye trade one brother for another?" she accused.

"No greeting?" Bronwyn said tiredly as she headed for the bed. "I bring you a new child and you can give me no fond greeting?"

Morag's wrinkled face grinned. "That's my sweet Stephen. I knew he was a man."

Bronwyn lay down on the bed and didn't bother to argue with Morag. "Go and meet the other Englishman

I brought you. You'll like him." She pulled a quilt over her. All she wanted to do was sleep.

The weeks came and went and all Bronwyn did was sleep. Her body was exhausted from the turmoil and the changes that the baby was making. Miles came one morning to tell her he was returning to England. He thanked her for her hospitality and promised to make her apologies to Judith and Gavin. Neither mentioned Stephen.

Bronwyn tried not to think of her husband, but it wasn't easy. Everyone asked questions about him. Tam demanded to know why the hell she left England so suddenly. Why didn't she stay and fight for him? His mouth dropped open when Bronwyn suddenly burst into tears and ran from the room. After that fewer people asked questions that she couldn't answer.

Three weeks after she returned home, one of her men told her a guard of Englishmen was approaching Larenston.

"Gavin!" she cried and ran upstairs to change her clothes. She donned the cloth-of-silver dress Stephen had given her and stood ready to greet her brother-in-law. She was sure it was Gavin approaching. He'd been to Scotland before, and he would be the one to give her news of Stephen. Perhaps Stephen had forgiven her and was coming to her. No, it was too much to ask.

Her smile faded when Roger Chatworth walked into the Great Hall. She was appalled at what she'd done. She'd ordered the visitor to be allowed entrance to Larenston without actually knowing who he was. And her men had obeyed her with no questions. She looked at the faces of her men and saw their concern for her. They would do anything to make her return to herself again.

She tried to cover her disappointment and held out her hand. "Lord Roger, how nice to see you again."

Roger dropped to one knee and took her hand, held it to his lips. His blond hair was darker than she remembered, the scar by his eye even more prominent. He brought back memories of the time at Sir Thomas Crichton's house. She'd been so lonely then, and Roger had been so kind, so understanding. He'd even been willing to risk his life to do what she wanted.

"You are more beautiful than I remembered," he said quietly.

"Come now, Lord Roger, I don't remember you as a flatterer."

He stood, his eyes on hers. "And what do you remember about me?"

"Only that you were willing to help me at a time when I needed help. Douglas," she called, "make Lord Roger and his men welcome."

Roger watched as the man obeyed her instantly. He looked around at the bare, unadorned walls of Larenston. The road into the peninsula had been lined with very poor little houses. Was this all the wealth there was to the MacArrans?

"Lord Roger, come to my solar and talk with me. What brings you to Scotland? Oh, but I forgot that you have relatives here, don't you?"

Roger lifted one eyebrow. "Yes, I do." He followed her upstairs to another bare room, where a small fire blazed cheerfully in the fireplace.

"Won't you sit down?" Bronwyn gave a curt look at Morag, then asked the disapproving little woman to bring them wine and refreshments.

When they were seated and alone, Roger leaned toward her. "I will be honest with you. I came to see if you needed any assistance. When I saw Stephen at King Henry's court and—"

"You saw Stephen at court!" she gasped.

He watched her face. "I thought perhaps you didn't know. There were too many women near him and—"

Bronwyn rose and went toward the fire. "I'd prefer not to hear the rest of what you have to say," she said coldly. She was beginning to remember all about Roger Chatworth. He'd stabbed at Stephen's back once before.

"Lady Bronwyn," he said desperately. "I meant no harm. I thought you knew."

She whirled on him. "I've matured a great deal since I last saw you. Once I was easy prey for your handsome ways, and I was childishly angry because my husband was late for our wedding. But now I am older and much, much wiser. As you have guessed, I'm sure, my husband and I have quarreled. Whether we will settle our differences or not I don't know, but the quarrel will remain between us."

Roger's dark eyes narrowed. He had a way of tilting his head back so he seemed to be looking down his narrow, aquiline nose. "Do you think I've come here to carry gossip like some fisherman's wife?"

"It would sound so. You've already mentioned the women around Stephen."

Roger began to smile slowly. "Perhaps I did. Forgive me. I was only surprised to see him away from your side."

"So you hurried to tell me of his . . . escapades?"

He stared at her, his handsome face warm and alive. "Come and sit down, please. You weren't always so hostile to me. Once you even asked that we be married."

She took the chair beside him. "That was a long time ago. At least it was long enough for lives and feelings to change drastically." She watched the fire and was silent.

"Aren't you curious as to the real purpose of my journey here?" When she didn't answer, he continued. "I have a message from a woman named Kirsty."

Bronwyn's head shot up sharply, but before she

could speak, Morag came in with a tray of food. It seemed hours before she left. The old woman insisted on adding wood to the fire and asking Roger questions.

Bronwyn wanted to ask questions too. How did he know Kirsty? What message could he have? Did it have something to do with the message the MacGregor had sent Tam saying he wanted to meet Bronwyn?

"If that's all, Morag!" Bronwyn said impatiently, then ignored the old woman's look as she left the room. "Now! What have you heard from Kirsty?"

Roger leaned back in his chair. This Bronwyn wasn't what he'd expected. Perhaps it was being in her own country or maybe it was Montgomery's influence, but she wasn't the easily manipulated young woman he'd first met. He'd heard part of the story of Bronwyn and Stephen in the MacGregor's land by chance. A man, poor and hungry, had asked to join his garrison. One night Roger'd overheard the man telling of his adventures in Scotland with the ravishing MacArran laird. Roger'd taken the man upstairs with him and gotten the whole story. Of course, it was only a part of the story, and Roger had spent considerable money finding out the rest of it.

When all the pieces were together, he knew he could somehow use it. He laughed at Stephen for foolishly parading himself before these crude Scots in a manner and dress as crude as their own. He sipped his wine and thought again with hatred of the time Stephen had dishonored him on a battlefield. Too many people had heard of that fight, and often he heard whispers of "the back attacker." He'd repay Stephen for that new nickname he now had.

His plan had been to seduce Stephen's wife, take what he'd fought for. But Bronwyn had fouled his plans. She was obviously not a woman who followed a man easily. Perhaps if he had time. . . . But no, he had no idea how long Stephen would be away.

Then a new plan began to come to him. Oh, yes, he thought, he'd repay Montgomery in full.

"Well!" Bronwyn said. "What was the message? Does she need me?"

"Yes, she does," Roger smiled. And I need you even more, he thought.

Chapter Seventeen

BRONWYN LAY IN BED, STARING AT THE UNDERSIDE OF THE canopy. Her entire body was tense with excitement. For the first time in weeks she felt like she was alive. Her sleepiness was gone, her nausea had passed, and now she was pleased that something was about to happen.

When she'd come home and Tam had told her of the MacGregor's message, she'd ignored it. She'd been too wrapped up in her own problems, her own misery, to even consider anyone but herself. Stephen said she was selfish, that she never listened to him or learned from him. Now she had a chance to do something that would please him. He'd always wanted her to settle her differences with the MacGregor, and now Kirsty had opened the way.

When Tam had first told her of the MacGregor's message, she'd half-heartedly talked of meeting him. The protest from her men shook the walls. Bronwyn had easily dismissed the matter and settled back into her mood of feeling sorry for herself.

Now that was all over. She saw a way to win Stephen back. She must prove to him that she had learned something from him, that she wasn't a selfish person.

Roger Chatworth had told her an incredible story about meeting Kirsty and Kirsty asking him to tell Bronwyn that a meeting had been arranged. The MacGregor and the MacArran were to meet alone, just the two of them, tomorrow night. Kirsty said the MacGregors were very much against the meeting, just as she was sure the MacArrans were. Therefore she'd made every effort to arrange a private meeting. She sent Bronwyn and Stephen her love and begged her to do this for the sake of peace for them all.

Bronwyn threw back the covers and went to the window. The moon hadn't set yet so there was still plenty of time. She was to meet Roger Chatworth outside Larenston Hall, by the mews, and she would lead him off the peninsula. There were horses waiting for them, and together they'd ride to meet Kirsty and Donald.

It wasn't easy to wait. She was dressed long before it was time. For a moment she stood over the bed, caressed the pillow where Stephen usually slept. "Soon, my love, soon," she whispered. Once there was peace between the clans, she could hold her head up before Stephen again. Maybe then he'd think her love was worthy of having.

It was easy to slip out of her room. She and David had often, as children, sneaked out to the stables, sometimes to meet Tam or one of Tam's sons. Rab followed her down the worn stone steps, sensing from his mistress the need for quiet.

Roger Chatworth stepped from the shadows as quietly as a Scotsman.

Bronwyn nodded to him curtly, then gestured Rab to be quiet. The dog had never liked Roger and made no secret of it. Roger followed her along the steep, dark path. She could feel the tension in his body, and more than once he grabbed her hand to steady himself. He clung to her and stood still until he got his breath.

Bronwyn tried to conceal her disgust. She was glad she now knew that not all Englishmen were like this one. Now she knew there were brave, courageous men like her husband and his brothers. They were men a woman could cling to and not the other way around.

Roger began to breathe easily once they reached the mainland and the horses. But they couldn't speak until they were out of the valley of MacArrans. Bronwyn led them around the valley by the sea wall. She went slowly so Roger could steady his horse. The night was black, and she led by instinct and memory rather than sight.

It was close to morning when they halted on the ridge that overlooked her land. She stopped in order to allow Roger to rest a moment.

"Are you tired, Lady Bronwyn?" he asked, his voice shaky. He had just been through what, to him, was obviously an ordeal. He dismounted his horse.

"Shouldn't we go on?" she urged. "We aren't very far from Larenston. When my men—"

She stopped because she didn't believe what she saw. Roger Chatworth, in one swift, fluid motion, took a heavy war axe from his saddle and struck Rab with it. The dog was looking at its mistress, concerned more with her than Roger, and so reacted too slowly to miss the lethal blow.

Instantly Bronwyn was out of her saddle. She fell to her knees at Rab's side. Even in the dark she could see a great gaping hole open in Rab's side. "Rab?" she managed to gasp through a thickened throat. The dog moved its head only slightly.

"It's dead," Roger said flatly. "Now get up!"

Bronwyn turned on him. "You!" She wasted no more energy on words. One instant she was on the ground, and the next she was flying through the air, her knife drawn and aimed for Roger's throat.

He was unprepared for her action and staggered

backward under the weight of her. Her knife blade cut into his shoulder, barely missing his neck. He grabbed her hair and pulled her head backward just as she brought her knee up between his legs. Roger staggered again, but he held on to her, and when he fell to the ground, he took her with him. She jerked her head to one side and bit him until he released her hair. When she was free, she charged him again with her knife.

But the knife never made contact because four pairs of hands grabbed her and pulled her away.

"You took long enough!" Roger snapped at the men holding Bronwyn. "Another minute and it might have been too late."

Bronwyn looked at Rab, silent on the ground, then back at Roger. "There was no message from Kirsty, was there?"

Roger ran his hand across the cut she'd made in his shoulder. "What do I care about some damned Scot? Do you think I'd deliver messages like some serf? Have you forgotten that I am an earl?"

"I had forgotten," Bronwyn said slowly, "what you are. I had forgotten the way you attack a person from behind."

They were the last words she spoke for quite some time, for Roger's fist came flying toward her jaw. She was able to move to one side quickly enough that he clipped her cheek instead of smashing her nose as was his aim. She crumpled forward in an unconscious heap.

When Bronwyn woke, she had trouble knowing where she was. Her head pounded with a black fury that she'd never experienced before, and her thoughts were disorganized. Her body ached and her mouth was immobile. She gave no more than a few attempts at thought and went back to sleep.

When she woke again, she felt better. She lay still and realized that half of her pain came from a gag around her mouth. Her hands and feet were also tightly tied. She listened and felt and knew she was in a wagon, thrown onto a heap of straw. It was night, and she knew she must have slept through the day.

There were times when she wanted to cry from the pain of not moving. The ropes cut into her, and her mouth was dry and swollen from the gag.

"She's awake," she heard a man say.

The wagon stopped, and Roger Chatworth bent over her. "I'll give you some water if you swear you won't scream. We're in a forest and no one could hear you anyway, but I want your word."

Her neck was so stiff she could barely move it. She gave him her word.

He lifted her and untied the gag.

Bronwyn knew she'd never felt anything so heavenly in her life. She massaged her jaws, wincing at the bruised place Roger's fist had made.

"Here," he said impatiently, thrusting a cup of water at her. "We don't have all night."

She drank deeply of the water. "Where are you taking me?" she gasped.

Roger snatched the cup from her. "Montgomery may tolerate your insolence, but I won't. If I wanted you to know anything, I'd tell you." Before she could stop looking with longing at the cup he'd taken, he grabbed her hair, tossed the half-full cup aside, and replaced the gag. He shoved her back into the straw.

Through the next day Bronwyn dozed. Roger threw burlap bags over her to hide her. The lack of air and movement made her lightheaded. Her senses drifted about, and she was in a state of half awareness, half sleep.

Twice she was taken from the wagon, given food and water, and allowed some privacy.

On the third night the wagon stopped. The bags were taken off her, and she was roughly lifted from the wagon bed. The cold night air hit her as if she'd been thrown into icy water.

"Take her upstairs," Roger commanded. "Lock her in the east room."

The man held Bronwyn's limp form almost gently. "Should I untie her?"

"Go ahead. She can scream all she wants. No one will hear her."

Bronwyn kept her eyes closed and her body limp, but she worked on regaining consciousness. She began to count, then she named all of Tam's children and worked at remembering their ages. By the time the man placed her on a bed, her mind was functioning quickly. She had to escape! And now, before the castle could settle into a routine, was her best time.

It was difficult to remain still and lifeless as the man gently untied her feet. She willed blood into them, using her mind instead of moving her ankles. She concentrated on her feet and tried to ignore the thousands of painful needles that seemed to be shooting through her wrists.

The gag came last as she closed her mouth and moved her tongue over the dryness in her mouth. She lay still, her mind beginning to race as the man touched her hair and her cheek. She cursed his touch but it at least gave her body time to adjust to the blood that was once again beginning to flow.

"Some men get everything," the man said with a wistful sigh as he heaved himself off the bed.

Bronwyn waited until she heard a footstep and hoped the man was walking away. She opened her eyes only slightly and saw him lingering by the door. She turned quickly and saw a pitcher on a table by the bed. She rolled toward it, grabbed it, and slung it across the room. The pewter clattered noisily against the wall.

She lay still again, her eyes open only a slit, as the man rushed toward the noise. Bronwyn was off the bed in seconds and running toward the door. Her ankle gave way under her once but she kept going, never looking at the man. She grabbed the handle on the heavy door and slammed it shut, then slipped the bolt into place. Already she could hear the man pounding, but the sound was muffled and weak through the heavy oak.

She heard footsteps and just had time to slip into a dark window alcove before Roger Chatworth came into sight. He stopped before the door, listening to the man's pounding and the indistinct voice for a moment. Bronwyn held her breath. Roger smiled in satisfaction, then passed her as he went toward the stairs.

Bronwyn allowed herself only seconds to calm her racing heart, and for the first time rub her aching wrists and ankles. She flexed her bruised jaw repeatedly as she slipped silently from the shadows and followed Roger down the stairs.

He turned left at the bottom of the stairs and entered a room. Bronwyn slipped into a shadow just beside the half-open door. She could see inside the small room quite well. There was a table and four chairs, a single fat candle in the center of the table.

A beautiful woman sat with her profile to Bronwyn. She wore a brilliant, flashing gown of purple-and-green striped satin. The delicate features of her face were perfect, from her little mouth to her blue, almond-shaped eyes.

"Why did you have to bring her here? I thought you could have her any time you wanted," the woman said angrily in a sneering voice, so unlike her lovely face.

Roger had his back to Bronwyn as he sat in a chair facing the woman. "There was nothing else I could do. She wouldn't listen to what I meant to tell her about Stephen."

"Wouldn't listen to you?" the woman taunted. "Damn the Montgomery men! What was Stephen doing at King Henry's court anyway?"

Roger waved his hand. "Something about petitioning the king to stop the raids in Scotland. You should have seen him! He practically had the whole court weeping with his tales of the noble Scots and what was being done to them."

Bronwyn closed her eyes for a moment and smiled. Stephen! she thought. Her dear, sweet Stephen. She came back to the present and realized she was wasting time listening to these two. She must escape!

But Roger's next words halted her. "How the hell was I to know you'd choose this time to kidnap Mary Montgomery?"

Bronwyn stopped dead still, her whole body listening.

The woman kept her face turned as she smiled broadly, showing crooked teeth. "I meant to have his wife," she said dreamily.

"By that I take it you mean Gavin's wife, Judith."

"Aye! that whore who stole my Gavin!"

"I'm not sure he was ever yours, and if he was, you were the one who discarded him when you agreed to marry my dear, departed older brother."

The woman ignored him.

"Why did you take Mary instead?" Roger continued. They may have been discussing the weather for all the interest he showed.

"She was returning to that convent where she lives, and she was conveniently at hand. I'd like to kill all the Montgomerys one by one. It doesn't matter which I begin with. Now! tell me of this one you captured. She is Stephen's wife?" Still the woman did not turn. She kept her profile to both Roger and Bronwyn.

"The woman has changed. In England, before she married, she was easy to manipulate. I told her an outrageous story about some cousins in Scotland." He paused to give a derisive laugh. "How could she believe that *I* am related to a filthy Scot?"

"You got her to ask for a fight between you," the beautiful woman said.

"It was easy enough to put ideas in her empty head,"

Roger said. "And Montgomery was willing enough to fight for her. He was so hot for her his eyes were burning out of his head."

"I've heard she's beautiful," the woman said with great bitterness.

"No woman is more beautiful than all that land she owns. Had she married me, I would have sent English farmers in there and gotten some good out of the land. Those Scots think they should share the land with the serfs."

"But you lost her and the fight," the woman said quietly.

Roger stood, nearly upsetting the heavy chair. "The bastard!" he cursed. "He ridiculed me. He laughed at me—and he's made all of England laugh at me."

"Would you rather he killed you?" she demanded.

Roger stood in front of her. "Wouldn't you rather have been killed?" he asked quietly.

The woman bent her head. "Yes, oh, yes," she whispered, then her head came up. "But we will make them pay, won't we? We have Stephen's wife and Gavin's sister. Tell me, what do you plan for the two of them?"

Roger smiled. "Bronwyn is mine. If I can't have the lands, I must make do with the woman herself. Mary is of course yours."

The woman put up her hand. "She is poor sport for anyone. She's terrified of everyone and everything. Perhaps I should send her home like this," she said with hatred as she turned her face so Bronwyn could see her fully.

It was a combination of the sight of the woman's hideously scarred cheek and the words about Mary that made Bronwyn gasp. Before she could move, Roger was at the door and had her by the arm. He pulled her into the room.

Bronwyn winced with pain as Roger's fingers bit into her skin.

"So! This is the laird you captured," the woman sneered.

Bronwyn stared at her. The once beautiful face was distorted on one side, long ridges of ugly scars drawing the eye down, the mouth up. It gave her an evil, sneering look.

"Look your fill!" the woman screeched. "You should see it, for you'll help pay for what you've done."

Roger released Bronwyn and grabbed the woman's hands. "Sit down!" he commanded. "We have more to settle than your immediate hatreds."

The woman sat down, but she continued to stare at Bronwyn.

"Where is Mary?" Bronwyn asked quietly. "If you release her, I will not try to escape again. You may do with me what you want."

Roger laughed at her. "How very noble of you. But you have nothing to bargain with. You won't be given a second chance to try to escape."

"But what use can Mary be to you? She's never hurt anyone in her life."

"Do you call this nothing?" the woman screamed, her fingers running along her scars.

"Mary didn't do that," Bronwyn said with conviction. She was beginning to believe the scars showed the woman's true nature.

"Quiet, both of you!" Roger said. He turned to Bronwyn. "This is my sister-in-law, Lady Alice Chatworth. Both of us have reason to hate the Montgomerys, and we have sworn an oath to destroy them."

"Destroy!" Bronwyn gasped. "But Mary—"

Roger grabbed her arm. "Have you no concern for yourself?"

"I know what men like you want," she spat. "Can't you get a woman without lies and treachery?"

Roger drew his hand back to slap her, then stopped at Alice's cackle. "That is what you went to Scotland for, isn't it, Roger?" she laughed. "Why was it necessary to bring her back tied in a wagon?"

Roger looked from one woman to the other, then grabbed Bronwyn and pulled her from the room. He half dragged her up the stairs, paused in front of the bolted door, then pulled her farther down the hall. He pushed her onto the wide bed in the center of the rich room. Dark brown velvet hung from the bed canopy. Brown velvet draperies covered the window. Gold braid elegantly trimmed the brown.

"Undress!" he commanded.

Bronwyn smiled at him. "Never," she said in a friendly way.

He returned her smile. "If you value Mary's life, you will obey me. It will cost her one finger for every second you delay."

Bronwyn gaped at him, then began to unfasten her brooch. Roger leaned against a high, carved chest and watched her with interest.

"Did you know I got drunk on your wedding night?" he asked. "No, of course you didn't know. I'll wager you never gave me a thought. I don't like being used. You used me in some sort of game with Stephen Montgomery."

She stopped, her hand on the buttons of her shirt. "I never used you. Had you won the fight, I would have married you. I thought you were being honest when you told me you cared for my clan."

He snorted in derision. "You're stalling. I want to see what has cost me so much pain and dishonor."

Bronwyn bit her lip on her words. She wanted to tell him he had brought his own dishonor.

Her hands were shaking on her buttons. She'd never undressed before any man except Stephen. She blinked back tears. Stephen would never love her again if another man took her. He was already so jealous that he mistrusted her every action. How would he be after Roger Chatworth got through with her?

She stood, unfastened her belt and her skirt, and let them slide to the floor. And how would she react to Roger's touch? Stephen had only to look at her and she fairly attacked him. His merest touch would set her to trembling with passion. Would Roger be able to do the same?

"Hurry up!" Roger commanded. "I've been waiting months for this."

Bronwyn closed her eyes for a moment and took a deep breath as she let the shirt fall to the floor. She kept her chin high and her shoulders back as Roger took a candle and came toward her.

He stared at her, his eyes roaming over her satin skin, her high, proud breasts. He touched her hip gently, ran his finger along the soft pad of flesh around her navel. "Beautiful," he whispered. "Montgomery was right to fight for you."

A sudden knock on the door made them both jump. "Quiet!" Roger commanded as he glanced at the door.

"Roger," came the voice through the door, a young man's voice. "Are you awake?"

"Get in the bed!" Roger said under his breath. "Stay under the covers and don't make a sound. Do I need to threaten you?"

Bronwyn obeyed him quickly, glad for any excuse to hide her nude body from his sight. She buried herself under the furs and coverlets while Roger hastily drew the curtains around the bed.

"Brian, what is it?" Roger asked in a completely different, gentle voice as he opened the door. "Did you have another bad dream?"

Bronwyn moved silently so she could see through the curtains. Roger lit several candles on a table by the bed. He stepped aside, and she could see the young man who entered.

Brian was probably twenty years old, but his slight build made him appear to be little more than a boy. He walked with a hesitant step, as if one leg were stiff but he'd learned to walk with only a slight limp. He was obviously Roger's brother, a younger, weaker, more delicate version of his strong, healthy older brother.

"You should be in bed," Roger said in a kind voice, a voice Bronwyn had never heard from him before. Roger's love for this boy was apparent in every word he spoke.

Brian eased himself into a chair. "I was waiting for you to return. I couldn't even find out where you went. Alice said . . ." He stopped.

"Did she upset you?" Roger asked earnestly. "If she did—"

"No, of course not," Brian said. "Alice is an unhappy woman. She is miserable over Edmund's death."

"Yes, I'm sure she is," Roger said sarcastically. He changed the subject. "I visited my other estates to see that the serfs were not robbing us blind."

"Roger, who is the woman who keeps crying?"

Roger's head shot up. "I . . . I don't know what you mean. There isn't any woman crying."

"For three nights now I've heard someone crying. Even during the day I catch just a bit of the sound."

Roger smiled. "Perhaps the house has a ghost. Or maybe Edmund—" He stopped abruptly.

"I know what you mean," Brian said flatly. "I know more about our elder brother than you think. You were going to say that perhaps the crying is the ghost of one of Edmund's women. Maybe it was the one who killed herself on the night Edmund was murdered."

"Brian! How do you hear of these things? It's late and you ought to be in bed."

Brian sighed, then allowed Roger to help him out of the chair. "I think I will go to bed. Will I see you in the morning? Alice is so much better when you're here, and I miss Elizabeth already. Christmas is much too short."

"Yes, of course, I'll be here. Good night, little brother. Sleep well." He stood for a moment after the door closed.

Bronwyn didn't move as she watched Roger. Roger may be a liar, he might attack a man's back, but he loved his younger brother.

Roger turned and threw the bed curtains aside. "Did you hope I'd forgotten you?" His voice was cold again.

She held the bedclothes to her neck and backed toward the far edge of the bed. "Who is Elizabeth?"

Roger gave her a smirking look. "Elizabeth is my sister. Now come here."

"Is she older or younger than Brian?" She was talking rapidly.

"Would you like to see my family tree?" He grabbed her arm, pulled her to him. "Elizabeth is three years younger than Brian."

"Is she—" Her words stopped as Roger pulled her into his arms and began to kiss her hungrily.

She was quite still as he kissed her. His lips were firm and pleasant, his breath sweet even, but there was no fire. He ran his mouth down her neck as his hands caressed her back. His fingers played down her spine, then gripped her buttocks and pressed her to him. He was fully dressed, and the padded velvet of his clothes felt good against her cool, bare skin.

But aside from a pleasant sensation, there was no fire. She felt like an outsider, as if she observed what was happening rather than experienced it.

"You do not fight me?" Roger asked in a throaty whisper, a hint of humor in his voice.

"No," she said honestly. "I—"

Again he stopped her words with a kiss. Gently he lay her down in the bed and began to kiss her neck as his hands freely caressed her breasts. His lips followed his hands.

"No, Roger, I don't fight you," she said, her voice full of honesty. "Truthfully, I find there is nothing to fight. I must admit I was curious about how I'd react to another man touching me. Stephen says I am after him so often he hasn't enough time to recover."

She gave a little laugh, stared at the canopy, and put her hands behind her head. "Not that Stephen *always* told the truth," she chuckled. "But I find it's just not the same. You touch me in the same places Stephen touches me, but with you I feel nothing. Isn't that odd?"

She looked with innocent eyes at Roger, who was bending over her, his hands still, his eyes wide. "I'm really sorry. I don't mean to offend you. I'm sure some women like you. I guess I just happen to belong to one man alone."

Roger raised his hand to strike her, and Bronwyn's eyes turned cold. "I'll not fight you nor will I react to your lovemaking. Does it anger you that you aren't half the man Stephen Montgomery is? Either in bed or out of it?"

"I'll kill you for that!" Roger growled as he lunged for her.

Bronwyn rolled away from him, and he landed on his face in the soft mattress. She jumped from the bed and looked about for a weapon but could find none.

Roger stopped as he started after her. Damn, but she made a startling sight. Her black hair swirled about her like a demon cloud. Her proud, strong body taunted him. She was breathtaking, like an ancient primitive queen, arrogant, defiant, threatening him with her small strength.

Every word she'd said about her husband screamed at him. She knew men well, didn't she? With each word he'd felt his passion shrink. What man could take her when he knew she laughed at him? If she feared him he would rape her, but this laughter of hers was too much.

"Guards!" he bellowed.

Bronwyn knew he planned to release her from the duty of his bed. She grabbed her clothes and by the time the door opened, she was wrapped in her plaid, the rest of her clothes under her arm.

"Take her to the east room," Roger said tiredly. "And I will have the man's head who lets her escape."

Bronwyn did not breathe easily until she heard the bolt shoot home and she was alone in the room. The guards had released the man she'd locked in the room hours before.

She sank down on the bed and instantly began to tremble. Her body ached from having been tied in a wagon for three days. Her fear for Mary tormented her, and now the episode with Roger further weakened her.

Once when she was just a girl she'd gone riding with one of her father's men. They'd stopped to rest the horses, and the man had tossed her to the ground and began to undress her. Bronwyn had been extremely innocent and very frightened. The man undressed himself, and when he stood over her he thrust his manhood out at her as if he were massively proud of the thing. Bronwyn, who'd only seen horses and bulls, began to laugh at the man, and before her very eyes he'd deflated. She'd learned several lessons that day. One, to never ride alone with just one man, and two, whereas fear seemed to excite the man, her laughter only crushed him.

She never told her father about the encounter, and three months later the man was killed in a cattle raid.

It should have been good to see Roger hurt as she'd hurt him, but it wasn't. She fell down onto the covers of the bed, hiding her face, burying her head. She wanted Stephen so badly, needed him so much. He was the foundation of her being. He kept her from doing stupid, impulsive things. If he'd been with her, she would never have left Larenston. Rab would be alive and she wouldn't be held prisoner by Roger Chatworth.

Stephen was with his king, pleading with the man to

stop the raids on her country. Her country! Hadn't Stephen proved he was a Scot? He deserved the title more than anyone else.

Bronwyn had no idea when she began to cry. The tears just began to flow silently at first, then with deep, wrenching sobs. She swore that if she ever managed to get herself out of this mess, she'd be honest with Stephen. She'd tell him how much she loved him and needed him. Oh, yes! How very, very much she needed him.

She cried for Mary, for Rab, for Stephen, and most of all for herself. She'd had something so beautiful and she'd thrown it away. "Stephen," she whispered and cried some more.

When her body was dry and she could cry no more, she slept.

Chapter Eighteen

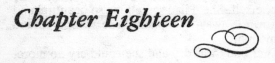

BRIAN CHATWORTH WAS VERY QUIET AS HE MADE HIS WAY down the stairs to the cellar. The Chatworth house had been built over an old castle, a place his grandfather had conquered and destroyed. Some people said it was bad to have built over the home of an enemy.

Brian thought of his brother's words about a ghost and smiled. Roger was so protective of his little brother and sister. When they were children, they needed protection from their older brother. But now, since Edmund's death, there was no need of hiding and lying. There was a woman crying, and Brian meant to find out about her. It was probably a kitchen maid who'd fallen in love with Roger and now cried because Roger didn't return her love. Brian realized that Roger thought his little brother knew nothing that went on between men and women. To Roger, Brian was still a frightened, hiding little boy.

He paused at the bottom of the stairs. The cellars were dark, full of wine barrels and casks of salted fish.

As he listened he heard a roll of ivory dice and a couple of guards laughing and cursing. He slipped between the barrels and went toward the back where he knew a locked cell was. He had no idea why he sneaked about except that he'd learned to be good at it when Edmund was alive. Besides, he'd rather Roger didn't think Brian had no faith in his brother.

The crying became louder as he neared the cell door. It was a soft, wrenching sound that came from inside a woman's heart. Now he knew why the guards moved to the far side of the cellar: they didn't want to hear the constant crying.

Brian looked inside the cell. In a formless heap in one corner lay a woman in a nun's habit.

Brian could only gasp as he grabbed the key from the nail by the door and unlocked the door. It swung open on well-oiled, silent hinges.

"Sister," Brian whispered as he knelt beside her. "Please let me help you."

Mary looked up at him with fear in her eyes. "Please release me," she whispered. "My brothers will cause a war because of this. Please! I could not bear to see them hurt."

Brian looked at her in bewilderment. "Your brothers? Who are you? What have you done to make Roger take you as his prisoner?"

"Roger?" Mary asked. "Is he the man who holds me? Where am I? Who are you?"

Brian stared at her. Her oval face was swollen, her soft brown eyes red and irritated. She suddenly reminded him of his sister, Elizabeth. Elizabeth was as perfectly lovely as an angel, and this woman looked like the Madonna. "I am Brian Chatworth and this is my home, the Chatworth estate. My brother Roger owns this house."

"Chatworth?" Mary said, sitting up. "My brother was once in love with a lovely woman but she married a man named Chatworth."

Brian sat back on his heels. He was beginning to see some link to this woman's imprisonment. "You are a Montgomery!" he gasped. "I knew only of the four brothers. I had no idea there was a sister."

"I am the eldest child, Mary Montgomery."

Brian didn't speak for some minutes.

"Tell me what you know. My brothers protect me too much sometimes. Why am I being held captive? Why should your brother hate my family?"

Brian immediately felt a kinship with Mary. "My brother also protects me. But I listen and I hear things. I will tell you what I know. A young woman named Alice Valence was once in love with your brother, the oldest one, Gavin is it not?"

Mary nodded.

"But for some reason I do not know, they did not marry. Alice married my eldest brother, Edmund, and Gavin married—"

"Judith," Mary supplied.

"Yes, Judith," Brian continued. "My brother was murdered one night." He stopped a moment. He did not tell of the evilness of his eldest brother, the way everyone lived in terror of him. He didn't mention the lovely young girl who cut her wrists the night Edmund was killed.

"And Alice was a widow," Mary said quietly.

"Yes, she was. She, I believe, made some attempt to win Gavin back to her. There was an accident and hot oil spilled across her face. She was scarred badly."

"Do you think there is some connection between this and why I am here now? Where is this Alice now?"

"She lives here. She had no one else." He thought of the kindness of his brother Roger. "This fall Roger had a public fight with another brother of yours. They fought over a woman."

"That could only have been Stephen. Bronwyn never said a word." Mary rubbed her hand across her face. "I had no idea this was going on. Oh, Brian, what are we to do? We cannot let our families war with each other."

Brian was startled by her words. What did she mean "we"? How could she assume that he was on her side? Roger was his brother. Of course, he'd take Roger's side. There must be a good reason why Roger was holding this quiet, gentle woman a prisoner.

Before Brian could say a word, Mary spoke again. "Why do you limp?" she asked quietly.

Brian was startled. No one had asked him that in a long time. "My leg was crushed by a horse," he said flatly. Mary just looked at him as if she expected more, and Brian found himself transported back to a time he didn't like to remember.

"Elizabeth was five," he said in a faraway voice. "Even then she looked like an angel. One of the woodcarvers used her for a model for all the cherubs in the chapel. I was eight. We were playing in the sand in the jousting field. Our brother Edmund was already grown then, twenty-one years old."

Brian paused a moment. "I don't remember everything. Later, they said Edmund was drunk. He didn't see Elizabeth and me as he charged onto the field."

Mary gasped in horror.

"We would have been killed if it weren't for Roger. He was fourteen and big and strong. He ran right in front of Edmund's horse and grabbed both of us. But the horse's hoof hit his left arm and he dropped me." Brian looked away for a moment. "The horse crushed my leg from the knee down." He gave a weak smile. "I'm lucky I didn't lose it. Elizabeth said it was Roger's care that saved the leg. He stayed beside me for months afterward."

"You love him very much, don't you?"

"Yes," Brian answered simply. "He . . . protected both Elizabeth and me all our childhoods. He put Elizabeth in a convent when she was six."

"And she's there now."

Brian smiled. "Roger says he's looking for a man fit for her but he's not found one yet. How can you find a husband for an angel?" He laughed in memory at something Elizabeth had said. She'd suggested Roger find her a devil. Roger had not found Elizabeth's statement humorous. Too often, Roger didn't laugh at Elizabeth's sharp remarks. Sometimes her tongue was at odds with her sweet looks.

"We can't let our families fight," Mary was saying. "You've shown me that your brother is a kind, loving man. He's just angry at Stephen. And no doubt your sister-in-law is angry too."

Brian almost laughed at that. Alice's half-crazy rages were more than anger. Sometimes she was totally insane and sleeping herbs had to be given her. She screamed about Judith and Gavin Montgomery constantly.

"You've said so little about yourself," Brian said quietly. "Here you are held prisoner, you've been crying for days, yet you ask about me. Tell me, why have you been crying? For yourself or for your brothers?"

Mary looked at her hands. "I am a weak, cowardly thing. I wish I could pray as I should, but my brothers have taught me realism. When they find I am gone, they will be so angry. Gavin and Stephen will calmly prepare for war, but there will be nothing calm about either Raine or Miles."

"What will they do?"

"No one can tell. They do whatever seems good at the moment. Raine is usually so gentle, a great bear of a man, but he can stand no injustice. And Miles has a horrible temper! No one can guess what he will do."

"This must be stopped," Brian said, rising. "I will go to Roger and demand that he release you."

Mary stood beside him, shorter than he. "Do you think demands will make him angry? Shouldn't you ask?"

Brian looked at her, her soft roundness, her great liquid eyes. She made him feel as strong as a mountain. He'd never asked Roger for anything—except his very life. She was right. How could he make demands of someone he loved so much?

He touched Mary's face. "I will take you from this place. I promise you that."

"And I believe you," Mary said with great trust. "You must go now."

Brian looked about the small, damp cell. There was straw on the floor and it was none too clean. The only furniture was a hard cot and a bucket in a corner. "This is a foul place. You must leave with me now."

"No!" She backed away from him. "We must be careful. We cannot anger your brother. If he is like mine, he may say things he will regret later, but then he will be forced to hold to them. You must wait until morning when he is rested and then talk to him."

"How can you concern yourself with my brother when it means another night for you in this hell-hole?"

She answered him only with the look in her eyes. "Go in peace now. You needn't worry about me."

Brian stared at her a moment, then grabbed her hand and kissed it. "You are a good woman, Mary Montgomery." He turned and left her.

Mary looked away as she heard the door locked once again. She hoped she hadn't let Brian see how very frightened she really was. Something scurried across the floor and she jumped. She shouldn't cry, she knew, but she was such an awful coward.

Roger looked at his little brother with shock.

"I want her out of that cell," Brian said quietly. He'd done as Mary'd said and waited until morning to confront Roger. Not that Brian had slept any, nor had Roger from the look of the dark circles under his eyes.

"Brian, please . . ." Roger began in that voice he used only for his younger brother and sister.

Brian didn't relent. "I still haven't heard why you have her prisoner, but whatever the reason, I want her out of that cell."

Roger turned away from Brian so the pain in Roger's eyes couldn't be seen. How could he explain his humiliation at the hands of the Montgomerys? It had hurt him when his sister-in-law threw herself at Gavin and was rejected by him. Later Bronwyn had chosen him and he'd felt redeemed. But Stephen had gotten in a lucky blow that had sent Roger sprawling. He'd been so angry, he hadn't thought but had attacked Stephen's back. Now he wanted to let the Montgomerys know he couldn't always be beaten.

"She won't be harmed," Roger said. "I promise you I won't harm her."

"Then why hold her? Release her now before there is a full-scale war."

"It's too late for that now."

"What do you mean?"

Roger looked back at his little brother. "Raine Montgomery was leading several hundred of the king's soldiers to Wales when he heard I had Mary. He turned the men and led them toward here to attack us."

"What! We are about to be attacked? We have no defenses. Doesn't he know he can't lead men like that in these days? We have courts and laws to protect us from attack."

"The king met Raine before he could get to us. The king was so angry at Raine's use of his men in a personal fight that King Henry declared Raine an outlaw. He has retreated to the forest to live."

"Good God!" Brian breathed, easing himself into a chair. "We have no defenses such as that massive fortress of the Montgomerys'. If we release Mary—"

Roger looked at his brother in admiration. "I had not meant to include you in this feud. You must leave here. Go and stay at one of my other estates. I will come to you soon."

"No!" Brian said firmly. "We must settle this quarrel. We will send messages to the king and to the Montgomerys. Until then I will personally look out for Mary." He stood and limped from the room.

Roger glared at the door after Brian closed it. He ground his teeth in anger, then grabbed a war axe from the wall. He slung the weapon across the room, where it sank into the oak door. "Damn all the Montgomerys," he cursed. He was glad the king was angry at them. They did nothing but take. They'd taken his sister-in-law's beauty and half her mind as well. They'd taken all those lands in Scotland that should have been his. And now they worked to take away his brother's admiration. Brian had never before defied Roger, had never done anything to contradict him. Now Brian thought he could make decisions and tell Roger what to do.

The door opened and Alice entered. Her gown was of emerald-green satin trimmed with rabbit fur that had been dyed yellow. A veil of tissue-thin silk covered her face. "I just saw Brian," she said in a quarrelsome voice. "He was helping that Montgomery woman up the stairs. How can you order her from the cellar? A woman like that should be thrown to the dogs."

"Brian found her on his own. It was his decision to care for her."

"Care for her!" Alice screeched. "You mean you're going to treat her like a guest like that one upstairs?" She smirked in laughter. "Or are you no longer giving the orders in this house? It looks like Brian is the man of this household now."

"You should know all the men, shouldn't you? From all reports, you've had all of them."

Alice smiled at him. "Are you jealous? I heard you sent Stephen's wife from your room last night. Couldn't you 'perform' with her?" she taunted. "Perhaps you should send Brian to do that for you too."

"Get out!" Roger said in a low voice that left no doubt of his meaning.

Bronwyn stared out the window at the snow in the courtyard below. She had been Roger Chatworth's prisoner for a month, and in that time she saw no one except a maid or two. They brought her food, firewood, clean linen. Her room was cleaned, the chamberpot emptied, but she spoke to no one. She tried to ask the maids questions, but they looked at her with great fear and tiptoed from the room.

There hadn't been a method she hadn't used in attempting to escape. She'd tied sheets together and let herself down the side of the house. But Roger's guards had caught her when she reached the ground. The next day a man had come and put bars over the window.

She'd even started a fire to create a diversion, but the guards held her as they put the fire out. She'd made a weapon from the handle of a pewter pitcher and wounded one guard. The two guards were replaced with three, and Roger came and said he'd tie her if she caused him any more problems. She begged Roger for news of Mary. Did the Montgomery brothers know the women were being held captive?

Roger answered none of her questions.

Bronwyn sank back into her loneliness. The only thing she had to occupy herself was her memory of Stephen. She had time to go over every moment of their life together, and she knew where she'd make changes. She should have realized a whole race of people couldn't be as bad as the men who ogled her at Sir Thomas's house. She shouldn't have been so angry because Stephen was so interested in her person and not in her clan. She shouldn't have trusted Roger's stories so completely.

No wonder Stephen had said she was selfish. She always seemed to see just one side of a problem. She thought of Stephen with his king, and she knew that when—if—she left Roger Chatworth's alive, she would go to Kirsty and try to arrange peace with the Mac-Gregor. She owed that to Stephen.

"Brian, they're lovely," Mary smiled, accepting the little leather shoes from him. "You spoil me."

Brian looked at her, and the love poured from his eyes. They'd spent most of the last month together. He'd never again asked Roger to release Mary, because Brian didn't want to see her go. For Mary took away the loneliness in his life. Too often Roger was off to some tournament, and Elizabeth was always locked away in her convent. As for the other women, Brian had long ago learned that women made him feel shy and awkward. Mary was ten years older than he and as unworldly as he. Mary never giggled or asked him to dance or expected him to chase her around the rosebushes. Mary was quiet and simple, demanding nothing from him. They spent the days playing a lute, and sometimes Brian told stories, stories that had always been in his head but he'd never told anyone. Mary always listened and always made him feel strong and protective, something more than just a younger brother.

It was this new feeling of protectiveness that kept him from telling her that Bronwyn had also been taken as a prisoner. He wasn't as blindly trustful of his brother as he once was, and he asked the servants questions, wanting to know what went on in his own house. He'd immediately demanded Bronwyn's release, and Roger had quickly obliged. Now only Mary was held captive.

"No one could spoil you enough," he smiled.

Mary blushed prettily and lowered her lashes. "Come and sit by me. Have you heard any news?"

"No, nothing," Brian lied. He knew Raine was still

outlawed, still living in a forest somewhere, the head of a gang of ruffians if Alice was to be believed. But Brian never told Mary of Raine's plight. "It turned colder last night," he said, warming his hands at the fire in her room. By mutual agreement they never mentioned Roger or Alice. They were two lonely people who came together out of mutual need. Their world consisted of one large, pleasant room on the top floor of the Chatworth house. They had music and art and joy in each other, and neither of them had ever been happier.

Brian lay back against the cushions of a chair before the fire and thought for the thousandth time how he'd like this to go on always. He never wanted Mary to return to her "other" family.

It was that evening that Brian spoke of his dreams to Roger.

"You what?" Roger gasped, his eyes wide.

"I want to marry Mary Montgomery."

"Marry!" Roger staggered back against a chair. To be allied with a family he considered his enemy! "The woman is of the church, you can't—"

Brian smiled. "She's taken no vows. She lives with the nuns as one of them, that's all. Mary is so gentle. She only wants to help the world."

The two men were interrupted by Alice's high laugh. "Well, Roger, you have certainly done well. Your baby brother wants to marry the older sister of the Montgomerys. Tell me, Brian, how old is she? Old enough to be the mother you've always wanted?"

Brian had never had any reason to experience rage before. He'd always been protected by Roger from most of the unpleasantries of the world, but now he snarled as he went after Alice.

Roger caught his slight young brother. "There's no need for that."

Brian looked into Roger's eyes. For the first time in his life Brian didn't think his brother was perfect.

"You're going to let her say those things?" he asked quietly.

Roger frowned. He didn't like the way Brian was looking at him, so coldly, as if they weren't the closest of friends. "Of course, she's wrong. I just think you haven't thought about this thoroughly. I know you're young and you need a wife and—"

Brian jerked away from Roger. "Are you saying I'm too stupid to know what I want?"

Alice screamed with laughter. "Answer him, Roger! Are you going to let your brother marry a Montgomery? I can hear all of England now. They'll say you couldn't get Stephen in the back one way so you got him another. They'll say the Chatworths take only the leavings of the Montgomerys. I couldn't get Gavin. You couldn't get Bronwyn, so you sent your crippled brother after their old-maid sister."

"Shut up!" Roger roared.

"The truth hurts, doesn't it?" Alice taunted.

Roger clenched his jaw. "My brother will not marry a Montgomery."

Brian pulled himself up to his full height. He was half the size of Roger. "I *will* marry Mary," he said firmly.

Alice laughed again. "You should have put him in charge of the other one. He might have spent his lust on her but at least he wouldn't be talking of marriage."

"What are you talking about, you hag?" Brian demanded. "What other one?"

Alice glared at him through her veil. "How dare you?" she gasped. "How dare you call me a hag? My beauty was so great that once I wouldn't have looked at a crippled weakling like you."

Roger took a step forward. "Get out of here before I scar your other cheek."

Alice snarled at him before she turned to leave. "Ask him about Bronwyn upstairs," she laughed before she hurried from the room.

Roger turned to meet Brian's cold eyes. He didn't like the way Brian was looking at him. It was almost as if Brian no longer worshipped his big brother.

"You said you released her," Brian said flatly. "How many other lies have you told me?"

"Now, Brian," Roger began in that special tone he always used for his little brother and sister.

Brian moved away from him. "I am not a child and I will not be treated as one! What a fool I've been! No wonder the Montgomerys don't attack us. You hold two of their women, don't you? How could I have listened to you? I never even questioned that whatever you did was right. I was too happy with Mary to even think for myself. But then I've always been too busy to think for myself, haven't I?"

"Brian, please . . ."

"No!" Brian shouted. "For once you're going to listen to me. Tomorrow morning I'm going to take Mary and Bronwyn back to their family."

Roger could feel the hair rising on the back of his neck. "They are my prisoners and you will do no such thing."

"Why are they your prisoners?" Brian asked. "Because you attacked Stephen Montgomery's back? Because you were beaten by him?"

Roger staggered backward. "Brian, how can you talk to me like this? After all I've done for you?"

"I'm sick of hearing how you saved my life and Elizabeth's! I'm sick of being grateful to you every moment of my life. I've served my time of being your little brother. I'm a grown man now, and I can make my own decisions."

"Brian," Roger whispered. "I never meant to ask gratitude from you. You and Elizabeth have been my whole life. I have no one else. I never wanted anyone else."

Brian sighed and his anger left him. "I know you

didn't. You've always been good to us, but it's time now to leave you and get out on my own. I want to marry Mary, and I mean to do it." He turned away. "Tomorrow I will take the women home."

Roger began shaking as soon as Brian left the room. No battle or tournament had ever left him as weak as this confrontation with Brian had. Moment by moment he'd seen his dear, sweet little brother change. He'd seen Brian's blind adoration of his big brother leave him.

Roger collapsed in a chair and stared at the tiled floor. Brian and Elizabeth were all he had. The three of them had stayed together, a strong force against Edmund's evilness. Elizabeth had always been independent. Her angelic face hid a strong nature, and she'd often stood up to Edmund. But Brian had always looked to Roger for love and protection. Brian was content to allow Roger to make all his decisions for him. And Roger loved the role. He loved Brian's worship of him.

But tonight he'd seen that adoration drain away. Brian had changed from a sweet, loving young boy into a hostile, demanding, arrogant man.

And all because of the Montgomerys!

Roger didn't know when he started drinking. The wine seemed available, and he took it without a thought for what he did. All he could remember were Brian's cold eyes and that the Montgomerys had even cost him his brother's love.

The more he drank, the more he thought of all the troubles the Montgomerys had caused him. Alice's lost beauty seemed to be a direct insult to him. After all, she was his relative. Judith and Gavin had toyed with Alice; worst of all, they'd laughed at her—just as they laughed at Roger. He could hear the taunts of the men at court, where he'd gone after his battle with Stephen. "I hear you made a play for that little chieftess of

Montgomery's. Not that I blame you from what I heard, but were you so hot for her you sought her at the cost of Stephen's back?"

Over and over the words came back to him. King Henry's son had just married a Spanish princess, and the king did not want his good mood spoiled by Roger's unchivalrous activities.

Roger slammed down his pewter tankard on the chair arm, and a piece of the carving fell away. "Damn them all!" he cursed. Brian was ready to throw away years of love and loyalty for a woman he hardly knew. He thought of Bronwyn's trick of laughing at him when he'd tried to make love to her. A whore's trick! Just like Mary's trick of telling Brian she wasn't of the church. Brian seemed to think Mary was pure, worthy of marriage, but she was clever enough to be able to seduce an innocent boy ten years her junior. Did she hope to use him to gain her freedom, or was she trying for the Chatworth wealth? The Montgomerys were making a habit of marrying great fortunes.

Roger rose unsteadily to his feet. It was his duty, as Brian's guardian, to show his little brother what lying bitches all women were. They were like Alice or Bronwyn. None of them were sweet and gentle, and certainly none were worthy of his brother Brian.

He staggered out of the room and up the stairs. He had no idea where he was going, and it was only when he reached Bronwyn's room that he paused. A vision of her black hair and blue eyes floated before him. He remembered every curve of her lush body. He put his hand on the door bolt before he remembered the way her cleft chin jutted up at him in defiance. He moved away from the door. No, he wasn't drunk enough to be able to withstand her ridicule of him. It wasn't possible to get that drunk!

He went up another flight of stairs to the top floor of his house. His problems were caused by that slut who

dressed as a nun and enticed his little brother. Her evil
ways were causing the break-up of his family. Brian
said that tomorrow he was leaving the Chatworth
estate. He was going to marry a Montgomery and leave
Roger. As if the Montgomerys didn't have enough
family already, they were going to take Roger's!

Roger lifted the bolt from the door of Mary's room.
The moonlight was streaming through the window, and
a night candle burned by the bed.

"Who is it?" Mary whispered, sitting up in bed.
There was fear in her voice.

Roger tripped over a chair, then sent it crashing
against a wall.

"Who is it?" Mary said louder, her voice beginning
to shake.

"A Chatworth," Roger growled. "One of your jail-
ors." He towered over the bed, looking down at her.
Her long brown hair was twisted into a braid. Her eyes
were wide with fear.

"Lord Roger, I . . ."

"You what?" he demanded. "Aren't you going to
welcome me to your bed? Isn't one Chatworth as good
as another? I can release you as well as Brian. Come,
let's see what you have that has enticed my brother so
much."

Roger grabbed the cover Mary held clutched to her
neck and tore it from her. He stared in a glazed way at
the prim cotton gown she wore. Most women wore
nothing to bed, yet this woman, a harlot supreme, wore
a gown. For some reason this only angered Roger
more. He grabbed the collar of the gown and tore it off
of her. He didn't notice her body or listen to her when
her terrified screams began. All he could hear was
Brian saying he was leaving his home for this woman.
He'd show Brian what a whore the woman was and that
she wasn't worth his dear little brother's affection.

He fell on Mary's plump, innocent body in a mindless state. He removed only enough of his clothes to perform the deed. Her legs were held rigidly together and he had to pry them open. Her screams had subsided into a whimper of terror. Her body was as rigid as a piece of steel.

It was no pleasure to rape her. She was dry and tense, and Roger had to pound against her to gain admittance. It was over in seconds. The drink and the emotion he'd spent worked together to exhaust him. He rolled off of her and collapsed on the bed beside her. Now Brian wouldn't leave him, he thought as he closed his eyes. Next Christmas, Brian, Elizabeth, and he would be together, just as they always had.

Mary lay quite still as Roger rolled away from her. Her body felt violated, unclean. Her first thought was of her brothers. How could she face them again when she was what Roger had called her over and over, a whore? Brian could never again sit with her, talk to her.

Very calmly, she rose from the bed. She ignored the pain in her body and the blood on her thighs. With great care she pulled her only gown over her head. It was a simple thing of dark blue wool, a gown the sisters had made for her. She looked about the room for one last time, then walked to the window.

The cold night air blew into her face, and she breathed deeply of it. She lifted her eyes toward Heaven. She knew the Lord could not forgive her for what she did, but then neither could she forgive herself for what had happened. "Good-bye, my brothers," she whispered to the wind. "Good-bye, my Brian."

She crossed herself, put her hands across her breasts, and jumped to the stones below.

The animals of the Chatworth estate sensed something wrong before the people did. The dogs began to bark; the horses became restless in their stalls.

Brian, upset and unable to sleep, threw on a robe

and made his way outside. "What is it?" he asked a stableboy who was running past him.

"A woman threw herself from a top-floor window," he called over his shoulder. "I've got to find Lord Roger."

Brian's heart stopped at the boy's words. It had to be one of the women who was held captive. Please let it be the woman he didn't know, Bronwyn, he prayed. But even as he thought the words, he knew who lay dead.

He walked calmly toward the side of the house that contained the window to Mary's room. He pushed through the crowd of servants peering down at the body.

"She's been raped," a woman said quietly. "Look at the blood on her!"

"It's just like when Lord Edmund was alive. And here I thought the younger one was going to be better."

"Get out of here!" Brian shouted. It made him sick that they felt free to look at his beloved Mary. "Did you hear me? Get out of here!"

The servants weren't used to taking orders from Brian, but they recognized the tone of authority when they heard it. They turned quickly and left to hide in the dark corners and stare at Brian and this woman they'd never seen before.

Brian gently smoothed Mary's clothes. He straightened her neck from its unnatural angle. He wanted to carry her into the house and even made a few attempts, but he wasn't strong enough. Even his weakness seemed to feed the anger rising in him. The servants assumed Roger had raped her, but Brian didn't believe them. One of the guards! he thought.

As he stood he began to imagine tortures for the man, as if it would help bring his Mary back.

As if in a trance, he walked up the stairs to Mary's room. The guards started to hinder him, but they stepped back when they saw Brian's face. He pushed open the door to Mary's room.

He stared for some moments at Roger's form, dead asleep, snoring, as he lay in Mary's bed. He didn't seem to have any thoughts, only a feeling that ran through him. He seemed to grow and strengthen with each passing moment.

With great calmness he turned and took a pitcher of cold water from a table. He poured it over Roger's head.

Roger groaned and looked up. "Brian," he said groggily with a faint smile. "I was dreaming of you."

"Get up!" Brian said in a deadly voice.

Roger became alert. He was war-trained and knew how to control his senses when he felt there was danger. "What has happened? Is Elizabeth—" He broke off as he sat up and realized where he was. "Where is the Montgomery woman?"

Brian's face didn't change from its look of steel. "She lies dead on the stones below."

A flicker went across Roger's face. "I wanted to prove what kind of woman she was. I wanted to show you—"

Brian's low voice cut him off. "Where is Stephen Montgomery's wife?"

"Brian, you must listen to me," Roger pleaded.

"Listen!" Brian gasped. "Did you listen to Mary's screams? I know she was a timid woman and I'll wager she screamed a lot. Did you enjoy it?"

"Brian . . ."

"Cease! You have said your last words to me. I am going to find this other woman you hold, and we are leaving here." His eyes narrowed. "If I ever see you again, I will kill you!"

Roger fell backward as if he'd been struck. He watched numbly as Brian left the room. He looked at the blood on the sheet beside him and thought of the woman lying dead below. What had he done?

It didn't take Brian long to find Bronwyn. He knew

she'd be in the room where Edmund once kept his women. Again the guards outside the door didn't challenge him. The undercurrent of the night's tragedy was being felt even through the walls.

Bronwyn was awake and standing ready when Brian entered her room. "What has happened?" she asked quietly of the hard-looking young man before her.

"I am Brian Chatworth," he said, "and I am taking you to your family. Are you ready?"

"My sister-in-law is also being held prisoner. I won't go without her."

Brian clenched his jaw. "My brother has raped your sister, and she has killed herself."

He said the words flatly, as if they meant nothing to him, but Bronwyn sensed something deeper. Mary, she thought, sweet, dear, gentle Mary! "We cannot leave her here. I must take her back to her brothers."

"You need not worry about Mary. I will take care of her."

Something about the way he said "Mary" told Bronwyn a lot. "I am ready," she said quietly and followed as he left the room.

Once they were outside in the cold night air, Brian turned to her. "I will arrange for a guard to accompany you. They will take you wherever you want. Or you may return with me to the Montgomery castle."

It didn't take Bronwyn long to make a decision. She'd had a month to think about it while she was confined in the room alone. She had to make peace with the MacGregors before she could see Stephen again. She had to prove that her love was worthy of him. "I must return to Scotland, and I want no English guards. I will travel more easily alone."

Brian didn't argue with her. His own misery and hate occupied all of his thoughts. He nodded curtly. "You may have a horse and whatever provisions you need." He turned to leave but she caught his arm.

"You will care for Mary?"

"With my life," he said from deep within him, "and I will revenge her death also." He walked away.

Bronwyn frowned as she thought how Mary would hate any talk of revenge. Suddenly she looked about her and realized her freedom for the first time. She must go as quickly as possible, before more violence erupted in this place. She had much work to do. Perhaps the saving of lives, even Scot's lives, would please Mary's ghost. She turned toward the stables.

Chapter Nineteen

BRONWYN LEANED HER HEAD AGAINST THE WARM SIDE OF the cow as she milked it. She was glad she'd come to Kirsty's parents' cottage instead of returning to Larenston. Kirsty and Donald had taken little Rory Stephen and returned north to their home. Bronwyn turned back to her horse and started to mount when Harben caught her arm.

"Ye'll stay with us, lass, until ye've met with the MacGregor. That is, if ye still want to."

She looked from Harben to Nesta and back again. "How long have you known?"

"Donald told me after ye left. I always suspected something, though. Ye don't talk like an ordinary woman. Ye have more . . ."

"Self-confidence?" Bronwyn asked hopefully.

Harben snorted. "More like as it's more insolence." He stared at her. "The MacGregor will like ye." His eyes went to her expanding stomach. "I see that man of yers enjoyed my home brew."

She laughed at him.

Harben led the way into his little cottage. "One thing I don't understand. I can see that you're the MacArran, but I can't see that that man of yours is an Englishman. I'd rather believe in a MacArran than an Englishman."

They went into the cottage, laughing, Nesta smiling at both of them. It was Nesta who kept the farm going and saw that Bronwyn and Harben worked while they argued.

It had taken a few days to arrange a meeting with the MacGregor. He agreed to tell no one and to bring no men with him, just as Bronwyn did. The next morning, at dawn, in the mist of the moors, they would meet.

She pulled harder on the cow and brushed at a stray strand of hair that bothered her. She finished the milking, swatted absently at her hair, and carried the pail to the far end of the barn, noticing that it was already growing dark outside. Just as the last drops of milk splashed into the pail, she heard a noise that made her stop instantly.

There was a little bark, just a small sound, but something about it reminded her of Rab, and tears instantly came to her eyes. She remembered all too clearly seeing Rab on the ground, the gaping wound in his side.

The sound came again, and she turned, the bucket still in her hand. There, standing quietly, his eyes alight, his tail wagging, was Rab.

She just had time to drop the bucket because the next moment all one hundred and fifty pounds of the dog were upon her. The dog knocked her back against a manger and nearly broke her in half.

"Rab!" she whispered, hugging the dog in return. "Rab!" She laughed as he threatened to drown her in his exuberance. "Oh, sweet dog," she cried. "Where did you come from? I thought you were dead!" She buried her face in his fur.

Suddenly a low piercing whistle came, and Rab went

rigid. The next instant he stood on the ground in front of her. "What is it, boy?"

She looked up, and there stood Stephen. His hair was shorter but he wore the Scots dress. She looked him up and down slowly. It seemed she had forgotten how large he was, how strong and muscular he was. His blue eyes looked at her in an intense way.

"Do I get the same welcome as Rab?" he asked quietly.

She didn't think but leaped at him, her arms going about his neck, her feet off the floor.

Stephen didn't say a word but began kissing her with all the hunger he felt. It had been so very long since he'd touched her. He stepped backward, carrying her, and fell into a thick pile of hay. Even as they fell, his hands were on the buttons of her shirt.

"We can't . . ." Bronwyn murmured against his lips. "Harben . . ."

Stephen bit her earlobe. "I told him we planned an orgy for the rest of the day."

"You didn't!"

"I did!" he mocked, laughter in his eyes. Then the expression on his face changed. His eyes widened and he looked at her in astonishment. The next moment he was tearing her clothes off her and gaping at the hard mound of her stomach.

He looked up at her in question.

She smiled and nodded at him.

Stephen's shout of happiness scared the chickens from the barn rafters. "A baby!" he laughed. "Harben was damn right about his home brew."

"I was carrying the child before we met Kirsty, so Morag says."

He lay beside her and pulled her nude body close to him. "Then maybe it was me and not Harben," he said from some deep, inner joy.

Bronwyn nuzzled against him and rubbed her thigh between his. "It may as well have been the home brew," she said sadly. "I don't remember anything else that could have given me a baby."

He chuckled, then moved quickly as he pushed her face-down in the hay. In an instant he was out of his plaid. He kept his knee on the small of her back. When he was nude, he bent and kissed the back of her knees. "I haven't forgotten you completely," he murmured as he ran his teeth along her tendons. His hands caressed her legs as his mouth tormented her. She moaned under him and tried to turn over, but he held her fast as he continued his sweet torture of her.

His skin against hers sent shivers all through her body. His mouth traveled up to her spine, his legs against hers. The hardness and the hairiness of his thighs worked to excite her. His big hands caressed her back, played with the soft shape of her.

Just after she knew she could stand no more, he turned her over. He kissed her while his hand rubbed her stomach then inched up to her breasts. She arched toward him as his mouth touched her breasts.

He moved upward again, his teeth running along her neck. She grabbed at him, pulled him down on top of her. "Hungry, my laird?" he growled in her ear.

She bit at him, almost too hard, and the next moment he was on her. It had been so long since they'd been together, and Stephen's mouth on her knees had excited her to a fever pitch. It took only a few thrusts before both of them were shuddering in the throes of their love.

"Oh, Stephen," she whispered, clutching him to her. It was so good to feel safe again, to not be alone. She didn't realize when the tears started.

Stephen moved from atop her and pulled her into the haven of his strong arms. He covered them with his plaid, and Rab snuggled against his mistress's back.

The safety and security she felt made her cry even harder.

"Was it horrible?" he asked quietly. "We felt so helpless, but there was so little we could do."

She wiped her tears away and looked at him. "Mary?"

He pushed her head down. "Brian Chatworth brought her back to us." He was silent for a moment. Now was not the time to talk of his grief—and rage—at the death of his sister. Sweet, gentle Mary, who only did good in her life, did not deserve death in such a vile manner. Miles had been the one to nearly kill Brian before Gavin and Stephen could prevent him. When Brian's story was told, it rang true that even held captive, Mary gave love. Brian's grief was obvious as he held the lifeless body of the woman he loved.

"Brian went to find Raine, wherever he is now," Stephen continued. "We heard he was hiding in the forest. Why didn't you return to Larenston? Tam has aged twenty years in the last month. He knew so little about what had happened. They found Rab in the morning, and Tam was sure you were dead."

"I wanted to do something for Mary."

"For Mary? You came to Harben's because of Mary?"

Bronwyn began to cry harder. "You were right. I had so long to think about it. I'm so selfish and I don't deserve your love."

"What the hell are you talking about?" he demanded.

"What you said. When you were holding that woman," she sniffed disjointedly.

Stephen frowned as he tried to remember what she was talking about. Since they'd been married, he'd not touched another woman. Every woman he saw paled in comparison to Bronwyn's beauty and spirit. He smiled as he remembered the night at Gavin's castle. "Aggie!" he laughed. "She's the castle whore. I was sitting there feeling miserable and sorry for myself when she came in the room, opened her blouse, and threw herself across my lap."

"You certainly didn't push her off! You were enjoying her when I came in."

"Enjoying her?" he questioned, then shrugged. "I'm a man and I may be angry and upset, but I'm not dead."

Bronwyn grabbed a clump of hay and threw it at his head.

He pinned her arms to her side. "Tell me what I said that night," he insisted.

"You don't remember!" How could he forget something that meant so much to her?

"All I remember is us screaming at each other, then I got on my horse. I don't even remember where I was going. Somewhere along the way I fell on the ground and slept. In the morning I realized I'd probably lost you through my idiocy, and so I decided to do something to try to win you back."

"Is that why you went to King Henry? To win me back?"

"I didn't do it for any other reason," he said. "I hate court. All that waste!"

She stared at him, then laughed. "You sound like a Scot."

"King Henry also said I was no longer English, that I sounded like a Scot."

She laughed and began to kiss him.

He pushed her away. "I still haven't had an answer from you. All the time I was at court I thought you were with my brothers. Gavin was so angry he refused to write me. I think he assumed I knew you'd walked out of his house that night I left. You and Miles scared them half to death, you know."

"But not you?" she asked. "What did you think when you found out I'd returned to Scotland?"

"I didn't have time to think!" he said in disgust. "Gavin, Raine, Miles, and Judith lectured me for days. When they got through, they stopped speaking to me."

"And all the time I was in Scotland, you didn't even send a message to me!"

"But *you* left *me!*" he half shouted. "You should have sent a message to me!"

"Stephen Montgomery!" she gasped. "I did not leave you. You've just said you rode to King Henry. Was I supposed to sit and wait for your return? What should I have told your family, that you preferred a fat trollop to me? And after the things you said!" She looked away from him.

He put his fingers on her chin and drew her face back so she looked at him. "I want to know what I said. What made you leave me? I know you, and if it'd been only the wench you wouldn't have left. You'd probably have taken a hot poker to her."

"She deserved torturing!" Bronwyn said hotly.

Stephen's tone was firm, almost cold. "I want to hear what you have to say."

Although he was above her, she looked away. The tears came to her eyes easily. She'd never cried so much in her life, she thought with disgust. "You said I was selfish, that I was too selfish to love. You said I hid behind my clan because I was afraid to grow up. You said . . . you were going to find a woman who wasn't cold and who could give you what you need."

Stephen's mouth dropped open in astonishment, then he started to laugh.

She looked up at him in shock. "I see nothing humorous in my faults," she said coldly.

"Faults!" he gasped amid his laughter. "Lord! I must have been very drunk! I didn't know anyone could get that drunk."

She tried to roll away from him. "I will not be laughed at! Perhaps it's my selfish nature that causes me to be unable to see the humor in your words."

Stephen pulled her back to him. She pushed him, and for a moment he let her win the struggle, then, still laughing, he pulled her back under him. "Bronwyn," he said seriously. "Listen to me. You are the most unselfish person I ever met. I have never seen anyone care so little for herself and so much for others the way you do. Didn't you realize that that's why I was so angry when you went over the side of the cliff? You had the power to order anyone else to go, or you could have done as Douglas advised and regarded Alex as dead. But not you! Not my dear, sweet laird. You thought only of the life of one of your clan members, not of yourself."

"But I was so afraid," she confessed.

"Of course you were! That just emphasizes your courage—and your unselfishness."

"But why . . . ?" she began.

"Why did I call you selfish? I guess because I was so hurt, because I love you so much and you didn't love me. And to tell the truth you sometimes make me feel very mortal. I'm afraid I don't have half your courage."

"Oh, Stephen, that's not true. You're very courageous. You took on four Englishmen with only a bow when we were at Kirsty's the first time. And it took great courage to give up your English clothes and become a Scot."

"Become a Scot?" he asked, one eyebrow raised. He was very serious. "Once you said you'd only love me if I became a Scot."

He waited but she made no answer. "Bronwyn, I love you, and the closest wish to my heart is that you love me also." He put his finger to her lips and gave her a threatening look. "And if you repeat all that about 'of course we're fond of each other,' I may break your pretty little neck."

"Of course I love you, you fool! Why do you think my stomach aches and my head swims when you're near? And it grows worse when you're far away. The only reason I went with Roger Chatworth was to prove to you that I wasn't selfish. I would have done anything to make you love me."

"Running off with my enemy is not likely to prove you love me," he said coldly, then he began to smile. "Are you saying you love me or that I make you ill?"

"Oh, Stephen," she laughed, realizing he believed in

her. He didn't accuse her of sleeping with Roger Chatworth. He was beginning to master his jealousy!

Suddenly they both stopped and stared. A sharp movement in her stomach had been felt by both of them.

"What was that?" he asked.

"It felt like a kick," she said in wonder. "I think your child just kicked us."

Stephen rolled off her and reverently caressed her stomach. "Did you know about the baby when you left me?"

"I didn't leave you," she pointed out, "but yes, I knew about it."

He was quiet as he held his hand warmly against her bare stomach.

"Are you happy about our child?" she whispered.

"A little frightened perhaps. Judith lost her first child. I wouldn't want anything to happen to you."

She smiled at him. "How could anything happen with you around to protect me?"

"Protect you!" he exploded. "You never listen to me, never do anything I say. You drug me. You leave my family's protection in the middle of the night. You—"

She put her fingers to his lips. "But I love you. I love you very, very much and I need you. I need your strength, your level-headedness, your loyalty, and your peacemaking ways. You keep me and my clan from declaring war on our enemies. And you make us see that the English aren't all ignorant, greedy, lying—"

He gave her a soft kiss to quiet her. "Don't ruin it," he said sarcastically. "I love you too. I've loved you from the moment I saw you with your clan. I'd never seen a pretty woman, except Judith, who was any more than an ornament. It was a shock to see your men listen to you and see the way they respected you. It was the first time I saw you as something besides . . ."

Her eyes sparkled. "A good romp in bed?"

He laughed. "Oh, yes, most definitely that." He began to kiss her more seriously, his hands on her body.

"Stephen," she whispered as he kissed just behind her ear. "Tomorrow I meet with the MacGregor."

"That's nice," he murmured, moving down to her neck. "Very nice."

She moved her head so he could kiss her mouth.

Suddenly he jerked away from her. Rab gave a little bark of alarm. Stephen stared at his wife in horror. "You jest!"

She smiled sweetly. "I meet with the MacGregor at dawn tomorrow." She lifted her head and began kissing him again.

He rolled away, then jerked her upright. "Damn you!" he said through clenched teeth. "Are you starting again? No doubt the meeting is alone in some secret place."

"Of course it's alone. I can't very well ask my clan to accompany me. I intend to settle this war before I enter into it more fully."

Stephen closed his eyes for a moment and tried to calm himself. "You cannot meet this man alone. I forbid it."

Disbelief registered immediately on Bronwyn's face. "You what? You forbid it! How dare you! Do you forget that *I* am the MacArran? Just because I love you doesn't give you rights over my duties as chief."

"Will you shut up a minute?" he demanded. "You always believe I'm against you. Now listen to me. Who else knows of this meeting?"

"Harben is the only one. He arranged it. We were afraid to even tell Nesta that the time was set, for fear it'd get her hopes up."

"Get her hopes up!" he gasped. "Is that all you think of? Consideration for others?"

"You make it sound like something evil."

"In your case it sometimes is." He again tried to calm himself. "Bronwyn, don't you realize that you must, at times, think of yourself?"

"But I am! I want peace for my clan."

Stephen looked at her with great love. "All right, listen to me. Picture this if you will. You and the MacGregor meet in some lonely spot, no doubt in the fog, and the only person who knows about the meeting is Harben. What if the MacGregor decided to end his feud with the MacArrans by killing their laird?"

"That's insulting!" she gasped. "This is a peace meeting. The MacGregor wouldn't do that."

He held his hands heavenward as if for help. "I can't get you to see any middle ground, can I? Six months ago you hated everything about the MacGregor, and now you plan to turn your life over to the man."

"But what else can I do? If the MacGregor and I reach some sort of peaceful agreement, we can stop the killing. Isn't that what you wanted? Haven't you always said you wanted the feud ended? Our private war caused the death of your friend."

He grabbed her and hugged her to him. "Yes, I agree with you. I want all those things—but when I think of what it could cost! How could I let you go out there alone and meet with a man twice your size? He could kill you with one blow."

She lifted her head, but he pushed her down again.

"You won't go alone. I'm going with you."

"But you can't!" she exploded. "The message was for me to be alone."

"You already carry another person, so what does one more matter?"

"Stephen . . ." she pleaded.

"No!" He glared at her. "For once you're going to obey me, do you understand?"

She started to argue, but she knew it was no use. Truthfully, she was glad he was going with her. She lifted her face for his kiss.

He just touched his lips to hers then pulled away.

She looked up in surprise.

He nodded toward the window. "Unless I'm wrong,

it's about an hour before sunrise now. I think we should leave."

"We couldn't spare even a few minutes?" she asked wistfully.

"You're a naughty child," he teased. "Now let's get dressed and go conquer the MacGregor as you've conquered me."

She lay back in the hay and watched him as he dressed quickly. Too soon was his strong body covered. And to think she once thought of him as her enemy! "You, my lord, are my conqueror," she sighed, then reluctantly began to dress.

They sobered as they saddled their horses and prepared for the short journey to the meeting place. Stephen considered locking Bronwyn in the barn and going alone, but she, seeming to sense his thoughts, refused to tell him where she was to meet the MacGregor.

The meeting place was as Stephen had thought— secluded, enclosed by rock, lonely-feeling with its heavy shroud of fog.

As soon as he dismounted, Stephen felt the point of a sword at the base of his neck. "And who are you?" the MacGregor growled.

"I came to protect her," Stephen answered. "Laird though she is, she doesn't meet men alone."

The MacGregor looked at Bronwyn, tall, slim, beautiful. She held the enormous dog in check as he threatened to attack the big man. The MacGregor laughed and sheathed his sword. "I don't blame you, boy. Though she might need protection for some reason other than the one you mean."

Stephen turned to meet the man eye to eye. "I'll protect her in all ways," he said with meaning.

The MacGregor laughed again. "Come over here and sit down. I've given this idea of peace some thought, and the only way I can see is to unite the clans in some way." He looked at Bronwyn as she sat down on a rock. "I'm not married any longer. Had I seen the MacArran earlier I would have offered for her."

Stephen stood behind his wife and put his hand possessively on her shoulder. "She's taken and I'll fight—"

"Stop it, both of you!" Bronwyn demanded, shrugging Stephen's hand away. "You're like two rutting stags clashing. Stephen, if you do not behave you'll have to return to Harben's."

The MacGregor laughed.

"And you, Lachlan! I'll have you know there's more to the MacArran than a face! If you can't deal with me on an intelligent level, perhaps you can send one of your chieftains."

It was Stephen's turn to laugh.

Lachlan MacGregor raised one eyebrow. "Perhaps I don't envy you after all, boy."

"She has compensations," Stephen added smugly.

Bronwyn wasn't listening to him. "Davey," she whispered.

Stephen stared at her as he began to understand what she meant. "He tried to kill us," he said quietly, but Bronwyn's look stopped him. He understood what she felt: blood was thicker than water.

He turned to the MacGregor. "She has an older brother, about twenty. The boy is going crazy with jealousy. Rather than stay in a clan where his younger sister is laird, he's hiding in the hills somewhere. Recently he made an attempt on our lives."

The MacGregor frowned, nodded his head. "I can understand the boy. I would have done the same thing."

"Understand him!" Bronwyn said. "I'm his laird. He should have accepted what our father said. I would have accepted him."

"Of course," Lachlan waved his hand. "But you're a woman." He ignored her sputters.

Stephen smiled warmly at the MacGregor.

"I have a daughter," Lachlan continued. "She's sixteen and a pretty little thing and as sweet and pliable as a woman can be." He gave one look at Bronwyn. "Perhaps we could arrange a marriage."

"What else do you offer him besides your insipid daughter?" Bronwyn asked levelly.

Lachlan winced before he answered. "He can't be laird, but he can be chieftain. It's more than he has now, and he'd be the laird's son-in-law."

"He's a hot-tempered lad," Stephen said. "That's why Jamie MacArran didn't name him as chief."

"You've never even met him!" Bronwyn said. "How do you know what he's like?"

"I listen," Stephen said in dismissal.

"I can handle him," Lachlan asserted. "I'll not die as early as Jamie did and leave the boy alone. I'll keep him with me always and teach him the right ways. I'd rather have an angry young man than a placid one. I can't abide a man, or woman," he smiled at Bronwyn, "with no spirit."

"I can vouch for the spirit of the MacArrans," Stephen laughed.

"I'll wager you can," the MacGregor chuckled. "This Davey should make my daughter happy if he's anything like his sister."

Stephen grew serious. "What will your clan say when you bring in a MacArran?"

"They'll not say anthing to me, but they'll have a lot to say to young Davey. Let's hope he can handle it."

Bronwyn stiffened. "My brother can handle any Mac-Gregor."

Lachlan laughed, then put out his hand to Stephen. "It's settled then."

The MacGregor turned to her. "Now you, young woman, I owe you for a B I still carry on my shoulder." He grabbed her and kissed her on the mouth heartily.

Bronwyn looked quickly at her husband, worried about his jealousy, but Stephen was looking at them fondly. They stood together as Lachlan rode away.

Bronwyn turned to him. "In the future I wish you'd remember that *I* am the MacArran, as I have shown you tonight."

Stephen smiled lazily. "I plan to change that."

"What is that supposed to mean?"

"Didn't I tell you I petitioned the king to change my name?"

Bronwyn stared at him stupidly.

"My name is now Stephen MacArran. Aren't you pleased?"

She threw her arms around his neck and began covering his face with kisses. "I love you, love you, love you! You are a MacArran! This will prove to my clan that you can be trusted."

Stephen hugged her and laughed. "They never doubted me. It was only you." He pulled her closer. "Bronwyn, we're not enemies any longer. Let's try to be on the same side."

"You're a MacArran," she whispered in awe.

He stroked her hair. "Everything will be all right now. I'll go find Davey and—"

"You!" She pulled away from him. "He's my brother!"

"The last time you saw him he tried to kill you!"

Bronwyn dismissed this. "He was angry then. All my family has a temper. He won't be angry when he hears my plan."

"Yours! I believe it was a joint effort."

"Possibly, but Davey will still only listen to me."

Stephen started to speak but then kissed her instead. "Could we continue this later? I suddenly feel something's come between us."

She looked up at him innocently. "My stomach?"

He grabbed her hair and pulled her head back. "How does it feel to kiss the MacArran?"

"*I* am the MacArran!" she said. "I . . ."

She couldn't say any more because Stephen's hand had slipped down to the back of her knees.

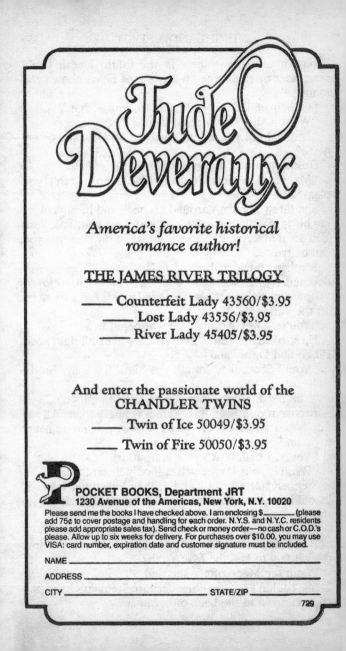